Getting to Happy

"TERRY McM[...]
FINEST [...]
AMONG [...] WOMEN."
—*San Francisco Chronicle*

PRAISE FOR THE NOVELS
OF TERRY McMILLAN

Getting to Happy

"[McMillan] reveals, in her characteristic don't-you-dare-feel-sorry-for-yourself way, how the women have fared over the past fifteen years."

—*O, The Oprah Magazine*

"*Getting to Happy* again hits a chord that will resonate with readers. McMillan does an excellent job of aging her characters, remaining true to the personalities she created. . . . Once again I felt these women could step out of the book's pages and into my own circle of friends." —*Chicago Sun-Times*

"McMillan clearly respects her characters and her readers too." —*The Washington Post*

"Signature McMillan: written in the earthy, funny, personal voice that some say created the 'girlfriend novel.'" —*The Raleigh News & Observer*

"McMillan fans won't be disappointed. . . . Still in a struggle to make sense of life and relationships, the women are older, a bit wiser, and . . . they soon learn that while bad things in life keep happening, they now have the wisdom and strength to forgive and to take control of their own happiness." —*The Dallas Morning News*

"Raw and cutting, the book mirrors the everyday life of real folk." —*Minneapolis Star Tribune*

continued . . .

"As usual, McMillan's snappy ear-to-the-ground dialogue drops you right into the centers of her characters' lives." —*The Chicago Defender*

"A phenomenal read for anyone looking for a happy place—or just the right groove."
—*San Francisco Bay View*

"Spending time in McMillan's world with these familiar characters is like sitting around in a comfortable pair of sweats with your old girlfriends, being their best cheerleaders and critics, listening patiently, and walking them through tough times. McMillan knows her audience and they will delight in this touching, philosophical, and oftentimes funny chronicle of women in the prime of their lives." —Suzanne Rust, MSNBC

"[McMillan is] fantastic at capturing the lives of African-American women." —*BookPage*

"Fans of *Waiting to Exhale*, many now middle-aged themselves, will want to cheer on the women in this sequel." —*Library Journal*

"Without missing a beat, McMillan writes these women seamlessly into the next phase of their lives."
—Curled Up with a Good Book

Waiting to Exhale

"Hilarious, irreverent . . . thought-provoking, thoroughly entertaining, and very, very comforting."
—*The New York Times Book Review*

"Terry McMillan has created a well-written, truthful, and funny story of four African-American women . . . and the sometimes volatile world of Black female–Black male relationships." —Spike Lee

"Sharp, dynamic, and funny as hell."
—*New York Daily News*

ALSO BY TERRY McMILLAN

Mama

Disappearing Acts

*Breaking Ice: An Anthology of Contemporary
African-American Fiction*
(editor)

Waiting to Exhale

How Stella Got Her Groove Back

A Day Late and a Dollar Short

The Interruption of Everything

GETTING _to_ HAPPY

Terry McMillan

A SIGNET BOOK

SIGNET
Published by New American Library, a division of
Penguin Group (USA) Inc., 375 Hudson Street,
New York, New York 10014, USA
Penguin Group (Canada), 90 Eglinton Avenue East, Suite 700, Toronto,
Ontario M4P 2Y3, Canada (a division of Pearson Penguin Canada Inc.)
Penguin Books Ltd., 80 Strand, London WC2R 0RL, England
Penguin Ireland, 25 St. Stephen's Green, Dublin 2,
Ireland (a division of Penguin Books Ltd.)
Penguin Group (Australia), 250 Camberwell Road, Camberwell, Victoria 3124,
Australia (a division of Pearson Australia Group Pty. Ltd.)
Penguin Books India Pvt. Ltd., 11 Community Centre, Panchsheel Park,
New Delhi - 110 017, India
Penguin Group (NZ), 67 Apollo Drive, Rosedale, Auckland 0632,
New Zealand (a division of Pearson New Zealand Ltd.)
Penguin Books (South Africa) (Pty.) Ltd., 24 Sturdee Avenue,
Rosebank, Johannesburg 2196, South Africa

Penguin Books Ltd., Registered Offices:
80 Strand, London WC2R 0RL, England

Published by Signet, an imprint of New American Library, a division of Penguin
Group (USA) Inc. Previously published in Viking and New American Library
editions.

First Signet Printing, August 2012
10 9 8 7 6 5 4 3 2 1

Grateful acknowledgment is made for permission to reprint an excerpt from
"March" from *A Village Life* by Louise Glück. Copyright © Louise Glück, 2009.
Reprinted by permission of Farrar, Straus and Giroux, LLC, and the Wylie
Agency, LLC.

 REGISTERED TRADEMARK—MARCA REGISTRADA

Printed in the United States of America

PUBLISHER'S NOTE
This is a work of fiction. Names, characters, places, and incidents either are the
product of the author's imagination or are used fictitiously, and any resemblance
to actual persons, living or dead, business establishments, events, or locales is
entirely coincidental.
   The publisher does not have any control over and does not assume any responsibility for author or third-party Web sites or their content.

Dedicated to Mrs. Helen Johnson,
who deserves as much happiness as she can stand

Nothing can be forced to live.

The earth is like a drug now, like a voice from far away,
   a lover or master. In the end, you do what the voice
   tells you.

It says forget, you forget.

It says begin again, you begin again.

—from "March" by Louise Glück

We create ourselves by our choices.

—Kierkegaard

AUTHOR'S NOTE

For those of you who may have seen the movie that was based on my novel *Waiting to Exhale*, please be aware that it was indeed a movie. As one of the screenwriters, I acknowledge that we strayed from the book, took many liberties and ended it the way a film should leave you: hopeful and somewhat pleased. Well, sorry to say that after these women left that campfire on New Year's Eve 1990, way out in the middle of nowhere surrounded by nothing but one another and a pitch-black desert in Phoenix, they found out that apparently exhaling is a relative state that is difficult to sustain. Like the rest of us, I assumed they flourished and floundered over the years. To be honest, all four of them got on my last nerve long after their shelf life and I forgot about them each time I met a new set of characters to worry and care about. Fifteen years later, however, these women suddenly began to reclaim their place in my heart, and, like old friends you haven't seen since college, I wondered how they might be faring now. And, like a good bottle of vintage wine—when aging is savored because it usually enhances the flavor—I had hoped that their lives might now be easier, smoother, solid, joyful. A lot happens in fifteen years. And like the rest of us, I realized that these four women are still trying to get to happy.

THE WOMEN

Savannah Jackson
Bernadine Harris-Wheeler
Robin Stokes
Gloria Matthews-King

CONTENTS

The Deep End | 1

Making the Cat Walk Backward | 22

Shake, Rattle & Roll | 39

Fourteen Years | 61

Love Don't Live Here Anymore | 81

If I Sit Still Long Enough | 95

Coming Clean | 109

Thunderstruck | 123

Icebreakers | 136

You Need to Watch Dr. Phil | 151

Four-Way | 162

Soap Opera Digest | 178

You Can Never Be Too Sure | 194

Good Vibrations | 206

Grocery Shopping | 220

The First One's Free | 232

Things Couldn't Be Better | 245

140/90 | 257

I Need a Fucking Vacation | 269

Returns | 284

Play Areas | 294

Blockbuster Night | 305

I'd Rather Work at Walmart | 328

Stick a Fork in Me: I'm Done | 338

Is That Your Final Answer? | 349

Thank You | 360

Blind Date | 374

Recovery Road | 387

Bonjour | 398

Velvet Handcuffs | 411

Payments | 422

Today I Got a Letter | 429

Choosing a Future | 438

Breathe | 446

White Dress | 453

Everybody Dance Now | 456

Acknowledgments | 471

The Deep End

"Are you sure you don't want to come to Vegas with me?" my husband asks for the second time this morning. I don't want to go, for two reasons. First of all, it's not like he's inviting me for a hot and heavy weekend where I'll get to wear something snazzy and we'll see a show and casino-hop and stay up late and make love and sleep in and order room service. Not even close. It's another exciting trade show. Isaac builds decks, fences, gazebos and pergolas, and as of a few months ago, playhouses. He's in love with wood. Can I help it if I don't get worked up hearing about galvanized nails or color-clad chain links and break-throughs in screws and joists?

I don't bother answering him because he's known for weeks I'm under a deadline for a story I'm doing on the rise in teenage pregnancy in Arizona—Phoenix in particular—which is the other reason I can't go. I've been sitting in front of my laptop in my pajamas for the past forty minutes waiting for him to leave so I'll finally have three and a half days to myself to focus. But he is taking his sweet time.

"I didn't hear you." He's looking for something. I dare not ask what. "You'd have the room all to yourself for most of the day. You could still work."

"You know that's not true, Isaac." I take a sip of my lukewarm coffee. I've been to so many of these conventions, trying to be the supportive wife, but I always get stuck with the wives, most of whom just want to sit around the pool all day reading romance novels or *People* magazine while they sip on margaritas and eat nachos, or linger in the malls for hours with their husbands' credit cards, trying on resort wear for the cruise they're all going on in the near future. I'm not crazy about cruises. I went on one with Mama and my sister, Sheila, and those long narrow hallways gave me the creeps because I've seen too many horror movies where the killer jumps out of a doorway and pulls you inside. After two or three days of being out in the middle of the ocean with no land in sight until you wake up not knowing what country you might be in front of, by day four I was ready to jump off our balcony and backstroke home.

And then there are those obligatory convention dinners. I'd sit there in one of the hotel ballrooms at a table full of contractors and their now-gussied-up wives, trying to be sociable, but I was basically making small talk since they never discussed anything that might be going on in the world. Call me elitist, but this often made me feel like an alien who'd been dragged to another planet by my husband because he, as well as they, didn't seem to think producing television shows about cultural and social issues was as interesting as all the things they could build out of lumber.

It truly irks Isaac that people don't respect or appreciate the role wood plays in our lives. That we aren't aware of how much we take it for granted—as if it'll always be here—and how much we rely on it yet overlook its value to the point where we ignore it and its beauty. It would be nice if he still saw me the same way. For about eight of the past ten years it felt like he did.

As Isaac passes behind me, he smells like green apples and fresh-squeezed lemons. For a split second it reminds me of when we used to linger in the bathtub surrounded by sage and lemongrass candles, my back snug against his chest, his arms wrapped around me and our toes making love. Those were the good old days.

I snap out of it.

Now he's pushing my favorite mustard-colored duffel across these terra-cotta tiles with those size-fourteen boots, leaving black scuff marks behind him as he simultaneously pulls a white sweatshirt over a white undershirt. It's a V-neck and shows the top of a black forest on his chest. "If I could, you know I would," I say while checking my e-mail. Of course there are back-to-back messages from Robin: a joke I don't bother to read and an attachment about a new motionless exercise she told me and Gloria about last week that almost had us choking from laughter. She believes almost everything she sees on TV.

"You just don't want to go," he says, and starts looking through his pockets to make sure he has everything. He doesn't. I know just about all his patterns. "Why don't you just come out and say it?"

"Because it wouldn't be true." I rarely lie, although I'm not always a hundred percent honest. This is one of those times.

"Then I guess I'll see you on Tuesday. After rush hour." He walks over, presses his palms against my shoulder blades, gives them a little squeeze, bends over and gives me a peck on the cheek. I don't feel a thing except the scratchy new growth on his face.

"You have everything?" I ask.

"What if I don't? Would it matter to you?"

"Of course it would matter to me, Isaac."

Right before he gets to the door leading to the garage, he turns and looks at me as if he doesn't believe me. Isaac knows we're on shaky ground. "I'm seriously beginning to think you might be racist."

He's trying to find a button to push. I'm not falling for it. Part of our problem is he's forgotten how to talk to me. He's forgotten how to ask me a question that doesn't put me on the defensive. All those sessions with the marriage counselor—for some of which he played sick, or was too busy drilling or hammering—aren't saving us. I'm tired of this war, which is why I'm ready to hold up a white flag. "Aren't you supposed to be picking up somebody?"

"So now you're trying to get rid of me—is that it?"

"Yes. How's that for an honest answer?" I feel my body stiffen, using the truth to lie. "Have a good time, Isaac. Wait a second! Did you remember to make the loan payment?" I only ask because he seems to have had a little bout of amnesia off and on the past six or seven months. It's the cause of brand-new friction. I have no idea what he's been doing with his money. It's not gambling—that much I do know. He stays away from the Indian casinos and usually dreads these conventions when they're in Vegas. He thinks gambling is too much of a gamble because most people lose. That's not really it. Isaac is just too cheap.

"Yes, I made it. As a matter of fact, I paid two."

"Thank you. And have a good time," I say, without moving my fingers, which are frozen two or three inches above the keys. I cosigned for this loan to help him start his business. After it took off, he took over the payments. Unfortunately, I've discovered by default that Isaac isn't as proficient managing his finances as he is at building. To this day he refuses to hire a bookkeeper, which is one of the reasons his taxes are always late.

"Good luck on your research," he says, and heads for the garage. He is so disingenuous. He hardly ever watches my shows anymore. For years he pretended he was interested, but over time he couldn't fake it anymore. He thinks my stories show problems that can't be solved, so what's the point?

I finally hear the door shut. I turn around and stare at it. It's red. My bright idea. I'm hoping to hear the garage door go up. There it is. Then the engine roars in his truck. Instead of turning my attention back to the screen, I wait for the handle to turn. Sure enough, in he comes.

"I forgot my cell phone." He dashes down the hallway to our bedroom. To this day Isaac reminds me of a black Paul Bunyan, except he's finally getting a few strands of gray. His mustache and goatee look like they've been sprayed with silver dust. He's still sexy as hell, which is a shame, because it doesn't seem to be serving any purpose. I shouldn't dog him too much. Isaac is a good man. I just think marrying each other wasn't the best thing we could've done for each other.

He stops dead in his tracks, pivots, comes over and

kisses me in the exact same spot. This time he lets his lips stay a millisecond longer. I appreciate the gesture. "I'll call when I get checked in."

———

I make myself some French toast, put a few strips of bacon in the microwave and sit back in front of my laptop. My mind isn't on teen pregnancy, so I bookmark the sites I may want to look at later. I'm thinking about the man who just left. The one I once loved harder than any of the others.

I was a forty-year-old love-starved black woman who'd never been married and didn't think it was still possible. I met Isaac in church. He was tall, dark and handsome. (Aren't they always?) I was sitting near the front and found myself going deaf as the minister delivered yet another guilt-laced sermon about the evils of temptation, because I was slowly being hypnotized by Isaac Hathaway's soft black eyes up there in the third row of the choir. This was a small church. It was as if he'd appeared out of nowhere. I certainly would've noticed him before. Not that I went to church every Sunday. And not that I didn't have faith in God. I did, and still do. I'd been on a whole lot of folks' prayer lists and God had known for years my address was still 111 Unlucky-in-Love Avenue. On this particular Sunday, this man followed me down those church steps to the parking lot and seduced me with my clothes on after he smiled at me, introduced himself and in a slow baritone said, "You are absolutely beautiful." I blushed brick red because he was lying through his teeth. I was not then, nor am I now, even remotely close to beautiful.

Now, I've been known to be attractive on special occasions, and I do my best to project as much beauty as I can muster from deep inside, though I often fail. On this particular day, I was wearing a boring brown dress I thought was perfect for church since it's not a venue for which I dress to draw attention to myself. Back then, I hadn't gotten into the habit of exercising on a regular basis, and my dress didn't conceal enough of my curves for my taste, so Isaac couldn't possibly have been moved by my breasts since they were and still are close to nonexistent. The pearls were noticeably fake, which should've given him a clue I wasn't loaded, although I made out okay. Besides, who under fifty wears real pearls to church?

I never did hear him sing solo. I would later think God had saved the best for last. Any woman in my position would've felt the same way and probably done the same thing: parachuted into his arms. Or was it his bed, first? Who can remember? Who cares? He was intoxicating, and any fool would've wanted more of him. All I know is he made me feel brand new. Lit a fire in me that burned bright orange. His smile reduced me to mashed potatoes. I loved that he held my hand wherever we went and stroked my palm with his thumb.

We prayed together. A few months later, he moved into my house. I knew I'd gotten lucky, because I'd found a man who wasn't afraid to admit his faith in God and also came with his own tool belt. Nothing stayed broken for long. Isaac had magical hands. He would shampoo and condition my hair, brush it at night and oil my scalp. He massaged my feet while I read and he watched television. He put lavender and ylang-ylang oil in my bathwater and let me lean way back. I could've lived forever in his arms. He made me feel safe, necessary, to the point I started believing I *was* beautiful. For years, he kissed me twice a day. Every single day. And not a peck, like that bullshit he gave me today, but a warm, slow, succulent kiss complete with arms I dreamed about when I was alone in a hotel bed on a business trip. Isaac is the best kisser in the world. And to date, the best lover I've ever had in my life. He was my Mr. Wonderful. I thought he was going to be my Mr. Once-and-for-All.

There was no escaping the hold he had on me or the spell he'd put on me. After a year of complete bliss, I surrendered and said of course I'll be your wife. When he lost his job putting up the fence along the Arizona-Mexico border because the company had gotten busted for hiring illegals, I wasn't worried. He was only twenty-six units shy of getting his degree in engineering.

Unfortunately, my world started shrinking not long after I married Mr. Wonderful. Since I didn't have kids, I was used to doing what I wanted and going where I wanted. I ate out at least two or three times a week. Enjoyed going to plays and live concerts and dance performances. Loved foreign films. Didn't mind the subtitles. In fact, I used to go to the movies at least once a week except in August, when the slashers came out. I loved reading in bed. Unfortunately, Isaac couldn't fall asleep without the television blaring. Turns out he wasn't keen on eating in restaurants except Denny's and the Olive Garden. I never saw him open a book but he couldn't get enough of *Outdoor Projects* or *Dream Decks & Patios* or *Wood Magazine*. He didn't like taking bona fide vacations because it was a waste of good money. He was also afraid of flying, which meant everywhere we went had to be by car. We rented movies, except during holidays. Isaac also liked fish, so once a month we went to the aquarium. Yahoo.

Last August, I flew to Chicago for the Democratic National Convention and was able to hear the young senator Barack Obama give a speech that sounded like it might go down in history. Flying wasn't the only reason Isaac didn't want to go. Right before the 2004 primaries, I inadvertently opened his absentee ballot. He had the nerve to be registered as a fucking Republican! I couldn't believe my eyes. I don't know any black Republicans. I was not only offended, but confused. I felt like I was married to a Nazi or something.

"Of course you have the right to align yourself with whatever party you so choose," I said when I confronted him. "But what on earth would possess you to support the Republican party, Isaac?"

This was Mr. Millionaire's answer: "Because they make sure we get the best tax break."

I left his ass standing in the bathroom dripping wet, since he was waiting for me to bring him a towel. So it was his dumb-ass vote that helped reelect that dumb-ass George Bush. Twice. I wondered who in the world I was really married to. It worried me.

I can't lie. I spent a lot of energy trying to give Isaac as much love as I possibly could as often as I could for as long as I could. Right after he lost his job, I tried to make him feel valued. I asked him to share his dreams with me. I listened. He changed his mind about getting his degree in engineering, opting instead for a construction management program. I paid his tuition. When he talked about all the things he wanted to build one day, I shared his enthusiasm. I also slowed down, said no to some travel. The Olympics in Australia was the biggest. I cooked almost every day. Washed and folded his work clothes. Took pills for car sickness. Everywhere we drove: "You see that sagging fence right there? That's a sign of a rookie." Watching the History Channel and *This Old House* was like foreplay. And wrestling: like witnessing phony cavemen perform acrobatics. I went to football games, which I didn't like because it was violent and took too long to make a fucking touchdown. I went camping and fishing but I didn't like getting dirty and putting stinky things on the end of a pole, and grabbing a wiggling fish that was headed for a hot skillet gave me the heebie-jeebies. Did I complain? No, I did not. I tried to do what made my husband happy.

Over the years, Isaac stopped showing interest in what I felt or what I did. I had to bribe him to go to or do anything that didn't have an outcome. Whenever I wanted to talk about my stories, he always seemed to have the remote in his hand. I'm tired of not feeling respected. Since he's become a successful entrepreneur, Isaac's arrogance has pierced right through his beauty, which is why I don't like him.

Make no mistake, I still love Isaac. I haven't been *in* love with him for quite some time. It's not an easy thing to admit. I'm not one of those women who feels I need a man to *complete* me. I also don't think there's just one person in the world meant for you. Sometimes you luck up and sometimes your luck runs out. I'm beginning to wonder if a good marriage is even possible. What I do know is I'm tired of feeling navy blue when I have a right to feel lemon yellow.

Ever since I turned fifty I've become more aware of the passage of time and what I'm doing with it. If I dropped dead today, what legacy would I leave? Would I have done a lot of the things I wanted to do? Seen some of the places I wanted to see? And would I—if I took a few minutes to think about it—feel as if the time I was blessed with was well spent or had I just bullshitted my way through it?

Even though I have an interesting job, it still feels like I should be doing more. All I ever wanted was to do something with my life that would have a positive impact on other people. To do something to make us look in the mirror or slow down long enough to see what our behavior really says about us. Mostly about our inhumanity, since it leaves red marks. I believe the only way to evaluate how we're living is how we're not living.

This is why I'm on a mission to start doing things that make me feel good. I've made a vow to start eating healthier and exercising on a regular basis because I know better. I'm twenty-five pounds away from being fat. I don't want to have to start buying all my clothes in *Encore* at Nordstrom. My goal is to be fit at fifty-two and sixty-two and seventy-two. I want to feel better than I look. I'm not trying to be a middle-aged centerfold. I just want to look at myself naked and not be disgusted. It may sound naïve, but I always thought as you got older the quality of your life would improve, that things would be smoother, calmer, and you could finally exhale.

If only.

I'd probably be in the nuthouse if it weren't for my girlfriends: Bernadine, Robin and Gloria. Fifteen years ago, we thought we were hot shit. I was thirty-six and had just moved here from Denver, where I'd been a publicist for the gas company. Thrill thrill. Bernadine and her then husband, John, talked me into moving here after a visit, when a position in PR opened up at a local television station. The three of us went to Boston University together. I was her bridesmaid. She worked in finance for a real estate developer, had become a CPA. She introduced me to Gloria, a single parent who had her own hair salon. And Robin: Miss Congeniality. She worked in an executive capacity at an insurance company but was still on the verge of becoming a slut. She was and still is a hoot.

After years of our being casualties of love, Gloria is the only one who's happily married. Times have certainly changed. We're all busy. We don't hang out like we used to, don't run our mouths on the phone half the night the way we used to, don't gossip about each other the way we used to. We send e-mail or text. Who can be bothered reaching out all day long like teenagers? Forget about happy hour. (Do they still have them?) We haven't been drunk since 1999. Haven't set foot in a nightclub since Rick James had his last hit. We dance at home. Apparently, we're too damn old to have fun in public places.

I don't know why we stopped being social creatures, but it's why Gloria came up with the idea of having Block-buster Night. Once a month we kick up our heels at one of our houses. It's something to do. Bernadine cooks, since she's our black Julia Child. We make our husbands and children disappear. We don't care where they go, as long as they're gone for at least four hours.

———

I finally get out of my pajamas and take a cool shower. I put on a pair of purple running pants and a pink sweatshirt and grab a bottle of cold water from the fridge. I go back to my laptop and start looking at some of the sites I'd bookmarked. I hit ENTER. The screen turns cobalt blue, then goes completely black. I lean back in the chair thinking the battery must be dead, but I always plug the laptop in when I'm at home, and when I look under the counter, it is. I power off and wait for it to reboot. I don't hear that low blender sound. I don't hear anything. I hit the power button again, this time praying I'm not a victim of one of those apocalyptic viruses. I've got tons of irreplaceable information inside the soul of this computer. Nothing I do resuscitates it. I'm glad I have a backup disk at work.

I walk down the hall to Isaac's office. The tiles are cold on my bare feet. It amazes me how neat he keeps it in here. There's a picture on one wall of giant redwood trees in Muir Woods in northern California. On another, a bulletin board with photos of his recent projects. I sit at his desk, a beautiful maple-colored door turned table-top. I click on the browser and type in the last site I visited and hit ENTER. My site isn't what comes up. My heart is pounding as I see before my eyes a screen full of color photographs and video clips of women giving men blow-jobs and three and four of them piled on top of one man and some pleasing each other. I know this is a porn site, but I didn't make a mistake when I typed. I close it and retype the same address. I don't believe it when I see these same nasty people again! I do this a few more times, get the same results.

I call my godson, who also happens to be my pretend nephew, John Jr., who also happens to be Bernadine's son who goes to MIT. He's a computer geek. I explain to him what just happened to my laptop and now this. "Sounds like Uncle's browser's been hijacked. Porn sites are notorious for doing this."

"How do you know that?"

"It's kinda the norm."

"But what could've caused it?"

"Well, it could be a virus, although I doubt that. I think Uncle's been very busy checking out these sites."

"How would I know that?"

Over the next fifteen or twenty minutes he talks me through a process that gives me access to temporary files which make it quite clear my husband has been having cybersex with hundreds if not thousands of women and the son-of-a-bitch has two names. He's Isaac Hathaway to me. But EbonyKing to all these nasty bitches he's been jerking off with and having virtual sex with via the little webcam attachment I gave him last Christmas. I've watched porn with Isaac and before I met him, but what I'm looking at takes it to a whole new level.

My teeth feel cold. My fists ball up on their own. I yank open a file drawer and start rummaging through his credit card statements only to discover he's a fucking Gold Card member. Not just on one site, but on quite a few others. To the tune of a few grand a month. I sit here for the longest, more pissed off than hurt, more disgusted than anything, trying to figure out how long he's been doing this shit. It's cheating, any way you look at it, except this feels much worse. It's sneaky as hell. I wonder how Isaac would feel if he saw me masturbating in front of a webcam for men, or hell, how about other women? So this is what he's been doing in here while I was sitting up in bed engrossed in a good book.

I print out the home pages of twenty or thirty of these sites and Scotch-tape them on the walls of this freakazoid den Isaac's been fronting as his home office. Without thinking about what I'm doing, I crawl under the desk, yank the plug out of the socket, carry the computer like a corpse through the great room, outside, right across this beautiful redwood deck he built, down the four steps and over to the pool, where I drop it into the deep end. This does not make me feel better.

I dry off where I got splashed and sit on the edge of the bed for almost an hour. When the phone rings, I answer it like someone who's just come out of surgery.

"Savannah?" I hear Sheila say. She's my baby sister. My only sister. I have two brothers.

"Hey," I say to Sheila in a cracked voice.

"Girl, what in the world is wrong with you? Did somebody die?"

"No. I just found out Isaac's been visiting a bunch of porn sites for the longest and I'm a little pissed off."

"I hope this isn't *all* you're tripping about?"

"If you saw the shit he's been doing and how much money he's been spending, I think you'd be a little more than pissed, too."

"Girl, all men spend money on porn sites. I'm grateful for 'em, if you want to know the truth. Saves me a lot of unnecessary energy. As soon as Paul thinks I'm asleep, I hear him tiptoeing down to the basement. I could care less."

"I'm filing for divorce."

"Not over this bullshit, Savannah. Come on."

"No. This is the cherry."

"Where is Isaac? You didn't throw him out, did you?"

"He's at a trade convention in Vegas."

"Don't do anything stupid, Savannah."

"Like what?"

"You didn't bust up his computer, did you?"

"No."

"Is it still intact?"

"Yes, it is."

"This silly shit shouldn't even qualify as grounds for divorce. The judge would probably laugh at you in court."

"I'm also miserable."

"Most married people are miserable but that's still no reason to get a divorce."

"I beg to differ with you, Sheila. Just because you and Paul have been living in marriage hell for twenty-something years doesn't mean everybody can tolerate it."

"I love Paul and he loves me. We've had our share of problems but everybody does."

"Well, I can't live like this anymore."

"Like what?"

"Isaac isn't just a freak—he's also boring as hell."

"Paul is, too. Being boring is also not grounds for divorce. And hanging out—no pun intended—on porn sites doesn't make him a freak."

"I'm bored, Sheila."

"Have you ever wondered if maybe you're the one who's boring? Look at all the great stuff he builds. Paul can barely snap Lego pieces together for our grandkids."

"Do you think I'm boring?"

"Hell, I don't know. I don't live with you and I don't know what you're like in bed—hee-hee . . ."

"Fuck you, Sheila."

"This is an issue in your house, baby cakes, not mine. I thank God for Viagra twice a month. And stop being such a prima donna, Savannah. It took more than half your life to find a man to marry, and Isaac is a good one. I know a lot of women who would love to have a husband like him."

"Then one can have him."

"I would cool my jets if I were in your shoes. You ain't exactly Beyoncé—no offense."

"I know how old I am."

"It's hard out there, Savannah. If you go through with this without really thinking about how you can save your marriage, you'll probably end up regretting it."

"Did I ever tell you he voted for George Bush?"

"I know you have got to be lying."

"He's a fucking registered Republican!"

"Tell me this is a joke, right?"

"No, I'm dead serious."

"Now, *this* is grounds for divorce! I could not fuck a Republican, let alone be married to one. He needs help."

I hear a click on the phone. "Oh Lord. Sheila, it's Mama calling me on the other line. Don't hang up."

I click her on. "Hi, Mama. How you doing? Is everything okay?"

"Everything is fine, but I had to call to tell you I had the weirdest dream last night about you and Isaac."

"I'm talking to Sheila right now. Can I call you back in a few minutes?"

"I'm on my way to see that Michael Jackson movie. *Finding Neverland*. You heard of it?"

"Yes, Mama, I have." I didn't feel like telling her it was a British movie with Johnny Depp and Kate Winslet and Michael isn't in it.

"Anyway, I'm going with Sheila and those little bad-ass grandkids, so tell her to make sure they go to the bathroom first and don't be late picking me up."

"I will, Mama."

"How is Isaac?"

"He's fine. Why would you ask?"

"Because in my dream, you all were getting a divorce over something stupid but the dream didn't give me no hints. You two doing all right?"

"We're good, Mama. Let me get back to Sheila so she can get over there on time. Love you. Talk to you later."

"What did she want?" Sheila asks. "I'm supposed to be walking out the door in a few minutes. The kids think this movie is about Michael Jackson's ranch, and I'm not telling them any different! Anyway, you were saying . . ."

"I was saying I know how hard it is out here. It was hard fifteen years ago. I'm not letting this stop me from living my life."

"Oh, please. You're half-a-damn-century old, Savannah, okay? You've had all the time in the world to live your damn life. Well, guess what? This *is* your life, and it's not a bad one. You're just never satisfied. That's always been your problem. Enough is never good enough for you. Go ahead and say it."

"What?"

"Fuck you, Sheila."

"I wasn't going to say that. Go to hell, Sheila."

"And I love you, too. Can we change the subject real quick and then talk about your marriage or divorce tomorrow?"

"I don't have anything else to say about it."

"You know I've been having problems with GoGo, don't you?"

"How would I know that? What kind of problems?"

"First, let me say this: Mama's got a big mouth and you know if you want to keep your business to yourself, don't even think about telling her."

"As if I don't know this."

"And please don't tell her about this, okay?"

"Tell her about what, Sheila? Get to the damn point, would you? You know Mama's sitting in front of her window staring at the curb."

"I'm on my cell phone. To make a long story short. Hold on a minute. I'M COMING! GO GET IN THE CAR! WAIT! AFRICA, TAKE THE LITTLE ONES TO GO MAKE PEE-PEE FIRST. Anyway, you know GoGo just turned eighteen even though he's in the eleventh grade, but you remember when I had to hold him back in kindergarten because he lacked social skills, right?"

"No, I don't, Sheila." The truth is I don't know which one GoGo is. I thought he was a she. Sheila and Paul have five or six kids. I can't remember. I dare not ask what GoGo's real name is.

"Anyway, he's been hanging around with the wrong crowd here and he got suspended for smoking weed, and I think he might be selling it or his girlfriend might be selling it, but I was kind of hoping maybe if he could come out there and spend a couple or three weeks, or part of the summer, with you and Isaac—but since Isaac may or may not be in the picture, maybe just with you. GoGo could be a big help around the house and keep you company. What do you think?"

I love my sister to death but she always puts me on the spot like this. If I said no, she'd be pissed or disappointed. I'm not in any position to be thinking about having my nephew whom I don't even know, who also happens to be a pothead, coming for a summer stint. I don't know how to talk to kids, let alone teenagers. "Let me deal with my marriage issue first, Sheila, and then let me think about if and when it might be a good time for GoGo to come out."

"That's cool. Have you ever thought about counseling?"

"We tried it. Counseling only works if both people want to save their marriage. I don't."

"Just don't do anything stupid when he gets home. Cut the man a little slack, Savannah. Could you try to do that?"

"I'll try," I say. "And could you please try to keep *your* big mouth shut?"

"I'm the Ziploc queen. Love you, sis."

Before I can put the phone in the cradle, it rings in my hand. It's Isaac. "You made it."

"I did and I'm beat. Traffic was bumper to bumper

for almost two hours. That's why I'm just getting around to calling. Is everything going all right?"

"My laptop crashed."

"For real? I'm sorry to hear that."

"Would you mind if I used yours?"

"I think I might have a virus. Didn't I tell you?"

"No, you didn't. Why would you think that?"

"Every time I try to visit any Web site, it keeps taking me to these porn sites."

"Why would you think it's a virus that's causing it?"

"What else would make it do this?" he asks. "I wouldn't chance it."

"Then I won't bother."

"You do have a backup disc at work, don't you?"

"Thank God. What about you, Isaac? Do you have one?"

"No, I don't."

"You should," I say. "You just never know when you might need it."

Making the Cat Walk Backward

"Mom, you should sign up for one of those online dating sites, because at the rate you're going, you're never gonna get laid ever again in life, and you're not even like completely over the hill or anything," Sparrow says to me out of nowhere.

Most mothers would be shocked to hear this coming out of their daughters' mouths, but sometimes Sparrow acts like she's my mother. We're best friends, and talk about most everything. This topic, however, is off-limits. I ignore my daughter's comment and just keep my eyes on the nontraffic as I back out of the driveway. We're on our way to the DMV so she can take the test for her learner's permit. She turned fifteen and a half this morning. She will take the driving test on Thursday, June 16, 2005: six eternal months from today. The only time these kids wait longer than twenty-four hours is if their birthday falls on a weekend.

"Mom, did you catch what I just said?"

"I'm not deaf, Sparrow. My love life and my sex life are none of your business. Put your seat belt on."

"I'm very aware of that, Mom," she says, and clicks

it in place. "But it's not normal to live the way you do." She crosses her arms.

It's true, times have changed. Twenty years ago, I couldn't go more than two weeks without having some kind of orgasm, and feeling desperate wasn't even a concern. I'd just pick one out of a lineup and call it a night. Back then we also didn't have to worry about AIDS or vaginal dryness. What my daughter doesn't know is I've been so preoccupied raising her and working long hours so she could take ballet and karate and now violin (which she happens to be getting quite good at), and trying to make sure my mom stays comfortable in that facility down in Tucson, that I forgot all about romance. I can't even remember the last time I was in love. I also can't believe I've never been married, when just about everybody I know has been divorced at least once. I'm beginning to wonder if it's too late. If it is, it seems unfair that all the good stuff only happens to you when you're young.

I find myself gripping the steering wheel a little harder than necessary. "So tell me what's normal in the teenage world, these days." Not that I'm blind. I just want to hear how she sees it. I already know she's done it. It's hard to stop them. Plus, after showing me a handful of colored condoms a couple of months ago, Sparrow came right out and told me: "Mom, I know you don't want me to do this yet, and I've tried not to, but it was difficult, almost impossible to say no, so I'm trying to be smart about it. Please don't worry, okay?" I wanted to slap her back to twelve, but I couldn't/didn't. I simply asked her who she'd been intimate with, praying it was *just* the one boy, Gustav, she'd been so crazy about for six consecutive weeks.

"It's not about my world, Mom. It's yours. You don't have a life. You're too smart and pretty to live the way you do. My friends think you look like a movie star! That's what you should do, Mom! Live your life like you're starring in your own movie!"

"And who'd direct it, Miss Eye on the Sparrow?" I'm trying to go along with this little game of charades.

"You waste like ten amazing hours a day going to a dull job you get nothing out of, which is why I'm surprised you're not popping ADs like Auntie Bern. In fact, maybe you should borrow some from her since going to the gym isn't doing much for your endorphins. I mean, you're in great shape, but what good does it do you if no one ever gets to appreciate it?"

"*I* do. And how do you know your auntie is taking antidepressants?"

"Taylor told me."

"How does Taylor know?"

"Because she found her stash. By accident when she was over there. That's not all she's on."

"What else is she *on*?"

"Ambien and Xanax."

"What exactly is Ambien?"

"Where have you been all your life, Mom? It's a sleeping pill and it's really no big deal. Everybody's on something. Most of the kids at my school get their meds from their parents' and grandparents' medicine cabinets."

"Are you telling me you've looked in my medicine cabinet for drugs?"

"No . . . well, yes. I just wanted to see what gets you

through the day besides exercise. But you're clean—I'm happy to say."

"And what have you tried?"

"Ritalin. But I didn't like feeling all wired up and zingy. Plus, I'm not running from anything. I haven't had anything tragic happen to me yet, so I'm cool with my own head."

How this child thinks amazes me and what comes out of her mouth is often astonishing. I never know what to expect but I'm thankful she has a mind of her own. "What about marijuana?"

"Now, that I like. I can't lie."

"You mean you smoke it?"

"No, I do not. I said I like it, which is why I refuse to do it. Anything that alters my mind can't be cool. Too many of my friends at school are like totally zonked because they're stoned all the time. Can't study like that."

"Damn" is all I can say. When I see a bank I remember I don't have any cash and forgot to give her lunch money. I swerve into the parking lot. "I have to stop at the ATM. I'll be right back."

I take my debit card out of my purse, and right after I push it in the slot and it asks me for my password, I lift my hand to punch in the numbers but my mind draws a blank. I don't believe this. I can't remember my fucking password! I stand there a few more seconds trying to think hard and keep coming up with all these other configurations, but not the one I need.

Sparrow honks the horn and sticks her head out the window. "What's wrong, Mom? Is it out of money or are you?" She chuckles.

I'm now perspiring. My forehead is beading wet balls. My deodorant isn't working and I suddenly feel like someone turned a furnace on inside me and put it on a hundred degrees. Damn it! I don't think I can go through this much longer. It's unfortunate I'm still having periods, and I'll be glad when they stop. I blow a tunnel of air out of my mouth and pretend I remember the password. This time I place my fingers on the buttons and let them press whatever numbers they are inclined to. When I see the screen change I'm ecstatic. I get sixty bucks and hand twenty to Sparrow when I get back in the car.

"Thanks mucho gusto," she says and tucks it inside her bra. "Anyway, Mom, I'm on your side, okay? We've been card members from day one."

"I get your point, okay?"

"But we haven't even gotten to your social calendar. It's totally blank unless you count my lovely aunties and your bimonthly DVD outings, but all of you guys live too much by the book. I mean, when you get to be, like, fifty, isn't this when you should, like, really be kicking up your heels and kicking ass?"

I take my eye off the road and loosen my grip on the steering wheel. "What did you just say?"

"I went too far. I meant what I just said and I apologize for using that profane word. It was completely out of line, but you get my drift, don't you, Mom?"

"Why are you on my case today?"

"Because it's a beautiful morning and I'm about to enter a whole new zone in these few short years I've been on this planet and I was just your little girl in braces and thank you for these knockers, Mom—but have I grown up faster than the speed of light right before your very eyes or what?"

"Yes, indeed you have."

"My point is that if I can see how fast it's going, then I know you should be about ready to, like, let it rip! I mean, don't you look at yourself some mornings and think, Damn, Robin—I mean, darn it, Robin—is this *it*?"

"Of course."

"Then how do you respond, Mom?"

"That is not something I feel like sharing with you."

"Why not?"

"Because I don't—that's why."

"Is it something you're ashamed of?"

"No!"

"I mean, do you ever think: Wow, I feel like a cat trying to walk backward?"

"What in the world are you talking about, Sparrow?"

"Never mind," she says with a sigh, as if she just can't get what she wants or needs to get out of me. I just wanted the girl to get her driver's permit this morning, not put my life under a doggone spotlight for her inspection. I mean, who does she think she is? She's the daughter. I'm the mother. What makes her think her opinions or her little teenage insights are worth their weight in gold? I know she means well. And there's a small chance she may be right. But you shouldn't let your kids know when they know more than you do.

"What I mean is, do you ever wish you could go back and do things differently?"

"Of course I do."

"Like what, for instance?"

"I wish I had chosen a different career and been better at picking men."

"Well, it's not too late, is it?"

"I don't know what else I'd do to make a living other than what I've been doing."

"Have you ever given it any thought?"

"Yes. I mean no. I don't know."

"When I tell my friends you're, like, an underwriter it's hard to explain. But it sounds boring."

"It isn't boring."

"But what do you get out of it?"

"Let's skip the subject. Anyway, I'll think about trying online dating."

"Good, because I've already set you up on three sites. You can go in and edit your profiles, Mom, even though I told, like, major lies about you. I had a hecka good time pretending to be you. And for the record, please don't lie about your age like some of my friends' moms do, please."

"I don't have to lie about my age, and I said I'll give it some thought."

"You think long, you think wrong. Let's be honest here, Mom. The only true loves in your life besides me are those stupid little dogs."

"Romeo and Juliet are not stupid!" They happen to be my teacup terriers, who together weigh about seven pounds and are cute as can be.

"They don't serve any purpose—all they do is bark and you spend a fortune on them. Plus, they don't protect us from anything. A robber could climb over the fence in the backyard and walk right into our house and they'd probably lead him straight to my room." She bites what's left of her royal blue nails. Of course they're chipped. Which drives me up the frigging wall. She has no idea what tacky means.

"They're called pets, Sparrow."

"Well, they get on my nerves, but you love them, so forget I said it. The point I'm trying to make here is that times have changed, Mom. Okay? You have to look for a guy the same way you look for a job. Online is the way to go."

"How do you know so much about this?"

"Mom, this is 2005 in case you weren't aware. Anyway, seventy-five to ninety percent of my friends' parents are divorced, and their moms are always meeting cool dudes with paper and very little baggage, except for those monthly support payments. This, of course, is not something I've had the privilege of experiencing firsthand since my dad is a jailbird and all, but I don't blame you for that. I just want you to be happy! I want you to fall into that deep hole called love I know nothing about except what I've seen on TV. Until then, can't you at least get laid?"

"Didn't you wear that yesterday?"

"You shouldn't limit your options to just black men, either."

"Who do you think you're talking to?"

She leans forward, turns her head to the side and points one of those blue nails at me.

"Just because you only like white boys, don't try to get me to follow in your footsteps, sweetie."

"I don't like them because they're white, Mom. I just like them. A lot of black guys at school aren't attracted to girls like me."

"And what kind of girl are you?"

"I'm my own person. I don't fit the mold."

"Oh, so you're saying that white boys don't mind your not fitting it?"

"They make me feel special. Unique. To be honest, they make me feel even prouder than I already am to be black."

"To each his own."

"Have you ever even dated a white guy?"

"No."

"Why not?"

"Because I've just never thought about it. I have always been attracted to black men."

"Yeah, and look where it's gotten you."

"What did you say?"

"Nothing, Mom."

"I've never been attracted to white men."

"It's because you didn't look at them as men because they were white. I've heard that inside, they're all just guys."

"You still haven't answered my question. Didn't you wear that getup yesterday?"

"And?" she asks, looking down at this potpourri of clothing even I know is a *Glamour* Don't. She's rolling the window down and I swear I wish every stitch she has on would fly straight out of this car into one of those trash bins lined up along the curb. Even though it's January, she's wearing too much of everything: a dingy white sweater that was once mine, jeans cut off at the knee and purple tights with holes or runs in them, and she has the nerve to wear them with teal blue hightop sneakers. She is clearly confused. As are a lot of teenagers. They don't care how they look. Sparrow's five ten. An inch taller than me. So she looks twice as bad as most of her girlfriends, most of whom happen to be white, which doesn't bother me, but she's a black Valley Girl even though all of Phoenix is a valley. All I know is the more mismatched they look, the cooler or more original they think they are. I have never had good taste, but I know from tacky. The only things on her that do make sense are the clusters of twisted hair that fall like branches of a weeping willow all over her head and over her eyes so she's constantly pushing them to the side, more for effect than anything. Like using a bobby pin would kill her.

"I am trying to be a conservationist, Mom, in case you aren't aware of our dwindling ozone layer. Look at that clay-colored cloud out there. Don't you want me to live long enough to see that disappear?"

"Shut up, would you, Sparrow? You're starting to get on my nerves and it's not even nine o'clock. I'm going to be late for work as it is, and you better pass the stupid test or I might make you walk back to school."

"I'd call the cops on you."

"I'd pretend like I didn't know you so they'd have to go to prison and ask to have your dad sprung so he could come get you."

"Mom, you're not playing fair! You promised never to bring him up when we play like this. You just broke one of our rules."

"I'm sorry, my little birdie. You should know Russell's getting out in a few months."

"Mom, that's, like, soon."

"I know. Don't go getting all in a tizzy. He's always going to be your dad, plus he doesn't even qualify as being a real criminal. He's just done some really stupid things over the years that he should be more embarrassed about than anything."

"He's a drug addict, Mom."

"It's a disease, Sparrow."

"Isn't there a cure for it?"

"No, there isn't. Abstinence. And you know how hard that is, don't you?"

She gives me the eye.

"Can I ask you something? And I want you to give me an honest answer."

"Oh, God, Mom, not one of these?" She lifts her right hand over her eyes like she's about to salute and shakes her head.

"Are you ever embarrassed because I've never been married and your dad's incarcerated?"

She drops her hand in her lap and looks at me with the utmost sincerity. "Absolutely not! First of all, Mom, it was your choice and your right to be a single parent, which makes me proud of you, to be honest. Haven't we, like, had this conversation before?"

"Not really. I tried explaining to you when you were little why your dad wasn't in your life. I don't remember explaining why I didn't marry him. Or anybody for that matter."

"Well, I haven't exactly been broadcasting that my biological has been living behind bars. I've told a few of my semiclose friends he's dead, because to me, he has been."

"Sparrow, that's kind of stretching things, don't you think?"

"Maybe. Most of my friends have never asked because they don't care. Everybody's families are, like, either so screwed up or like a really good mixed salad. I've got friends whose parents are lesbians or gay men, with kids that are white as snow to black as me and every shade of brown in between. Nobody cares anymore, Mom. Get it? We are who we are and it's all good. So, does that answer your question?"

"I suppose."

"Cool."

"On a lighter note, I'm giving you a friendly heads-up that if for some reason unbeknownst to you your GPA falls below that three-point-oh, you can forget about any make or model with an engine. Understood?"

"No worries, Mom. I'm taking AP geo this summer."

I turn into the DMV parking lot, but before pulling into a space, I stop the car. "Get out," I say. "I'll be right behind you."

She doesn't move. "Mom?"

"What is it now, Sparrow?"

"Are you crying?"

"No! I am not crying. Now would you go!" I pop her seat belt and give her a little shove.

"Mom, would you do me a favor?"

"What now, Sparrow?"

"Wait in the car. This won't take any time, believe me."

"What if I don't want to wait in the car?"

"I just want you to chill for a minute. I didn't mean to upset you."

"You didn't upset me and I wish you would stop trying to act like you're my mother. Now go pass your test. I don't want to go in there anyway."

She slams the door hard. She is such a Cancer. She is also a spitting image of my mother when she was young. I wipe my eyes on my sleeve and park. I don't bother turning off the engine and just stare out the window at nothing in particular. My mom and dad were married for fifty-two years, which is pretty amazing. They loved each other with a kind of urgency and grace I have never felt. I haven't loved anybody in a long time. And nobody has loved me. It's not the hand I thought I'd be dealt. I don't think I really loved Russell. He was just good-looking, a good lay and more like a hard fish to catch rather than the kind of man I imagined spending the rest of my life with. I should've thrown his ass back. Deciding to kick him to the curb after I learned I was pregnant was a major step in owning up to just how bad my judgment had been about him. And other men. I was tired of chasing ghosts, hollow men who were outside my comfort zone, men who had nothing to give me except a rush. It was all I asked for, and all I ever got.

The one thing I've always wanted to do is get married and wear a wedding dress. A white one. With pearls all over it. And enough crystals to make me sparkle. I'll be fifty in a matter of minutes and I've never even tried one on. My three best girlfriends have had rings on their left fingers, one of them twice. At this stage of the game, I seriously doubt if I'll ever meet the man of my dreams, even on the Internet. I don't know what the man of my dreams adds up to. I just know what I don't want: losers.

Back in the good old days, I was a little loose, if I want to be honest with myself. The longest relationship I ever had was with Russell. All we did was pimp each other for pleasure. Back then I confused passion and orgasms with love. It took me years to realize the two weren't synonymous.

Raising Sparrow made me shift my focus. I felt a kind of love for her that was better than any romantic kind. Once you bring a life into the world, your priorities change. You change. What you do becomes more important than who you are. I always wanted to be a good mother. I wanted my child or children to be proud of me. I wanted them to know I could manage my life.

Maybe I haven't turned out to be the smartest mother. I've probably made things too easy for Sparrow. I've spoiled her, and it's becoming obvious. Not saying no to your children can be a curse. She anticipates my saying yes to just about all of her requests: "Yes, you can go to the concert even though it's a school night. Yes, you can stay out until midnight and when you stroll in at one, I won't ground you. Yes, you can get a new cell phone even though there's nothing wrong with the one you have. Yes, you can use my Visa to buy whatever it is you need at Hot Topic and Wet Seal. Yes, the housekeepers will clean the scum off the tile in your shower and get that spot off your carpet after you spilled your root beer float on it." And the list goes on. Bernadine told me Sparrow needs a part-time job at someplace like Jack-in-the-Box. Savannah and Gloria think I've created a cross between a little Oprah and Annie Oakley. My daughter has chutzpah and a lot of insight for her age. She also thinks she knows everything.

I've told her hundreds of times she can't learn everything there is to know about life from *Real World* and *Survivor*.

I can't hide behind Sparrow anymore. Time has run past me and now here I am forty-nine years old, with no love life and no prospects of bumping into a man that might increase my joy over the next however-many years. Add to it eighteen years of working at a job I feel no enthusiasm for, and where does that leave me? How on earth do you start over? And where? I can't ask Sparrow. My girlfriends can't help me on this one. Savannah's been waffling for years about whether her marriage is worth saving. Gloria is happy, content, because Marvin loves her right and has kept her smiling for more than fifteen years. Bernadine is just the opposite. She's like a block of ice when it comes to men and love.

I could use a hobby. Besides shopping. I don't know what I'm interested in or what I'm good at. I can't make anything. I can't cook. I can't sew. In fact, I don't think there's a creative bone in my body. Which is why some of us do other things. I crunch numbers.

How long could this stupid test take? I've been waiting out here now for forty-five minutes with the engine running, since there's a serious chill in this January air. I decide to go check on her, but as soon as I open the door, my cell phone rings. It's Norman Nielson, from my office. We're both senior underwriters, VPs. He's a real senior. Norman is over sixty and should be retiring soon. I don't think he has plans for the rest of his life outside the office. We've worked together forever: like eighteen years. "Hi, Norm. Did everybody forget I was coming in a little late this morning or what?"

"No, not at all. I just wanted to give you a heads-up about something."

"Is something wrong?"

"I'm not sure, but a deal that was supposed to close yesterday fell through without much explanation."

"And?"

"Well, you know this is unusual, Robin. Plus, there's a buzz going around that we may be getting bought."

"This wouldn't be the first time, Norm."

"You never know how it might work for or against us in this industry."

"Remember the last time? They just changed the terms of some of our benefits and what have you. Until something actually goes down, we should just keep doing what we've been doing. By the way, is Fernando in yet?"

"Doesn't look like it."

"He's pushing his luck. Just because he's smart he thinks it's his ace in the hole. I might shock him and let him go if he keeps this up. Dare I bother to ask if Lucille has given you the printouts?"

"She has indeed. I think there must be another dance coming up soon, because she's got a stack of tickets on her desk."

"Oh, Lord."

"I might go to one, one day, Robin. Do you know how many tickets I've bought from her over the years?"

"I think I do, Norm."

"I'd probably stick out like a sore thumb. Being white. That would be a hoot."

"You'd be surprised how many white folks are at these dances."

"You're funny, Robin. See you soon."

Since my calendar is clear this morning, as soon as I drop Sparrow off, I think I'll head over to Macy's. They're having a one-day sale. I can beat the crowd, plus I need to return a pair of sandals I got at the Mills Outlet a few days ago. They looked good on me in the store but not when I got home. They're still in the trunk, which is where I store a lot of my returns. The outlet stores are my drug of choice—and in and around Phoenix they're everywhere. And good ones. I'm talking Saks, Bebe, Nieman's, Nordstrom, and even Victoria's Secret. I find a reason to shop at least two to three times a week. The best rush in the world is getting something at 80 percent off. One day I'm going to say no to myself. But not today. I'm going to try to limit how many times I whip out Mr. Visa or Ms. Gold American Express, and I promise not to buy Sparrow another anything.

I turn on the radio and what's her name who won American Idol last year—Fantasia—is singing her new song "Free Yourself." I kinda like it but her voice is a little too high-pitched for me. Hell, if the company does get sold, this could be a good thing. Sometimes these takeovers can mean a raise or a promotion and new career opportunities, even though I doubt it. But I can't worry about any of this stuff right now. My baby girl is about to start driving.

Shake, Rattle & Roll

Bernadine was lying in bed watching *Jeopardy!* when the phone rang. "Hello," she said after noticing the number was blocked on the caller ID. She prayed it wasn't a telemarketer. If so, as soon as she heard the unfamiliar voice ask for her she would do what she always did and hang up.

"Is this Bernadine Wheeler?" a woman who was obviously black asked. She also had a Southern accent. Bernadine had relatives all over the South. Maybe this was one of them.

"Who wants to know?" Bernadine asked. She sat up straighter and pressed MUTE on the TV remote.

"Belinda Hampton."

"I don't know anyone by that name."

"Well, you do now. You might want to sit down, honey."

"Why?" Now Bernadine was beginning to feel curious along with suspicious.

"I just want to know how long have you been seeing my husband?"

Bernadine didn't think she'd heard her right. She couldn't have. "You *must* have the wrong number. I'm a married woman myself. Goodbye."

"Hold on a minute! Is your husband's name James Wheeler?"

"Yes it is, and I'd really like to know who you are and how you got my number and why you're calling my house."

"He's both of our husbands, sweetheart. I got your number off of one of his cell phones last night right after he called you. He did call you last night, didn't he?"

"Yes, he did." Bernadine pressed the OFF button on the remote, swirled her legs off the side of the bed and stood up. She didn't think this shit was funny.

"From D.C.?"

"Yes. But what business is it of yours?" Her voice dropped an octave.

"Well, I hate to lay so much on you at once and completely out of the blue and everything but I have not been able to figure out a decent way to tell you this: his name is Jesse Hampton."

Bernadine inhaled but couldn't breathe out. She started fanning herself to generate some air, even though the ceiling fan was whirring on high right above her.

"You still there?"

"Is this some kind of prank?" Bernadine asked after finally being able to exhale.

"What would I get out of it?"

"I don't know. But I don't believe this bullshit. Maybe this is some kind of scam. What is it you really want?"

"He's the scam artist, honey, not me. I just accidentally found his other wallet under the front seat of the car when I took it to the car wash, and there was the name

James Wheeler on all kinds of credit cards. So, I realized this son of a bitch has been playing me, too. How much has he hit you up for and how long have y'all been married?"

"You know, I don't have time for this," Bernadine said as she got up from the bed and started walking around in circles. Her head was beginning to feel like it was full of cotton. And what if she just hung up? She flopped back down on the edge of the bed, dug her toes into the pale gray carpet and decided to listen, if for no other reason than entertainment.

"How long have you been married to him?"

"That's really none of your business. Why don't you tell me, since you seem to know so much about us."

"Not *us,* him," she said. "I can prove this is no childish prank, sweetheart. Ask me something about him. What'd he tell you about his family?"

Bernadine thought about this for a minute, but it was all too surreal. If, however, this woman *was* telling the truth, then she really did want to know. Even still, Bernadine was praying this was just one big misunderstanding and in a minute, she was going to get to the bottom of it, cuss this woman out for wasting her time and playing a game that wasn't even close to being funny. But for some reason, she heard herself spew out: "He takes care of his elderly mother because his five brothers are all trifling and in prison."

The woman actually started laughing. "What a dirtbag. First of all, Jesse's mama's been dead and gone since 1988, okay? And all *six* of his brothers are college-educated and some of the most well-respected black men in D.C. Jesse's the black sheep."

Bernadine felt a lump the size of a walnut forming in her throat. This had to be somebody else's nightmare she'd been dragged into. But she was beginning to realize it could in fact be hers.

"Bernadine?"

"Yes," she said, more to let this woman know she now had her undivided attention even though Bernadine was becoming fearful of just how much personal information this woman had about her and her husband.

"You mind if I call you Bernie?"

"Yes, I do mind. I don't know you. Do you mind if I call you Billy?"

"No, I don't mind. In fact, that's what my friends call me."

"Are you almost finished, Belinda, because I've got things to do."

"Not make dinner for your husband, that much I do know. I'm sorry. That was mean. Anyway, what'd he tell you he does for a living? I'm dying to hear this."

"He's a civil rights attorney."

"Right. Well, let me tell you this. He not only isn't anybody's lawyer and has never been to anybody's law school, Jesse didn't even finish college."

This was almost too much to handle all at once, but now Bernadine's curiosity had been aroused and she wanted to know just how much this Belinda did know about James. If she could cause her to stumble, then Bernadine would know this was some kind of premeditated scam, even though she couldn't for the life of her imagine why a grown woman would want to pull something as heartless as this. "What about his wife who died from cancer? The white one."

Belinda laughed again. "Jesse doesn't even like white people. Girl, he really had you believing all this mess, didn't he?"

"I guess he did."

"Well, he's a charmer—that's for damn sure. And he's good at getting people to believe just about everything he tells them. He's a pathological liar, and I think they call people like him psychopaths or something. What's really sad is he's got genius genes that just got all mixed up. Which is why he's probably like this. It's still no excuse for what he does to other folks, and especially women. I'm a hard bitch to fool, and you sound like you could be smart, too, but smart doesn't have a damn thing to do with it."

"And how long have you been married to him?"

"Five years, and I've got two of his kids to prove it."

"You know, I'm having a real hard time believing this. You have some nerve just calling my house out of the blue with this kind of outrageous bullshit, and this isn't funny."

"Want me to prove it?"

"How?"

"I can do a three-way. I really am finally glad to bust him because he's been doing this shit a long time and he needs to be stopped."

"Is he close by?"

"He's just across the bridge in D.C. I'm in Alexandria. Virginia. Just stay on the line and I'll click back when he's on, but promise me you won't say anything until you can hear for yourself what a sleazy human being he is, okay?"

"Okay." It felt like her heart was about to explode. While she waited, Bernadine ran downstairs to the kitchen and got a Corona out of the fridge. She drank half of it in one long swallow. When she sat the bottle on top of the center island, her hands were shaking and she knocked it over. The gold liquid flowed over the edge of the counter and between her toes. Bernadine grabbed a dish towel, dropped it on the floor, stepped on top of it and just stood there.

This whole ordeal was downright frightening. This was the kind of stuff you saw in movies or on soap operas. Not in real life. Not in her life. Not in anybody's life she knew. Of course there are the cheaters, like her ex-husband, John—but this kind of deception and betrayal was light-years beyond cheating. This was just plain evil. And if it turned out all of this was really true, who in the hell did James think he was and what gave him the right to use her life like she was a damn coupon?

John had been bugging her for years about something being a little "off" about James. That he fell too hard for her too soon. That his civil rights work was suspicious, especially since she'd never been in his local "field" office because she couldn't get "security clearance." His so-called *required* travel back and forth to D.C. twice a month. Why it purportedly took him a year to take the Arizona bar. It had taken a few years for her to realize she had confused his sense of self-importance for confidence. John may have been demanding, but James expected her to prove her love by how much she was willing to tolerate. Ironically, John was the one who insisted Bernadine not marry him without a prenuptial agreement. James signed without any qualms.

"Hey, baby," she heard Belinda say.

"Hey back."

"What time do you think you'll be home?"

"I'm running a little behind schedule. It's been crazy. Are the girls asleep already?"

"I'm putting them to bed in a few minutes. You know what I've been meaning to ask you, baby?"

"I'm listening."

"Where are you thinking of taking me for our sixth wedding anniversary?"

"I don't know. That's five whole months from now. You pick the place this time. How's that?"

"That's fine. Let me ask you something else, baby. Do you know a woman named Bernadine Wheeler?"

"That name doesn't ring a bell. Why?"

"Because she called me."

"What do you mean, she called you? When? About what?"

"She said you're her husband."

"That crazy bitch lives out there in Phoenix, and she's been stalking me ever since I started going out there for work. I think she might even be locked up somewhere. Did she call you from a pay phone? If so, it means she's finally in a facility. Don't believe a word that bitch says. And how'd she get your number?"

Bernadine took a breath. "This crazy *bitch* didn't call your wife, James or Jesse, whatever your real name is! She called me. I don't even believe this shit is really happening. I don't—"

"What the hell is going on here? You mean to tell me both of y'all broads have ganged up on me? What kinda bullshit is this? Bernie, don't believe a word—"

"You know what, James, I'm going to let you in on a little secret. Bigamy is a felony. Which means you can go to prison for it. So, I'll tell you what. I dare you to bring your lying ass anywhere near the Arizona state line. I dare you! Try it and you'll be behind bars in a New York minute. I still can't believe this is happening, but thank you, Belinda."

"Thank you, Belinda?"

"You're welcome," Belinda said in a warm voice, as if she was giving Bernadine a high five through the phone. "Women need to stick together and stop sorry men like Jesse from getting away with so much. They want us to be enemies, when they're the ones who try to pit us against each other. You okay, girl?"

"I'm fine. What about you?"

"Now y'all getting chummy! What is this shit?" James yelled, but then the pitch in his voice changed to nice, a falsetto, the one he'd used the entire time he'd been married to Bernadine. She could hear it as plain as day now: the phoniness. Why hadn't she noticed it before?

"Look, baby, I'm leaving the office right now and I'll be home in about a half hour."

"I don't think so," Belinda said with conviction. "Your key doesn't work, and I'm filing to have this bogus marriage annulled in the morning. Bernadine, you know you can do the same. I already looked into it."

"You can't do that. We've been married too long."

"Hey," Bernadine said, "since you're the big-time lawyer, James, you should know how this works."

Belinda was laughing again.

"What's so damn funny, Billy? And what about my kids? You can't stop me from being with my kids. And plus, that's my house you're living in. My car you're driving."

"You want me to cut it all down the middle and give you your half—is that what you want, Jesse?"

There was complete and utter silence. He was in a corner and he couldn't lie or whine or cry or weasel his way out of this one.

"I'm sorry," he said. "To you both. I didn't mean to hurt either one of you—can't you understand that?"

"I'm sorry, too, Jesse James, sorry I ever met your lying ass. You really should be ashamed of yourself. God made a huge mistake when he wired you."

Bernadine hung up.

———

This happened six years ago. To Bernadine, sometimes it feels like yesterday. "Fuck!" she says when she opens her eyes and looks around her bedroom. A wave of fear paralyzes her and she can't move. Her heart is racing, as if she's been running. Her forehead is wet and so are her pajamas. It's not from night sweats. She finished with that almost two years ago. Her hands are tingling but she can't shake them. Not yet. She can blink, which she does until she's batting her eyes—anything to send the pain of the past back where it came from. She doesn't dream about the whole ordeal anymore. Occasionally, it just shows up and jumps inside her. When it does, she waits the five or ten minutes it takes for her breathing to slow down and she can feel the blood flowing into her fingertips.

Right now, the sun is peeking through the space between the shutters. Bernadine knows she needs to get her act together because her daughter and a friend are flying in from Oakland this evening. They're students at Mills College, and it's Martin Luther King, Jr., weekend. They're coming to interview for summer camp counseling jobs in Tucson.

She counts to three, rolls on her side and opens the drawer to the night table. She reaches for two prescription bottles. Swallows the Zoloft dry. She almost doesn't know why she still bothers taking it every morning, because her spirits don't seem to have gotten any higher. Next, she grabs the Xanax. When she shakes it, nothing rattles. Her doctor prescribed them years ago to help her get through episodes like this. She doesn't usually take them every day, but she feels better knowing they're here.

She could use one now. "Shit!" she says, pulling the drawer all the way out, hoping there might be an old bottle lying behind the others. But she knows this isn't the case. She speed-dials the pharmacist for a refill, and without taking a shower, slips on a T-shirt and some shorts, then decides to brush her teeth and wash her face. In less than ten minutes, Bernadine is standing in line behind a little redhead girl who she takes to be about three. Her pale legs are dangling through the slots in the grocery cart. She has a black baby doll squished between her belly and the metal bar separating her legs. She's sucking her thumb. Suddenly, she pulls it out of her mouth and it falls on top of her baby's curly head. "Hi," she says to Bernadine, smiling, her small teeth already protruding.

Braces are in her future, Bernadine is thinking as she smiles back. "Hi," she says to the little girl. Her dad, a stocky guy on the verge of being fat, is at the counter, paying as well as listening to how best to administer this medication which is clearly for his daughter.

"I haven't seen you in a long time!" the little girl says to Bernadine. She is smiling as if they go way back and she's delighted to see her.

"I know," Bernadine says, knowing she has never seen this little girl before. "How have you been?"

"Fine," she says. "You need medicine, too?"

"Yes, I do."

"Me, too. My belly is always hurting. Does your belly hurt, too?" she asks.

"No, my belly doesn't hurt but I sure hope yours feels better soon."

"What hurts for you?" she asks.

"Emma," her dad says to her. "Just say bye-bye to the nice lady."

"Bye-bye," she says to Bernadine.

"She's very friendly, as you can see," the dad says. "She says the same thing to everybody. Have a great day." He pivots the cart to Bernadine's right and whisks down the pet food aisle.

————

Bernadine is still mad at herself for marrying James before the ink had dried on her divorce from John. She was feeling like an empty parking space and James simply pulled in. John was her first husband. They were married eleven years. Fell in love in college back in Boston. Had two children: Onika and John Jr., both now in college. Back in 1989, Bernadine was taking hot rollers out of her hair because they were getting dressed to go somewhere, though she can't remember where, when out of the blue John told her he wanted a divorce. She does remember snatching those rollers out of her hair and hurling them at him after he told her it was Kathleen, his bookkeeper, who was ten years younger than her, and white. For years, Bernadine hated John for the premeditated way he slung this news in her face. They had made a pact in college that if their feelings toward each other started to deteriorate they would let the other know before either of them cheated. John obviously broke his side of the promise. It made her feel like a homicide victim. But there was no funeral.

This felt like the second time she'd been killed.

Her friends had a hard time accepting all of it. Belinda Hampton kept her word and sent Bernadine all the legal documents proving she was indeed married to James, too, and not long afterward, Bernadine's marriage was annulled. She removed James Wheeler's name from everything and was surprised to find out how intertwined their lives had become during the six years they were married. It was about this same time Bernadine discovered James had been systematically robbing her for years. That she had paid for all those trips back and forth to D.C. This was when she went to see her doctor. She started having trouble falling asleep. Having anxiety attacks. In the beginning she worried if he hated her enough that he might try to harm her. It took years for her to stop worrying, but by that time, she was mad at herself for having been such a fool. She has not seen or heard from him since.

Pills have helped her fake it. Helped her to smile when she was supposed to, to hold back tears when they were inappropriate, to forget she hasn't been kissed in six years, not been touched in six years and not had an orgasm in six years. All this trying to forget only made her remember more. That she's lonely. That she often feels like she weighs a ton.

Today is one of those days she has to put the bullshit on the back burner, which won't be hard to do because her daughter is coming home tonight. For three days Bernadine will be happy. She'll be a hands-on mother and her smiles will not have to be manufactured. Over the next nine or ten hours, Bernadine will clean all the rooms the housekeeper ignores—especially the nooks and crannies in the kitchen—and she'll give Onika's room extra-special attention. She'll spend hours in Bed Bath & Beyond where she'll buy an espresso maker she can't afford, but it'll be a surprise since Onika's always having one at Starbucks. She'll also buy new towels and a matching rug for her daughter's bathroom. She'll go up and down every aisle in the grocery store just to be sure to get all the ingredients for some of Onika's favorite meals. She hasn't cooked for her daughter since last Christmas.

By seven o'clock, Bernadine lies across the bed to take what she likes to call a nap.

"Mom, where are you? I'm home! You better not be in bed! It's only eleven-thirty!" Onika yells as she and her girlfriend barge into Bernadine's bedroom. She thought she'd heard them running up the stairs, but by the time she's able to slide her head from under the pillow, the two girls are standing over her. Bernadine rolls over and tries to open her eyes but they flutter and close again.

Sleeping pills will do that.

"Mom, wake up! We're here!" Onika says even louder this time, and starts rocking Bernadine back and forth.

"Hi there, baby girl," Bernadine mutters as she slowly sits up and gives her daughter a peck on the lips. She knows she looks disastrous, because she can see from the mirror her hair is smashed flat on the side she'd been sleeping on, the mascara has given her black baseball smudges under her eyes and to top it off, she still has her clothes on: a white wifebeater and goldenrod capris.

"Hello, Mrs. Harris," Onika's friend says. "I'm Shy."

As Bernadine combs her fingers through her hair and gets up, this young lady is towering over her. Onika looks even more petite than her five feet two inches standing next to her. "You don't have to be shy around me, sweetheart."

"It's short for Cheyenne," she says.

"That's a pretty name. And since you're my daughter's best friend, you can call me Mom if you want, or Auntie's fine with me, too."

"Thanks then, Mom!" Shy says as she bends down and gives Bernadine a soft kiss on the cheek. "And thanks for having me. I've heard a lot of amazing things about you."

"Well, O's prejudiced. Even though I'm not her real mother, I love her just the same."

Shy is obviously taken aback hearing this and glances over at Onika.

"I'm just teasing. Very nice to meet you, Shy."

"Whew!" she says.

Bernadine can now tell that Shy's dreadlocks are bright red. It also looks like she's probably mixed with something. Her skin is the color of sand. She's pretty in an odd sort of way. She also looks athletic. "Well, you sure look like an athlete," Bernadine says, mostly to see if her assumption is right.

"Soccer it is," Shy says, proudly.

"When did you cut your hair off?" she asks Onika, since it's almost as short as Bernadine's was centuries ago when she chopped it off close enough to see her scalp. She did it to piss John off after he'd told her he wanted a divorce. He never liked short hair on women, especially his wife.

"Shy cut it for me, last week. We were just fooling around. Do you like it?"

"I do."

"Look, we didn't mean to interrupt your zees, and you do look tired. I just wanted you to know that we got here okay. Didn't you get my messages?"

"No. When'd you leave them?"

"Right before we got on the flight. A few hours ago."

"I haven't checked the voice mail at home and I can never hear that cell phone because I always have it on vibrate."

"It's all good, Mom. We couldn't get on three flights. Standby from Oakland to Phoenix is really hard. We couldn't even get seats together, but we made it."

Onika smells like blueberries. Bernadine spots the

new tattoo on her forearm. It looks like Chinese but she doesn't want to ask her what it means right this minute. It can wait. Besides, she knows Onika will tell her anyway. There are rings on eight of her fingers. Thin and thick silver bands of various shapes. Onika's fingers are short, too short for all this jewelry. But she's young. Bernadine reminds herself to keep her middle-aged, maternal thoughts to herself. "Aren't you guys hungry? I'll fix you something really quick."

"No, it's okay, Mom. We had a slice at the airport. We'll find something to snack on. I want to show Shy around the crib. And our killer view. This is her first time ever in Phoenix."

"Okay, but if you change your mind, let me know. I could stir-fry something. It'd only take a few minutes."

"Go back to sleep, Mom. We'll see you in the morning. We're pretty wiped out, too. Six hours in that airport was taxing. Every college student in the Bay Area was either going skiing or heading home."

Bernadine looks at her daughter. She can't believe her baby is going to be a junior in college and she's old enough to buy booze. From the time Onika was in high school she'd told Bernadine she knew she wanted to go to a women's college. At first it was Barnard and then Smith but she wanted to be close to home so she chose Mills. She's majoring in social anthropology with a minor in book art. "It's really about the fine art of bookmaking," she'd said. She'll never get a job, but Bernadine wouldn't dare say it.

"Thanks anyway, Mom," Shy whispers, and puts

both hands on Onika's shoulders and slowly shuffles her out the door.

After Bernadine watches the news she remembers she forgot a few items she needed to make Onika's favorite omelet: fresh crabmeat, sour cream, tomatoes, black olives, scallions and yellow and red bell peppers. She'd been so busy thinking about dinner, she forgot about breakfast. She brushes her teeth and washes her face and hears Jay Leno saying something about Katie Holmes and Tom Cruise getting engaged. "It'll never last," she says, turning to the screen.

She leaves the TV on and runs downstairs. It's freezing in here because she forgot to turn the heat up after she'd finished cleaning. She grabs a bottle of sparkling water from the fridge, and on her way to the garage spots the girls' backpacks leaning against the door. They look like penguins.

God, she envies them. Being able to dream about their future. Do whatever they want to do. That their biggest worry is their GPA. Bernadine hopes her daughter and son cherish these years. John Jr. is a first-year graduate student at MIT. His primary interest in life fits into urban studies and planning. Bernadine has had to sit and listen to him lecture her about this stuff as if he's a commentator on CNN or like he's explaining what happened on *Lost*. He's headed for Washington. She can feel it.

When she gets back from the grocery store, she puts everything away and spots the washed and folded towels she bought for Onika still sitting in the laundry basket. She forgot to put them in her bathroom! She tiptoes upstairs, and since Onika's door isn't completely closed, quietly pushes it open with her hips. She's not sure at first if her daughter and Shy are just lying very close together or if they're in fact wrapped in each other's arms. As she walks past the bed, she can see that this is exactly what they're doing. Holding each other. Out of all the times Bernadine used to sleep over with her girlfriends, she'd never held any of them like this. In fact, they'd always fought over the blankets.

She must've been standing there longer than she realized because the girls break apart as if they suddenly feel her presence. She knows why they were holding each other this close. She's not stupid. And she's suspected this about her daughter for years. Onika has never had a real boyfriend that she was ever aware of, and Bernadine never asked why. She always assumed that if her daughter wanted one she would've gotten one.

"I didn't mean to wake you two," she says after she sees their eyes pop open. "I just wanted to put these in your bathroom, O. Go on back to sleep."

They sit up straight. Like soldiers at attention. Now, they're leaning against the headboard and wearing a fearful look. Bernadine sees they're trying to inch away from each other without making it apparent. It is apparent. There was no space between them and now there is.

"I sleep very hard, sometimes, Mom," Onika says.

Shy looks scared shitless, like a child used to being abused—as if Bernadine might hit her or something. Shy decides to play it another way. "We're just used to sleeping in those twin beds at school. It's really tight."

"I didn't know you two were roommates."

"We're not, but we will be in the fall," Onika says.

"You two like each other a lot, then, don't you?"

"Yes," Onika says.

"Yes, Mom, I mean Auntie," Shy says.

"Look, girls, I just want you to know I think it's healthy when you acknowledge who you like."

They look a little surprised and not sure if Bernadine is saying what they think she's saying as she heads on into Onika's purple-and–sky blue bathroom, places the purple-and-blue towels over the rack, picks the damp ones off the floor and tosses them into the basket.

"Mom, why aren't you, like, freaking out?"

"Why should I be freaking out?" she says, standing in the doorway.

"Well, just because."

"Just because my daughter happens to like girls?"

"Yeah, my parents would flip," Shy says.

"Well, I'm not going to flip or freak out. Plus, I wasn't born yesterday, Onika."

"I can't believe you're not angry or anything."

"What's to be angry about? Just don't get too comfortable. I'm still your mother. Now go back to sleep. I'm making your favorite omelet in the morning. Shy, I thought you were going to call me Mom while you're here?"

"I will. I mean I am, Mom."

"Are you a vegetarian, too?"

She shakes her head no. The two of them look as if they're the ones who're thunderstruck. As she turns to leave, the girls sit there frozen in place. Bernadine isn't shocked. In fact, she's grateful this is finally out in the open. Maybe now her daughter can feel good about who she is and stop hiding it. After she closes the door, Bernadine wonders if John knows.

———

At nine-thirty the following morning Bernadine drags herself out of bed, goes to the grocery store, then stops by the lender to pick up a set of loan documents. Thanks to James, she's almost broke. For the past couple of years she's been living on the fumes from her divorce settlement, and what was left of her investments is almost depleted. Bernadine has never been in this position before. She has just enough money to cover her expenses for nine or ten months. She's scared.

If the bank doesn't give her a loan or she can't come up with a major source of income between now and then, she may be forced to put her home on the market. She's lived in this house for twenty-five years. Her kids grew up in it. Of course, she's been thinking about downsizing since they went away to college and only come home for holidays, and not even full summers anymore. She doesn't need all this space. But what if she were to get grandkids?

The court had granted her title to the house free of all encumbrances on top of almost a million dollars. John could afford it. He owned a software company. Still does. The settlement allowed Bernadine to quit her job as a controller at the real estate investment company where she'd worked for years. And rather than start the catering business she'd thought about having one day, she used a good share of the money to open a café: Bernadine's Sweet Tooth. She invested the rest. But that was fifteen years ago. Before James/Jesse.

She doesn't miss her café. For fourteen years, Sweet Tooth thrived. She'd served the finest coffees and teas and personally baked most of the soulful specialties: blackberry cobbler, peach cobbler, sweet potato pie, bread pudding, banana pudding, rice pudding, lemon meringue pie, Seven-Up and Sock-It-to-Me and Red Velvet cakes.

After James/Jesse, her attitude toward Sweet Tooth changed. The baking became monotonous. There was no more joy, no delight in running the café. It was hard work. There was also no room for variation: a sweet potato pie was a sweet potato pie. A peach cobbler had to be a peach cobbler. As much as she was grateful for all the years it was profitable, Bernadine closed the café four months ago. Business had been steadily falling off. With four years left on the lease and the rent at $3,800 a month, it no longer paid for itself. Times had changed. People were more conscientious about what they ate. She was selling sugar.

When she gets home, Bernadine is surprised to find the girls already gone. Onika has left a note: "Mom, thanks for understanding about me and Shy. You have *no* idea how good this makes me feel. After you left my room last night, we were both blown away by your very cool attitude about us. I love her. And she loves me. We'll see you later. Love, O."

What the hell is she talking about? *I love her. And she loves me.* Bernadine is wondering if she went into Onika's room last night, what in the hell it was she witnessed. She honestly couldn't remember anything except getting up this morning to go to the lender. She'd seen their backpacks and assumed they made it in okay. Yesterday evening, when she hadn't heard from Onika by seven, she remembered taking a sleeping pill and lying down to take a nap so she'd be awake by the time they got there.

It was that fucking sleeping pill.

Now she feels shaky. Apparently she'd acknowledged to her daughter she was fine with her being a lesbian—which she is. Bernadine has suspected it for years, but didn't want to ask Onika. She always felt if it was true, then Onika would tell her when she was ready. Now she has. And Bernadine missed it. All because of a stupid sleeping pill?

Bernadine is ashamed and afraid because all this self-medicating has turned her into a different person. Where's she headed if she keeps living like this? She does not want to entertain that thought. She wants her life back—that much she does know. The one she's in charge of. She's tired of keeping the pain of the past present. Doesn't want to keep missing out on the good things. Bernadine begins shaking her head back and forth until she feels dizzy. When she stops, an image of John Jr.'s stupid guinea pigs pops into her head. The ones she accidentally left out in the sun. They spend their whole lives running in place. Bernadine shakes her head one last time. She has no intention of ending up like them.

Fourteen Years

On the morning her doorbell rang, Gloria was in the back-yard, on her hands and knees, pulling weeds and digging in dirt. She removed her cowhide gloves, wiped the sweat from her brow, took a sip of her Pepsi and yelled, "Be there in a second!"

Gloria whistled and skipped up the three steps because she was happy. It was her and Marvin's anniversary. For the past fourteen years they were guilty of filling each other's lives with so much love, they often thanked each other for it. And no matter what day of the week their anniversary fell on, Gloria always took two days off from Oasis—her hair salon—and let Joseph and the girls run things. Right now, Marvin was over at Clarkson's Nursery buying flats of ocotillo, red yucca and baja ruby fairy dusters along with mulch and Bumper Crop. For at least a decade, they marked their anniversary by planting a single hue of flowers indigenous to the desert. This was their red season.

The soles of her rubber boots were caked with mud so Gloria kicked them off before entering the kitchen. She could smell the oxtails beginning to stew in the Crock-Pot she'd filled with water and garlic, onions and celery, and probably a dozen spices. This was Marvin's favorite dish.

On their anniversary, she always gave him what he wanted. Last year Gloria gave him an iPod and since Marvin loved him some Marvin Gaye, she had Joline—the little white girl who does weaves down at Oasis—load it up with every song he'd ever made. Lately, he'd gotten addicted to John Legend so Joline was about to add all the songs from his CD except number five, which was about cheating. Marvin didn't agree with that one.

Gloria walked through the family room. Thanks to Marvin—with the help of Savannah's handy husband, Isaac—the two had brought this fifty-year-old (as of 2005) ranch-style house complete with one-foot-square tiles and skylights, white oak floors and distressed wood cabinets, along with plenty of smooth granite tops. The house was small, not big enough for more than one adult houseguest, since only a daybed fit into one of the three bedrooms. Gloria had fixed up the other room for her three grandkids when they slept over.

Before she reached the front door, she could see a few long-stemmed birds of paradise and pink ginger peeking through the glass. Gloria was tickled. Marvin always had them delivered early. Wanted her to know she was still being wooed. It's definitely date night. They'll have dinner around six. By candlelight. A couple of glasses of champagne and a bubble bath. By candlelight. Then they'll turn the lights on to read their cards to each other since neither of them can read without their glasses. Gloria will wear a pretty nightgown. She's thinking about the crimson one, since she's managed to maintain the size fourteen she walked her way down to from an eighteen. She'll spray his favorite cologne in the air and then walk through it. Marvin will wear his plaid cotton bottoms and a white undershirt. By nine o'clock they'll most likely curl up under the covers and watch *Titanic*—or try to—since they've never managed to make it to the end. Over the years, Gloria has thought about fast-forwarding it, but then that would feel like cheating. Besides, they know how it ends.

Gloria opened the door and glanced over the delivery boy's shoulder. She smiled at the boat parked in the driveway. As soon as Marvin had left this morning, she called Tarik to drive it on over. He had hidden it in his backyard for two days. The small Mexican boy didn't look a day over fifteen and couldn't be an inch over five feet. There was a hint of black peach fuzz below his nose and he was the one driving that van, so what did she know? "You are Gloria Matthews?"

"I am, indeed."

"*Bueno*. These flowers for you." He handed the tall vase to her but it was obvious it was too heavy. "I take in for you?" he asked, first with his eyes.

Gloria stepped aside. "Thank you."

"Happy birthday to you," he said, as if he'd memorized it.

"Oh, it's not my birthday. Anniversary!"

"*Si!* Concrashulations!" he said proudly.

"*Muchas gracias!*" She ushered him across the room to the nook, where he set the vase in the center of the white table. The tissue paper around the base was wet but she didn't care. "*Muchas gracias,*" she said to the boy again, and signed the delivery receipt. As he turned to leave, Gloria reached into what she called her everything drawer and pulled out a ten-dollar bill. "Wait! Tip for you!" she yelled as if he were deaf.

The young man looked shocked when he saw it was a ten. He took a step forward as if he wanted to hug her but knew it was inappropriate. This woman had made his day. And night. He knew he had made hers, too.

After he'd gone, Gloria remembered she'd forgotten to take her blood pressure medication again. She took her daily aspirin before she went to bed. She'd had a heart attack back in '89, right after she met Marvin. This was when he became her personal trainer and nutritionist. He saw to it Gloria walked almost daily and ate wisely. The only time she cheated was during holidays and their anniversary. She was looking forward to having a little gravy this evening.

As she lifted the top off the oxtails, Gloria knew it would still be a couple of hours before she could add the carrots, tomatoes and butter beans. Butter beans? She didn't see any of those cans on the counter because she hadn't taken any out of the cabinet. Shoot. She called Marvin.

"What's going on, baby?" he said, singing it like Marvin Gaye.

"Yes, Mr. Gaye, would you mind picking up a few cans of butter beans on your way home?"

"I thought you were my butter beans?"

"I am, but I'm not in a can. How soon before you think you'll be finished?"

"Are you rushing me, woman?" he asked, trying to sound harsh, which was almost impossible. "I'll be there when I get there!"

Gloria tried to hold back her laughter. "You know Tarik and Nickida are planning to stop by for a hot minute in about an hour or so with the kids. They made us something."

"I hope she didn't have to cook it."

Nickida doesn't have any cooking skills. Gloria and Marvin haven't been able to figure out how they're all still alive. She refuses to follow a recipe, and Gloria has tried to teach her the basics since her own mama apparently forgot. Nickida still can't make a decent tuna sandwich. Even eggs give her problems.

"The kids made it," she said while stirring. "Something out of clay. Again."

"Then make some room on the shelf by the fireplace. It's funny how these masterpieces never seem to break, huh, baby?"

"I'm telling you the truth, but they're our grandbabies and our house is their museum. So there you go."

"Didn't you hide that volcano that looked like a perforated green penis?"

"I sure did," Gloria said, and started laughing. "I have to find it. It was too hard explaining to folks. I keep forgetting to pull it out when they come over. But they don't seem to notice. Anyway, that beige eruption that sat on the tip of it fell off and broke into so many pieces I cut my toe on it. I cannot for the life of me remember where I hid it. Anyway, baby, are you finding some pretty ones or is that a silly question?"

"It's a silly question, Lady Glo. It is truly amazing how many different shades of red there are. God wasn't joking when he made flowers. And you, Baby Girl. Happy anniversary one more 'gain. Anyway, I'm about to start loading the truck. I have one more little stop to make, and do not ask me where that might be. I'll swing by the grocery store right afterward. I should be home in the next forty-five minutes to an hour, tops. If that's okay?"

"That's fine. Marvin, I hope you remember what I asked you not to do?"

"I can't hear you!"

"I'm not kidding, Marvin. Don't you spend a dime on me! Do you understand?"

"I can't hear you! Did you say you're gonna drop a dime on me?"

Gloria stomped her foot. She knew she was too late. This just meant he wouldn't be so mad at her for going a little overboard and getting him that twenty-six-foot day cruiser he'd been fantasizing about for the past three years. He needs to fish. And they need to know what it feels like to sleep below the deck on a lake and rock with the waves. Marvin was going to flip. At first he'd be upset. She could hear him now. "Have you lost your mind, baby?" And she would simply say, "Yes, and so what?" And he would say, "It's beautiful and it's a dream come true, but I can live without this. We could use this money on a lot of other things." And she would say, "I know that, but this is what I spent it on. It was my money. Now go on out there and touch it and then stand at the helm and be quiet." She already had a berth, and this boat was going to get parked in it.

Plus, Gloria could afford it. The past four years at Oasis had been quite profitable. Since she hired Joline to do weaves for white hair, business jumped. Adding a few more braiders who specialized in natural styles also made a big difference. They'd just recently started cutting and dyeing men's hair, since they seemed to spend as much time primping as women did. Metrosexuals is what Joseph said they're called. Hot-lather shaves had become so popular Gloria had Monique and Twyla specially trained.

It's taken almost ten years to update her services and Gloria still can't keep up with requests for spa treatments. Everybody wants everything waxed. They don't want hair on their bodies. They live to exfoliate. Crave glycolic peels. They want to be touched, which is why deep tissue, shiatsu and hot stone massages top the list. Cellulite treatments aren't far behind. And then there are body wraps, scrubs and polishes. Folks want to glow, to leave their worries and dead skin behind.

For months, Marvin had been helping her search for a bigger space, one that wouldn't require much work. They knew plumbing would probably be the most extensive thing they'd have to do. Marvin was excited he and Isaac could build those "treatment rooms" with their eyes closed. They thought of them as walk-in closets. However, if Gloria was finally going to have a full-fledged day spa along with her hair salon, they wanted to do it right. Her lease was up in August, eight months from now. So they had a little time. No more strip malls for Oasis Hair & Beauty. Gloria wanted it in a nicer area, one with healthy palm trees and expensive landscaping. Next to a boutique or a hip new restaurant serving food that needed to be explained. Even a Starbucks wouldn't hurt. So far, no luck. This was just one of many reasons why she bought Marvin that boat. He'd been looking out for her ever since they met.

———

Gloria was back outside when she heard her grandkids running on the gravel walkway along the side of the house. They didn't know how to walk. They sounded like little ponies.

"Slow down, Blaze!" Nickida yelled. Blaze is four. Nickida yells a lot. She's six years older than Tarik, which puts her at thirty-eight. She gets on everybody's nerves except his. Gloria doesn't know if it's because she's so pretty that he tolerates her or because she acts like she needs him for everything. Tarik is forever rushing her to the emergency room. She is such a phony. Even Marvin can see right through her. "What's she got now?" he always asks her after Tarik explains how Nickida couldn't breathe or she thinks she's getting an ulcer. She thought she had cancer on her scalp once but it turned out to be dandruff. It's always something. Gloria has tried to love her but Nickida makes it difficult. Millions of people hate her because she works in the collection department at the IRS. Tarik is her second husband. She also has a son by her first. Brass is twelve. He lives half-time with Nickida and Tarik and the other half with his dad, Luther, whom Gloria has never met. Brass is cocky, acts more like he's fifteen, which is why Gloria and Marvin are glad when they come over without him.

Considering Tarik is a police officer, Gloria wishes he'd apply the skills he uses on the force in his marriage. He never questions anything Nickida does, believes every-thing she tells him. She certainly knows her power. It's both sickening and sad for Gloria to see how docile her son acts around his wife. Even Marvin, who has a very high tolerance for bullshit, finds her hard to take in large doses. For this reason, whenever they're around her, they pretend she's really sweet and just having a bad hair day.

"Hi, Gawa!" Blaze yelped.

"Easy now, Blazie," Gloria said, draping her arms around this little pint-size person. Blaze, of course, was wearing a blue dress because everything she wears is blue. She refuses to wear pants—and only wears shorts when the temperature is over a hundred.

Gloria didn't see Tarik, probably because he was lugging stuff out of their brand-new Sequoia. Next to appear was Stone. He's six. The oldest of the three. His afro looks like black cotton. He has the nerve to be wearing a wifebeater, baring muscles that look like chocolate Easter eggs. Diamond's cheeky face hides behind a cascade of braids. She's almost three and doesn't talk. She did up until a year ago; then she just stopped. She's a sweet little devil. Says everything with her eyes, especially "no." She was diagnosed as autistic, but Nickida refuses to believe it. "She'll talk when she has something to say."

"Hi, Gawa," Stone said as he tried to hog a hug from Gloria. He's tall for his age, and a little on the pudgy side. "Where's Grandpa?"

"He's at the nursery, buying flowers for us to plant."

"Can we plant some?" he asked. He's a mini-me of Tarik, even down to a mole on the left side of his neck. He's also smart, smarter than Tarik was when he was little.

"Let's wait until Grandpa gets here and see what he has that might be easy for you. How's that?"

"Okay." He plopped down on the bottom step of the deck and already looked bored.

"Happy anniversary, Mom," Nickida said. Those three-inch heels slowed her down. Nickida doesn't look like she's had three babies in four years. Her stomach is flat but Gloria suspects that Tarik gave her money to have a tummy tuck and her breasts lifted, because they look the same as when she breast fed.

"Thank you, Nicki." Gloria pushed her hand into the soil and struggled a little to stand up. The kids rushed to help her. They immediately started giggling, digging their hands in the dirt and throwing huge clumps at one another.

"Stone! Blaze! Stop that right now! You know better! Now go over there and turn on the hose and wash your hands."

"It's okay," Gloria said.

"It is not okay. Anyway, Tarik's getting the things out of the truck, Mom. We have a big surprise for you and Pops!"

"Shouldn't we wait for Marvin?" Diamond walked over to Gloria, looked up and smiled. Her little teeth are so perfect they look like baby dentures. Gloria picked her up. She couldn't weigh more than thirty pounds. Gloria rubbed her nose against Diamond's—something Gloria knows she loves—and sure enough, she laughed.

"Well, sure. But we can't stay long because the kids are going to two separate birthday parties. One starts at noon and the other starts at one."

Tarik finally appeared with two grocery bags. He's as tall and black and handsome as he ought to be. He walked over to Gloria, bent down and gave her a warm kiss on her forehead. He kissed Diamond, too, or she'd have had a fit. "Happy anniversary, old woman! Where's Pops?"

"Thank you, sugah. He's still at Clarkson's."

"You guys sure like to live by the book, huh?"

"But it's our book, baby."

"That is the honest-to-goodness truth, Mom. Stone and Blaze, turn that hose off! You're getting all wet and dirty, and you cannot go to your parties if you're not clean!"

Tarik smiled, as if Nickida were such a great mom. He was starting to look so much like his father, David. It's funny how that works. The father who turned out to be gay, and to whom Tarik has not spoken to or about for more than fifteen years. David had tried reaching out to him but Tarik jumped back, said he couldn't handle having a dad who was a fag. Gloria told Tarik his dad was homosexual, not a fag. That he wasn't gay because he chose to be. He was born that way and had simply fought it for years. The last Gloria had heard, David was still living in Seattle.

"Mom, do I smell oxtails?"

"You know what you're smelling."

"Are they ready to be taste-tested?"

"They need another hour or so. When Marvin gets here I can add the butter beans and tomatoes. But go ahead and taste 'em if you just have to." She untied her bibbed apron and tossed it into a wheelbarrow. "Don't get too close to me, because I'm dirty and stinky!"

The kids ran up behind her and yelled, "Stinky Gawa! Gawa's dirty and stinky!"

"Gawa's been gardening. She smells like the earth and that is clean dirt on her, not the other kind," Ms. Martha Stewart said. "Come inside where it's cool and help get your Gawa and Pops's anniversary presents out of the bags!"

Off they went. Her wonderful grandchildren. Stone. Diamond and Blaze: human rock, carbon and fire. Although she wasn't one to criticize, Gloria couldn't help but ask what some of these parents are thinking about when they name their children. Years ago, black people gave them African and biblical names but then they just seemed to stop and started making up the most ridiculous combination of sounds and syllables, most of which didn't make any damn sense. They were just tongue twisters.

Nowadays, parents were naming babies after anything and everything: numbers, letters of the alphabet, trees, spices, flowers, the weather, seasons, colors, perfume, cars, designers, alcoholic beverages and a slew of other inanimate objects. Gloria's friend Robin was no better. She named her daughter Sparrow. So now there are two birds in their house. White folks have gotten worse than black people, as if they're trying to outdo one another to see who can come up with the weirdest names ever. Pets are the ones getting all the human names: Jake, Jo, Bo, Max, Romeo, Juliet, Chloe, Annie, Lizzy, Bill, George, etc., etc. Gloria feels sorry for some of these kids although she's gotten used to and has even grown rather fond of her grandkids' names.

"Nicki didn't tell you our good news, did she?"

"What good news?" Gloria asked, praying to God Nickida wasn't pregnant again.

"I haven't had time to tell her about your promotion or our winning the trip to Hawaii."

Tarik, who was dipping the ladle into the Crock-Pot and scooping out a small oxtail, just gave her a look. "Well, maybe next time I have a surprise, I might be able to tell it."

"I didn't tell her!"

"Who got a promotion?" Gloria asked. "And what kind of raffle was it that you won a trip to Hawaii?"

"I made lieutenant, Ma."

"Oh, my Lord! That's just wonderful, baby," Gloria said without having to fake her enthusiasm. "When?"

"I've known for a few months but it became official yesterday."

She walked over and gave him the kind of hug she used to give him when he made the honor roll or after the first time he played his saxophone in a parade. "I'm so proud of you, Tarik. So proud."

"I know you are, Ma. Anyway, Nicki bought five dollars' worth of raffle tickets from the kids' school, and we just found out a couple of days ago that we actually won! An all-expenses-paid trip to Honolulu. Can you believe that?"

"I guess you two need to pinch yourselves to make sure this is real, then, huh? This is fantastic! I've never won anything in my life."

"Neither have I," Nickida said.

"I think I won a case of Pepsi once at a picnic, but I left because the grass was killing me. Anyway, Ma, we went online and got the hookup, and it looks like we can both get off the second week in June, and we were wondering if you think you and Pops might be able to watch the kids for us that week. Actually, it's ten days all told."

"Don't give it a second thought."

"You know we've never been on a honeymoon?" Nickida asked like it was a statement. Gloria did know. They were broke back then. Tarik was paying off the last of his student loans and had finally decided he might not ever be any Branford Marsalis or Kenny G, and sold his saxophone.

"I do recall that being the case," Gloria said. "Just e-mail me the exact dates so I can give Joseph a heads-up."

"Are you sure they can run that place without you?" Nickida asked.

"Joseph's been helping me run Oasis for more than twenty years, Nicki. Plus, the kids like going to that place we call a hair salon."

"Well, if they just have to get their hair braided, could you make sure they don't mix that synthetic hair with theirs?"

Gloria was trying to stop herself from rolling her eyes at this child, but she simply blinked and said, "I wouldn't dream of it, especially without asking you first, Nicki; you know that."

"I was just . . ."

"Gawa!" Blaze yelled. "Come see!"

Gloria turned the corner, and there in the middle of the dining room table were two more clay masterpieces, the colors and shapes unrecognizable, but Gloria mustered up her sense of delight and surprise by saying, "They are just beautiful! Thank you so much for making these for us!"

"Wanna know what mine is?" Stone asked, pointing at the ugliest of the two, which looked like a grayish brown coffin with a lid that didn't quite fit. "Guess, Gawa, guess!"

"A lot of things come to mind."

"Okay. It's a thing for butter."

"Oh," Gloria said. "I was thinking that might be what it was. I just wasn't sure. I like it. I hope the butter fits."

"Just break the butter in half if you have to. I won't mind."

"Do you like mine, too, Gawa?"

"I do indeed. Isn't yours a saucer?" Gloria asked, praying she was right.

"It's a cat dish," Blaze said proudly. "For your cat."

"But I don't have a cat."

"It's for when you get one." She had a look on her face that said, "I'm way ahead of you."

"Who knows, maybe one day we will, but I think Pops is allergic to cats."

"Then get a kitten."

"We will give that some thought. But thank you both so much for our lovely gifts."

"Okay, kids, give Gawa a hug, because we need to get going," Nickida said.

"What time is it?" Gloria asked.

"Almost eleven-thirty."

"Marvin should be here in a minute."

"Well, if we miss him, we also wanted you guys to have this," she said and handed Gloria a small gift bag from Blockbuster.

"What on earth . . ." Gloria said, and peeked inside the bag. She could see it was a CD or a DVD.

"You can go on and look at it, Ma. We thought you guys might want to consider not getting on the *Titanic* tonight and instead consider watching *Casablanca,* which is not three hours long."

"Why, thank you for being so thoughtful."

The doorbell rang.

"I'll answer it," Stone said and started heading toward the door.

"Hold it right there, mister. What have I told you about answering the door? First of all, this is Gawa and Pops's house, and if anybody answers the door, it should be her or him. Now just cool your heels."

It rang again.

"You want me to get it for you, Ma?"

"Sure, go ahead. I hope it's more flowers!"

"Come on, kids, let's get everybody strapped in. We'll wait for you in the car, Tarik. Happy anniversary again, Mom." Nickida gave Gloria a quick peck and squeezed her hands, something she rarely did.

"I have to peepee," Blaze said. Little Diamond crossed her hands down there to indicate that she had to go, too.

"I didn't have to go, but now I think I do," Stone said and ran to beat them to the bathroom.

"Use the one in our room," Gloria said, and off they went.

Tarik not only didn't put the top back on the Crock-Pot but had dripped gravy all over the counter. Some things just don't change. After Gloria wiped it up, she went to get four eggs out of the carton to start the corn-bread and her foot slipped on a few drops of gravy she hadn't noticed. All eighteen eggs hit the floor. Gloria just shook her head, grabbed a handful of paper towels and got down on her knees to clean them up. Tarik could sign for the flowers.

When her son opened the door, instead of another floral delivery, there were two uniformed police officers standing there to greet him. They were surprised to see him. "Hey, Tarik, what are you doing here?" the younger of the two officers asked him.

"My mother and stepfather live here. What's going on, guys? I know this isn't a social visit."

"Can you step outside for a minute, man?"

"Yeah," Tarik said. He was suspicious because he knew this wasn't going to be pleasant. Police officers don't ring your doorbell unless it's bad news.

"Is your mother at home?"

"She's in the kitchen. Talk to me, fellas."

"Slow down a second. Anybody else here with you?"

"My wife and kids. What's going on?"

"Look, you're an officer of the law, Tarik, and we're going to need your assistance in this."

"Has something happened to Marvin? Does that have anything to do with why you're here?"

They gave him an affirmative look.

"Marvin King, your stepfather, was killed about an hour ago in a drive-by."

"What?" Tarik asked, backing away from his colleagues as if the space would make room for the truth. But he knew this was the truth.

"We're really sorry, man. Right now we need you to bring out that law-enforcement soul. Do you hear me?"

Tarik wiped his eyes and stood erect. He'd been drilled on exactly how to deal with death without breaking down, without taking it personally. But Marvin was the only father he'd ever really known. "I hear you," Tarik said. "It's their anniversary."

"Oh, wow, man. We're really sorry."

"This is going to destroy my mother."

"It's probably better if a family member tells her."

He was the only family member she had. It fell to him, then, to tell her. Right then, Tarik's heart didn't have a badge on it. From inside the house he could hear the kids running down the hallway. He knew they were heading straight toward the front door. "Nicki! Get the kids! And don't let them come outside!"

She appeared inside the open doorway. "What's going on? I need to get them to their parties, and we're going to be late as it is. Hi, Doug. Hey, Jose."

Both officers tipped their hats and nodded hello to her. She wondered what they were doing here. Whatever it was, she knew it wasn't good.

"Go talk to your wife," the older of the two officers said. "And ask her to get the kids out of here or take them to a back bedroom."

"Give us a minute, Nicki. And please, just go back in the house and stay with Ma for a few minutes. I'll be right in."

"Is everything all—"

"Please, just do it! Okay?"

"Okay."

"So, exactly what happened, guys?"

"The only information we have is that your stepdad was an innocent bystander. Right there in front of Clarkson's Nursery. There were twenty-eight rounds exchanged between gangbangers and six stray rounds struck your stepdad. Three in the head, three in the chest. He went down at the scene, man."

"Do you have anybody in custody?"

"Not yet. When we got to the scene, they were of course already gone. You know how they do this shit, man. And we're really sorry to have to be here. Several eyewitnesses have been interviewed by Homicide and they're still over there. Some are just in shock."

"Do you have any idea which gangs they were?"

"That's not known to us right now, Tarik, but we're pretty sure it'll be easy for us to ascertain. You know we've been having problems in that area and a couple of these groups are at war."

"Aren't they always," Tarik said, nodding his head slowly. He, of course, knew all of this already. "Where is Marvin?"

"Right now he's on the way to the coroner's office."

"He's on his way to the coroner's office," Tarik repeated.

The younger officer wanted to reach out to squeeze Tarik's arm or something, but knew this wouldn't help his blue brother, at least not right now. Plus, this wasn't in the codebook. "We'll just wait out here until after you tell her."

"Tarik," Gloria said. She was standing in the doorway and eyeing the officers suspiciously. "Is something wrong?"

Tarik opened his eyes as wide as possible, hoping the air would ventilate them and evaporate the moisture and redness. He wasn't sure if it worked. All he knew was that he needed to be strong right now. As he turned to look at his mother, he saw her take in sips of air and a look of terror was filling up her eyes.

She already knew.

Love Don't Live Here Anymore

"I don't want to spend the rest of my life with you," I say to Isaac as soon as he walks in the door. I'm sitting on the love seat in the Great Room. Two cold crab cakes sit on a paper plate on the cocktail table. The salad is wilted, the French fries hard. I thought I could eat.

"How about, 'Welcome home, Isaac'?"

"Welcome back, Isaac. I meant what I just said."

"What in the world are you talking about?" He sits down on a stool at the counter. His legs are long. They're crossed at the ankle. The lace on one of his running shoes is undone. I'm tempted to tell him, but then that would mean I'm creating some kind of intimacy, which is the last thing I want to do. I need to keep my distance because of course you don't stop loving someone on a dime just because they do something you might find unforgivable. I want to hate him, so I have to keep the focus on how pissed off I am more than on how much I am hurt. Falling apart would give him just the room he needs to touch me. Not this time, buddy.

"What if I walked in here and said, 'Savannah, I don't want to spend the rest of my life with you.' How would you feel about that?"

This gives me a jolt. "Is that how you feel, Isaac?"

"Look, can I just get a glass of water and take a hot shower before you read me the riot act and tell me what I've done this time that's so deplorable? I'm beat, Savannah."

"Take your time." He doesn't look the least bit tired. In fact, he looks quite rested. There's something different about him. He's wearing the same look on his face that I've seen right after we've had great sex. I'm surprised I can still remember. I'm not going to think about this because I almost don't care. He did something in Vegas besides touch wood. That much I do know.

When he pushes himself up to a standing position and takes a step, he almost trips over the shoestring. I feel bad but not that bad. "I see you got a new laptop."

"That I did." It's on the kitchen table.

"You like it?" he asks.

"They're all the same when you get right down to it."

"Were you able to recover all your stuff?"

"Pretty much. You might want to look at yours after you get out of the shower."

"Why, did you try to use it?"

"I did, but I had the same problem you had."

"Really," he says, rather suspiciously.

"Really."

I can see he's tempted to go into his office but he's afraid to open that door. I think he knows I know what he's been doing in his so-called office. "Why don't you go on and take your shower."

"Maybe I will."

This whole thing feels weird. This is not how you

end a marriage, is it? I'm wondering deep down inside if I really want to end it or if I just want to break up the monotony. I wish I could keep the parts of Isaac I still love. I wish I could pretend I never saw what I saw, that I don't feel so let down. I wish we still excited each other. But which one weighs more?

He turns down the hallway. I hear his office door open. My heart is beating fast and now I'm anxious. I'm tempted to lunge off the sofa but for some reason I don't. I want to confront him from where I'm sitting. I want him to stand still and look down at me, so his eyes can't avoid mine.

"Savannah!" he yells. "What the hell did you do with my computer and what's all this shit on the wall?"

Out he comes. He doesn't have the look I imagined. There's anger in his voice but not rage. After all, I invaded his space. Violated his world, the one he thought was secret. The next thing I know he's standing over me. "I had no idea you were such a freak," I say.

"I'm not a freak. What did you do with my computer?"

"It's in the pool."

He looks outside as if he might see it floating or doing laps. "You threw it in the pool?"

"That's what I just said." I stand up like a soldier. "You are one sneaky, lying son-of-a-bitch, Isaac, and I wish I'd known I couldn't trust you from here to the corner."

"I haven't done anything wrong."

"Yes, you have. And you know it." I'm trying not to cry but it feels like I'm crying anyway. He takes a few steps toward me. I jump back. "Don't even think about fucking touching me."

"Savannah, come on, now. Maybe I went too far. But none of this has anything to do with how I feel about you."

"Fuck you, Isaac."

"It's just something we do for kicks."

"Who is 'we'?"

"Guys."

"I don't care what guys do, Isaac. How would you feel if you found a bunch of naked men on my laptop, huh?"

"They'd probably be gay."

I just roll my eyes at him.

"Look, Savannah, I'm sorry."

"Sorry?"

"Okay, so maybe I have a little problem."

"But it's your problem, Isaac, not mine."

"I'd be willing to stop, I swear. It's wearing me out anyway, living at night the way I have been."

"You've been having sex with these women, Isaac."

"No, I haven't."

"Yes, you have. I've seen some of what you've been doing, and you can just keep on getting your dick sucked in cyberspace or whatever else you may do with all these freaky-ass women. I couldn't even watch some of the weird shit you've been doing, not to mention the money you've been spending. I get it now."

He sits on a stool and stands up again. I've backed away from him as far as I can go and am leaning against the doors that lead outside. The glass is cold but I welcome it.

Isaac gets a bottle of water from the fridge and drinks it in two swallows. This time he leans on the counter and peers over at me. "Well, you know what, Savannah? What if I told you that as much as I still love you, I think I might be tired of being married to you, too? I'm tired of you being in charge of my life."

This stings. He may as well have shot an arrow right in the middle of the blood vessels that lead to my heart. "How in the world am I in charge of your life, Isaac?"

"You try to be. Just because I don't like what you like."

"That is not true and you know it."

"You've never tried to come over to my side. You always expect me to come over to yours." He sits on a different stool. It seems as if he's been waiting a long time to get this off his chest.

I could've gone down the list of all the things I've done over the years just to keep the peace, but it didn't feel like it was worth it. "What you just said isn't true and you know it, Isaac. I've tried to be as supportive as I possibly could. Who was it that helped you start your business?"

"We both know the answer to that. That's not what I'm talking about."

"I can't help it if I'm not as gung-ho about fences and decks and playhouses as you are!"

"You don't have to be gung-ho about them, but at least show some respect for what I do."

"I don't even believe this! You don't even watch my shows!"

"Because they're boring, Savannah. There's no punch

to them. You're just reporting what you see—what we all see—and what we already know. That's why I don't watch them!"

This is just the kick in the stomach I needed. "You know what? Fuck you, Isaac! If they were so boring then how have I been able to keep my job all these years, huh? If everybody felt the way you do, huh?"

"Look, it's my personal opinion, okay? I didn't mean to say it the way that it came out. I'm sorry. I know you're good at what you do, Savannah. That's not what this is about, is it?"

"No, it's not, Isaac. Not even close."

"Then tell me what's wrong with us."

"I can't tell you what's wrong with us. But I can tell you why I'm not happy."

"I'm listening."

"You don't seem all that interested in me anymore."

"That's not true."

"You don't seem to care if what you do pleases me or not."

"That's probably true."

"Why is that?"

"I can't honestly say."

"Yes, you can."

"People's feelings change, Savannah. Sometimes you can't do anything about them."

"What's that supposed to mean?"

"It could mean that I don't feel the same kind of love I once felt for you even though I want to."

I'm trying my hardest not to start crying again but it's impossible. I bend my head over and yank my T-shirt up to wipe my eyes before they get wet. Did he just say he doesn't love me anymore? Isn't that what he just said? I pull myself together as best I can and lift my head back up. "You know something, Isaac?"

"What?" he asks, moving over toward the sofa, almost directly across from me. "Let's not turn this into a wrestling match, Savannah, okay? I don't want you to hate me."

"Why would I hate you, Isaac?"

"Because even though I love you and will probably always love you, maybe it would be a good idea if we did get a divorce."

I can't believe he just said that. "You mean you want a divorce, too?"

"I don't know what else we can do at this point. Why do you want one?" He's looking at me as if I'm about to disclose some deep secret.

"Because I'm bored. Because these past couple of years you've made me feel dispensable, unimportant, like an afterthought. Because you haven't tried to do things that make me happy. Because you've deliberately done things you know won't bring me joy. Because it seems like you've become my adversary instead of the warm, thoughtful, loving and considerate man I married ten years ago. Because I don't like who you've become. Because you've forgotten how valuable I am, and I know how valuable I am and I can't live with someone who makes me feel bad, especially when you were the one person I could rely on to make me feel good. You've been killing me inside, and I don't want to die like this. This is why I want a divorce. Even though I still love you."

He looks at me as if I've said the unthinkable. I see his eyes begin to glisten and now they're a glassy red. Tears fall from his eyes. I've never seen Isaac cry in all the years I've known him. "Well," he says, dusting his face dry. "Okay." He stands up. "That's ten for the home team."

"Well, you asked."

"That I did. I will say this, Savannah. I wish I could still love you, because you've been the one constant in my life. You've been my anchor. But you didn't hold on to me. Your grip loosened except when it came to things you wanted me to do. Things I suppose made you value me. It was basically all the stuff I could do that you seemed more excited about. Not what was inside me. You seemed to think I was what I did but it wasn't true, and you never bothered to look any further than the surface. That's why I started drifting away from you. It's how I ended up here."

"Which is where?"

"I've met someone who does look inside and likes what she sees, and she understands me."

"Did you meet her with her clothes on or off?"

"That's not even cool, Savannah."

"Was she swinging on a rope or slithering around a fucking pole? Did she dry-fuck you or maybe you met her in a brand-new online church?"

"Does it really matter where I met her?"

"Yes, it does matter. What matters more is how long have you been seeing the bitch?"

"She's not a bitch. And how long I've been seeing her is not important right now."

I walk over to him. "It is important, Isaac. It's very important. It means if you've been sleeping with me and fucking her at the same time I want to know how long you've been doubling your pleasure, you sneaky son-of-a-bitch!" I push him but not hard enough for him to lose his balance.

"About a year. Does that make you feel better?" He looks down at me like he's getting some kind of sick pleasure telling me this.

With all my might I ball up my fist, charge toward him and sock him in the nose. It feels like I might have broken my hand, but I pretend not to feel any pain. When he grabs me by the wrist, I see a drop of blood trickling from his right nostril. It gives me instant pleasure. Now I know how love can make you violent. "You lying, sneaky bastard!"

"Take it easy, Savannah." He walks into the kitchen and gets a paper towel.

I stand here waiting for the bell to announce the next round but the only sound I hear is ringing in my ears. I cannot believe my boring husband of ten years just had the nerve to say he still loves me but he's not in love with me anymore—which really is a nice way of saying he doesn't love me and he's found it somewhere else with somebody else. "Did you see her in Vegas?"

He takes a few baby steps but keeps his distance while he thinks about this for a second and then says, "Yes, I did."

"Then why did you keep hounding me about coming?"

"Because I knew you wouldn't."

"What if I had said yes, Isaac, I'll come with you or I'll meet you there?" Now these stupid tears are calling the shots, and as much as I don't want them to appear anywhere on my face, they are rolling down my cheeks, so now I head for the kitchen to get a paper towel of my own, and he takes a giant step to the side to make room for me to pass.

"You're too hung up in your world to come into mine. I knew you wouldn't change your mind."

"So why'd you bother asking me?" I wipe my eyes dry. Since they're feeling the same anger as the rest of me, most likely there will be no more tears.

"Because I was hoping if you had an inch of respect left for me then you would try to show it. And if you did, then it would've or could've possibly started to restore some of my love for you. It's not gone, Savannah. It's just been put on ice."

"I want you to leave."

"Leave?"

"Yes, go. Like get out."

"I suppose I will."

"Right now, Isaac!"

"Right now?"

"Yes, right now."

"Wait a minute. I can't—"

"I want you to get the fuck out of here!"

"And where am I supposed to go?"

"Go live with your bitch or your mama! I don't care! But I want you out of my house!"

"Oh, so it's *your* house?"

"It was my house when I met you, and the last time I checked you have yet to make a mortgage payment, so whose house do you think it is?"

"Yours," he says, hunching his shoulders. "It's yours."

"I can't stand to look at you right now, Isaac. And the thought of—"

"What if I said I don't want to leave?"

"It doesn't matter what you want. Just go! And I don't really care where!"

"Okay. Take it easy, Savannah. Don't blow a gasket. You got a good punch in, and I hope it makes you feel better."

I just roll my eyes at him.

"I'll take off for now to give you a chance to cool down."

"I don't need to cool down. You've made yourself crystal clear, Isaac."

"And so have you."

"Yeah, but the difference is I'm not the one who's been having an affair behind your back while fucking you at the same time, have I?"

"I don't know that."

This time I grab a paperback off the counter—*Sugar* by Bernice McFadden—and throw it at him, but he's quick and dodges it. "You do know! You're making me sick to my stomach! Now go! I mean it, Isaac!"

"So this is how we end our marriage? Like a boxing match?"

"You're the one who hit below the belt. You're the one who didn't play by the rules. Not me. And for the record, if I hadn't cared about what made you tick I never would have married you in the first place. I certainly wouldn't have helped you start your business. But I did it because I had faith in you and because I had something you didn't have at the time, and that was resources and money, and I showed you something else you still don't seem to understand, and that was patience and compassion because I understood how hard it is to be a black man with talent and skills, and so I gave you my shoulder to lean on and all I wanted was for you to let me lean on yours."

"I thought I was."

"That's what the problem was, Isaac. Your shoulder was synthetic. You went through the motions because your heart wasn't in it. So just go. Please. Go."

"I'm sorry you feel this way."

"I'm sorry I do, too."

I walk over toward him but this time he just stands there. He looks down at me and I cannot look at him. I look down at his feet and then push him toward the door leading to the garage. Touching him burns.

"What about all of my stuff?"

"You can get it while I'm at work. And please leave the key on the table."

"Leave the key on the table?"

"I don't care. Keep it. I'm going to be changing the locks anyway," I say, not having thought about any of this until this very moment.

He looks at me as if he just remembered something. "I'm not a burglar, Savannah."

"Yes, you are."

Now his black eyes are glistening. "I'm really, really sorry, Savannah."

"No, you're not," I say, and slam the door. I turn the

lock so hard I break two nails. I then lean my back against the door and slide until I'm in a sitting position. The tile is ice cold against my bare thighs. I sit here for the longest and count the number of tiles I can see, over and over and over. It becomes obvious to me that some things just don't add up, because I keep getting a different number.

I think I knew it was over when we celebrated our eighth wedding anniversary. I remember looking at him across the dinner table in a restaurant we'd eaten at the previous seven. That's when I realized we had flat-lined. Being married to Isaac was like walking on a sidewalk that suddenly stopped. There was nowhere else to go. Little did I know he was apparently feeling the same way.

But here I am. Fifty-one years old. I've been out here on this raft of love and the love boat so many times it's not even funny. This time is different. Isaac is my husband, not my boyfriend. I don't have a Plan B because I never thought I'd be needing one. Based on the urgency and strength of our love in the beginning, I thought we were going to keep blooming. But here we are, like two dead roses.

It doesn't seem to matter if you're thrown overboard or you jump ship. Both lead to sorrow. I think it might weigh more now than it did at thirty-six. So many people think because we're older we should be used to failed relationships and bad marriages, but especially disappointment. How do you get used to it? This is the complete opposite of what I was led to believe I could expect when I grew up and became a woman. Back in the '70s I wasn't preparing for the worst that could happen. I was preoccupied with the best that could happen. I didn't know some men could be such big liars and such good liars because neither I nor my girlfriends saw anything redeeming about lying. We were honest. About most things, but definitely our feelings. We didn't cheat on our boyfriends, especially if we loved them. We never thought some guy would deliberately fill our hearts with brown sugar and then pour hot water over it. We thought boys would grow up to become decent men who would love us as hard as we loved them.

I push my shoulder blades against the grooves in the door. I'm going down in an elevator that's not going to stop. But then it does. The doors open and here comes heartache. I feel it right now. That thud. These acid tears. The tear inside my chest. My elbows are getting heavy. I can't stop myself from keeling over, so I go ahead and roll into a knot but find myself unable to stop rocking. I want to sit back up, but I just can't. Even when I suddenly feel like I'm freezing, I can't get up. All I can do is look around the room and hear how loud the silence is already. My marriage is over. I live alone now. This is not the way I dreamed it. This is not what I had hoped for, what I asked for. I want to skip this part. I want to push the fast-forward button until I get back to happy. In fact, I wish Isaac would walk back inside this house and wrap his arms around me and hold me close, the way he used to, because even though I know he's the source of this brand-new pain, he's really the only one who can stop it.

If I Sit Still Long Enough

What Gloria remembered about that day was falling. First to the floor. Then being picked up by her son. And then falling into his chest. She remembered him saying something about Marvin being shot. With bullets. Stray bullets. Aimed at someone else. Aimed at another gangbanger. That he was caught in crossfire. She melted. Then her body stiffened and froze. Her teeth would not stop chattering. She bit her tongue trying to silence them. And she went looking for her car keys anyway, because she figured Marvin would need a ride home.

"Where on earth did I put those damn keys?" she asked Tarik as she walked from one room to the next, looking for them. They were, of course, in the same spot they always were: hanging on a hook by the door that led to the carport. Her grandkids wanted to help Gloria locate them. Nickida just shook her head back and forth in disbelief and grabbed Gloria by the wrists, then wrapped her arms around her mother-in-law as tight as she could.

"Ma," Tarik said, bending over and pulling her close and with a firmness that made it hard for her to move. "You don't need your keys."

"But I have to go get Marvin," she said, wiggling her way out of his grip. "It's our anniversary and he's going to want to eat his oxtails before he goes anywhere. That much I do know."

"Ma, you've gotta calm down."

Gloria looked at him as if he were crazy. "Can you give me a ride, baby? I think he's going to be so surprised to see that boat in the driveway! But first, I need to finish cleaning those eggs up off the floor. After we get Marvin I might need you to pick up another carton because he cannot eat oxtails without cornbread. And I need to take a shower because I'm filthy. Can you give me ten minutes? I should call him and let him know I'm on my way. Where's my cell phone?"

"Ma." Tarik sighed.

That's when she remembered Tarik breaking down and drooping as if he didn't have a muscle in his body. He folded his arms on the kitchen counter and his head dropped on top of them. Gloria heard him wail, then whimper. She wanted to hold him and help him feel less pain than she was feeling, but she had collapsed on the sofa and could not get up. She crossed her arms but they broke apart and fell into her lap. Gloria forced herself to blink enough to see through the tears and then pushed herself to the edge of the cushion and sat up straight. She closed her eyes and felt herself balancing. She was thinking that if she sat still long enough, maybe she could rewind this movie to the butter beans. She knew exactly how she would change it. She would call Marvin and say, "Baby, how soon before you head home?" And right after he said, "I'm about to start loading the truck . . ." she would cut him off and say, "Wait! Would you please go back inside the nursery and see if you can find some Red

Paramount or button cactus at a good price and call me back as soon as you see them?" She would not have even mentioned butter beans. "And take your time, baby. There's no rush."

This would've changed everything. Marvin would've come home and flipped when he saw the boat in the driveway. "Have you gone and lost your entire mind, woman?" he would've yelped, though standing there in awe, because Gloria knew he had always wanted a boat and now he had one. He would've given her a small pair of diamond studs from Zales, to replace the ones that were stolen out of their luggage when they went to Cabo last year, and she would've put them on immediately. He would've run back to the grocery store to get the butter beans and another carton of eggs and she would've made the cornbread and Po' Folks Pie, and by six o'clock they would've started their official date night.

———

Tarik called Bernadine first. She did not answer, and he didn't want to ask his mother for her cell number. He left a message. "Auntie Bern, this is Tarik. I'm here at Ma's. Something has happened to Marvin and it would be nice if you could stop by. I'll try to get in touch with Auntie Robin and Savannah. Thanks."

He then dialed Sparrow's number; she answered on the first ring. "Everything is up in the air."

"I'm not so sure about that."

"You need a babysitter, cuz? Fair warning: my rate has gone up because of inflation. Heard of it?"

"I have. And I don't need a babysitter, Sparrow. Where's your mom?"

"At work. You want the number? You sound weird. What's going on?"

"Marvin is gone."

"Where'd he go?"

"Probably up. He got shot by some gangbangers and didn't survive."

"You mean he's dead?"

"That's what it amounts to."

"Oh, fuck! You mean to tell me Uncle Marvin is really dead for real?"

"I'm afraid so. I don't want to call Auntie Robin at work to lay this on her, so maybe I'll call back. What time does she usually get home?"

There was no response.

"Sparrow?"

"What?" She is obviously angry and she's also obviously crying because she—like everybody else—adored Marvin. He was the father and uncle and brother none of them had been fortunate to have. They all claimed him. "How is Auntie Gloria doing, or is that, like, a dumb question?"

"She's not doing so hot."

"If I had my driver's license I would zoom over there right this very second and hold her hands. I swear to God, I would, Tarik."

"I know, sweetheart. But just wait until your mom gets home—could you do that for me?"

"I will. I will do that. But I hope when I hang up the phone that this was just a prank call. Love you, cuz. Bye."

Tarik dreaded the next call. Auntie Savannah didn't know how to take bad news. And Uncle Isaac. He and

Marvin were tight. They built things together, smoked cigars on the deck Isaac helped him build, watched March Madness together, all the NBA playoffs. The Super Bowl. And Tiger. Hell, they were buddies. Tarik wasn't sure who would be the hardest to tell.

"Tarik, why on earth are you calling me? You never call me! What's going on, and it better be good news!" she said.

"I'm afraid it's not."

"Please don't tell me something has happened to Gloria? It's not her heart, is it? Please tell me it's not her heart."

"It's not *her* heart."

Savannah let out a sigh of relief and then said, "What do you mean?"

"It's Marvin's heart."

"What do you mean by that, Tarik?"

"Okay. Earlier today Marvin was accidentally shot by some gangbangers."

"I know you're not telling me Marvin is dead, are you?"

"I'm afraid he is."

Tarik heard her scream.

"Noooooooooooooooo! No no no no no NO! Not Marvin! Not today! Please. Come on, Tarik. Not our Marvin. Where is Gloria? Who's there with you and her?"

"It's just the two of us here now."

"I'm on my way."

"Is Uncle Isaac at home?"

"He doesn't live here anymore, but I'll figure out a way to get this—"

"What do you mean he doesn't live there anymore? Why not? And where'd he go?"

"This is not the time to talk about me or Isaac, okay?"

"Okay."

"Where did this happen?"

"In front of Clarkson's Nursery."

"But how? Even though I think I already know."

"I'll tell you later. I've got a few more calls to make."

"Where is Gloria right now?"

"I think she's asleep."

"Poor Marvin. Poor Gloria. And today of all days. On their goddamn anniversary! Which gang was it? Oh, never mind. They don't even know what they're fighting over, do they? Turf they don't fucking own. Drugs! Drugs! Drugs! This isn't the Wild Wild West. It's fucking Phoenix and it's 2005, isn't it, Tarik?"

"I know, Auntie, I know."

"I'm sorry for swearing."

"Why don't you wait until you calm down and maybe come over tomorrow. I wouldn't want anything to happen to you in this state. Ma's okay for right now."

"I can't stay in this house. I'll drive slow. Please don't say anything about Isaac to Gloria. It's not important right now."

"So she doesn't know?"

"No."

"How long has he been gone?"

"Not long enough," she said. "Tarik, who else knows about Marvin?"

"I left a message for Auntie Bern, asking her to stop

by to see Ma, and Sparrow is going to tell Auntie Robin when she gets home from work."

"That was a mistake. I'll call them," she said. "What about Joseph and the girls down at Oasis—do they know?"

"I'm about to call them after I hang up. This is so surreal, it's hard to believe."

"You're telling me. Lord, have mercy. Just like that, huh? Your life can be snatched away from you. In a split second."

"That's the whole truth."

"And how are *you* holding up, Tarik?"

"I'm doing the best I can," he said. "Trying to be strong for my mom."

"You don't have to be strong when it comes to something like this. None of us do."

———

As it turned out, Robin had gone straight to the gym after work and forgotten her cell phone in her locker and she wouldn't hear about Marvin until she got home. It was after nine.

Savannah and Bernadine arrived minutes apart. They didn't ring the doorbell, just walked in. Tarik was sitting in a chair near the door. "Hey, Aunties," he said, standing up to give them both a much-needed hug.

Savannah had a balled-up tissue in her hand. When she opened her mouth, her voice cracked. "Where's Gloria?"

Tarik pointed to the family room. Gloria was sitting at the far end of the chocolate brown sofa as if it were full of people. She was in a white robe. Her elbow was on the arm and her face was held up by her palm. Her eyes were blank, even though it looked as if she were staring at something on the floor. Savannah eased next to her and put her arms around her. Bernadine knelt down on the floor and began to rub her bare feet. When Robin got there, the three of them helped Gloria get into bed. They took her robe off, only to discover she was fully clothed. One by one, they removed her socks, pants and T-shirt, and each of them wet washcloths and bathed her lying down. When they finished, Robin saw the crimson nightgown hanging on the closet door, but opened one drawer after another until she found a short, pink cotton gown, and the three of them propped Gloria up and pulled it over her head. They kissed her on her forehead, tucked her in and sat on the bed until she fell asleep.

They did not say a word.

———

The house filled up with people almost overnight.

Joseph closed Oasis for three days, and just about all of their clientele showed up for the memorial service, which was short because years ago Marvin had made Gloria promise him that if he checked out first, not to spend too much of her precious time grieving over him. "Don't stop living because I'm not around. And please don't have no sad funeral for me, Glo. I mean it! Make it a party and help me celebrate my life! I want you to chuck my ashes on one of these fine golf courses because I believe that's where my heaven is, somewhere close to the eighteenth hole!"

Gloria would follow his wishes to a T.

Tarik had done his best to comfort his mother but he had lost the only father he had ever really known, so he, too, needed to be comforted. Nickida did the best she could. Gloria didn't know how she would've been able to fill out all those damn death papers if it wasn't for her friends. The first few weeks, when Gloria could barely get out of bed, they cooked for her and massaged her hands. They helped her get up. They helped her lie down. They held her when she moaned and when she screamed. They cleaned the house. They took turns sitting with her, watching her do nothing and listening to her not say a word.

Gloria couldn't sleep. She just couldn't get warm. Marvin's side of the bed was empty and cold. She had never slept in this bed without her husband, except for the time he had to go to Oxford, Mississippi, when his brother called to tell Marvin a long-lost relative had left them some property. She missed him lying beside her, but she knew he was coming back. This was just a big mistake. Until then, she'd sleep in her grandkids' room, on the lower bunk bed. She took Marvin's pillow in there and hugged it until the feathers flattened.

———

It took a while before she was able to walk into Oasis, and even when she did, she couldn't bring herself to go through all her mail. Gloria didn't know what she'd do without Joseph. "Don't you worry about a thing, baby," he'd told her when she tried coming back a few days after it happened and she had to go back home.

Gloria wanted to return the boat, but of course she couldn't. The dealership couldn't care less that it was a gift for her husband and he had died. So Gloria gave it to Tarik, who gladly accepted it but on the condition that he take over the payments. With his new raise, and with Nickida's income, it wouldn't be a hardship.

It had been only a few weeks when Gloria got a certified letter from Marvin's insurance company with a check made out to her for $300,000. She was not moved. In fact, that check would stay in the envelope, in a slot on the kitchen island, for weeks.

She sleepwalked through the days down at Oasis. It was like being at one long wake.

"Girl, let me give you a hug."

"I'm so sorry for your loss."

"Can I give you a hug?"

"I lost my husband a few years ago, baby. Time is the only healer."

"He's in a better place."

"God doesn't give us more than we can handle."

"Can I give you a hug?"

Gloria was grateful for the ongoing show of sympathy but she was also glad she didn't do hair anymore. She couldn't concentrate or focus on too much of anything for more than a few minutes at a time. She avoided all paperwork. Couldn't fill out forms. Why were they so long anyway? She often forgot to order inventory. Her snail and even e-mail was often backed up for weeks. Robin's corny jokes didn't make her crack a smile.

Coming home from work was the hardest. She hated the silence when she walked in, which was why she left both TVs on: the one in the family room and the one in their bedroom. They kept her company. Sometimes when she pulled into the driveway, she hoped to smell a steak sizzling on the grill or some kind of fish searing in a hot skillet or bow-tie pasta or spinach noodles boiling in chicken broth and chopped garlic, since Marvin did most of the cooking on the days she worked.

Way back in '90, Marvin King—whom Gloria would learn was a recent widower and retiree—had moved into this ranch-style house, which was right across the street from where she and Tarik lived. Back then, Marvin had no idea there was any more love available to him. In fact, he thought he'd used up that card, and was ready to settle into his living room with the remote control. Before he could get acquainted with all the channels on his new satellite TV, Gloria Matthews—being neighborly and glad to see another black family finally moving into the neighborhood, and thinking he had a wife and family—had gone over to introduce herself and bring them her famous sweet potato pie.

Gloria's knees felt a little wobbly after Marvin told her he was a widower, mostly because he was handsome and she found his stark white teeth surrounded by that mixed-gray mustache and goatee dangerously sexy. Plus, Gloria hadn't wobbled in years. No one was more surprised than she was when she found herself adding a little rhythm to her stride as she headed back across the street, where on a platter she created mountains out of collard greens, candied yams, her famous honey cornbread, chilled potato salad and enough slices of ham to feed a family of four.

When she met Marvin, Gloria was fat. She hadn't thought or cared how she looked until she had to buy a bigger size. On the day she felt something churn inside her chest, she was up to an eighteen. Her blood pressure was off the chart, but Gloria never thought she would or could possibly have a heart attack. Until she had one. She was thirty-seven years old. Marvin was there. He helped her walk her way down to a healthy weight. Taught her how to eat, and how to cook to save her life.

———

Over the next six or seven months Gloria would discover how quickly time passes when you're happy and how slowly when you're sad. She found herself crying when she tried so hard not to. She lived in constant twilight, despite the comfort of her friends and the long hours she had started putting in at Oasis. She was the one who felt dead.

They would catch the boys responsible for Marvin's death; of course they would. The idea that the three young men would spend the rest of their young lives in prison was not at all gratifying to Gloria. It wouldn't bring her husband back. Their young lives were over, too, except they had to die every day while still breathing. These were boys who would probably never grow up to live as free men. She did not—could not—go to their trial. Her girl-friends would.

———

Gloria was sitting at her desk, watching Joline, Twyla and Joseph weaving, braiding and cutting hair, when Tarik walked in. She was surprised to see him here. He rarely came to the salon. She prayed nothing was wrong. He looked good. At peace. He was obviously on duty, because he was in his dark blue uniform, with a holster around his waist and a gun in it.

"Hey, Tarik," Joseph said. "How you doing, man?"

"Pretty good, all things considered. Hi, everybody," he said to the other stylists and the seven or eight customers who were under hair dryers, being shampooed or just waiting their turn. He waved to his mother as he walked back to her office, then stood at the open doorway and knocked. "May I come in?" he asked.

"Is something wrong, Tarik?"

"No, Ma, nothing's wrong." He gave her a kiss. "I just wanted you to know that me and Nicki canceled our trip."

"You did what?"

"We can go another time. You don't need to deal with the kids yet."

"That is not your decision to make, Tarik. Why didn't you talk to me first?"

"Because we just decided. Even though things have calmed down a little bit, it doesn't feel right, asking you to watch the kids. We also don't feel much like celebrating."

"Is it too late to reinstate it?"

"Ma—"

"I want you to go, Tarik. The one thing I've been looking forward to is spending time with my grandkids. Don't do this. And don't change your plans. Would you do that for me? Please?"

"Are you sure?"

"They brighten my day, and I was looking forward to them getting on my nerves."

"I'll see what we can do. Thanks, Ma."

"And next time, call first. You scared the daylights out of me."

When Gloria got home that evening, she walked into the living room, sat down on the sea foam sectional, leaned her elbow against one of the cushions and looked out into the backyard. She twirled her wedding ring around her finger. She was not about to take it off just because her husband was dead. As far as she was concerned, she was still married. Marvin's presence was everywhere. There were pictures of the two of them all over the house. They had been strategically placed on walls, tables and certain shelves, so they would always be able to wink at the other. There were some of him catching a fish or barbecuing or just being handsome. Thanks to Marvin, the water in the bean-shaped pool was lavender and in an hour would be periwinkle, but during the day it was always turquoise. Marvin was good with lights. Butter yellow strobes were aimed at the house. Soft blue beamed from the trunks of palms in blocked brick boxes. That white pergola was sheltered from the scorching sun by one of two shade trees Isaac had helped him plant when arthritis had moved into Marvin's hands. He had done an amazing job remodeling this house. What was the point of it now that he wasn't in it? Gloria felt like a visitor in here. She didn't feel like gardening all by herself. Or cooking for herself. In fact, the house seemed to be growing. It took longer to get from one side to the other, and this house was small. She wasn't sure if she could live here without Marvin. And as for work, who really cared if she had a spa or not? Right now, she certainly didn't.

Coming Clean

I had Isaac served at his mama's house a few days ago, since it was the only address I had for him. We haven't spoken since he came and picked up all of his stuff. Mostly clothes and some of his tools. His key didn't work anymore. It was horrible to have to let him in. He lived here for ten years and now he was a guest. It was heartbreaking. He looked like he hadn't slept in days, but we were both cordial. I was a nervous wreck and tried to act busy as he made one trip after another out to his truck. I put a few dishes into the dishwasher and turned it on. I dusted the artwork and the plants, which of course didn't need it. The housekeeper does a pretty good job. As usual, he seemed to be taking his sweet time, but I didn't want to rush him. We made small talk. Like people do who don't really have much to say to each other.

Right before he was leaving he stopped and looked around. "It's amazing how little I actually have after all this time. All of this stuff is yours: the furniture and artwork. It was all here when I got here."

"Well, you left your mark outside, Isaac. You made the exterior beautiful."

"I wish that had been the case with us."

I sat down on a stool and laid the feather duster

across my lap. "You know what? I think we did the best we could for a while."

"Look, Savannah. I know you hate my guts but can—"

"Wait a minute. I don't hate your guts, Isaac. I have no reason to hate you. You disappointed me and you've made me angry as hell, but hate? No."

"Well, I'm glad at least to hear you say it. Look, Savannah, can we not do this like everybody else?"

"You mean make it ugly?"

"Precisely."

"I'm so glad to hear you say that, Isaac. I mean, this is hard enough as it is, and I've been praying that if we could just be civil it would make things so much easier on us both."

"Then let's," he said. "I can tell you this right now so we can be clear about it. We both know what you came into our marriage with, so I'm not going to try to take you to the cleaners by asking for anything I don't deserve."

"Well, I want to be fair, too."

"I mean, let's face it, Savannah, you far out-earn me even with my business and—"

"This is a community-property state, Isaac. You know that."

"Yeah, I do. But whatever the court decides I'm entitled to, I'll take it and be happy. Seriously."

"Like I said, I just want to be fair."

"Okay, then. I guess that's pretty much it."

"You want to know what I just found out?"

"What?" He was still standing in the open doorway. His jacket was missing a button and his T-shirt looked rough-dried. I used to fold and smooth them with my hands until they were flat. I wonder if he notices what I used to do for him. If he cares.

"We can be divorced sixty days after we file as long as we don't contest anything. Did you know that?"

"No, I didn't. That soon, huh?"

"That soon."

He picked up a black contractor's trash bag and wrapped his arms around it as he headed down the sidewalk toward his truck. I couldn't believe he didn't live here anymore. I was wondering where he was going. If he missed me. If he wished we could turn back the clock.

———

It has taken me almost a month to file even though the form was simpler than filling out a job application. Easier than applying for a credit card. On the day I did, red hearts were everywhere. I had forgotten it was Valentine's Day until I handed it to the clerk, who actually looked up as if she knew I meant business.

We had both gotten attorneys but decided to use a mediator instead of going through the whole divorce court setting. This process is called "Divorce with Dignity." We liked the sound of it, plus it's a whole lot cheaper.

I forgot my cell phone at work yesterday and was surprised to see a message from Isaac. I had my coffee and bagel and for some reason was afraid to listen to it. I even read my snail mail. Including the junk. Cleaned off my desk. Looked over my notes for a possible story about domestic violence. Then another about how dysfunctional the foster care system is. Sometimes I get worn out looking at how much is wrong in the world, and I've been thinking maybe I might want to start shifting my focus to some of the good things people do. But it's hard to make news out of that, so they say. Nevertheless, I'm still grateful to have the kind of job that allows me to paint portraits of our lives, good or bad. We need to be able to see how we behave instead of ignoring it.

I finally decided to play it. "Hi, Savannah. I got the papers and of course it's all good. Would like to talk to you about something. Don't worry, I'm keeping my word, so it's not anything adversarial. I hope you're well. Call me as soon as you can. I might be moving to Vegas when this is all over."

"Moving to Vegas? Have you lost your mind, Isaac?"

"Who are you talking to, Savannah?" Sally, one of the other producers, asked while passing my office. She's six foot two and gorgeous. Her hair is black and her eyes are blue. Her husband is five ten. He's fine as hell, so maybe that makes him appear taller. Or maybe she doesn't care.

"I was talking to myself, like I always do."

"Well, tell yourself a good joke and laugh it off," she said. "You might want to take an early lunch because Thora's bringing in her two demon seeds in about an hour."

"No! I am not in the mood for them today." These would be the four-year-old twins that our boss, Thora, had at forty-six, after years and thousands of dollars of in-vitro attempts until finally two of those eggs stuck. They were the strangest-looking babies and they're still odd-looking. They have not been trained and behave like wild animals. They must weigh fifty pounds each and they still wear those pull-up diapers at night and suck on their pacifiers like cigars. Thora couldn't care less what anybody thinks about it either.

"Thanks for the heads-up." I was trying to figure out how to disappear very soon. I dialed Isaac, and as soon as he answered I just said, "What do you need to talk to me about?"

"Hello to you, too, Savannah."

"Hi, Isaac. Are you worried about something? Is that why you called?"

"Everything is fine on the divorce front. I saw the numbers and I'm fine with them. Just like I told you I would be. But I was wondering what you're doing for lunch?"

"Lunch? You want to take me out to lunch?"

"Sort of. I need to talk to you about something that's kind of important."

"You can't tell me over the phone?"

"It would be better in person. If you don't mind."

"Where?"

"How about I pick up some sandwiches and we meet at the aquarium?"

"Are you tripping on something?"

"No, it just seems like a peaceful place to meet. It won't hurt, Savannah."

"Okay. In about an hour."

"Do you want your usual?"

Why did he have to say that? And just because, I decided to change up. "No, I'll have a turkey club on whole wheat with mayo and extra mustard and a splash of balsamic vinegar, chips and an iced tea with lemon."

"Wow. You are moving on. That sounds delicious. I might try it, too. See you in a minute."

———

I was sitting inside on a long concrete bench, watching four sharks swim back and forth, when Isaac tapped me on the shoulder, almost giving me a fucking heart attack. "Here you go," he said. He looked like his old handsome and sexy self, and part of me was relieved but the other part wished he still had a little bit of a haggard look.

I took the bag and could already smell the bacon and the mustard and vinegar. There were quite a few groups of school-age children being led by their teachers. Isaac and I used to come here a lot and watch the colorful fish in the reef tanks. We had always planned to get one but never did.

"Do you want to move away from the sharks?" he asked.

"I'm not reading anything into sitting here," I said, and actually smiled without looking suspicious.

He sat down next to me, leaving enough space between us for the bags. We placed our sandwiches on top. I took a bite and then waited for him to say something.

"You know we did have some great years, didn't we, Savannah?"

I had to stop myself from rolling my eyes at him. "I know you didn't ask me to meet you here to stroll down memory lane. At least I hope not. But to answer your dumb question: Of course we had some great years, Isaac."

"Okay, this is the deal. Because we've been filing our

returns separately since I got the business, there's some things I haven't shared with you."

"Like what?"

"Well, I've had a few tax problems."

"And what does this have to do with me, Isaac?"

He looked intently at the sharks, then down at the concrete floor. It didn't seem to be as dark in here as it used to. "I owe them a decent amount of money which I'm in the process of trying to pay back and working out a payment plan because the penalties and interest are killing me."

I took a few chips from the bag and offered him some but he shook his head no thanks. As soon as I started chewing, the sound they made seemed like I had made a mistake. I was being rude, so I stopped chewing and let them stay on my tongue until they started to get soft. "I'm listening." And then I swallowed.

"Well, I know since we've both signed the papers we could be divorced—ironically enough—on tax day, and if I were to get the settlement around that time, the IRS would take almost every dime of it without fail."

"So what are you asking me, Isaac?"

He took a deep breath and blew it out. He had yet to touch his sandwich. "I was wondering if you would be willing to postpone the final divorce decree until July first?"

He didn't look at me.

"Okay." What difference did it really make? I wasn't trying to hurry up and get married again, and no one but us would even have to know. Not only that, but some people battle it out in court for years. What's a few more months?

"Are you serious? You'd be willing to do that for me?"

"I would, but I have to tell you, Isaac, you better be glad I was already preapproved for the second mortgage I have to take out on the house to pay you. I still have time to postpone it. But how much do you . . . Oh, never mind. It's none of my business and I don't really want to know."

"Thank you, Savannah." He looked like he was on the verge of leaning over to give me a kiss, and I was about to let him when it hit me what we were doing and I backed away.

"And you're sure you'll be able to resolve all this by July first?"

He nodded and finally reached for his sandwich and took a big bite. Chewed. "I'm actually already working with someone but it takes a minute to set it up. It's looking good. It's so much you have to disclose, and I can't afford to have that kind of money showing up in my account until I get this worked out."

"And is that when you're planning on moving to Vegas?"

"I'm just thinking about relocating. I'm getting a little tired of Phoenix. I've been here all my life and could use a change of scenery."

"Does your girlfriend feel the same way?"

"Can we not talk about any third parties, because it might spoil the tone, and right now I'm feeling nothing but gratitude toward you, Savannah."

"No problem. I don't want to know, anyway."

"You look good," he said out of nowhere, which threw me off guard. He's always been good at that.

"So do you, Isaac."

And then we just sat there and ate. "This is a really good sandwich," he said after he had devoured it and treated himself to too many of my chips. "What time do you need to be back?"

I just looked at him. He knows I'm not on a clock, that no one cares as long as I do my job. I took a sip of my tea and wanted to get up and prepare to say goodbye, until next time, but of course it dawned on me that there might not be a next time. We don't even have to sign the papers together and the same will hold true even with the amended date. Our divorce will just happen on the day we designate. We could be anywhere, doing anything.

"You know what, Savannah? I don't know when we might see each other again or if we'll ever have a chance to talk, but I want you to know that I have absolutely no regrets about being married to you. None."

I was surprised to hear him say this. But I figured if this was his way of coming clean, then we should both do it. "In spite of everything, Isaac, I'm glad you stalked me at church until I went out with you, and I loved you up to the last minute."

"What made you stop?"

"Don't ask me that."

"I would like to know. And I didn't stalk you. I followed you out to the parking lot but that was only because you were staring at me up in the choir."

"You couldn't sing a lick, and I don't know how you ever got in the choir. I stopped loving you because you stopped making me feel important."

"When was that?"

"When did your porn fun get deep?"

"A couple of years ago."

"There you go. You stopped listening to me when I talked."

"Savannah, all you did was talk."

"Okay, I have to agree. But when I do, I try to make sure I have something to say."

"But sometimes it's good to be quiet, too. Everybody doesn't need to know what you think. At least not on an hourly basis."

I reached over and punched him on the shoulder. "You know what I miss about you?"

"I do not."

"These," I said and squeezed his shoulder, and then, "These," I said, and pressed my fingers gently against his lips, and "That," I said, and rubbed the palm of my hand across his hard belly. "I'll stop there."

"No, don't. Please. Keep going."

"Shut up, Isaac."

"Come on, Savannah."

"Okay. So you're the only man that has ever made me come four times."

"You're the only woman I've ever made come four times, but that's because I loved the way you made me feel."

"Okay, let's skip this part. I loved how comforting you could be."

"I loved how you used to watch me when I was building something. Like you were really interested."

"But I was. I didn't know how you did it. I thought you were brilliant."

"Really? You never told me that."

"I did so."

"I beg to differ with you. I would remember that."

"Well, I'm telling you now."

"I miss watching stupid television shows with you and you rubbing your feet across mine during the whole show. I was always glad when it was an hour program. I hate to say it, but I loved watching you jump up and down when you disagreed with something on *Sixty Minutes* or when something you read in the paper or saw on the news really upset you. I liked that you were compassionate and empathetic. Not very many women I've ever met get worked up about social and political stuff."

"You didn't seem to feel that way about a lot of the stories I did, and it hurt my feelings."

"I'm sorry, Savannah. I wasn't dismissing them or their relevance. I just wanted you to take it a step further."

"Meaning?"

"Offer up some solutions."

"But I don't have the answers."

"You've got opinions—this we all know. You should make them known. That's what'll get people to thinking."

"You might have a point. But maybe not. I respected what you did, even though I didn't go ga-ga over fences and decks. I sure loved ours. The bed in the backyard is still kick-ass."

"I hope you never make love to anybody else on it. But then again, I'll never know, will I?"

We sat there silent for a minute or two. Maybe five.

"You want to know what I don't miss?" I asked.

"I'm afraid to say yes."

"Camping and fishing. It's not as much fun as you think it is, Isaac."

"No comment."

I pushed him this time.

"I'm beginning to wonder if divorce is making you violent, young lady."

"I like the sound of that: young lady."

"You are young, Savannah. Your heart is young and so is your spirit."

"I wish that was true."

"Please. You and those crazy girlfriends of yours won't be senior citizens for years to come. I'm glad you have them in your life, and they should be glad to have you in theirs."

"We are. You always liked them, didn't you?"

"I did. Robin is a hoot. Gloria's just sweet. I don't know how she's managing without Marvin when I'm having a hard time accepting he's gone. I feel for her. I don't know who I'm going to watch games with. I really miss him. I hope you stay close to Bernie, too, Savannah. She's been bitter too long and it seems to have taken its toll on her."

"Well, some people do really rotten things that can make getting over it and moving on a little harder."

"I know. You know what else I want you to know?"

"I'm listening."

"That everything doesn't always have to serve a purpose."

"I know that."

"I don't think you do. If you meet somebody else—and I pray that you do, Savannah, seriously—loosen up and lighten up. Be as silly as you can be sometimes. Waste time. Don't try to fill up every minute with shit you think is important because everything isn't."

"As for you. Take a phobia class so you can get your old ass on a plane and go somewhere you can't get to by car. You are missing out, Isaac. There's a world out there worth seeing and I sure wish we could've seen more of it together."

"I'll consider it."

As the sharks were being fed, we sat there and watched them rush to eat.

"I started going to PAA meetings."

"That's really good to hear. I hope it helps."

"You want to know how it got started?"

"Not really, but spill it."

"When I was about fifteen one of the neighbor kids shared some of his dad's porn stash with me. Of course I liked it. Had never seen anything like it. We laughed about it and even bragged about it. Fast-forward to the Internet, and I never in a million years would have thought of it as addicting until you busted me, really. Well, it had gotten way out of hand and I knew it, but I couldn't talk to you about it."

"But you didn't know that, did you? I don't think it's something to be ashamed of and I would much rather you'd told me than have me find out the way that I did."

"I know. My poor computer. You were serious, weren't you?"

"I was. I couldn't believe my eyes, and I think I was more hurt that you were sharing so much of yourself with these strangers, and of course, over time, you ended up not being as warm toward me. But it's water under the bridge. I think I better get going now, though."

We both stood up and stretched.

"I'll always love you, Savannah. Know that."

"That's nice, Isaac. Now here," I said and gave him a quick peck on the lips, but before I was able to back away he slid those long arms around me like he used to and squeezed me so tight I didn't think I was going to be able to breathe.

Thunderstruck

Bernadine is sitting inside a nice little bistro, sipping on a cup of coffee, waiting for Gloria. She's a half hour late. She wants to call to see what the holdup is, especially since Gloria has canceled on her three times in the last month. But she doesn't feel like harassing her. Marvin's been gone four months now, and Savannah, Robin and Bernadine have been doing their best to help her get through this. They've been trying to get her out of the house to do some of the things they used to do—lunch, brunch, shop, anything—but she has resisted.

"What do you feel like doing today?" they've asked her.

"I'm doing it," she'd say. Which was nothing.

The last one to see her was Robin. That was over a month ago when Joseph tightened her weave. "Gloria looks like she's packing it on," Robin had said. Bernadine hasn't brought up this topic. She knows grief takes its own time, that it can end up on your plate or in a pill but you still can't swallow it. After weeks of cajoling and warm threats, Gloria finally agreed to meet her for brunch.

Bernadine is staring out the window at those heat waves wiggling. At that giant sun. The cloudless sky. The breeze is so hot you don't want to inhale.

"Are you almost ready to order?" the waitress asks as she freshens Bernadine's coffee.

"Just give me a few more minutes. Thanks."

She calls Gloria. "Where are you, Glo?"

"Right around the corner. Sorry I'm late, Bernie. I just found out one of the girls has quit, so I had to call Joseph about rescheduling her Tuesday appointments."

"I hope it's not Twyla or Joline."

"No, thank goodness. Monique. I don't think you know her. She did mostly hot lathers. Anyway, she was flaky and not half as good as she thought she was."

"She quit on a Sunday afternoon?"

"Why are you acting like you don't believe me? She's moving to Seattle. Where she's from. Anyway, I'll be right there."

When she spots Gloria heading for her table, Bernadine is shocked and saddened by what she sees. Robin was right. Gloria has put on at least twenty pounds. She looks older, tired. "Hey, girl." She stands up and gives Gloria a hug. "You look good."

"I look like hell, so stop lying, Bernie."

"You don't look like hell. And that dress is pretty." She was also lying about this. It was the wrong purple and looked like a maternity dress.

"Thanks anyway. I'm starving. What are you having?"

"Maybe an omelet."

"I would love some banana pancakes and bacon," Gloria says.

The waitress brings more coffee and takes their order. They are quiet for a few minutes. They look out the window, then at each other. "So, how are you holding up, Glo?"

"I'm doing the best I can."

"I know this isn't an easy thing to go through."

"That's an understatement, Bernie. You have no idea what it feels like to lose your husband."

"I've lost two husbands."

"But they didn't die, Bernie."

"That depends on how you look at it. They didn't come back."

"Anyway," Gloria says, perking up. "My grandkids are staying with me for ten whole days next month. Tarik and Nickida are going to Hawaii."

"They'll keep you busy." Bernadine pours more cream in her coffee. "Tarik still deserves better."

"Let's not go there today, Bernie. My son loves the huzzie, so I have to tolerate her."

"And Tarik still doesn't think anything about that oldest boy—what's his name again?"

"Brass."

"That every year that goes by, he's looking less and less like his so-called biological father?"

"If he's figured it out, he hasn't said anything to me and I'm not saying anything to him. He loves that boy, regardless."

"It's his mama I don't trust from here to the corner."

"Well, Tarik thinks she can walk on water, so I've just pretended all these years not to know where she's been."

"How's your pressure and cholesterol these days, Glo?"

"They're both fine—thank you for asking."

"You know none of us want to see you go through anything like that again."

"Who is 'none of us'? Have you guys been talking about me behind my back?" She adds another package of sugar to her coffee and stirs it fast. "They are taking their sweet time with the food and it's not even crowded in here."

"Come on, Glo. Robin just mentioned that you'd started putting on weight and then we couldn't help but remember when you had your heart attack. We love you, Gloria, and just want you to be careful."

The waitress brings their food and gives Gloria's pancakes to Bernadine and Bernadine's omelet to Gloria. "I'll take that," she says to Bernadine, and swaps plates. "I've got all that under control despite how things might look. It's just been hard, Bernie. So you can report back to Robin and Savannah that they can stop worrying about me even though I appreciate the concern."

Bernadine eats some of her omelet. Maybe she shouldn't have mentioned this. Maybe she should just mind her own business. And maybe she should just change the subject.

"So what do you think about Savannah divorcing Isaac?" Gloria asks.

"I think it's sad."

"I think it's stupid." Gloria pushes an entire strip of bacon into her mouth.

"Why is it so stupid? He's a porn addict. He even admitted it. Plus he was cheating on her."

"You think all men cheat, Bernie."

"Not all of them. Most of them. Anyway, Isaac even admitted he was seeing another woman."

"First of all, don't you think it's a little odd that he didn't tell Savannah about this other woman until after she told him she wanted a divorce?"

"Well, it's not like men broadcast when they're having an affair, Gloria. Are you trying to say you think he made it up?"

"Sometimes folks throw darts when they're attacked."

"She didn't attack him!"

"The bottom line is, Isaac is a good man and he was a good husband. I love her to death but Savannah lives in her own idealistic world, you know. I'm surprised Isaac was able to hang as long as he did."

"What in the hell is that supposed to mean?"

"She treated him like she was superior."

"But she is," Bernadine says and props her fork and knife against her plate. "You're making it sound like she should've played down how intelligent she is just to make her friggin' husband feel secure. Please."

"She married him knowing exactly who he was."

"Then maybe she made a ten-year mistake, Gloria. It happens, you know."

"I think it's a knee-jerk reaction to a situation she's given more weight to than it deserves."

They continue to eat, Gloria cleaning her plate. "So what about you, Bernie? You're so concerned about everybody else's problems and worries, how's everything going with you? Are you going to be able to reopen Sweet Tooth anytime soon? How are the kids doing? Wasn't Onika here a few months ago? And how's John Jr.?"

"Slow down, Gloria! That's quite a mouthful. Maybe

I should just write a book and put all the answers in it."
Bernadine is surprised when Gloria chuckles.

"I'm listening."

"I'm good. Sweet Tooth had its day. It's time to move on to something else."

"Like what?"

"I'm weighing my options."

"You and me both."

"Onika is a lesbian," Bernadine blurts out.

Gloria reaches for a slice of honeydew from Bernadine's plate, takes a small bite and chews it. "It's about time that child came out with it. You can't sit here and tell me you didn't have a notion."

"I thought maybe."

"So how'd you find out?"

Bernadine wishes she could tell Gloria the truth but she can't. "She told me."

"Just out of the blue?"

"She brought a girlfriend home for the weekend and I put two and two together."

"Did you catch them doing anything?"

"No!"

"Are you disappointed about it?"

"No. She is who she is and I'm just glad she knows it."

"Did you tell her that?"

"Yes, I did."

"Good. So many parents freak out when they find out their kids are gay. When Joseph came out right after he started working at Oasis, his family disowned him. That was centuries ago, but there are still a lot of young kids out there who are terrified. How'd John take it?"

"Onika hasn't told him yet. He wasn't around the weekend she was here."

"You're not planning on telling him, I hope."

"Of course not. It's Onika's call, not mine."

"So what about John Jr.? Does he ever come up for air? I haven't seen that boy in over a year."

"He's doing fine. Lots of research, plus word on the street is that he's madly in love with some Southern belle and claims they might drive out here sometime this summer."

"How old is he now?"

"Twenty-four. Anyway, Glo, can I ask you a favor?"

"How big?"

"Not big."

"I'm listening."

"Are you still getting the bootleg DVDs?"

"You don't have to say it so loud, Bernie!" Gloria whispers almost as loud. "And don't ever mention this in front of Tarik or I could be in big trouble. Anyway, to answer your question: yes. What kind of favor?"

"Can we please start having Blockbuster Night again soon? We miss it. We miss you. We miss us."

Gloria looks down at her empty plate and then up at Bernadine. "I'll see what they have in stock and let you know. Give me a few weeks, okay?"

"Okay."

———

Not long after she gets home Bernadine is upstairs changing when she hears someone knocking at the front door. She does not rush to answer it. For starters, she has a doorbell, and second, there's a sign out front that says as plain as day in English and Spanish and in giant red letters, NO SOLICITORS.

It was good to see Gloria. Bernadine wished she could've told her the truth about how and why she hadn't remembered going into Onika's room. But what would she have said? That she was scared because she didn't know these sleeping pills caused her to black out? Bernadine didn't feel comfortable talking about her issues. The whole point was to provide a little comfort for Gloria, but it was clear she hadn't done a very good job of it.

She puts on a pair of shorts, and while pulling the tank top over her head, Bernadine can't believe it when she starts crying. She hasn't cried since Marvin's funeral. She doesn't know why, but then again, she does.

The person at the front door is now knocking hard, entirely too hard for any solicitor. She wipes her eyes and runs down the stairs. Bernadine is surprised to see John through the peephole. He has a worried look on his face. He has never dropped in on her, so she knows something is wrong. She opens the door.

"Bernie, you okay? I've been standing out here forever but I saw your car in the garage and I figured maybe you just didn't hear me. Can I come in?"

She steps away from the door and opens it wide enough for him to enter.

"What's going on, John?"

He shakes his head back and forth, but doesn't say anything.

"Is it Taylor? Nothing's happened to our kids, because I'd know. Talk to me."

"It's me who's not doing so hot."

"It's not your health, is it?" Bernadine asks, finally closing the door. John heads for the kitchen. He knows this house because he used to live in it. She follows him, praying that nothing is wrong with him. At the same time she's thinking that if there was ever such a category, John would certainly get top honors for being a good father to Onika and John Jr. Since their divorce, he'd been a hands-on dad. Bernadine also realized that he made a much better ex-husband than husband.

"No, it's not my health. And I'm sorry for dropping by like this, Bernie, but I'm not sure what to do about this situation." He leans on the counter and then stands up as if he's been ordered to.

"What situation?"

"Why are your eyes red? Have you been crying? Is this a bad time?"

"It's my allergies," she says.

"I'm sorry. I never knew you had allergies. Are you sure you're okay?"

"I'm fine." She's wondering if maybe she should take a Xanax, at least half of one, but decides against it. John looks like he might need her full attention.

When she sees tears rolling down his cheeks she gets nervous. "John, why are you crying? If it's not the kids or your health, then what's wrong? Is it Kathleen?"

He nods his head.

Bernadine wants to get him a glass of water but decides that maybe it's not what he needs right now. She stops in front of the refrigerator, turns around and faces him.

"Kathleen left me."

Oh shit. She swallows a mouthful of relief that she wasn't in some horrible accident and that she's not dead. "What do you mean, she left? And went where?"

"To be with someone else."

"Wait a minute. Are you standing here telling me that your wife has left you to be with another man?"

"That's exactly what I'm saying, yeah. Basically, that's the way it is."

Bernadine is thunderstruck by the irony, considering this is a replay of how their marriage ended, but she doesn't feel any gratification whatsoever. "Look, I'm really sorry to hear this, John. When did all this happen?"

"A couple of weeks ago."

"And were you, like, expecting this? I know she couldn't have just up and left."

"Of course I wasn't expecting it. True, things have been bad between us for the last six months or so, but I thought her frustrations with me were due to the long hours I'd been putting in. There's another man. And she did just up and leave."

"You mean she didn't take Taylor?"

"No, she didn't. She couldn't just *take* our daughter without getting permission from a court. But she doesn't want her."

"Hold up. Just wait a fucking minute here. What do you mean, *she doesn't want her*? Her own daughter? That's the most ridiculous-sounding shit I've heard yet. How can you say that?"

"Because she told me. She said she was burnt out on motherhood, me, Phoenix, everything. She said it would be better if I just finished raising Taylor."

"I don't fucking believe this."

"At first, I didn't either. But I do now."

"And I thought the stuff James pulled was deep."

"It *was* deep, Bernie."

"How could she leave her own kid? And what took you so long to tell me?"

"Because I didn't know what to tell you. I know you never cared for Kathleen."

"That was sixteen years ago, John. I don't have anything against Kathleen, and you more than anybody should know that by now. I've always been friendly toward her and I treat your daughter like she's part of this family, because she is. The kids don't think of her as their half-sister. She's their sister. Taylor has never felt like an outsider in this house, and you know it."

He's nodding his head in agreement. "I got served yesterday."

"It's probably just a power play. She'll be back. As soon as his spell wears off she'll come to her senses."

"She's in London."

"You can't be serious."

He just looks at me.

"But what about Taylor? How does she feel and does she know what's going on?"

Bernadine figures this might be a good time to get him and herself a bottle of water. John looks like he's in some kind of trance. He's staring at the floor as if there might be answers in the grout. "I'm not sure how to handle this, Bernie. I'm so fucking confused I don't know what to do from one minute to the next. Taylor is fourteen, and she's not stupid. She knows her mother's been fooling around for a while. Kathleen made her swear to secrecy, which is a terrible position to put your own kid in."

"I didn't think she was like this."

"You and me both."

"Well, maybe you should just chill for a minute before you go doing something you'll regret."

"She's the one who's going to regret this."

"What's that supposed to mean?"

"You don't abandon your own child. *Me*, I can understand. But not your child."

"I'll tell you, John, nothing surprises me anymore."

"She wants a lot."

"They always do. Your prenuptial agreement is valid though, right?"

"Absolutely. She'll get what she's entitled to since she left Taylor in my custody. I'm just not interested in taking care of her lover."

"I hear you."

"So that brings me to the other reason for my visit. I think I'd like to give you one of my properties."

"What are you talking about? I hope you're not trying to hide it?"

"Not at all. There's no need to. I've been thinking about this for a while. I know James took you to the cleaners. We all know it. JJ told me how tough it's been for you even before you closed Sweet Tooth."

"John Jr. doesn't know what he's talking about."

"I think he does. We're not all blind, Bernie. Plus, you can sell it, lease it or do whatever you want with it."

"Look, let's not talk about my situation right now,

John, okay? This is serious business. Is there anything I can do to help you with Taylor?"

"Anything you can do would help. I'm not sure I know what to do with a soon-to-be fifteen-year-old. I think you might know her better than I do. It would be nice if I could bring her over to spend a weekend or something."

"Sure."

"Onika sent me an e-mail telling me about being a camp counselor this summer. Sounds respectable."

"She's coming with a girlfriend."

"That's good. So she's doing okay?"

"She's doing fine."

"Good. I'll give her a call in a day or so. Bernie, thanks for listening. And for everything." He gives her a genuine hug. Bernadine hugs him back. She is surprised when she feels warmth. She forgot about that. Probably because she hasn't felt a man's body touch hers in six years.

Icebreakers

"Okay. So, I'm Tiger Lady," I whisper to Savannah.

"You cannot be serious," she says loudly, and takes a sip from the second bottle of water she's had in less than the hour we've been here. She must be dehydrated. This heat will certainly do it to you.

We're at a yoga class. Well, we're not exactly participating. We're standing outside the room, looking through the window at all these flowing bodies. We're trying to see how hard it is.

"There is no way in hell I could get my body to do any of those movements."

"They're called poses, Savannah."

"Whatever. And why aren't there any black people in there?"

"I don't know. Just be quiet and watch."

Maybe ten seconds pass.

"Did you just have to bring those dogs?"

"Are they making any noise? No, they are not." Romeo and Juliet are chillin' in their carrier, which is hanging over my shoulder.

Savannah rolls her eyes and doesn't even look at the people in the room. "So how long have you been doing this online dating stuff?"

"Why?"

"Because you haven't mentioned it to anybody, that's why. Are you embarrassed about doing it?"

"No! Why would I be embarrassed? I told you, didn't I?"

"You usually tell us all of your personal business—that's why."

"I do not tell you guys all of my personal business. Okay? Anyway, I wanted to wait until I met somebody nice, that's all. Plus I didn't want you guys dogging me and making me feel desperate."

"But you are desperate, aren't you?"

"Yeah, but so is everybody else."

"How long?"

"About a month or two."

"Do you really think you're going to meet somebody on an online dating service who's worth getting serious about?"

"I've tried everything else."

"Like what?" Savannah crosses her arms, waiting for me to come up with a decent lie.

"Okay, so I'm rusty. But you've been out of circulation for years, Savannah. We don't go to happy hour anymore. And who has parties anymore? Nobody. So tell me, where do you go to meet a guy in our age bracket? Not on the street. Not at work or you might lose your job. And not at the gym because the fine ones are usually gay. And thanks to Isaac, I'm not sure if I can even trust the ones in church. This is just one reason why I go to every single dance Lucille invites me to."

"Okay, you made your point. Do you know anybody that's had any luck doing this?"

"Not personally, but I've read a lot of testimonials."

"You can certainly rely on those."

"You know something, Savannah? I'm looking at this whole thing like I do when I'm shopping and trying to find the perfect black pumps or the perfect black dress. You have to try on different ones and walk around in them until you find one that fits."

"Whatever, Robin. Okay, this yoga class looks way too hard. Let's check out that hot one."

We follow the arrows and head downstairs. We stop on the first landing to use the restroom, and while washing our hands, Savannah says, "This is way out of left field, but I bet you can't guess who just popped into my head."

"You're right. I can't."

"Whatever happened to that guy Michael you dated for a hot minute way back in the stone age?"

"You mean mister pudgy-wudgy-no-can-fuck Michael?"

"That's mean, Robin. I thought he was nice and sort of handsome, and if I remember correctly, you kind of liked him."

"I did. But Michael was my rebound guy because I was trying to get back at Russell. Poor guy didn't stand a chance."

"But all of us remember how pissed you were when you saw him with that other woman after you kicked him to the curb. Who could forget that mess?"

"Anyway, Michael left the company about ten or twelve years ago because he got a major offer in Miami. To my knowledge, no one's ever heard a peep from him since."

We go down one more flight and finally reach

another class. The folks behind this glass are sweating something terrible. "I know that downward dog pose when I see it. They do that one a lot."

"Anyway, so have you met any potential potentials online?"

"First of all, I had to redo my profile and change my screen name."

"Why?"

"Because Sparrow signed me up on three different sites but she made me some kind of goddess—it was ridiculous—plus, she didn't get a lot of things right."

"Oh, so you think Tiger Lady is more sophisticated?"

"I'm a Leo, Savannah."

"Which would make you a lion, not a fucking tiger, Robin."

"Anyway, I like it. And I'm keeping it."

"Did you ask Sparrow to do this for you?"

"No. She was just trying to be helpful."

"She is too old for her age and you need to stop letting your teenage daughter run your life."

"She doesn't *run* my life," I say a little too loudly. "She knows me better than anybody."

"That's total bullshit and you know it. She shouldn't have enough information about you to fill in so many blanks on any form, especially when it comes to your social and personal life. Come on, Robin."

I ignore her and focus on the flowing bodies. Savannah and Bernadine get on my nerves when it comes to how I raise my daughter. Savannah never had kids, so what does she know about being a mother?

"Did she get her permit?"

"She failed the written test."

Savannah starts laughing and shakes her head. It is funny, but I don't want her to know I agree. I tried not to laugh when Sparrow came storming back to the car, totally pissed off at the test.

"How is that possible, as smart as Miss Thang is?"

"Actually, she got more wrong the second time than she did the first. I'm glad, to be honest. Saves me from worrying."

"How many times can you take it?"

"I don't know. Until you pass. It would help if she studied for it."

"Can she drive?"

"Somewhat. We've been practicing for almost a year. At this rate, she won't be driving until she's, like, twenty."

We turn our attention to the twenty or so shiny white people bending, swaying and lying on their bellies. They're dripping with sweat but they're also glowing and they don't look miserable.

"How hot is it in there?" Savannah asks.

"They say it's about one hundred five degrees."

"We're used to that. I don't understand what the point is."

"It loosens and relaxes your muscles."

"Well, I could stand to lose about ten pounds."

"I don't think this is for weight loss, Savannah."

"I'm not stupid, Robin. I know that. It's supposed to help you focus and relieve stress. But if you sweat like a pig and bend and stretch, you're bound to lose a few pounds."

"Well, I'm going to take a class. I've been wanting to for years. We should take one together."

"It doesn't look like much fun, and that music is almost creepy. I'll think about it and let you know."

"Well, I'm taking it with or without your ass."

"I said I'll think about it. I've got a lot of stuff going on right now."

"Is Isaac being difficult?"

"Actually, he's not. It's just weird getting used to the idea that our marriage is really over. Oh-oh! It looks like all these sweaty and probably stinky people are headed this way. Let's get out of here."

We dash out the exit door. Looking at us, you'd swear we were about to work out. Savannah is wearing some purple-and-white getup that I wouldn't have chosen for her. She has no boobs and her ass is big enough for the two of us, but I wouldn't dare tell her that. She really could stand to lose fifteen pounds, but I wouldn't dare tell her that, either. If she did, she could maybe be a high six or low seven again. I don't know what I am anymore, but I think I'm higher than her. Oh, who cares? She's getting rid of a husband and I've never had one. Who knows how big I'd be if I was getting divorced?

As soon as we get outside the dogs start squirming and making their silly we-want-out sounds. It's not a bark. They hardly ever bark.

Savannah puts on her sunglasses and then crosses her arms. "He's going to be entitled to some part of the house. But I really don't care."

I put Romeo and Juliet on their leashes and get off

this hot concrete and head over to a small patch of grass next to a rock garden filled with desert flowers. Romeo and Juliet do their business and run back inside their mesh home.

"Why do you buy clothes for those dogs, Robin? Would you please explain that to me?"

"Because it makes them look cute."

"Why don't you just get them a credit card and they can go to Macy's and pick out their own little outfits?"

"You should get a puppy. And so should Gloria."

"Anyway, I'm going to have to buy him out, but it's cool."

"No shit."

"Or sell."

"I know it's none of my business, but did he ever make any of the mortgage payments?"

"No. He made a lot of improvements and paid for a lot of other things that had to do with upkeep and the like, stuff you can't put a price on."

We're almost at the parking lot. I knew we should've come together; I can't remember where I parked my damn car. This happens a lot. Thank God for these keys that make your lights go on and off or your horn honk.

I think Savannah's more upset than she lets on about her marriage being over because Isaac didn't want to stay. I also think she's as lonely as Gloria, but Savannah does a good job pretending that she isn't. Who wouldn't miss somebody she's been with for ten years? I'm her friend, which is why I've listened to her whine for years. It's also why I suggested we try this whole yoga thing, since it's supposed to have magical powers, which we could all use a little of.

"Anyway, have you ever loved a man whose outsides didn't match his insides?"

"What do you mean?" I ask.

"When what you see is all you get."

"It took you ten years to figure that out?"

"Eight. You and Gloria and Bernie know how long I've been complaining about my marriage."

"You complain about everything, Savannah."

"I beg to differ with you. Anyway, Isaac is only partially to blame. I think I just wanted him to make me feel like Cinder-fucking-rella and Rapunzel and Sleeping Beauty and the Little fucking Mermaid."

"I thought he did, or you wouldn't have married him."

"I meant, like, forever."

"Don't we all?"

"I tried to make him feel like he was my superhero and I still got flack for holding the bar too damn high. Anyway, a man can't fill in all the blank spaces."

"Aren't you scared, Savannah?"

"Scared of what?"

"Starting all over. Being by yourself."

"*Scared* is too strong a word. I'm not really worried about being by myself. I know it's going to be different. And take some getting used to. I already miss him."

"Well, that's about the most honest thing I've heard you say."

"It is not. And before you ask, there is not a chance in hell that we'll get back together. Aren't *you* scared?"

"My daughter and my dogs keep me company."

"That's not what I asked you."

"Okay. So I'm a little scared that once Sparrow graduates and leaves for college—and chances are it'll be far away from Arizona—I'll feel a little anxiety about the thought of being by myself and working at the same old job, doing the same old thing."

"Then do something else."

Now I roll my eyes at her. "Like what?"

"I don't know, Robin. You more than anybody should know what you like."

"Well, my company might be merging with a bigger one, so there might be some new opportunities."

"I thought you've been bored working in insurance?"

"It's a job. And the pay is good."

"That's the wrong answer. You should try that downward dog pose when you get home and think about what you're hungry for."

"Maybe I will."

"Did you see my show on teenage pregnancy?"

"I Tivo'd it. I know it's good. All your stories are usually pretty interesting."

"Thanks, Robin. I might be doing one on gang wars."

"I'd be extra careful with that one."

"I don't intend to indict them. I just want to show how killing each other over turf they don't own or drugs doesn't prove or solve anything, and how it's become the leading cause of adolescent genocide. That's all."

"That's all? Like I said, just be careful. Where are you parked, Savannah?"

"Under that lonely tree over there."

"I have to hurry up."

"Where are you rushing off to? Wait. Don't tell me. Macy's or Nordstrom?"

"No. I have to get the dogs out of this heat. I will say this. After seeing what you and Bernie have been through—not to mention all the folks in Hollywood—it seems like the one thing that's pretty much guaranteed when you get married these days is getting divorced. Let's face it, I've never been good at picking good men."

"That's an understatement. You never answered the question I asked about a year ago. Have you met anybody decent yet online?"

"Sort of."

"What's that supposed to mean? Have you gone out with him?"

"Not yet. You communicate through e-mail and then talk on the phone."

"I know you don't give these guys your phone number, do you?"

"No, Savannah. I'm not stupid. I bought one of those throwaway cell phones. I did give the number to one guy and even met him for lunch, but he turned out to be a total loser."

"There are probably a lot of them."

"Yeah, but there might be one who doesn't fit into that category."

"And what's his name?"

"Dark Angel."

Savannah rolls her eyes.

"Don't even say it," I say. "Just keep your thoughts to yourself."

With her index finger she makes a Z across her lips and we head for our cars.

———

As soon as it cools down, I let the kids out of their carrier, take them for a fifteen-minute walk, and when I get back I head straight into my little office and log in to one of the sites. I lied to Savannah. I've really been doing this more like four months, and as much as I hate to admit it, I've gotten addicted to checking my in-boxes. I also expanded my search for love and registered with six different sites. I haven't even told Sparrow.

Let's see. Today I have about fourteen icebreakers. If just one of them is promising, it will make my day. I also didn't want to tell Savannah how many creepazoids I've "met" online: everything from convicted felons to religious fanatics, con artists who ask for loans, married guys with children, middle-age men who still live with their parents, senior citizens, the unemployed or unemployable, the uneducated or just plain dumb, a few who'd never had sex, and fat or ugly men—sometimes they're one and the same. I wish they'd read a few of the answers on my questionnaire before winking or tagging or breaking ice with me. And I also wish I had said absolutely no Pisces, Virgos or Scorpios. Russell was a lying, cheating, sneaky Pisces.

Anyway, Bernadine took a good picture of me when the four of us went to Vegas two years ago. I think I look the same, so I put it up. I show very little skin. I even paid someone to write my profile:

Tiger Lady Wants to Purr. My friends consider me to be loyal, honest, silly and smart. I love a good joke. I couldn't live without music and appreciate everything from jazz to R&B and even some hip-hop. I will dance to anything and love romantic comedies and live concerts, and I read as much as I have time to. I am partial to biographies because other people's lives fascinate me. I'm big on keeping fit but am not a fit-o-holic. I'm 5'9" so I'd love to meet someone I can look up to. I've won lots of prizes at amusement parks for my daughter and her friends because no one ever guesses my age: 42. I love most animals but especially my teacup Yorkies. I'm interested in meeting a gentle and fascinating man who believes that life is an adventure. So, if you laugh a lot, are kind, fun-loving, accountable and honest, give me a cyber-shout-out and let's take it from there.

Okay, so I lied about my age. Everybody does.

Actually, I would be shocked if I got an interesting or intriguing e-mail. They are rare. Here is a small sample of some waiting for me today:

якщо ви прийдете до, тися з вамиїв, би зустріХот. іви вродлит, я думаю їй країмо.

hello gorgeous you are one of the most beautifulest woman I have ever seen in the universe. I am a super-romantic man that would love to get to know you very much leave your number so we could talk.

you got what it takes to take what I got. Really love your profile.

wat up omg ur really hot r u into young dudes if so I'm like 23 and so into older mature women cuz ur the only 1s who do it 4 me LOL. Check out my photo. I can rock you btr than any 40 yr old. I will wait n u will not regret it.

I would like you to have my children one day. I am a great kisser. If you are ever in Miami, look me up. Here's my number. You'll think you're in Disney World after 15 minutes with me.

I'm crazy and funny at the same time. I am a deep thinker when not stressed by the world. I wish you were here right now. I could use a hug. Why don't you ever e-mail me back?

I love black women. I am Russian. Break some ice, baby.

Would you share your favorite joke with me? You can learn a lot about a person through their sense of humor. Plus a relationship should be 100%-100%, not 50-50. Let me know what you think about this.

Hey there. I am the answer to your prayers. You just don't know it. Women love me.

I like your profile. We are the same age. Forty. I love dancing, music, live shows, cds, dvds, the NBA, the NFL, etc. and have fun when I am with my son (on weekends) . . . he brings me so much satisfaction and joy . . . when I'm not working, me and his mom don't get along but I usualy enjoy whatever it is that I'm doing. How about you? What are you doing right now?

I would love to see you shake your groove thang baby. You seem like a sweet lady. Did you say you like little dogs? I do too. But not under six pounds.

tic toc tic toc. I've got nothing but time. You seem honest and I think you have a great smile. I'm very picky but you have passed the first test. You're quite a looker. And it seems like you have a brain. Let's find out.

"Oh fuck all of you, idiots! And not a single one of you is even cute!" I close this site. At least Dark Angel has more going on. We've been e-chatting almost every other night for about a month. His real name is Glenn. I don't know his last name yet. He's a Capricorn. He's thirty-eight. Six three. Reality-show handsome. Has a body waiting to be jumped on. Never been married. No kids and doesn't want any. An ex-Marine who did two tours in Iraq. He spent three years at Arizona State. Major: undeclared but was almost creative writing even though poetry is his real love. He's got an idea for a novel about being in a war you don't believe in, and is thinking of doing a memoir about his life growing up in foster care. He said he's been jotting down his thoughts for three years but he hasn't shared any of them with anybody. I think I'm ready to give him my fake cell phone number because he seems interesting enough.

I decide that one more peek won't hurt and click on the site Dark Angel uses. The protocol is you're never supposed to give them your real e-mail address until after you meet them, and it's suggested that the first date be in a public place and preferably in broad daylight—like Star-bucks. Well, well, well. There he is in my in-box. This is all that's there:

> Robin you are a blue-jay to me
> your wings release me to be myself
> because I see inside your soul
> nothing stands in the way of this easy flow.

> Your attitude is gratitude
> there is no surprise more magical
> than the surprise of being loved:
> Surprise! It is the finger of God
> On a man's shoulder and that
> man is me.

I'm no poetry critic, but this is an amazing poem. I'm totally blown away. Shoot, no one has ever written a poem for me. Not even Sparrow. I immediately reply. I tell him how much I loved the poem and how moved and flattered I am that his feelings are already strong. I don't give him my fake cell number but I do tell him to consider this e-mail a green light because I can't wait to meet him in person.

You Need to Watch Dr. Phil

I call in sick even though I'm not sick. I'm having a hard time getting out of bed. I miss Isaac but I don't want him back—that much I do know. I also have a good idea how I think Gloria might be feeling, especially at night. I have not curled up with anything except my pillow, and it's usually cold. I miss those long arms that made me feel like I was in a cocoon at night. I miss his breath. The way he smelled. His laughter. The sound of his voice. You spend almost every single day of your life for ten or fifteen—or hell, even a few—years sleeping in the same bed, eating at the same table, living under the same roof, and then one day they don't come home. Without wanting to, I still find myself waiting for him to walk in the door, grungy and yelling, "Baby, I'm home." But then another day goes by and then weeks and now months, and it begins to sink in that he's never coming back. Sometimes I lie awake and wonder what it was he did that was so terrible. Sometimes I forget all about the whole porn thing. I have asked myself if some of the things he said I didn't do were true or if the engine of our marriage just burned out and its nobody's fault. Possibly both. I don't really know. What I do know is sometimes we love the wrong people and sometimes we marry them. Regardless, you get attached to them so that when they're missing in action, you feel like a ghost. It is an empty feeling. One that's hard to get used to.

I'm surprised to hear my phone ring this early. I look over at the atomic clock Isaac forgot. It tells me it's not only seven-thirty but it's already eighty-six degrees outside. Of course, who else could it be but Mama? She's spry and testy and bitchy as ever at seventy-four, and she still talks to me like I'm eighteen. I hit the SPEAKER button, but as usual, she thinks she's getting my answering service so I just listen to her say: "Hello, Savannah, this is me, your mama calling."

"I know it's you, Mama. I can see your number on the caller ID. I've told you this a hundred times."

"Well, now it's a hundred and one. Are you up?"

"Sort of. But that didn't stop you from calling, now did it?"

"Ain't you supposed to be getting ready for work?"

"I'm feeling a little under the weather."

"What's wrong with you?"

"I've got a cold."

"It don't sound like you got no cold."

"It's just starting."

"Un-hun."

"So, how are you feeling, Mama?"

"I'm feeling pretty good. Walked for thirty minutes this morning with the Lieutenant and Mrs. Mercury."

"That's good."

"And before you ask, my glucose is steady. I'm staying in the one hundred thirty range."

"I'm glad to hear that. And how're you looking these days?"

"What difference do it make how I look? When you old, you ain't gotta impress nobody, plus people don't notice you. Especially young folks. We might as well not exist."

"You still didn't answer my question."

"I look old, Savannah. Like I'm supposed to. I did lose five pounds but I gained 'em back. You lost any?"

"No."

"Now that we got all the small talk out the way, why didn't you tell me you and Isaac are getting divorced for real?"

"Because I wanted to make sure it was already happening in case it took longer than I thought." I sit up, prop two pillows behind my back.

"That don't make no sense, what you just said. Anyway, you can tell your sister but not your own mama?"

"I didn't want to have to listen to your opinion."

"Oh, really? Well, Sheila's got lots of 'em. She thinks what you're doing is stupid. She thinks you're just bored but that ain't Isaac's fault. She thinks you can be a real bitch on wheels and she don't know how Isaac has been able to tolerate you all these years. And she said . . ."

"I don't care what Sheila said or thinks, Mama. She was supposed to keep her big mouth shut."

"Sheila tells everybody's business. You should know that by now. She ain't got nothing else to do but gossip. It's what keeps her going. She stay on the phone all day and night, talking about nothing to anybody willing to listen. And them kids of hers is enough to drive anybody crazy. Sheila said you was letting GoGo come out there and spend some time this summer—is that true?"

"I told her I'd think about it!"

"Well, she got him a nonrefundable ticket for sometime in July."

"That was back in January!"

"You going somewhere in July?"

I didn't feel like telling her the whole truth, so I didn't. "I'm going through a divorce, Mama, so I may not be in the mood for babysitting or entertaining this summer."

"Sheila said you already filed. Did you?"

"Yes, I did. To save money we got a mediator so we can do this in a civilized manner."

"This I gotta see. I ain't never heard of no civilized divorce. I think you might be moving too fast, don't you?"

"This wasn't an overnight decision, Mama."

"Anyway, you should call Sheila."

"I don't feel like talking to her right now."

"Well, GoGo been smoking those things called blunts like it's going out of style and his grades done dropped, and Sheila and Paul both are ready to strangle him."

"Well, I can't fix him."

"Sometimes a change in scenery can help. Let the boy come out there for a couple of weeks. It won't kill you. He might help you not think about how miserable you are."

"Who said I was miserable?"

"Sheila. Plus, what other reason do people get divorced?"

I did not feel like answering that question. I took a bite of the remaining banana—now brown—I had started last night. "Tell her to call me since she likes running her mouth so much."

"You got a point. I'll tell her when she picks me up to go to the mall later."

"I don't feel like talking to her today, though, Mama."

"Okay, okay! I'll hold off a week. Them tickets cost her and Paul over four hundred dollars."

"I didn't tell her to go run out and buy a stupid ticket, now did I?"

"You need to be more sensitive, Savannah. You can be mean."

"I don't mean to be. And I'm sorry. I'm testy right now."

"So, you really going to go through with this?"

"Yes, I am."

"And Isaac wants to part ways too?"

"Yes, he does."

"Well, maybe if you'da kept yourself up more he wouldn'ta wanted to have supersex with all them naked women on the Internet. What happened? Did he fall in love with one of 'em?"

Mama is right. Sheila's got a big fucking mouth. I also know she meant cybersex but this was not the time to correct her. Plus, I liked the sound of it. What I really wanted to know was just how much she knew. "What naked women on the Internet?"

"I wasn't born yesterday, Savannah."

"Well, that's the truth."

"You better watch your mouth before I hang this phone up."

"Where's your sense of humor?"

"Here in Pittsburgh. And it's boiling on the stove. Hold on a minute."

I look out the window at the orange Arizona sun. All of this seems so surreal, but I am not in the mood for a lecture. It's the reason you shouldn't tell your mama everything. Some things you need to keep to yourself. Some things you do because it feels like the right thing for you to do. I know Mama doesn't want me to suffer. But some things hurt. Some things have to.

"Anyway," she says when she comes back, "I been saying it for years: church is full of sneaky men posing as honest souls, and they are perpetuators out here looking for women just like you, with giant holes in your hearts, and they can smell when you got a good job and when you lonely as hell. But Isaac wasn't like them. He was nice enough. Decent. I liked him. For the most part."

I really want to change the subject. Before I can think of something neutral, Mama grabs the microphone.

"I would like to say this and just get it outta the way if you don't mind. You married beneath yourself, Savannah. I never wanted to say anything to your face, but what on earth did you have in common with a lumberjack?"

"He was a skilled carpenter, Mama."

"Everything he built he had to use wood and he had to saw it into pieces, so that made him a lumberjack in my book. Anyway, did he have a college degree?"

She already knew the answer to that.

"No, he did not. Did he make any money? Not enough to brag about. And since times have changed, now women who make more money than their husbands have to pay them alimony the same way men used to have to pay women. Is Arizona one of those states you have to give him half of everything? I hope not."

"Yes, but I won't have to."

"Thank you, Jesus. How much will he be able to walk away with?"

"That is none of your business, Mama."

"I know it. I wasn't asking for dollar amounts, but it irks the hell out of me when folks get what they didn't work for just because you was married to them."

"I know."

"You need to watch Dr. Phil. He woulda told you to get yourself a prenup, but noooooo, even being middle-aged and everything you was still stupid in love just like some teenager. Ain't no man worth losing your damn scruples over, especially when you got property. I ain't calling you stupid but I'm saying you just acted like you was stupid."

"Thanks for sharing, Mama." I swear I wanted to tell her Dr. Phil wasn't on television when I got married, but Lord only knows what kind of war of words this would've led to.

"This is why they used to say it's cheaper to keep her. It costs too much money to leave. You sure you and Isaac can't work this out?"

"I'm sure of it."

"Anyway, I would like to throw this out there—as

GoGo would say. You gon' be a senior citizen in a minute in case you forgot you aging like the rest of us, and at fifty-one . . . I don't know, but the odds ain't in your favor for finding a replacement for Isaac, and I would think long and hard if I was you before signing on that dotted line. Unless you want to take a chance on spending the rest of your life by yourself. Let me tell you, it ain't no fun being old and lonely. Take it from somebody who knows."

"I'll take my chances, Mama. Anyway, I need to lie down."

"I thought you was already in the bed."

"I was, but I got up to make myself some tea," I lied. I was tired of talking to her about all of this.

"Hold it a minute! Don't go yet! For somebody who's supposed to be sick with a cold I ain't heard you cough once or so much as sniffle, so a few more minutes on the phone with your mama ain't gon' make you no sicker. So just chill for a minute, sista girl."

"What did you just say, Mama?"

"You heard me right! Sheila's kids keep me up on the hippest of everything. They're trying to show me how to fax you my e-mail addresses and I'm dying to Google a text message to you from MySpace. You'll soon be hearing from me online, girlfriend."

I laugh. "I'll look forward to getting an e-mail from you, Mama."

"What you doing for the holiday?"

"What holiday?"

"It's Memorial Day weekend, Savannah."

"Oh. I forgot. I don't know. Nothing. It's just another day to me."

"That's a shame. Holidays used to mean something, and if nothing else it was when families got together. But times do change. Anyway, I love you, baby."

"I love you, too."

I hang up and roll out of bed. I walk like I'm just learning how and head toward the bathroom. I wash my face in cold water to wake up. Brush my teeth. Moisturize. For some reason, I find myself opening my workout drawer, which sounds like it could use some WD-40. I look down at a gray top and shorts but then change my mind and pick up a lavender-and-white outfit. The tags are still dangling from it. Maybe a walk wouldn't kill me. Maybe it might help me perk up. Maybe it might help me lose ten ounces. I put on my watch that doubles as a heart-rate monitor and check to see how alive I am: seventy beats per minute. I pull on ankle socks and tie my sneakers, then head for the kitchen. I eat a new banana, make a pot of strong coffee and walk back to my bedroom, where I slide under the covers and wait for it to drip.

Mama's right of course. But aren't they always?

———

A few days later, Thora stands in the doorway of my office. "How're you holding up?"

"I'm doing fine," I say.

"You couldn't possibly be. I've been where you are and it drains you of your best everything. Believe me. I'm on husband number three."

"It's not a fairy-tale ending—that's for sure."

"Is the house getting bigger yet?"

"Yes, it is."

"Hearing things?"

"Yes, I am."

"Longing for him at night?"

"Sad to say, but I do."

"This is stage one. You'll get over it. So, how long before it's done?"

"First of July. It looks like it's not going to be as complicated as I thought."

"Give him whatever he wants and then move on with your life. I'm not kidding."

"All he wants is whatever he's entitled to."

"What about his business?"

"He just barely pays his employees, to be honest."

"He'll want something. I'm warning you. Whatever happens, don't let it turn into a war."

"I won't. Did you dye your hair, Thora?"

"I did. Good eye. It's a darker red. My colorist mixed three shades. I'm loving it."

"It looks good on you."

"Thanks. So, when you're a free woman you're going to need to decompress, so first let me say that even though it's a little soon to think about starting over and dating again, believe me, you'll be back on the open market in no time, and Bert has a great guy he wants you to meet. His name is Jasper. They went to medical school together at Columbia. He's African American, just for the record. A super guy and a divorce also. I'll tell you more about him when the dust settles. But anyway, this is just to let you know that there is life after marriage death."

"Tell Bert thanks for looking out. But right now, I can't even imagine myself dating, Thora. I haven't been on a date in over eleven years. I haven't kissed anybody or had sex with anybody except Isaac for the same amount of time. Anyway, let me get used to the idea of being single and then we'll talk about a date."

"No worries. But I'm also letting you know right now that Bert and I have a lovely two-bedroom flat in Paris. Actually, it's a duplex. In Montparnasse. You're welcome to it."

"That's really quite sweet of you to offer, Thora. I love Paris. But I loved it even more when I was young and hot and single."

"Well, you're still young and hot and soon-to-be single again. So keep it in mind."

Four-Way

"We need to get together," Robin says to Bernadine and Savannah. They're on a three-way call.

"For what?" Bernadine asks.

"That's a stupid question," Savannah says.

"It is, but I'll answer it anyway. I miss seeing you guys face-to-face and the four of us haven't done anything together since Marvin's funeral, and that wasn't exactly a social occasion."

"Has anybody talked to Gloria lately?" Savannah asks.

"I have. Sparrow and I stopped by when her grandkids were there. That little one can't talk but she can sure put a puzzle together. I'm talking about a lot of pieces. They cracked us up. Telling jokes with no punch line. Singing songs they didn't know all the words to. And talk about dance! That little Blaze can bust a move. What was really nice was seeing Gloria laughing. She may have aged ten years in ten days, but she sure came back to life with them around. I guess kids don't give you enough time and space to feel sorry for yourself."

"It's called grieving, Robin," Savannah says. "There's a big difference."

"Well, how long does it last? It's been six months."

"There's no time limit. It's different for everybody," Bernadine says.

"I think I'm grieving," Savannah says, surprising herself.

"I think you're just lonely," Robin says.

"I've been grieving for about six years," Bernadine says.

"Now you're the one who's been feeling sorry for herself," Robin says.

"I have not! I was married to somebody who impersonated being my husband. You have no idea what that feels like."

"You sound like a broken record, Bernie," Robin says.

"I couldn't agree more," Savannah says. "I'm waiting for the day we have a conversation and he doesn't come up."

"When was the last time you guys had a man steal from you and ruin your credit?"

"Never," Robin says.

"But how long can you stay angry?" Savannah asks.

"It's like a termite has been living inside you for the past six years robbing you of all your joy," Robin says.

"Well, Zoloft was supposed to be my pest control."

"Well, it's obviously not working," Savannah says. "I don't think those things were meant to solve your problems."

"They've helped me feel better so I can deal with my problems," Bernadine says.

"And I repeat. They're not working."

"So many people at my job are on antidepressants

it's not even funny," Robin says. "I don't get it. They're still not happy."

"They don't make you happy," Bernadine says.

"Anyway, I just think there's stuff that happens to us that throws us off center and we have to figure out how to get through it the best way we can," Savannah says.

"Oh hell, are you ready to hear this speech, Bernie?"

"Shut up, Robin. It's true. We get divorced, we get conned, someone we love dies, or we can't find anybody to love us or somebody breaks our heart and we realize this fairy tale *ain't* fair. So we suffer. We feel like shit and we want it to hurry up and be over, but there are no shortcuts. I think a lot of folks take this stuff hoping it's a panacea, only to find out it's not."

"Well, they've helped me. Otherwise, I might not have been able to get out of bed in the morning."

"But you're still harping on the ordeal like it happened last week," Robin says. "I never liked him anyway."

"Me either," Savannah says. "I thought he was pompous and phony and I never trusted his ass."

"Since we're finally coming out with it," Robin says, "how could you fall for this guy in, like, breakneck speed when you didn't know shit about him?"

"Because after my marriage fell apart I felt like an empty parking space, and James just pulled into it. Anyway, fuck you guys, okay? I'm doing the best I can."

"No, you're not. We want you to do better so you feel better," Savannah says. "We're on your side, girl. You know that, don't you?"

Silence.

"Bernie." Savannah sighs.

"What?"

"We didn't mean to hurt your feelings or piss you off."

"Yes, you did. But it's okay. Points well taken. After all, what are friends for?" Bernadine says this with no sarcasm in her voice. "So. On a lighter note. Robin, how is Ms. Sparrow doing these days?"

"Getting on my last nerve. Ever since they started this texting thing on cell phones—I made a big mistake and got her one so she wouldn't be able to come up with excuses about her whereabouts—I betcha these kids are gonna have carpal tunnel or arthritis in their thumbs by the time they're old enough to drink."

"When does she get her license?" Savannah asks.

"Next month—God willing. It took three tries for the written. I just pray the driving test is a one-shotter."

"What's she gonna drive?" Bernadine asks.

"She wants that ugly Prius. And since I'm getting my bonus next month, I think I can swing it."

"I can't believe a sixteen-year-old wants a Prius," Bernadine says.

"She doesn't want to contribute more pollutants to the ozone. Okay, enough about my daughter! The reason I called you guys was to see if we could figure out something we could do together since Gloria's DVD guys have been MIA."

"Hey, wait a minute! We forgot all about Gloria!" Savannah says.

"But I can only do a three-way."

"Well, how about we try to narrow down the options

and then one of us calls her. She probably won't care or won't want to come anyway," Bernadine says.

"If we have to drag her out of the house, she's coming," Savannah says. "Let's hear some of your bright ideas, Robin."

"We could drive up to Sedona and have dinner and turn around and come back."

"It's beautiful but boring. After you look at those red mountains, there's nothing to do," Savannah says. "When are we talking about anyway?"

"I don't know. Let's decide where we want to go first and then find out everybody's schedule."

"Mine's wide open," Bernadine says. "I haven't been to Sedona in years, which is shameful."

"Bernie, now that Sweet Tooth is closed, what is it you do all day?" Savannah asks.

"Paperwork," she says.

"How long before you finish?" Robin asks.

"However long it takes. Wait. In all honesty, I surf the Internet looking for everything I can on successful catering companies. The most prestigious culinary programs. I read about top chefs all over the world, and the best restaurants, including their menus, to see what makes them great. And most recently, I'm learning how to stage a progressive dinner party. This is some of what I do all day."

"Right on, Bernie," Robin says.

"What's a progressive dinner party?" Savannah asks.

"I knew you were going to ask. It's a party where each course is eaten at a different person's home."

"What's the point?" Robin asks.

Bernie lets out a long sigh. "It's a very cool way of spending time with friends and meeting new people."

"Then let's have one of those!" Robin says.

"Yeah, since we're trying to come up with something interesting to do," Savannah says.

"I need a lot more time to plan it in order to do it right. And before you ask, Savannah, it's not like a frigging potluck, okay? I'd put a different spin on it. Come up with a kick-ass menu, send invitations to you guys, who in turn would invite a friend or two—folks the rest of us don't know: in our case, a few single friends wouldn't hurt. Anyway, I don't have it all figured out, so let's talk more about it another time."

"Sounds like it could be hecka fun," Robin says.

"Sure does. I'm game," Savannah says.

"Okay," Robin says. "This may sound like a stupid question, but when was the last time anybody went to the Grand Canyon?"

"I am not going to anybody's Grand Canyon," Savannah says. "I've been a million times with Paul Bunyan. I could probably give tours."

"I always got carsick," Bernadine says. "Think of something else."

"How about going to a casino?" Robin asks.

"And get lung cancer?" This is Savannah.

"I agree. You can't breathe in those places, let alone talk," Bernadine says.

"Who said anything about talking?" Robin asks. "Oh, never mind. How about a spa?"

"That would be kind of insulting to Gloria," Savannah says.

"She hasn't even found a place yet," Robin says.

"Look, Robin, why can't we just go to a cool restaurant and have a good meal?" Bernadine asks.

"You mean, like, dinner?"

"Yeah, and we could use, like, a knife and fork, too," Savannah says.

"You go straight to hell."

The three of them laugh.

"We need to get Gloria in on this conversation. It doesn't feel right excluding her," Bernadine says.

"I just thought of something!" Savannah says. "I can call her on my cell and put her on SPEAKER."

And she does. There's no answer.

"She's probably asleep," Bernadine says. "Call her back in a few minutes."

"I will. Oh, by the way, girls, the station won an award for best news program and I got one for the show I did on teen pregnancy." Savannah continues to dial Gloria's number over and over, hoping it'll get on her nerves and she'll pick up.

"You got a what?" Bernie asks.

"An award."

"Why didn't you tell anybody?" Bernie asks.

"I didn't think you guys would be interested in coming to the dinner. They're pretty boring."

"Let us be the judge of that," Robin says. "I already told you how good I thought the program was."

"I Tivo'd it," Bernadine says. "I'm embarrassed to say I haven't watched it yet. But I will!"

"What in the world are you huzzies talking about?" Gloria asks. "And why are you all calling me so late?"

"It's only ten o'clock, so wake your old ass up," Savannah says.

"Savannah got an award for the show she did about the rise in teenage pregnancy in Arizona and didn't tell any-damn-body," Bernadine says.

"Oh, I saw it. And so did everybody at Oasis. It was on target and right on time. But I told you that, Savannah. I need to splash some cold water on my face. I'll be right back."

"And be quick about it!" Savannah yells, loud enough for her to be heard in another room.

"Stop being so bossy," Bernadine says. "And the next time you get honored for anything, be considerate and give your friends a heads-up."

"I will. It's not like I get them all the time."

"Speaking of being awarded and not to change the subject but I'm changing the subject: How long before your divorce is final?" Bernadine asks. "Or are you keeping that a secret, too?"

"July first."

"And how do you know the exact date?" Robin asks.

"Because I agreed to give him an extra couple of months so he'd have time to get health insurance coverage." Of course she was lying about this. She also didn't feel like explaining how the divorce process works in Arizona.

"Well, that was awful nice of you," Bernadine says.

"I'm just glad you guys aren't acting like they did in *War of the Roses*," Robin says. "Want us to come to court with you?"

"It's not fun," Bernadine says. "I'll be there for you."

"Thanks, you guys, but it's not going down like that. We've signed the papers, agreed to the terms, so we don't even have to be there."

"Get the hell outta here," Bernie says. "Times have sure changed."

"What are you gonna do about your house?" Robin asks.

"Live in it."

"Isn't it, like, creepy being in there all by yourself?" she asks.

"Why would it be creepy?"

"You're up there in those dark hills with wild animals everywhere."

"I live up here in these same hills and the only time I've ever been afraid was right after . . . never mind. Anyway, I've never been bitten or eaten by any wild animals, Robin."

"Wait a second. Savannah, does it sound like Bernie is slurring?"

"I was just thinking the same thing. Are you over there hitting the bottle?"

"No! And I'm not slurring. I'm tired."

"From doing what?" Savannah asks.

"I've been running around all day."

"Well, join the rest of the real world," Savannah says. "You're on something. What is it?"

"I'm not *on* anything."

"We can hear it in your voice. I don't know who you think you're fooling."

"Okay, so I took half a Xanax."

"And we're supposed to believe that? Come on, Bernie," Savannah says.

"You can't still be taking those things," Robin says.

"Not all the time."

"What made you take it? What are you nervous about?" Robin asks.

"Nothing."

"Aren't those things addicting?" Robin asks.

"Why're you taking them? What are you so stressed about?" Savannah asks.

"Nothing."

"Then why'd you take it?"

"To relax. Sometimes I feel anxious."

"Don't we all? What are you anxious about that you need to take a pill to relax?"

They hear Gloria snoring.

"Gloria! Wake your butt up!" Robin yells. "We didn't even know you were back on the phone."

"I have to get up early," she utters.

"And do what? We know not to do anybody's hair."

"I'm having a mammogram." Gloria is not telling the truth. Her mammogram is a week from now. She just needed a good excuse to go back to sleep.

"When was the last time you had one?" Robin asks Gloria.

"Last year around this time."

"Has anybody had a colonoscopy or bone density test yet?" Savannah asks.

"I haven't," Bernadine says, grateful the focus has shifted away from her. Again.

"I know I should, and I will, but I haven't," Gloria admits.

"Well, they say by the time we turn fifty, we make more trips to the doctor than anywhere else. I had a colonoscopy last year, and drinking that nasty stuff was the worst. You have to go like there's no tomorrow, but you don't remember a thing about the procedure. And it can save your life."

"A lot of things can," Bernadine says.

"Well, I don't have to have another one for ten years, hallelujah. It's almost time for my annual everything, which I usually do around my birthday so I don't forget—which you guys all know is October fourteenth. As a little reminder I'll accept any and all gifts, small and large, preferably large."

"That means we should look at fourteens, then, huh?"

"Divorce fat sneaks up on you, Bernie, but I'll lose it. Not to worry."

"We don't have to look at your naked behind," Robin says.

"Apparently nobody does," Savannah says. "And Lord knows when someone ever will."

"So what do you guys think about Onika being a lesbian?" Gloria asks.

"A what?" Robin asks. "You can't be serious."

"A lesbian?" asks Savannah. "How is it you know this and we don't?"

"I had to tell somebody."

"And you picked Gloria?"

"I'm not the one with the big mouth, Savannah! It's

you who has to express her opinion about everything, Ms. Walkie-Talkie."

"Oh, really? But who just spilled the beans, Gloria?"

"I thought you told all of us."

"I told you in confidence. So thank you very much, Gloria."

"You should've said that. But you're welcome."

"It probably happened because she went to that all-girls college," Robin says, like this was a math problem she just figured out.

"You don't catch it, Robin," Savannah says. "I always had a feeling she might be."

"Sparrow told me she was but I didn't believe her. That's too bad, Bernie. I'm sorry."

"There's nothing to be sorry about."

"Thank you," Savannah says. "Robin, you should know better. You've got a teenager who's a little way out. Does that bother you?"

"I'm used to her. And it's who she is."

"And Onika is who she is. So shut up," Savannah says.

"Thank you," Bernie says. "It doesn't bother me in the least. Hiding it is probably worse than anything."

"So, does she have a girlfriend and everything?" Robin asks.

"She does. I met her and she's nice. And cute. Tall. Her name is Shy."

"I bet John isn't happy about this, is he?" Robin asks.

"She hasn't told him yet," Gloria says. "She will when she comes home for the summer. How's that for accuracy, Bernie?"

"Go back to sleep!" she says, laughing.

"What about that little Taylor? How's she doing?" Robin asks.

"I don't know, to be honest. I haven't seen her much since her mother split."

"I almost wanna say this is a white thing, but I'm aware of a few black women who've pulled a disappearing act too," Savannah says.

"Okay, so back to us, ladies. We have yet to figure out where we're going and when we're going. Is that about right?" Robin asks.

"I'm free on Tuesday," Gloria says. "Hold it. Where is it we're supposed to be going?"

"I don't know," Bernie says.

"Robin?" Savannah asks.

"Well, you guys said Sedona was boring and everybody agreed the Grand Canyon is out."

"Savannah said Sedona is boring, not me. And I—"

"Why don't we just go to In-and-Out Burger, get a double-double with cheese and a basket of greasy fries—and I'd kill for one of those creamy vanilla shakes—and let's call it a fucking day? I can do Thursday," Savannah says.

"I don't eat red meat anymore," Robin says. "Plus, I have an all-day meeting in L.A. on Thursday."

"When and why did you stop eating red meat? Never mind. Just eat the stupid cheese," Bernadine says.

"Can anybody do Friday?" Savannah asks.

"It's my mom's seventy-eighth birthday so we're going down to Tucson and I'm letting Sparrow drive part of the way, so pray for me."

"Onika and Shy are driving from Oakland, ‍I want to be home when they get here. I'm making gumbo."

"Please make enough for us, Bernie, please!" Savannah begs. "I'll pay for my own crab if necessary."

"I'll pay for everything," Robin says.

"I think you owe me twenty dollars, don't you, Bernie?"

"No! But no charge for you, big mouth."

"I think a little of your gumbo might help resuscitate me," Gloria says. "I haven't turned on the stove since that day. I've been eating nothing but takeout and frozen dinners."

"Well, that's kinda obvious," Robin says. "I didn't mean it that way."

"Yes, you did, but it's okay. I know I'm starting to look like a Thanksgiving turkey, but I'm just trying to get through this the best way I can."

"I hear you," Savannah says. "Don't pay any attention to Jane Fonda. She doesn't understand a thing about grieving."

"Well, what's your excuse, Savannah? You used to jog, you used to eat like you had some damn sense, and over the past year you've been slumming. What's that about?"

"Like I said, Robin, you don't get it. I hope you meet somebody and get married and then they fucking disappoint you and you have to go through a divorce, and then maybe you'll get it."

"That was cold, Savannah," Bernie says.

"You know I didn't mean that. I'm sorry, Robin. Really."

"All is forgiven."

"Anyway, how is your mom doing, by the way?"

"She's fine. In good health. Sound mind. Her spirits are high. She walks every single day and even golfs."

"I've been wanting to learn how to golf, like, forever," Savannah says. "We live where they have some of the most beautiful golf courses in the world."

"Then take lessons," Gloria says.

"Doesn't it take a really long time to learn?" Bernie asks.

"I don't know," Savannah says. "I'm not trying to win the fucking U.S. Open. I just want to learn how to hit that little ball in the hole and see what all the hoopla's about."

"Everybody who plays seems to get addicted," Robin says. "My mom and dad golfed when I was a little girl."

"When do you plan on starting, Savannah?" Gloria asks.

"After I lose ten pounds."

"There are a lot of overdeveloped people who golf."

"You go straight to hell, Robin. In a matter of months there will be less of me. And that's a promise."

"Okay," Gloria says. "I've just been listening to you guys yack like a bunch of old hens and I have not heard anybody figure out when we can get together, although I think we've pretty much covered everything else."

"You're right, Gloria," Robin says.

"Well, it sure was good to visit and just run our mouths," Savannah says. "So when will your DVD guys be coming back, Glo?"

"I won't know until they show up."

"Blockbuster Night's at your crib this time, in case you forgot," Bernadine says.

"I haven't forgotten," Savannah says.

"You think you'll be up for company?" Robin asks.

"Look, as my mama has always said, 'One monkey don't stop no show.'"

"That's true," Bernadine says, "but they damn sure know how to mess things up if they get out of the cage."

"Good night, ladies," Gloria says and hangs up.

"Take an extra Zoloft tonight," Savannah says to Bernadine. "And keep your eye on the road, Robin." She clicks off.

"No more Xanax. Promise," Robin says.

"I promise," Bernadine says, hoping to sound convincing but knowing she is lying through her teeth.

Soap Opera Digest

"You mean to tell me Marlena is still on *Days of Our Lives*?" Bernadine asks the TV as she stirs the roux for the gumbo. She really can't believe this soap is still on. Then again, real life is pretty much one long soap opera when she thinks about it. She hasn't watched one of these things since she was breast-feeding Onika. If she remembers correctly Marlena was the local shrink in Salem. She was pretty, soft-spoken and sensitive. But Marlena had her ups and downs. Over the years the poor thing was possessed by the devil twice. Fortunately an exorcism saved her. She'd had her identity stolen by her twin sister, who was sent back to the sanatorium. She'd been stalked and raped and held captive. She married the guy who saved her but then he died and she married a few more guys, including one who drugged her and one who put her in a coma for five years. Everybody thought Marlena was dead. Bernadine could relate. The last thing she remembers, Marlena somehow resurfaced. But then, after having a miscarriage by one of her new husbands, she kind of freaked out and started suffering bouts of hysterical amnesia. When her first husband strolled back into town, the one she loved better than all the others, the one she thought had been shot down over enemy territory on some kind of mission,

178

he was disappointed to learn that not only was Marlena happily married; she had no memory of him at all. Bernadine wishes she could be so lucky. Since making gumbo is an all-day affair, the absurdity of what Marlena and company will go through during the next hour will keep her entertained.

Onika and Shy should arrive early this evening, and at the crack of dawn Sunday morning head on down to Tucson for their first day as camp counselors.

She continues to stir. The roux is creamy white.

"Marlena, you sure look good, girl. You haven't aged a lick considering all you've been through." Bernadine laughs for talking to the screen.

She has already cracked and cleaned eight Dungeness crabs. They weighed close to three pounds each when she carried them home in the red Igloo. Right now, they're boiling in a huge pot with cut-up lemons. In about five minutes she will store them—except for the tiny claws, which are the cook's treat—in giant Ziploc bags. She takes three different kinds of shrimp from the cooler: the tiny ones used mostly for salads and medium raw and jumbo frozen shrimp, which she will start shelling and save for the stock. Bernadine doesn't like using fish heads and carcasses like her mother always did, nor does she use filé, because you can't reheat it and it gets too stringy. She prefers to offer it at the table.

Spread out on the island is just about everything she's going to need: an array of herbs and spices, bottled clam juice, chicken stock (with no MSG), canned clams (which will take her a few minutes to clean, just to make sure there's no sand in them), Cajun sausage and Louisiana hot links (which she will slice into small chunks and cook in the microwave, making sure to remove all the fat before putting them into the pot), frozen okra (which she will sneak into the pot because most folks don't even realize it's in there), canned Italian tomatoes and, last but not least, the "trinity": onions, bell pepper and celery.

It will take her three to four hours to finish making this gumbo—not that she minds—and over the next half hour she will finish her infamous roux: equal parts oil and flour, which she will put in the cast-iron skillet her grandmother gave to her mother, who gave it to Bernadine before she moved back to Boston. She will sit on a stool and watch Marlena smile or look upset, using a wire whisk to blend this mixture on medium heat and in continuous figure eights until it's the color of root beer.

All of this stirring and chopping and dicing and peeling is rather hypnotic, not to mention therapeutic, for Bernadine. She forgets about time when she cooks, especially when she knows it's for other people. The kitchen is the one place she feels safest. She's in control of what happens in here. Bernadine knows she's a phenomenal cook. It's her very own form of artistry, the one thing she never takes a pill to do. "What good is it doing me, Marlena?"

She swirls the whisk. The roux is beige.

Bernadine wishes she could cook entire meals for other people, not just desserts. One of her biggest fantasies is running a restaurant that has a changing tasting menu. She's made up menus, cooked some of the dishes, taste-tested them and tossed the ones that didn't make the cut out on the hill for the coyotes. The only reason she mentioned the progressive dinner party to her friends was to see if they would find it intriguing. One day soon she hopes to give some of these ideas her best shot.

When the show is over, Bernadine reaches for the remote with her free hand and turns the TV off. Silence can be nice. The roux is now the color of nutmeg. She notices the cooler is leaking. "Damn it!" If she stops stirring, the roux will burn and she'll have to start all over. Bernadine watches the water form a slow canal along the baseboard. She regrets putting in these stupid hardwood floors, although back in the eighties, it was the hip thing to do.

If Bernadine stays in this house, one of the first things she intends to do is replace them with tile. The upstairs air conditioner is temperamental. The irrigation system has a leak that has been causing water to trickle down the curb for over a year, which explains why her bill has been so high. To remedy this problem is a mere twenty thousand dollars because they have to dig up and then replace most of the landscaping in the front yard, which isn't even included in this price. And then there's the issue of transportation. Her black Tahoe is seven years old, seems to be graying, and is one minute away from needing dialysis.

She is surprised to hear the front door open, because Onika and Shy aren't due in for at least a couple of hours. The door locks automatically and only a few people have a key. She keeps stirring. "Is that you, O?"

Taylor appears in the doorway. "Nope, it's me, MomMom." She walks over and gives Bernadine a kiss on the cheek. "Gumbo! Yes! Talk about good timing!"

"What brings you here, Taylor? And how'd you get up here?"

"I drove."

"You did what?"

"It's fine. I didn't kill myself or anybody and I didn't wreck anything unless you count that hearse." She has the nerve to giggle. Maybe when she gets those braces off a year from now she'll come into her own. She must have about forty teeth, all struggling for attention. Taylor has that mixed-race hair: frizzy-curly, dusty brown or dirty blonde, depending on how you look at it. She's tall and lanky for fourteen and a half. She's among the unfortunate mixed-race children who got too many genes from one parent and not enough from the other. She is sweet, though, which makes her cuter than she is.

"Before you totally freak out, MomMom, I need a tampon so badly. Can I run upstairs and get one out of your bathroom?"

"I haven't used a tampon in two years and counting."

"Oh, in case you didn't know it, the doorbell's not working. . . . Why not?"

"I've been finished with all that."

"You mean as in menopause?"

"Exactly."

"But you're not that old."

"Yes, I am. I'm old as dirt, just cleaner. Anyway, check Onika's bathroom."

Before she turns her attention back to the now perfectly brown roux, Taylor flies up the stairs, and seconds later she's back. "Super," she says. "Did you know there's water on the floor?"

"I've been watching it travel but I couldn't stop what I was doing."

"I'll clean it up." She runs to the laundry room and brings back an armful of rags.

"Where's your father, Taylor?"

"At work, where else? Please don't call him yet. Please!"

"Are you standing here telling me you drove all the way over here on your own?"

She nods. "I can't live with my dad, MomMom. I just can't. Things are so screwed up in our house. He's never there, and then let's throw in my slutty mom who bails on her own kid just so she can get screwed by some British guy."

"Hold up, little girl," Bernadine says, adding the trinity to the roux and making sure it's thoroughly mixed in. "I'm not going to stand here in my kitchen and let you call your mother a name like that."

"Then what should I call her?" Taylor is on her hands and knees, swishing the wet rags into a pile.

"What you've been calling her: Mom." Bernadine pours the roux into the hot stock waiting for it in the pot. Not taking her eyes off the contents, she watches the brown liquid begin to thicken.

"Would you mind putting those rags in the laundry room sink, please?"

"Of course I mind," she says, winking at Bernadine as she gets up.

As soon as she leaves, Bernadine empties the okra into the pot. Nobody's allergic to it. Otherwise someone would have let her know after all these years.

Taylor leans against the cabinet when she gets back. "You've been more of a mom to me than she has."

"This, too, is not true."

"May I please come live with you?" She folds her hands as if she's praying and drops her weight on one knee.

Bernadine is sure she's not hearing her right. "Sit," she says, pointing at a stool. "Excuse me a minute, baby. I need to find my purse."

Taylor darts off and lifts it from the stairs because she'd just jumped over it. She hands the big black purse to Bernadine, who immediately starts digging around inside like she's on a scavenger hunt. "Looking for your pills?"

Bernadine's hand freezes. "What do you know about anybody's pills, but especially mine, Taylor?"

"I've seen you pop them. My mom popped everything. I've even popped a few, too. Vicodin's my fave."

"Have you been looking in my purse?"

"Of course not, MomMom. One time when I stayed over we were going to watch *Scary Movie*, and you were making us popcorn and I couldn't find the remote anywhere, so I looked in your side table and saw your little pharmacy. My mom was always digging in her purse but she would never let me see what she was hunting for. I figured it out. Plus, all of her scripts were on display in the medicine cabinet. This is where most of my friends get their stash to sell at school for spending money."

"Wait. You take Vicodin?"

"I used to."

"Used to?"

"It was a phase."

"You're fourteen, Taylor."

She nods.

"Have you sold pills, too?"

"God, no! I used to lift from my mom just for kicks but it wasn't fun after a while. Plus, if my dad ever found out, he would kill me. He gives me a pretty decent allowance so I'm not strapped for cash. I said a *lot* of the kids at school steal from their parents. Everybody knows this. Don't you watch *Sixty Minutes* or CNN, MomMom?"

"Of course I do."

"My dad makes me watch it. I hated it at first but now I feel like I know a lot of important stuff, fascinating stuff, actually. Plus Anderson Cooper is such a fox—gay or not."

Bernadine is standing in front of the steaming pot. She puts the top on and shakes her head in disbelief.

"So what are you on?" Taylor asks.

"I'm not *on* anything."

"Well, if you're strung out you should check yourself into a facility."

"I'm not strung out on anything either."

"Everybody's strung out on something. It's a sign of the times, I guess."

"And what do you know about the *times*?"

"A lot of my friends' parents—but mostly their moms—are always in the clouds. They're bored with their boring husbands who are workaholics like my dad. They're bored with their boring lives, sick of us kids and all this puberty and rebelling, so they pop pills all day long and shop and watch the soaps, and then when it all starts to fall apart they realize they just want to be happy again, so they go to rehab to clean up their act and then start fresh. Can you relate?"

"No, I can't. I take certain medications because I need them."

"What's wrong with you?"

Bernadine is trying to think of a good answer. "Sometimes I can't sleep."

"Even when you close your eyes for a long time?"

"My mind races."

"Mine does, too, but I just tell it to shut itself down."

"Sometimes I suffer from anxiety."

"You know, I still don't quite get this whole anxiety thing, even after I Googled it. Do you worry about a lot of stuff?"

"A few things."

"Like what?"

"You wouldn't understand, Taylor."

"Try me."

"I would prefer not to, because you're beginning to try me, as much as I appreciate your interest in my well-being."

"Well, I know it says that when people are always thinking about what's around the corner, mostly things that haven't even happened yet, they kinda freak themselves out waiting for it. Is that how you feel a lot, Mom-Mom?"

"No. But you're young and you don't have much to worry about yet."

"Duh. Just finals and driving and sex and drugs and boys and why did my mom desert me and my dad, and what do I want to be when I grow up and is there a college out there waiting for me and what box do I check when they ask my race? I could go on."

"Point made."

"Do you take this stuff every day?"

"No."

"What would happen if you just stopped?"

"I don't know."

"Would you go crazy or never get to sleep or something?"

"Of course not!"

"Have you ever tried meditating or yoga? Natural stuff?"

"No."

"They can cure you."

"I don't need to be cured. I'm not sick. And what do you know about meditating and yoga?"

"I told you. I watch all kinds of amazing things on TV. You can learn a lot of cool stuff if you pick and choose."

"Maybe I'll look into it. But do me a favor. Please don't tell your father about this, okay?"

"No worries. Promise you won't tell him I drove over here?"

"Are you trying to blackmail me?"

"No, it's called being fair. So, do you think I can live here with you? I promise not to get on your nerves."

"It's more complicated than that, Taylor."

"That's all I've been hearing for the past year. When are things ever simple, MomMom? That's what I wanna know."

When Bernadine hears the phone, she answers it before the first ring is finished. It's John. "How are you, Bernie?"

"Fine, John. And you?"

"Have you seen Taylor, by chance? She's not picking up at home, not answering her cell phone, and I just want to make sure she's okay."

"She's here."

"Thank God. Is she okay?"

"She's fine."

"How'd she get over there?"

"Wait. Are you still at work?"

"Yes."

"How much longer are you going to be there? Because I've made gumbo and I was going to send some home with Taylor."

"There is a God. We were having pizza again. Anyway, I've got a few more hours of paperwork but I should be out of here by seven. I can pick her up?"

"Either I or Onika will drop her off. But she's fine."

"What time is O expected?"

"Probably in the next hour or so."

"Can I speak to Taylor for a second?"

"She's in the bathroom, John. She'll see you when you get home if that's all right."

"It's fine. And thanks, Bernie. I'm looking forward to seeing Onika."

Bernadine hangs up and sits back down on the stool.

"Thanks for not turning me in, MomMom."

They hear the front door slam.

"You had no right to say any of those things to Josie, Shy! I don't care how long you've known her. It was way out of line and you know it!"

"I said I'm sorry a million times, O."

"You seem to say that a lot."

Bernadine holds her hand up to stop Taylor from running out to the foyer to greet them, especially after she hears those backpacks hit the hardwood floor. "I smell gumbo," Onika says before the two of them enter the kitchen.

"Hey, sis," Taylor says, and she gives Onika a kiss and a hug. Taylor towers over Onika by four or five inches. She turns to Shy. "And you must be the girlfriend. Welcome, Shy. I'm Taylor. And I'm going to be living here soon."

"No fooling?" Onika asks. "Since when? Too bad we're leaving tomorrow."

"Don't listen to her," Bernadine says. "I thought you guys didn't have to be there until Sunday?"

"We looked at the schedule wrong. We have orientation and all that."

"Oh yeah, you guys are going to be camp counselors and sleep outside and get eaten alive by bugs, right?"

"No," Shy says, laughing. "We sleep in cabins, where we'll be eaten alive by bugs."

"And for the record, it has not yet been discussed whether Taylor's going to be living anywhere but with John, and there are a lot of things to consider."

"Like what?" Onika asks. "I mean, Dad can't be much fun. And since Kathleen split, it's not fair to Taylor, I don't think."

"My feelings exactly. I'm a perfect example of the so-called new nuclear family. I'm a product of a broken home. I'm biracial—but isn't everybody these days? I'm not stupid. I know none of this shit is my fault, but it's still very f'd up that my mother bailed on me and my dad. Even though I'm a teenager, I'm still a child and I don't want to grow up and become a totally twisted grown-up just because I was deprived of some basic shit they say we need as children—like love and attention. Is that, like, asking for too much?"

"Hell no!" Onika gives Taylor a high five. "I totally hear you."

Shy looks like she wants to agree, but decides against it.

"You should both watch your mouths," Bernadine says.

"Sorry, MomMom. That slipped."

"Anyway, I would love to just say yes, but I may be going back to work if I decide not to reopen the restaurant."

"Work?" Onika asks.

"What restaurant?" Shy asks.

"It's none of your business, Shy," Onika says.

"Stop being rude," Bernadine says.

"Yeah, and you're probably embarrassing Shy. Have your little lovers' quarrels in private," Taylor says.

"Who said anything about anybody being lovers?"

"Yeah," Shy says.

"Nobody had to tell me anything. I've known you were a lesbo since like forever, O, but it's no big deal. Gay is the new straight, in case you haven't noticed. At least be a nice lesbian or you're going to give the rest a bad rap. You're a fox, Shy, and if my sister mistreats you, kick her ass to the curb and move on."

"Shut. Up!" Onika says.

Shy is grinning.

"Swear one more time, you won't even be visiting."

Taylor covers her mouth, apologizes with her eyes.

"Isn't that Dad's Beemer in the driveway?"

"That it is," Taylor says. "I drove it over here without a license and I will probably get arrested and go to prison for life. You two feel like helping a sistah out?"

"I could really stand a nice long shower first," Onika says.

"Me, too," Shy says. "We actually did some hiking this morning."

Taylor winks at them, and they look at her like she's reading more into this than is necessary.

"Would you mind driving Taylor home as soon as the gumbo's ready?"

"No problem."

The house phone rings and Taylor answers it. "Mom-Mom, it's some guy with an accent. I think it's a telemarketer?"

"I'll take it in the other room," Bernadine says, and she picks her purse up off the floor. "Just don't go near that pot!"

"What time will the gumbo be ready, Mom?" Onika asks as she and Shy head toward the stairwell.

"In about an hour. I just need to put the rice in the cooker and make the cornbread."

"Great! We're starving."

Bernadine is already noticing how much Onika uses "we" and prays her daughter doesn't get her heart broken or ends up doing the breaking. She goes into the parlor bath, closes the door and sits down on the toilet seat.

"Hello," she says, trying not to sound nervous. She wasn't expecting to hear from the lender until Monday. She worked in finance long enough to know how this works.

"Mrs. Harris?"

"This is she."

"David Osborn from Sherman and Lynch Loan. If I've caught you at a bad time . . ."

"No," she says and gets up from the toilet seat, which makes a loud suction sound. "This is fine. Is everything all right?" She already knows it isn't.

"Well, I wish I had good news, Mrs. Harris. We've gone over these figures and I've tried to crunch the numbers in every possible configuration that I could. However, it's just not panning out the way I'd hoped. You're somewhat overextended on the debt-to-income ratio and even though you've had an excellent credit rating in past years, your score has dropped considerably because of outstanding balances on credit card bills, and as much as our institution appreciates and respects your entrepreneurial background, you've only got about forty percent equity left in your home and we don't think it would be wise for you or us to get it any lower. Otherwise, should the time come and you wish to sell, you're not really going to walk away with much."

"What about a lesser amount?"

"We think you might want to try a different lender or, if possible, pay down some of the cards and get that score boosted up a bit and then give us a call back in a few months. I'm sorry, Mrs. Harris. I wish we could've helped. And good luck to you."

Without thinking about what she's doing, Bernadine

digs inside her purse until she finds the pillbox and takes out a small orange pill. She pops it into her mouth dry and then turns on the faucet and fills a Dixie cup with hot water. She swallows it, hoping it will explode inside her belly immediately. She sits there and waits, tapping her feet: heel toe, heel toe, heel toe. And then she starts wondering: How would Marlena get out of this one?

You Can Never Be Too Sure

"Slow down, Sparrow! You're speeding!" We're on Interstate 10, on our way to Tucson. I've been a nervous wreck since she got behind the wheel thirty-eight minutes ago. If it wasn't for the vast backdrop of mountains, John Legend's CD, and the outlet malls, I probably wouldn't be able to stand this long stretch of boring highway.

"I am not speeding, Mom! I'm only doing sixty-five. What's that you're reading?"

"A poem."

"Not that dreadful thing you got from that Dark Angel guy, I hope."

I drop the piece of paper in my lap. "You mean to tell me you've been reading my e-mail?"

"No. But you left it on the screen one day and I couldn't help but read it. I cracked up."

"What was so funny?"

"It was corny and I didn't even need my English teacher to tell me it was super-syrupy, and on top of everything, it didn't make any sense: 'Robin you are a blue-jay to me'? Get real. Don't tell me you liked it, Mom?"

"I thought it was a warm display of emotion."

"Is he in prison or something?"

"God, no! What would make you ask something like that?"

"Because it sounds like he writes poetry but he doesn't read any. I bet he's never heard of Langston Hughes or Sonia Sanchez or Gwendolyn Brooks. And how about Mary Oliver?"

"Who's Mary Oliver?"

"She's a poet, Mom." She presses a button to change the CD. I pray it's not rap except maybe that Ludacris boy—I like him.

I sneer at her. And here comes that little white girl Avril Lavigne, whom I cannot stand.

"She won a Pulitzer Prize and a National Book Award."

"Is she black?"

"No, but you might want to check her out anyway."

"I will. Have you ever read any of Nikki Giovanni's poetry?"

"Of course I have."

"Where?"

"In my English class."

"We didn't read anything by black writers when I was in high school."

"That's why we had the civil rights movement, Mom. To shake things up and make things right."

"Can you please change this?"

"What would you like to hear?"

"No swearing or screaming. Real music."

I'm grateful when I hear John Mayer. We both like him. Sparrow enjoys her share of hip-hop but she's not big on R&B. It doesn't seem normal to be black and not like soul music. Her top three: Aretha, Otis Redding and Curtis Mayfield. She'll listen to that Matchbox Twenty and Nickelback (whom I also happen to get a kick out of), and those Red Hot Chili Peppers and Fall Out Boy and Coldplay like they're never going to make another album. We both have a soft spot for country music. It's just the blues with a twang. The Dixie Chicks and Kenny Chesney can take my money.

"So what'd you get Grandma for her birthday?" she asks.

"It's a surprise."

"I made her a pair of earrings."

"I hope they're not weird, Sparrow." She makes jewelry. Frightening jewelry. She uses stuff like bark, dust, aluminum foil and broken glass, and I think she glued some old bubblegum and dead flies on a necklace once. Her friends fight over this mess.

"I think she'll like these."

"If she doesn't, you know she'll tell you." I suddenly feel like I've walked into an oven set at five hundred degrees, so I reach over and turn the air up as high as it will go. I fan myself with Dark Angel's poem. Beads of perspiration have magically formed across my forehead. More has started dripping over my eyelids and temples. I absolutely hate this shit and I don't think I can keep going through it for however long it might last. I might have to break down and ask my doctor to give me something to help me get through this. I'm tired of waking up through-out the night, kicking the covers off because I'm burning up, then pulling them back on a few minutes later because I'm freezing. Plus, my memory is failing me. Sometimes it feels like I'm getting Alzheimer's or something. I don't think it's worth going through all this if I don't have to.

"So where does he live?"

"Who?"

"Dark Angel! How soon we forget."

"In Arizona."

"Well, that certainly narrows things down. Mom, turn the air down a little, please. It's freezing in here."

I don't feel like talking about Dark Angel anymore. "Did you save me some gumbo?"

"Of course I did. Aunt Bernie outdid herself again. "Do you have an address for this guy?"

"We haven't gotten that far yet."

"When do you plan on going out with him?" She veers off the pavement onto the gravel and then quickly gets back on. "Sorry."

"Pull over."

"Mom, it's no big deal! *You* go over the line some-times."

"I said pull over."

She just keeps driving. I would like to slap her. That would give me so much pleasure. Just once. Smack her dead in her smart-ass mouth. Of course I wouldn't dare, because she's my daughter.

"How would you like to have a sweet-sixteen party?"

"Absolutely not!"

"Why not?"

"Because it is just so uncool. To celebrate turning any age is silly if you just think about it. Except for Grandma, of course. She has earned the right to celebrate every single day of her life if she feels like it. I mean, getting my license is a very big deal, but I think once you pass fifty you have more of a reason to celebrate because you're lucky to still be alive."

"What in the world are you talking about?"

"That came out wrong," she says.

"Anyway, I'm not celebrating turning fifty. And I think I have a few good years left, Sparrow."

"You're going to be a whole half a century old, Mom! How cool is that?"

"Too cool. Now pull over. You've driven fifty miles and apparently that's enough."

"Spoilsport. You're just mad because I peeped your boy. But seriously, Mom, tell him you want to send him something and make sure he doesn't have any numbers behind his name or it's not some post office box. That's how you'll know he doesn't live behind bars."

"Why are you so concerned about him?"

"Because you're my mom and I've already heard one horror story after another about how many losers and wackos you've met online, and of course I've been hoping you'd meet your Lancelot by now, but this guy's poem sounded so desperate I almost felt sorry for him."

"He's been to Iraq twice."

"How old did you say he was?"

"Thirty-eight."

"Isn't that kind of old to be going to war?"

"Pull over, Sparrow. It's the last time I'm going to say it before I grab the steering wheel and turn it myself."

And she does.

I had planned to stop at the outlets in Casa Grande

for a hot minute but I don't much feel like shopping now. I get behind the wheel and drive in total silence for the next forty miles. When we get to my mom's assisted-living facility, she's sitting under a gazebo in a wicker chair, out here in all this heat, waiting for us. She's wearing a blue cotton dress with white flowers on it. Her hair is white and fluffy and her skin is a beautiful shade of brown. It's smooth for eighty and wrinkles only show up around her eyes when she smiles. She waves when she sees us.

Sparrow jumps out of the car and runs toward her, bends down and gives her a big hug. "Hi there, sugar pie. Grandma was wondering if you guys were going to be on time. I only have about an hour, you know."

"What?" I ask.

"I told you they were having a birthday party for me and it starts at six, and I can't be late for my own party."

"Are we not invited?"

"I'm afraid not. You needed to RSVP, Robin. They don't really like outsiders to come to our celebrations, because it makes some people sad."

"That doesn't make any sense," Sparrow says.

"Who said it has to make sense?"

"I have something for you, Grandma."

"Did you make it?"

"I did."

"Oh Lord," she says. "You make such unusual things that just don't seem to fit inside my age bracket. Please don't take it the wrong way, sweetheart. Grandma appreciates your talent and your thoughtfulness."

Sparrow pulls a little bag out of her backpack and

hands it to her. Like me, Mom has never put on more weight than she needed. I'm still a size ten. She's still a size twelve.

As she begins to unwrap the yellow and blue tissue paper, she looks up at Sparrow, who's in her usual costume. "Why do you dress like that?"

"I can't explain it, Grandma."

"Try."

"Well, it's sort of my way of expressing myself without trying to look like a carbon copy of other people."

"You might want to consider it because you look like you're trying to say so much you're really not saying anything. You dressed better when you were a little girl. I don't mean any harm by this. Oh my," she says, holding up two strands of beaded blue earrings that happen to match her dress. "I like these a lot, sugar pie."

"I tried to tone it down some for you, Grandma."

"I'm glad you did. Can you put them on me, please? I didn't mean to hurt your feelings. If you like the way you look, that's all that matters. Unless you're looking for a job."

Sparrow just laughs. I've already explained to her that when people get older sometimes it's almost as if they have Tourette's. They say whatever comes into their mind, which more often than not is pitch perfect.

Mom looks at her watch and then up at me. "How's that computer dating coming along, Robin? Met any cool cats yet?"

"She met a poet."

"Did she ask you or did she ask me?"

Sparrow hunches her shoulders and blows air inside her cheeks to make them puff out. *Sorry. Just having fun.*

"Anyway, Mom, things are looking up and I have a date in a few weeks."

"You didn't tell me you had a date with him, Mom."

"Why is it any of your business? She doesn't need your permission, young lady."

Sparrow keeps her mouth shut. For once.

Mom turns her attention back to me. "A few weeks? What's the holdup?"

"Our schedules are just different."

"Then forget him. Who wants to be bothered with somebody that busy?"

"We'll see. Anyway, happy birthday, Mom." I hand her a small box.

"I wonder what this could be." She opens it, holds the tiny frame up close, sees it's an old photo of her as a little girl. "Where on earth did you get this, Robin?"

"It's my little secret."

"Was it Bessie or Beulah? Which one?"

These are her older sisters who still live in Biloxi. "It was Aunt Bessie."

"Lord, Lord, Lord. I was a cute little something, wasn't I?"

"You still are," Sparrow says.

"You are indeed, Mom." She stands up and I hug her and kiss her on the lips. She smells like talcum powder. She has also shrunk over the years; she used to be taller than me. But she's still alive and she's in good health, for which I am grateful.

"Well, I have to get going," she says, standing up. "It was sweet of you to drive all this way to help me celebrate. I'm very much appreciative. I hope you know that."

"We do, Mom. And have a great party."

"Did I tell you we have a band?"

"No, you didn't."

"All the band members are over seventy!"

"So you guys are going to party hard this evening, huh, Grandma?"

"It's over at eight. It sure would be nice if your dad could come."

"I'm sure he's probably going to be there, Mom."

"You can never be too sure," she says, and waves to us.

I decide to let Sparrow drive all the way home.

———

Romeo and Juliet bark up a storm until we're both inside. We ate burgers on the way home, so I don't have to worry about dinner. I almost tiptoe into my makeshift office, which is really a small bedroom. I close the door. Log in. There are a dozen winks and icebreakers but I'm not interested in opening any of them. I decide to reach out to Dark Angel:

Hello there, Dark Angel: Just checking in to see what you're up to. I'm psyched about our finally meeting in a few weeks and wanted to make sure we're still on for coffee. I've also been thinking about your poetry aspirations, which is why I want to send you something before we meet. Would you mind giving me your mailing address? It's not a big deal but I think you might like it. I'm looking forward to hearing back from you. Have you written any more poems?

Ciao!

Tiger Lady a/k/a Robin

P.S. I know your first name is Glenn but what's your last name?

There. I slide away from the computer and try to figure out what I can do to fill up the rest of the night or to make the time pass until I hear the computer letting me know I've got mail. I decide on laundry. I do three loads, including drying them and folding them. Nothing. I take a very long shower, wash and condition my hair. I'm due for a new weave and so I leave a message for Joseph at Oasis to let me know if he can squeeze me in sometime next week. He's usually booked months in advance. But he likes me.

"Mom, can I come in?"

"No, go away, Sparrow. I'm relaxing."

"Well, can I ask you a question?"

"You just did."

"What if I change my mind about a party?"

"Too late."

I hear her stamp her foot.

"How could it suddenly become cool to have a sweet-sixteen party in a matter of hours?" I say.

"I don't know. But I don't want to have, like, something huge. Just a few friends over."

"What made you change your mind? This sounds a little fishy."

"I don't know. Seeing Grandma. Maybe I overreacted. Turning sixteen is a big deal. Don't you think?"

"Of course it is."

"But there's a catch."

"What is that, Sparrow?"

"I'll only have one if you have one, too."

"Then forget it."

"Then I'll just be depressed. Thanks for caring. I'm going to sleep. Oh, sounds like you just got an e-mail."

I grab my bathrobe. Before I have a chance to tie the sash, I brush past Sparrow and head down the hall to collapse in front of the computer. I close my door and click on. I hear hers close, too. It is an e-mail from Dark Angel. My heart is beating so fast I almost can't stand it. I pray my daughter is wrong. I pray he is who he says he is. I don't care if he never becomes my boyfriend or my husband. I just want him to be legitimate.

I open it:

Hello there, Ms. Tiger Lady: Nice hearing from you. To answer your question, I haven't written a poem since the one I sent you, but I have more than enough for a book. Finding a publisher is hard when you're a poet. I've been thinking about self-publishing, although it's expensive. But you never know. I'm glad you liked the poem I wrote for you. It's kind of embarrassing to be so open about your feelings sometimes. So, yes, I'm looking forward to meeting you at our agreed-upon date and time and my last name is Cook. My address is 100 Seal View Drive, Chandler, AZ 85249. Anyway, I'm exhausted. Been a very long day. So I'll sign off for now. By the way, I'm going to visit my folks for a couple of weeks and may or may not have Internet service. They live outside of Baton Rouge. So if you don't hear from me until we hook up, don't freak out. Dark Angel.

"Yes!"

Good Vibrations

"Hi, Joseph," Gloria said from her car phone.

"Hey, Miss Glo. How are you this lovely morning?"

"I'm better today than I was yesterday. I think I must be losing my mind though, Joseph. I forget more than I remember. I meant to tell you my annual blood test and mammogram are today. I also forgot the vacuum isn't picking up anything so I'm going to stop by Home Depot and buy a new one. Anyway, I should be in before noon."

"Would you mind getting a couple of cans of Brasso? We're also low on lightbulbs if you are so moved, sweetheart."

"No problem. I'll see you in a minute, then."

"Wait! Glo?"

"Yeah."

"Could we chat a few minutes after we close tonight?"

"Sure, baby. Is everything all right?"

"I hope it will be."

"It's not Javier, is it?"

"No no no. He's fine. We're fine. It's nothing for you to be alarmed about. I just wanted to run something by you."

"You're not leaving, are you?"

"Hell no! After twenty years? You need to get right

with God. I said it's nothing to worry about so don't go getting yourself all in a tizzy."

"Wait a second! Did you see who's coming in today?"

"I haven't checked everybody's schedule yet but now that I know you'll be a little late, I will."

"Sister Monroe is back in town."

"I heard. Grandma Dearest herself. I hope she's calmed down with age. I also heard she not only had work done but she did the gastric bypass thing. So there's less of her to get on our nerves."

"We'll soon see, won't we?"

After she left the imaging office, Gloria felt lucky when less than two blocks away she spotted the sign for Good Vibrations Hardware. She pulled into a parking space right out front. Most of the industrial vacuum cleaners were priced the same, so she didn't need to drive halfway across town to Home Depot. This must be an upscale hardware store, she thought, after seeing that the glass was tinted a little darker than most establishments in Phoenix. She could tell they got hit with southern exposure, so it made sense. Unlike most hardware stores, this one didn't have flowers or lawn mowers or wheelbarrows or shovels near the entrance. Gloria was relieved because it was why she always ended up with gadgets she didn't need or had no idea how to use, especially since Marvin had been gone.

When Gloria stepped inside, her eyeballs opened as wide as they could and then froze. The first thing she saw was an erect pink penis sitting on an acrylic stand. It looked like it was floating. As her eyes traveled across the aisles, there was a chorus line of penises in various shapes and sizes. It was clear this was not the kind of hardware store she had in mind. Penises were everywhere, perched high and low on wooden shelves.

It seemed as if they might come to life and attack her. It gave her the creeps. She didn't, however, rush to leave, much as she was tempted to. Gloria was more afraid someone might recognize her and think she was desperate for things to have come to this. Of the fifteen or twenty folks in here, she was grateful no one looked familiar.

Reluctant to walk around, Gloria also felt a tinge of excitement at the thought that you could actually buy the kind of penis you always wanted. Not that she had been thinking about one. If she had, it would've been Marvin's. As things stood, she had accepted the fact that she might never be sexually active again. And it was okay. She had no idea how much a fake penis cost and wondered what their return policy was. She started chuckling at the thought that you can take anything back to Nordstrom no-questions-asked. What would a woman or a man say (not that she had any intentions of buying one of these things): "This didn't fit" or "This one didn't work for me"?

"May I help you?" she heard a male voice say from behind her.

When Gloria turned around, she was surprised to see a young woman. She was dressed all in black and both arms were covered with so many colored tattoos you couldn't see her skin. She had tiny barbells through holes where there shouldn't be any: the middle of her tongue, her chin, the side of her eyebrow. The scariest of all went through the center of her nose. What was the point of them all? Gloria wondered. "I thought this was a hardware store!" she blurted out.

"Well, it is, sweetheart. Would you like me to show you how some of them work?"

Gloria pressed the palm of her hand against her chest like a schoolmarm. "Oh no, that won't be necessary."

"Well, some work better than others."

"I've never been in a store quite like this before."

"No need to be embarrassed, sistah. We all have needs and sometimes we have to satisfy them."

"I suppose there's some truth to that."

"Feel free to turn them on. Some vibrate. Don't be afraid to hold them to see how warm they get."

Gloria lowered her head and looked at her feet. She didn't know this young lady, and here they were talking about penises. As she headed toward the door Gloria noticed a shelf full of clitoris stimulators. She must've walked right past them when she came in. Between the creams and oils, feathers and whips, plus stacks of movies, Gloria was a little weirded-out by it all. "Thank you very much," she said to the young woman, who now had a line at the counter.

"You're quite welcome. Have a nice day, and come back to see us soon," she said.

"I'll do that." Gloria got in her car and headed straight for the salon. She decided to keep her mouth shut and not tell anybody what a fool she had made of herself. Her girlfriends especially. They'd have a field day.

———

The music met her at the back door. John Legend, to be exact. At forty-three, Joseph still held down the music front. He often bumped heads with Twyla and Joline. They loved hip-hop. He tolerated it. They loved rap. He hated it, couldn't stand the language: everybody was a bitch, a ho, a motherfucker or a fag. Gloria would not allow any of it in the salon. Right next to the front door was a big sign that read:

No Profanity
No Unnecessary Gossip
No Loud Talking on Cell Phones
(turn off all ringers, including ringtones)
No negative comments about anyone based on
race, physical features, gender or sexual preference.
Absolutely no personal checks.
No hot food.
No dogs. No children under 9 or 10
(unless they are getting their hair done).
We reserve the right to refuse service to anyone.
So relax. We hope you enjoy our services.
(10–20% discount on all referrals)
The Management
OASIS HAIR & BEAUTY

"Good afternoon, everybody." Gloria waved as she headed toward her office.

"What up, Ms. Glo?" Joline asked, never expecting an answer. The tips of her blond dreadlocks were pink today.

"Hi there, cutie," Twyla said. She had greeted Gloria the same way each and every day for the past three years.

"Hey, Miss Thang," Joseph said. He gave her the two-cheek kiss even as he struggled, trying to cornrow

Chrysanthemum's one-inch snatch of hair so he'd be able to stitch an eighteen-inch bone-straight weft onto it. He was shaking his head so she couldn't see him.

"Hey, baby."

"You need some help with the vacuum?" he asked.

"Oh, shoot!"

"If you forgot my Brasso I'm going to beat you."

"I'm sorry, Joseph. They ran late at the imaging place and I was rushing to get back here."

"Rushing for what?"

"Yeah, rushing for what?" Joline asked.

"Just stuff I need to take care of. I'll pick everything up tomorrow. Promise."

"Well, I'll let you off the hook today, and we can make Twyla sweep up."

"I don't mind," Twyla said. She was prettier than most of the girls in those rap videos on BET. Her maple skin looked like satin. Today, her hair was pushed back and brushed up on top of her head like one huge comma.

"Not to worry. I'll do it," Joseph said.

When Sister Monroe walked through the door, Gloria almost didn't recognize her. She was half of her old self. She looked weird, as if her head was now too big for her body. Her hair was no longer flame red but burgundy. Her roots were silver and those three-inch stilettos she was famous for wearing had been replaced by hush puppies. She still limped as if she weighed three-hundred-plus pounds.

"Hello there, Sister Monroe," Joseph said. "You are looking fabulous! Those missing pounds certainly agree with you."

"Why, thank you, Joey. It ain't no fun feeling like you walking into church on a bed of hot coals."

"I hear you, Sister Monroe. And it's Joseph. But Joey is okay, too."

"You all can call me by my real name now, too: it's Johnnie Lee. I quit my old church a long time ago. I worship at a non-what is it? demo, deno—demoninational church where you don't have to prescribe to just one religion. Anyway, it's nice to see at least one familiar face in here, Joseph. I see you finally got married!"

He looked at his wedding band. "I did," he said, and left it at that. He and Javier were married in Costa Rica a few years ago. They'd been together ten. It took a while for some folks to accept their union, since Gloria had insisted Joseph not hide it. Today, however, he didn't feel like breaking it down to Sister Monroe or Johnnie Lee.

"You had any kids yet?"

"They're on the horizon."

"That's good," she said, and headed to Gloria's office. "Chile," she said without even thinking about knocking, "I need to give you a hug with all you been through. You know I loved me some Marvin and you have been in my prayers nightly, baby."

Gloria stood up and accepted her hug, all the time hoping Sister Monroe wouldn't be inclined to compare body notes. "It's so good to see you, too, Sister Monroe. You have certainly been missed around here. You were our live entertainment."

"I know you all had to miss me. I'm blessed and highly favored. I could feel your spirit all the way out there in the Mojave Desert. How you doing, baby? Hanging in there?"

"I'm hanging in there. You look fantastic. You truly do."

Sister Monroe tried and failed to blush. "I certainly try. I may not have but ten or twenty years left, but I'm going looking as foxy as I can. Lord willing." She decided not to bother telling Gloria her real name. It could wait. She turned and looked out at the salon. "I sure like what you've done to this new place. It's lively."

The walls were pale gray. The workstations were bold: chartreuse, cranberry and purple.

"Thanks. I was looking for a much bigger place so I could add a day spa, but a lot has changed. I'm not so sure now. I just have to see how it goes."

"Un-hun. The Lord doesn't give us more than we can handle. He will make a way when it feels like there is no way. Anyway, which one of them chil'ren is Joline?"

Gloria points to her.

"You mean to tell me that little white girl is supposed to do my hair? What is she doing in here?"

"Working, Sister Monroe."

"I was baptized Johnnie Lee, Gloria. And I would really appreciate it if you would call me that from now on. Why can't the pretty young girl"—moving her chin toward Twyla—"just standing there doing nothing—why can't she do my hair?"

"Because she's waiting for a client, Johnnie Lee."

"Look, I am not prejudiced. None whatsoever. You sure she knows what to do with my hair?"

"I wouldn't have her doing it if I was worried."

"Well, one way or the other, you'll be seeing me more often now that I've moved back home. You go to church any Sundays?"

"Some. I think Joline is waving for you." Gloria smiled and shook her head as Sister Monroe limped away. Johnnie Lee my foot, she thought, shaking her head. Before she had a chance to boot up the computer and start sifting through all the mail, the young men who sold the DVDs strutted into the shop with their black leather bags thrown over their shoulders. They waved to Gloria and ushered her to come on out.

Neither Gloria nor anyone in here had ever bothered to ask where or how these young men got these DVDs—most of which included quite a selection of movies that were often still in theaters. Sometimes they had copies days after the film had opened, and not the ones where you saw silhouettes of folks getting up to go to the bathroom or carrying big bags of popcorn. You didn't hear any laughter. No coughing. No babies crying or loud comments about what was happening on the screen. They boasted about how they had mostly "directors' cuts" because they "got it like that."

The last time they were here one of them had said, "In a minute, we gon' be getting all our DVDs in high definition, so you know that means there's gon' be a slight price increase. We should charge about thirteen but since Ms. Gloria and her customers are loyal patrons we gon' give y'all our special discount: one for eleven, two for twenty or three for twenty five. You can't beat that with a stick."

Like everybody else, Gloria was curious about what

up-to-the-minute movies they had today. She had wanted to see *Diary of a Mad Black Woman* and *Crash,* but she hadn't had the energy or the ability to be still for twenty minutes unless she was lying down. Gloria laughed at the thought that the last movie she and Marvin had seen was *Meet the Fockers,* and the last one she'd seen without him was when she took her grandkids to see *The SpongeBob SquarePants Movie.*

"Why haven't we seen you guys in so long?" Joseph asked. "You know we need our celluloid fix."

"We had family problems we had to deal with, and after we settled all that we needed a real vacation, brotha man. We went to Cabo. Sweeeeet! But them waves they got down there ain't no joke. They'll kill a brother, and can't none of us swim so we wasn't about to get in no ocean no kinda way. But. We partied like we was Prince. Loved it. Even stayed a few extra days. But we back. And here's the new printout of our inventory. Take a look-see. And hey, again, sorry for the inconvenience."

Some of the first-timers or irregulars were letting out squeals. Gloria had left her glasses on her desk. "Just tell me a few of the latest ones, baby."

"Well, we got *Crash, Star Wars: Episode III, Batman Begins* and . . ."

"Batman isn't on DVD yet," Chrysanthemum said.

Everybody just gave her a look.

"Go on," Joseph said, while pulling the thread at the tip of that curved needle just a little tighter through one of her cornrowed braids.

"As I was saying. Just this morning we got *Mr. and Mrs. Smith, March of the Penguins* and *Slutty Summer.*"

"I can only afford two," Joline said. Sister Monroe just stared at herself in the mirror, waiting for Joline to make one mistake so she would have an excuse to jump out of that chair.

"I'll take *Crash* and *Mr. & Mrs. Smith.* I heard they're both good," Gloria said. This would fulfill her promise to Bernadine and they would start having Blockbuster Night again.

"What's *Slutty Summer* about, I wonder?" Joseph asked, and he started laughing because he was looking directly at Sister Monroe.

"Ain't this illegal?"

The ten or twelve customers under dryers, being shampooed, getting cut or permed or just waiting on the long sofa reading *Jet, Essence, Ebony,* or *Black Hair* or *People*—including the salesmen—all gave her the most ridiculous look ever.

"No, it is not illegal, ma'am," one of the young men said.

"Then I spoke out of turn. Would somebody mind picking a couple out for me?"

No one said a word.

"I will," Twyla said.

"Check it out, Miss Gloria. And by the way, we are so sorry about your loss. How you feeling these days?"

"I'm feeling much better. Thank you for asking."

"That's wonderful. Okay, looka here. We got *The Longest Yard, Monster-in-Law*—that's the one with old fine Jennifer Lopez in it. Then we got *Inside Deep Throat*— Wait. Scratch that one—we got *Because of Winn-Dixie . . .*"

"Because of win-who?" Gloria asked.

"Winn-Dixie! It's some corny white movie, but a lotta black folks seem to dig it. Anyway, we got the Pooh movie for the little ones, *The Pacifier* for the bigger ones and *The Ring Two* for anybody who like scary movies, but this one is just white folks tripping on some weird stuff that don't make no sense and it ain't all that scary but you didn't hear it from me. Anyway, for anybody looking for some real excitement we should have *War of the Worlds* tomorrow. That one's been hard to get. Don't be scared to check out our backlist. Our inventory is huge. My cell number is on the bottom, so if we don't have what you want on us, we deliver. Same day. Just give us a two-hour window. Two dollars. Gas is going up up up. Ms. Gloria, may I use your restroom, please?"

"Yes, you may."

"And for being so nice, yours are free today."

"Thank you. And tell me your name again, young man?"

"Marvin. The same as your husband's. Don't you remember me telling you that a while back?"

"I do now."

———

After everybody was gone, Joseph started sweeping up pounds of hair until it looked like he had enough for a bonfire. Gloria was sitting on the sofa, flipping through the pages of *Jet*. "Did you know that Bobby Brown is getting his own reality show?"

"Don't get me started," Joseph said.

"I wonder what he's gonna be doing?"

"Being Bobby Brown, Glo, that's what. I can't wait

for Whitney to kick his ass to the curb and get her life back. I swear."

Gloria put the magazine down. "Okay, so I'm all ears," she said and looked up, trying not to look suspicious or too anxious.

"All I can say is some of these white folks kill me how they do business."

"I agree," Gloria said, not sure what he was hinting at.

"They certainly don't mind throwing you out on the street if you can't pay your bills as long as they can still make a dollar."

"I agree."

"So what are we gonna do?"

"About what?"

"About this?" he said and swirled his free hand in the air like those models do on game shows.

"What do you mean?"

"I mean, maybe we should think about becoming partners. I mean, we've been together longer than some couples, and I think it could take some of the pressure off of you and make us both work a little harder to make the salon everything we've always dreamed of. It's just a suggestion. I'm amenable to it if you're amenable to it." Joseph released his grip on the broom handle and let it fall inside the crease of his forearm.

"You know I appreciate what you're saying and everything, but tell me something, what brought this on, Joseph?"

"Aren't you a little nervous about the terms of the new lease?"

"I haven't gotten around to reading it yet."

"Well, I did. When I was trying to help sort through your mail. I figured it might warrant your immediate attention. I thought you read it and just didn't know what to say or do."

"About what? I know there's always a slight increase."

"Gloria, the bastards tripled the rent. Starting in September. Three short months from now."

"I know you have got to be lying to me." She marched straight to her office, spotted that manila envelope, opened it and scanned down until she saw the new monthly rent: $15,000. Her mouth opened wide. She threw the lease on the floor, then picked it up and tossed it in the trash. Gloria flopped down in her chair and rocked back and forth. She didn't know if this was a sign that it was time for her to bow out or if Joseph was going to be her new partner.

Grocery Shopping

"What do you mean, GoGo can't come out there?"

"Stop yelling in my ear, Sheila. And hold on a minute. I'm at the grocery store."

I point to a rib-eye steak and nod a "that's all" and mouth "Thank you" to the butcher. "It's not a good time, Sheila."

"When is it ever a good time? How do you think I ended up with a house full of kids?"

"I told you I was going through a divorce. It's kind of a big deal. And a first for me."

"People get divorced every day, Savannah. A hundred times a day. What makes you think yours is so special?"

"Did I say that?"

"You're making it sound like this is so traumatic but the bottom line is you're the one who wanted the stupid divorce, so you're just getting what you wanted!"

"I wish it was that cut and dry."

"You complicate everything, always have, and this is no exception. Men cheat. They lie. They love porn. They don't respect you and don't care if they hurt you. It's the fucking breaks. Women divorce 'em 'cause we can't tame 'em or train 'em or control 'em like we do household pets. End of story."

"You should get your own talk show, Sheila. You're just full of insight."

"I know what I'm talking about. GoGo will not get on your nerves. He is very mature for his age."

"Look, Sheila. Nobody told you to run out and buy GoGo a damn airline ticket without conferring with me first."

"It's all good, sis. But. Let me just put this out there and you can take it any way you want to. We're your god-damn family. You seem to go all out of your way for your silly-ass friends and what have you—and don't even get me started on that little Hollywood-in-Phoenix job you've been working at forever: the one you kill yourself for just to come up with all these stories about problems that can't be fixed. Mama shows 'em to me. After hundreds of 'em you still aren't even on TV. So how are we supposed to see how well you're aging since you don't exactly break your neck coming to Pittsburgh—*where you were born and raised*, in case you forgot. The only time we see you is when somebody dies or you just feel guilty and—"

"That is not true and you know it!"

"It is true. When was the last time you came home?"

"Two years ago. And nobody had died."

"Yeah, but Mama had hip surgery."

"Who died, Sheila?"

"You needed a reason. That's my point."

"I'm not *on* camera because I'm *behind* the camera, Sheila."

"That's what I just said!"

"But it's by choice."

"Who in their right mind wouldn't want to be like Oprah?"

"I don't."

"Then something is wrong with you."

"Look, can I call you back when I get home?"

"No. Pull the cart over and park it. We're going to finish this."

"I've been standing in the frozen food section for the past ten minutes and it's cold as hell in this entire store and I've got on short sleeves."

"Then push the cart over to the produce section. Fruit and vegetables aren't cold."

She has a lot of nerve, telling me what to do, but I find myself pushing the cart in that direction, tossing stuff into it I know I don't need. Foods that scream, "You will see us on your waist and hips next week." I park in front of the melons. "Okay, now make it snappy. I'm working on something and I need to get home to look over my notes."

"What's this one about? I liked that teen pregnancy one, I won't lie. You oughta come to Pittsburgh. These young girls here act like they never heard of birth control. They get excited about being pregnant. A diploma is not their ticket to financial freedom. A baby is income. I'm so glad I didn't have any hot-in-the-ass daughters, 'cause I would've strangled her ass if she came in here bringing a baby at fourteen."

"Is this where I should say thank you?"

"I guess so."

"Thank you. Anyway, I just want you to know you're being very inconsiderate and selfish about this whole thing, Sheila."

"I think you got it backward, sis."

"Look. My life as I've known it and lived it for the past ten years has changed, Sheila. Can't you try to understand how this might feel?"

"You know how many times me and Paul split up? How many hotels and motels I've dragged these kids to over the years? So don't tell me anything about breaking up your life. Besides, you don't have any kids. So the only person you have to worry about is Savannah."

"So does having a hysterectomy and not being able to have children make me selfish?"

"I bet you don't even know my kids' names."

"From the sound of it, you probably don't either. Even on the back of their school pictures you put their nicknames!"

"It's what everybody calls them."

"What is GoGo's real name, by the way?"

"JaQuan."

"How on earth do you get GoGo out of JaQuan and why couldn't you simply call all five of them by their real names?"

"Six. Because they like their nicknames. Everybody does. It tells you who they really are or what they're like. GoGo used to run everywhere when he was little. Wouldn't walk anywhere. And he hasn't changed. So his name fits him to a T. Now Bean Head—"

"I get it, Sheila. Anyway, this is just one more reason why I would feel weird having your son in my home for how long?"

"Two or three short weeks."

"I don't know him!"

"You can get to know him. First, you need to be under the same roof and then in the same room with him. Eat at the same table and look at each other. He can talk about anything. He was getting nothing but A's until he started smoking that stuff. Anyway, he's a nice young man who just needs to get away from these thugs for a minute so he can see there's a better way to live. That's all I'm asking, Savannah. This ain't for me. It's for GoGo."

"What are you doing right now, Sheila?"

"Why?"

"I'm just curious. If you're busy."

"We getting ready to go to the drive-in."

"The what?"

"The drive-in. We take the van. Just in case you forgot, I only got two kids left at home—well, if you wanna count Bisquit—since him and his wife are on and off from one week to the next. You know they got two kids now."

"No, I didn't. I also didn't know they still had drive-ins."

"They do here. We love going. As soon as the weather change from spring to summer, we there. I fry chicken and we take potato salad and baked beans and put our drinks in a cooler and we spray ourselves with Off! and get our lounge chairs and just chill. Just like we did when we were little kids. Remember?"

"I remember." I sure wish I could go with them. I'm curious if they have them here in Phoenix. I would love to sit in my truck—well, it's an SUV—and recline the seat, eat a hot dog with relish and mustard and some soft French fries and slurp it down with a Diet Pepsi. I'm going to look into this. "Anyway, Sheila, does GoGo really want to come out here or are you forcing him?"

"He's excited. Unfortunately, he's only been as far as Philly and New York City on a field trip. Boston doesn't count. He has never been on an airplane, which is my fault, but you know paychecks can only go so far when you trying to clothe and feed six growing kids and a greedy-ass husband. GoGo is not a hoodlum. He will not steal from you. He is respectful. I'm telling you, he can fix anything that's broke around your house and he knows how to give tune-ups—even on foreign cars."

"Just give me a few days to figure this out, Sheila. Seriously. I'm not trying to be funny or anything. There are a lot of things I'm trying to do right now, and that's making it hard for me to think."

"Have you seen Isaac since he's been gone?"

"Once."

"And what happened?"

"We talked."

"Do you still hate his guts?"

"I never hated him. He pissed me off. I just wish he had closed one door before he opened another one."

"Most men do it this way. Because they don't know what to do on their own. Anyway, don't you miss him?"

"No."

"Stop lying."

"Well, it was a stupid question, Sheila. Of course I do, sometimes. But it seems logical to miss somebody you've lived with for ten years. Look, I'm going to have to go. Anything else you want to tell me?"

"Did you hear about Luther Vandross?"

"What about him?"

"He died."

"When?"

"Today."

"What's today's date?"

"It's Friday, July first, 2005, Savannah."

"It can't be." I cannot believe this date has slipped up on me like this, and even though I'm saddened to hear this about Luther, today is also the day my divorce is final. I cannot fucking believe this. Just like that. I'm not married anymore. And here I am in the grocery store. I don't feel like sharing this with Sheila right now.

"Time flies for all of us. Anyway, sis, I just want you to be happy when you get right down to it. And if Isaac can't make your lights come on anymore, somebody else just might."

"Okay, so back to GoGo because I'm at the checkout and I need to get home."

"Slow down, damn. Why are you in such a hurry all of a sudden? Anyway, I told you this is a nonrefundable ticket and we don't have the kind of money to be throwing it out the window so if you don't want GoGo to come, maybe I will. I could use a break. Think about it and let me know. Send me an e-mail. Love you. Bye."

The thought of Sheila coming out here made my heart race. I think I'd take GoGo—whoever he is—over her, which is pretty sad to admit. I suppose we're a lot alike when it gets right down to it. We are our mother's daughters. Right now I can't believe I'm officially free to do anything I want. Go anywhere I want. With whomever I want. Or I can do nothing at all. And I don't have to answer to anybody. I've been so busy thinking about my future and now it's here.

My cart is full of all kinds of fattening stuff I should never have even considered buying. Who am I fooling? And what does Sheila know about what I do and don't do at my job? I have worked hard over the years to produce shows I—and apparently my bosses—considered compelling and thought-provoking. She sounds a lot like Isaac. You can't even think about solving problems if you pretend like they don't exist. I just try to paint an accurate picture and put it out there. It's not like my ratings are through the roof, but I did get an award. I've even been asked to speak to junior and high school kids about teen pregnancy in November. I didn't feel like telling Sheila. In fact, I haven't told anybody. What's the point?

Sheila knows how to get under my skin. She also knows how to dish it out but she can't take it. Family members are the only ones who seem to be good at this. She's one of the main reasons I've sent Mama tickets to come out here to visit instead of going back there so much. The way Sheila's been struggling for the past twenty-odd years breaks my heart. She has settled for so little—it's like she never had any dreams.

My cell phone vibrates in my hand. It's Isaac. "Hello," I say like I'm a detective or something.

"Hey, Savannah. Sorry to bother you but I was wondering if you could do me a big favor."

"I've already done it."

"What do you mean?"

"Don't you know what today is?"

"Yeah, it's July first."

"And?"

"We are officially divorced. You couldn't possibly have forgotten, Isaac."

"Actually, I didn't want to think about it. So, should I congratulate you?"

"Whatever. But since this obviously isn't the reason you called, what's going on?" I have to remind myself that he is not my husband and I am not his wife.

"Is there any way you could possibly lend me two or three—preferably, three—thousand dollars until I get the settlement?"

"Don't tell me you've got a gambling problem now, too?"

"Of course not."

"Have you moved to Vegas or what?"

"Not yet. I decided to wait awhile."

"So what's the problem?"

"Well, business has been extremely slow. Materials are going up. Gas prices affect everything, Savannah. I've had to lay off a few workers, and there's only so much Enrique and José and I can do between us."

"You mind telling me what you need it for?"

"I'm behind on a few bills."

"And this is my problem?"

"Of course it isn't. If it wasn't serious, Savannah, you know I wouldn't be asking you—under the circumstances."

"Why can't you borrow it from your girlfriend?"

"She doesn't have it like that."

"What makes you so sure I have an extra three grand to lend you, or anybody for that matter?"

"Savannah, do you know who you're talking to?"

"I know you were the man I was married to for ten years—you mean him?"

"That's me. I thought we agreed to be friendly."

"Lending money to your ex-husband on the day he becomes your ex—is that how you measure friendliness?"

"No."

"I never said I wanted to be your BFF. Be glad I don't hate your guts."

"I am glad."

"To be quite honest, I think you have a lot of fucking nerve putting me on the spot like this, considering today is the day we're no longer husband and wife and I did you a favor by even waiting to make it official. I haven't heard a peep out of you for months and you still want something from me."

"My attorney suggested I lie low to give you a chance to get used to your new life."

"What new life?"

"The one without me in it."

If only he knew. "Speaking of which, how's yours?"

"I'm adjusting."

"So if I agreed to do this, Isaac, how would I get it to you?"

"Could you leave a check in the mailbox?"

"You mean at my house?"

"How many mailboxes do you have these days?"

"The same old one."

"If it's a problem . . . Wait. Have you got somebody living with you already?"

"Please, Isaac. It's been six months, but unlike you

I like to wait until I finish one thing before I start something else."

"Ouch. Even though it's not the way you think it is."

"Whatever. Look, it's all water under the bridge, and you know good and well that whatever her name is wasn't the reason we parted company."

"No, she wasn't. So, how do you want to do this?"

"First tell me how you intend to pay me back."

"You can deduct it from the settlement."

"The check is going directly to you. You should be getting it fairly soon now. Can I trust you to pay me back when you get it?"

"Of course you can. And thank you, Savannah. You're a lifesaver."

I can't believe he just said that. But he did.

"I'll mail it. Are you still living at your mama's?"

"No, but that'd be the best place to send it. If you don't mind."

"Why would I mind, Isaac? Is there anything else I can do to help you? Are you sure this is enough? How about a million dollars? Anyway, I hope it solves your problem."

"It will definitely help. Thank you from the bottom of my heart."

I put the phone in my purse. I do not for the life of me understand why I agreed to lend Isaac any amount of money. We haven't been divorced twenty-four hours and he's still able to talk me into doing something I don't want to do. As usual, he caught me off guard, and here I am in the grocery store, at the checkout, holding up the line even though there's nobody behind me, listening to my

newly minted ex-husband ask me if he can borrow money
so he can probably spend it on his new woman. But what
the fuck. It could be something he's too embarrassed
about. Maybe I'm the only one he could call. Let's just
see if he pays me back after he gets that check.

I finish emptying everything from my cart onto the
conveyer. "Did you find everything you were looking for?"
Mary asks. She is probably my age. And looks tired. She
smokes a lot. I can smell it. Her skin looks rough. Her
hair could stand to be shampooed and deep conditioned.
A good cut would help. There is no ring on her left finger
and it doesn't look like she's ever worn one. Mary looks
like she lives alone. I imagine she has a house full of cats
because there is a film of white hair all over her olive green
sweater.

I swipe my debit card. "I'm sorry, what did you just
ask me?"

"Did you find everything you were looking for, Mrs.
Jackson?" she asks when my name pops up on her screen.

"It's Ms.," I say politely. "As a matter of fact, I
didn't. What aisle are good husbands on, Mary?"

She chuckles. "I wish I knew, honey. I wish I knew."

The First One's Free

I can't believe it. I'm actually going on a real date. With Dark Angel. Finally. Ten long hours from now. Actually, we're just having a cappuccino at a Starbucks not far from my house, which of course he doesn't know. It still feels like a date. I actually took the day off so I could make sure I look as snazzy as possible. I want his mouth to water when he sees me in person, since he liked my pictures so much. Today is all about preparation. I already bought something jazzy to wear but I might change my mind at the last minute. I'm getting a new set of acrylics and you can never have too many pedicures. I'm also going over to Oasis to let Joseph tighten up my weave, since baby birds might be nesting on the crown of my head for all I know.

Right now, I'm giving myself a rejuvenating clay facial and whitening my teeth with those strips. I think I need to get waxed, too. Romeo and Juliet just ran out of here because the blue mask scares them. Sparrow just ran downstairs to back my car out of the garage so I can get out before the exterminators get here. They have to park their truck in the driveway in order to pull the hose around the back of the house. Then she'll drive herself to school since, by the grace of God, she finally managed to get her driver's license. She also came to her senses. Instead of that Prius, she decided on a black Honda Civic hybrid—which is pretty hard to say.

Sparrow isn't exactly psyched about my date with Dark Angel. She is excited I'm finally meeting him so I can hurry up and put him on the Never in This Lifetime list and move on to someone who doesn't write bad poetry. I pay her no mind. In fact, when she realized I was serious about not having a birthday party, she decided not to have one, too. I told her she could have a few friends over if she wanted to, but she just said, "It was only a passing thought, Mom. No big deal. I'll live." Well, we both did.

Oh hell, here we go again: hot flash #1,000! The clay was just starting to get hard! Shit shit shit. Broiling from the inside out with no warning off and on all day and night had gotten on my nerves so bad I finally begged my doctor for some hormones. I just started taking them a few days ago but it would sure be nice if they kicked in sometime in the next few minutes. I want my memory back. I need help unscrambling some of the puzzles that aren't really puzzles. I do not for the life of me understand why God had to make menopause so complicated. I mean, what was the point of dragging it out and making you feel like a mental case. Why couldn't He or She have just picked a date for your period to stop and then let us move on with our lives? As if bleeding once a month for thirty-five years wasn't bad enough.

My first stop this morning is the dentist. I hope I can sit in that chair for forty-five minutes without squirming. It feels like I'm getting ready for my prom or something instead of just having a cappuccino. I'm getting impressions made for those new invisible braces, since my teeth have started moving because I'm getting old and I'll be damned if I'm going to die with spaces between my teeth. Of course, I don't feel like going today but he charges a fifty-dollar cancellation fee if I don't give him twenty-four hours' notice.

I feel a little cooler as I walk over to the window, hoping the mask can now finish hardening. I'm tempted to stick my head in the refrigerator, but Romeo and Juliet would freak out for sure. I can tell by the cluster of dark clouds that the monsoon season is shifting into third gear. I love the heavy winds. The dust storms. The loud thunder. The yellow and violet lightning. But mostly the rain. I love the way it smells, the sound it makes pounding on the clay roof and how it gushes out of the gutters like narrow waterfalls. Although it can sometimes be dangerous if you're driving near a wash or a gully, I love the way the flooding forces me and Sparrow to stay inside. We often curl up on the sofa, get a pizza—out of the freezer, since delivery is often out of the question—and watch stupid movies: a romantic comedy and we both cry, or a horror movie and we both scream while munching on microwave popcorn. She most likely will have an Arizona iced tea and I usually nurse a mojito. Or two.

I hear my cell phone ringing. I hope it's not Norman calling from work. He's such a worrywart. We did get our bonuses last month like we always do, which is how I was able to pay cash for Sparrow's new ride. Everybody knows corporate does not like to give away free money if they don't have to. I pull the strips off and wipe my teeth with my fingertips. "Hello," I say with my mouth half closed.

"Good morning, Robin, it's me. Fernando."

"Is something wrong?"

"No, nothing's wrong."

"Then why are you calling me at home on my cell?" I grab a tissue and wipe all of the foamy stuff off my teeth so I won't have to swallow it.

"Well, I meant to call you last night, but I didn't get a chance. I was wondering, since things have finally slowed down, if it would be possible for me to take a half day."

"And what time would that be, Fernando?"

"About eleven."

"That's not a half day. It's almost eight o'clock right now. What's going on?"

"Well, my cousin Lupe is getting out of prison today at eleven-thirty and I offered to pick him up. He wants me to take him to play a round of golf."

I just look at the phone. I know damn well I couldn't possibly have heard him right. "Did you just say he wants to go play golf?"

"I did."

"And how long has Lupe been in prison?"

"Just two years. A few too many DUIs."

"So, did they have a driving range at the prison he was in or something?"

"No, that's funny, Robin."

"Well, this might be even funnier. If you think taking your ex-convict of a cousin golfing as a welcome-home gift is a good reason to ask your boss for time off—and on the same day, no less—then you have lost your damn mind, Fernando. Maybe you should consider taking— what's his name again?"

"Lupe."

"Maybe you should think about taking Lupe to play a few holes of miniature golf. But make his first stop the employment office, which is where you might be headed if you keep this up, Fernando. I mean, come on. Every other week it's something different with you."

"It was just a thought. I'm cool."

It was just a thought. My face is cracking. A few shards of blue clay fall on my beige duvet. I try to pick them up but they smear. Damn it. Before I can ask if there's anything else, he says, "I know it sounds ridiculous. And I agree. It's just that Lupe hasn't been around family so I was just trying to be nice. Maybe I can get my brother to pick him up. I'll take him golfing tomorrow morning. I thought it would be fun."

"Fun. Bye, Fernando. And do me a favor: don't ever call me on my cell phone to ask me some stupid shit like this, clear?"

"*Comprendo.* Have a nice weekend, Robin. See you on Monday."

Now, here comes Bernie. I'd left her a message earlier. But I need to hurry up and get this stuff off my face before my skin turns blue. "Okay, so don't make me laugh," I say to her.

"Why would I try to make you laugh?"

"I've got a mask on that's hard and if I laugh it'll crack."

"So you're finally going on a date with Hark Angel after a hundred years of online dating, huh?"

I want to laugh but I don't. I feel myself smiling, which I immediately stop doing. "His name is Dark Angel, not Hark."

"Whatever. I'm just suspicious of men who look for

women online, and especially black ones. Anyway, explain to me what it is you want me to do?"

"Okay. My date is at six. From everything I've read, sometimes the guy can turn out to be a total loser or nothing like you thought, so if I want to bail without being rude I suddenly have an emergency."

"I'm the emergency?"

"Well, first of all, I've already asked Savannah."

"So you anticipate having two emergencies?"

"No! Her call would come fifteen minutes after he gets there to see if it starts out okay. I'd say something that would let her know I'm not disappointed. Yet."

"Okay. And?"

"And then, say, about a half hour later you call and if I say something like 'Oh, really? I'm really sorry to hear that. Sure I will. I'll get there as soon as I can.' That's how you'll know he's a total dud."

"Okay. Consider it done. What are you wearing?"

"Why?"

"Just remember you're not auditioning to be a Vegas dancer, so tone it down for everybody's sake. Call me if anything changes. Bye. And good luck. I swear to God, what some of us will do to get laid."

"I'm looking for love, not sex, Bernie, so shut up!"

"And you think you can find it at Starbucks?"

I hang up and wash this stuff off my face. I hear Sparrow run up the stairs and down the hallway and stop outside my door.

"Mom," she says, like she's out of breath. "We have a problem."

I grab a hand towel. "What kind of problem?"

"Your car ran through the garage wall."

"The car did what?"

"Okay, so this is what happened. When I went to put the car in reverse I accidentally put it in drive and I looked over my shoulder like I'm supposed to but when I put my foot on the accelerator the car went forward instead of backward."

"And you're serious?"

She nods. She looks fine. Mostly shaken up. "Are you okay?"

"I'm fine, Mom. But your car isn't. And the garage got a little damaged, too."

"Come over here and look at me." I cup her face in my palms. "Did you bump your head or hurt anything on your body?"

"No, Mom. I'm just a little freaked out because it happened so fast. I can't believe I did this. I'm in major trouble, I know."

"Shit happens, Sparrow."

"But can't I lose my license since I just got it?"

"I don't think so. Plus, this was my fault, not yours."

"It is not your fault. Aren't you pissed?"

"Not right now. Let's just go downstairs and see."

I finish drying my face, tighten the sash on my robe and follow behind her as she slowly leads the way. The dogs try to sneak out but I make them stay inside. When we get in front of the garage, I don't know why but I cover my mouth with my hands and actually start laughing. First of all, there's a huge hole in the wall and particles of drywall are splattered all over the top of the car. The hood, which is really the trunk, is wrinkled like navy blue cellophane.

I'm standing here trying to picture Sparrow driving through a wall when she's supposed to be going backward. Of course this isn't funny but I start laughing and can't stop.

"Mom, what's so funny?"

I shake my head. "I'm just trying to figure out how in the world you passed that driving test."

Her little Honda hybrid is just shining away on the other side of the garage. "I need to borrow your car today," I say, knowing my insurance will cover a rental. I don't feel like going through the paperwork this morning.

"You can have it," she says. "Here, please take the keys."

And I do. "I can drop you off at school. . ."

"Mom, can I please stay home today, please? Today is a half day and I've already missed first period. I can't believe what just happened here. I mean, I just barely got my license and I've already had my very first accident and I ran into a stupid wall and I have like totally ruined your car, not mine. I'm sorry."

"It's okay, baby. This is why God created insurance," I say, letting her off the hook again.

She walks over and hugs me. Neighbors drive by slowly doing double takes. I wave, forgetting I'm still in my bathrobe and my hair is piled on top of my head like Marge Simpson's. After we close the garage door, Sparrow runs into the house and I feel the first ten or twenty raindrops begin to fall. I turn my face toward the sky for a few seconds and then rush inside just as the exterminator pulls up.

———

Because I always go to the drive-up window at Starbucks, it feels weird to actually pull into a parking space. I do not like driving a hybrid. Something is missing in this car. First of all, you can't even tell it's running. It feels like a big toy, but it got me here. With the rain coming down like crazy I thought I might hydroplane. It appears to be slacking up. Of course I called my insurance guy, since I know him personally because we went to U of A together years ago. He told me not to worry about anything. He suggested that the next time I drove without shoes and with wet toenails to just be careful. Since my homeowner's policy is also with him, he'd call someone to patch up the hole in the garage wall.

I canceled my dentist appointment and was shocked shitless when the usually bitchy receptionist told me that under the circumstances they'd waive the cancellation fee. She said she hoped my daughter wasn't too shaken up. Joseph wasn't pissed after I told him what had happened. He suggested I squirt some Sea Breeze on my scalp, put a little gel on my edges, pull my hair into a tight ponytail and call it a day. When I looked closer, my nails were still shiny. My heels weren't crusty and the peach polish not even close to chipping. All told, if this was a test, I think I could still pass it.

It's ten to six. I'm not interested in trying to be fashionably late just so that Dark Angel will have to wait for me. What's it prove? I'm also not worried about appearing too anxious if I beat him here. Thank God the rain is letting up. I pray Dark Angel doesn't have any problems getting here and that I don't have any getting home.

I check myself out in the mirror one more time, then get out of the car and run my hands down my hips to make sure everything is smooth. I have to be honest. I do love attention. Who doesn't? I have a reputation for going a little overboard to get it. I've also got three black Golden Girls who remind me when I do. I'm working on dressing less flamboyantly. I'm getting too old for it. Besides, I've finally realized other women aren't my competitors. Even before Bernie opened her big mouth, I had already chosen a pair of New Religion jeans that fit me to a T and topped it off with a white T-shirt that has a few simple rhinestones in the shape of a question mark on the front. I also decided on a pair of flats just in case Dark Angel isn't as tall as he said he was. Some guys are known to exaggerate.

When I walk in, it's crowded. I have never been inside this Starbucks now that I think about it. But then again, they're all the same. I'm trying to act poised and nonchalant as I slowly peruse every table that's not empty. There are only three black people in here. I don't see a black man who looks anything like Dark Angel. It's five after six. I check to make sure my throwaway cell phone is in my purse. It is. So is my real one. I buy a bottle of Ethos water and sit at a table by a window. Rain or not, that red sun is still out there.

"You're looking good, girl."

I'd know that rusty voice anywhere. Even after all these years. When I look up, sure enough, it's Russell, Sparrow's long-lost father. He looks old enough to be *my* father. Now it looks as if two convicts have been sprung, but this one doesn't look like he's been playing any golf. "Russell! What are you doing here?"

"Needed a Frapuccino. What about you? You drinking alone? Can I sit?"

"No!" I say a tad too loud. "I mean, no, I'm not

drinking alone. I'm waiting for someone. I'm a few minutes early."

"Take it easy. I'm not going to bite you."

"You're the last person I was expecting to see. When did you get out?"

"Why?" He has a smirk on his face like he's flirting.

"I thought you had more time left."

"Got out a little earlier. Good behavior. Not going back. I'm in a program. Getting my life on track for real. Tired of living behind bars. How's my daughter?"

I cut my eyes at him. "She's fine."

"I want to see her as soon as I get myself together."

"That looks like it might be a while," I say too soon. I'm watching the door. It's now pouring down again. "Anyway, it was nice seeing you, Russell."

"Nice seeing you, too, Tiger Lady."

"What did you just call me?"

He smiles. It's wicked and sinister.

I'm trying to figure out how in the world this bastard knows my screen name. "What do you know about any Tiger Lady, Russell?"

"I'd say it was you," he says, sipping the foam off the top of his drink and peering at me with those big black eyes.

"And who might you be?"

"I'm Rough-n-Ready, baby. It's so nice to finally meet you in person."

I almost don't know what to say. I remember getting an icebreaker from a Rough-n-Ready a couple of months ago but I don't think he ever attached his photo. Now I know why. "This isn't cute, Russell. You're too old to be playing these kinds of games."

"It was all in good fun. I like your picture. You're still looking watermelon sweet. Seriously though. My being in here. Purely coincidental."

"Well, don't let me stop you from leaving. I'm waiting for someone and I certainly don't want him to have to meet you."

He looks at his cheap watch. "What time is he supposed to be here?"

"None of your business."

He then acts like he wants to bend down to give me a kiss. I push myself deeper into a corner like he's about to electrocute me.

"It's like that then, huh? Well, maybe I'll see you around or give you another wink, Tiger Lady."

He has the nerve to wink at me. And off he goes. I wait until I think he's in the parking lot before looking out the window. I see him run through the rain and get in his ugly car that's some color and make I don't recognize. I sit here for ten more minutes. My real phone rings.

"I thought I'd give you guys a five-minute window. So is everything cool?" Savannah asks.

"He's not here yet."

"Has he called or anything?"

"Nope. Not yet."

"He'll be there. It's pouring, as you no doubt can see."

"Girl, you will never in a million years guess who I just ran into."

"Russell."

"How'd you guess?"

"It's always the ex. You should know that by now, Robin."

"Anyway, he's still a poor excuse for a man, but let me go in case Dark Angel walks in."

"Have fun," she says.

I order a nonfat mocha Frappucino with no whip and sip on it for the next fifteen minutes until Bernie calls.

"Is it an emergency or not?"

"He hasn't shown up."

"Not even a phone call?"

"Not yet."

"Then I'd leave. Get up right now and get the hell out of there."

"It's raining too hard."

"Well, as soon as it lets up some, get your ass in that Porsche and beeline it home and delete this bastard from whatever you call that wish list."

"Whatever." I felt like saying, "I'm driving a black Honda Civic hybrid," which sounds like it would've rolled right off my tongue. I sit for another five or ten minutes, then chuck the empty Ethos bottle into the receptacle and walk out into the downpour. Some men really try too hard to ruin your life. And none of this bullshit is worth the price of admission.

Things Couldn't Be Better

Bernadine is on her way to meet John at a stable where Taylor takes riding lessons and boards her horse. He bought her a new saddle and wants to surprise her since her grades were so good, considering the circumstances. She is, after all, headed for high school in September and he hopes this saddle will serve as an incentive for her to continue doing well. Yesterday, he sent Bernadine a text message and said he wanted to talk to her about Taylor and a few other things. Would she mind meeting him out here? Bernadine didn't have any other plans. The forecast called for a dry afternoon, and she loves the drive.

She turns the volume up on the radio when she hears Macy Gray singing "Get Up and Do Something." She couldn't agree more. Three days ago Bernadine decided the only pill she was going to take was the antidepressant. She wanted to see how long she could go before feeling any withdrawal symptoms. The longest she's gone without Xanax is two days. She normally took one in a twenty-four-hour period—two, tops, and the lowest dose. The only time she has trouble falling asleep is when she's got a lot on her mind. Usually money issues.

She's through playing this game of hide-'n'-go-seek with herself and from herself. She does not feel any better.

246 | Terry McMillan

The past is still the past. Now her friends are able to tell when she's on something. It didn't used to be this way. They've lost patience with her. They're tired of feeling sorry for her, tired of her drone. She doesn't blame them one bit.

It would be so much easier if she could just stop hating James, but she can't. If she could forget all that happened, but she can't. She doesn't know where to put the past. And the lingering pain. Doesn't know what to do with either one. Whatever it takes to free herself, she's willing to do it. After their marriage was annulled she had no reason to be in touch with him but she called him, hoping he would at least apologize for what he'd done. She just wanted to hear him say "I'm sorry." She didn't care if he didn't mean it. But his cell phone was disconnected. She wrote him a nasty letter thinking it would make her feel better. It didn't. It came back undeliverable. She has never heard from James since.

Her cell phone starts vibrating, moves across the seat and falls on the floor. Bernadine can't reach it so she pulls off the two-lane road onto the gravel shoulder. She puts on her flashers. When she reaches to pick up the phone it feels like something is suddenly spinning inside her head. Shit. She takes a deep breath, exhales quickly. It's John Jr. She presses TALK. "Hi, baby! This is quite a nice surprise. Why are you calling me in the middle of the day? What's going on?"

"I've got some very good news, Mom."

"I love good news," Bernadine says and turns the radio down. She pulls back onto the road. Within minutes, she sees people riding on some of the trails.

"I'm going to be a father."

"You're going to be a what?"

"A dad. And Bronwyn and I are getting married."

"Married? When?"

"In three weeks."

"Three . . . wha—" Bernadine is speechless. She knows Bronwyn has been in the picture since last year and John Jr. is crazy about her, but he'd been crazy about fifteen other girls, too, so Bernadine thought she'd just been added to the list. But maybe one finally stuck. Even still, a baby? You don't just call your mother on the phone without any advance notice and say, guess what, I'm going to be a father and somebody's husband. Didn't he just leave for college a few weeks ago?

"Anyway, we're coming home for the nuptials. I'm going to put my thesis on hold. Bronwyn's going to keep working on her dissertation. Don't ask, Mom. I'll let you know all the details when we get there. Aren't you happy for me? Don't you think this is outstanding news?"

"Well, of course it is, JJ, but there's so much going on right now around here, I just wasn't expecting anything like this when I picked up the phone. But you certainly sound happy about this, and that's good enough for me."

"I'm ecstatic, Mom. I've loved Bronwyn from the moment I met her, as corny as it sounds. I want her to be my wife and the mother of my children, and I want to be her husband."

"It sounds wonderful, JJ. Just wonderful. Where do you two plan on living?"

"Well, that's another reason I'm calling. We wanted to know if we could possibly stay with you for a month or so, until we get our finances squared away and I find a job—which shouldn't be a problem—and it would give us a little time to spend with you, Grandma-to-be, plus, we want to look around to see where it might be best to raise our child. You know what I mean? Is this doable, Mom?"

Bernadine wants to say, "What the hell is going on in the universe! Let's just turn this into the Little Old Lady Who Lived in the Frigging Shoe. Everybody can move right on in: my ex-husband's child, my son and his fiancée, my unborn grandchild. Am I leaving anybody out?" What she does say is, "Of course it's doable, JJ. You're my son, and Bronwyn's going to be my daughter. So, tell me, how pregnant is she?"

"Ten weeks. It's so cool, Mom. She throws up and everything."

"That's just great. Have you told your dad?"

"Not yet. I thought I'd tell you first."

"You won't believe this, JJ, but I'm on my way to see your dad right now. He's waiting for me at the stable where they board Herman."

"What's going on?"

"He got Taylor a new saddle and he wants to talk about a few things, so I agreed to meet him out here. I can't believe you're going to be a father. And you're sure about this?"

"You should know me by now, Mom. When I say I'm sure, what does that mean?"

"You're sure. So, I'm going to be a grandmother."

"Get used to the idea," he says. "Look, Mom, I'm at the lab and have to close up, but we'll talk in the next day or so. Is that okay?"

"Do you mind if I tell your dad?"

"By all means. Go right ahead."

"Quick question. What are you going to do about finishing school?"

"That's an easy one. I've already talked to department heads at ASU and U of A. A thesis is a thesis as long as it's publishable."

"Okay, then."

"Is everything going good out there with you?"

"Things couldn't be better."

"I'm glad to hear that, Mom. Have you been thinking about what you want to do now that Sweet Tooth is closed?"

"I've got a few ideas but I'll hold off talking about them until I do a little more research."

"Well, let me know if I can help in any way. Send a shout out to everybody and pop Onika for me. I heard she's going to be a camp counselor and she's in love."

"So she told you about Shy?"

"Mom, she's my sister. We grew up in the same house. I've known for years but it was her call. So I guess she finally felt safe."

"It was by accident."

"I don't need details. I just want to know if you're upset."

"It's not upsetting."

"So you're cool with it?"

"I'm cool with a lot of stuff, JJ."

"I know O must be relieved. What about Dad?"

"He doesn't know yet."

"How is it possible you know and he doesn't?"

"Onika hasn't seen him and it's not the kind of thing you tell your parent over the phone. I'm sure she'll tell him when she gets home."

"How do you think he'll take it?"

"I have no idea."

"I think he's going to freak at first, but he'll eventually come around. Plus, he doesn't have a choice. She is who she is. Anyway, you are the absolute coolest mom. Gotta scoot. Love you. Bronwyn sends some, too."

Bernadine clicks END. She's not sure if she's in shock or elated. She's going to be a grandmother? Is she old enough to be one? She decides to call John. When he answers, he sounds weird. There's a lot of noise in the background, like glass clinking or something. "John, are you at a bar?"

"Kind of."

"Are you drinking?"

"I've had a beer and will probably order another."

"I'm pulling into the parking lot but I don't see your car."

"I'm at the clubhouse. It's the green building. I ordered you a sparkling water with lime."

She can see it from here. She parks and walks in that direction, passing one beautiful horse after another, some being ridden, some being led. There are youngsters in corrals practicing jumps. Once she gets inside, John is standing at a tall table. He's aging well, she thinks, as she gets closer. Sometimes it's hard for her to believe she was once madly in love with this man. That she was once married to this man. That he is the father of her children. It's also hard to believe they've known each other since college. God, how many years ago was that?

"Well, Herman's getting a test drive in his new saddle. How are you, Bernie? And thanks for coming." He gives her a kiss on the cheek. His lips are warm. Bernadine is surprised she can feel it.

"No problem. I think I may be coming down with something, though. Feeling a little light-headed."

"You should've told me that. We could've talked over the phone."

"No, it's fine. It might not be anything."

"I hope not."

He takes a sip of his beer.

Her head is beginning to feel like she's wearing a headband that's too tight. She can handle this.

"So have you given any more thought to Taylor's request?"

"I have. I have to admit I'm a little conflicted about it. I mean, you know I love Taylor like she's my own daughter, but I'm just not real sure about how this will all play out. I've also got a lot of things going on right now."

"Like what?"

"I don't want to talk about it right now."

"Why not?"

"Because I just don't."

"She misses having her mom here, Bernie, and I'm dealing with a little prostate issue of my own."

"Please don't tell me you've got prostate cancer?"

"No, but I've got an enlarged one. And it's kind of been freaking me out."

"When did you find this out?"

"A few weeks ago."

"Were you having symptoms or did you find out from a routine checkup?"

"For the past five or six months, I'd been seeing small amounts of blood in my urine and it was becoming somewhat painful to go."

"So what does it mean?"

"It's not cancer, I assure you. What it means is I may have to have surgery but right now there are some lifestyle changes I need to make first. If that doesn't mitigate it, then they'll try medication. Surgery is the last option."

"Wow. I'm really sorry, John." Bernadine takes a sip of her sparkling water.

He pushes his beer glass toward the center of the table as if there's a bull's-eye in the middle. Bernadine wishes she could have a drink, something to take the edge off. A Tylenol might help. She'll stop on the way home.

"There is a possibility I might be selling the company. The stress and traveling are taking a toll on me. And Taylor. If you would give this some consideration, I'd be indebted to you, Bernie. I mean, I know—"

"Slow down, John."

"I'm sorry."

"You're going to be a grandfather."

"Come again? Wait. Don't tell me Onika's pregnant?"

"Not even close."

"What's that supposed to mean?"

"Nothing. It's JJ. His girlfriend is two and a half months and they're getting married in three weeks. Out here. Congratulations."

"Wait a second, now. Which girlfriend is this?"

"Her name is Bronwyn. She's been on the scene about a year. He e-mailed her picture a few months ago."

"You know how many there are in the album I created for him? Does he have a clue about what he's getting himself into?"

"He seems to have it all figured out."

"Of course he does. He's got book smarts but, my Lord, it doesn't always translate into common sense. What's he going to do about his PhD program? And what're they going to do for money? And where are they going to live, for crying out loud?"

"I'll let him tell you. But not to worry."

"Is he twenty-five yet?"

"Almost, but for right now, he's still twenty-four."

"We were younger than that," he says. His eyes are glassy and dreamy-looking.

"Yeah, and look where it got us."

"Don't go turning the cup upside down, Bernie. Come on. We were once madly in love and it lasted longer than we give ourselves credit for. We should cherish that. Don't you think?"

"I've cherished it a million times, and even prayed to get something like it back, but no such luck. I'm beginning to feel like everybody else is looking forward to something, except me." Bernadine cannot believe she just said that. She doesn't mean it. It came out wrong. Now her head feels like cotton candy is inside it, just spinning away. She's beginning to wonder what symptoms might be next. What she does know is she needs to get her behind home and in a hurry. It's a thirty-five-minute drive and she doesn't need to lose her cool while she's behind the wheel.

"Bernie?"

"Yeah," she says, almost absentmindedly.

"What's going on with you? Why would you say something so ridiculous? You've barely touched your water. Why don't you take a sip? Can I get you anything?"

"I'm fine, John. You know what I was trying to say."

"No, I don't. You just told me we're going to have a grandchild, our son is in love and getting married, and even though I'm a skeptic, it's still worth getting excited about. Isn't it?"

"Absolutely."

"Then I don't understand."

"I've been stuck in muck and I feel like I haven't been able to climb to the surface."

"What on earth are you talking about, Bernie?"

"Nothing."

"Is this still about what's-his-name? If so, you should be over him by now, Bernie. He was an evil person and he's probably behind bars somewhere. Which is where he belongs. I would've thought you'd have locked him inside a compartment in your head and thrown that key away."

"Sometimes he opens it and haunts me."

"Then go talk to someone about how best to lock him out for good. I'm not kidding. By the way, I haven't forgotten about the promise I made you. About the property?"

"I'm not worrying about it, John."

"I know that. I want you to know the court has frozen all my assets so I can't sell or give anything away until it's done. It could be a while."

"Like I said, whatever's clever. I'm grateful you

care." Bernadine rubs her head. Now it feels like an accordion. She takes a big sip of sparkling water. The bubbles tingle in her throat. They don't feel so good on the way down. It feels like she could throw up. Not here, she tells herself. She swallows over and over until the sensation goes away.

"By the way, Taylor told me she drove the car over there."

"We promised her we wouldn't tell."

"Don't ever trust her with a secret. She eventually tells me anyway."

"I'll keep that in mind."

"Taylor also said Onika has a very cool surprise for me when she gets back from Tucson next month. Do you have any idea what it might be?"

"No, I don't."

"You mean Onika doesn't have a surprise for you?"

"Not that I know of."

"You love surprises, Bernie."

"Not like I used to. Taylor didn't give you the slightest hint?"

"Nope. She just said it has something to do with lipstick." He scrunches his shoulders.

Bernadine has to give it to Taylor. She is clever.

"She also said you might be going on a trip."

"I didn't tell Taylor I was going on any trip."

"She said you might be going to Tucson for like a month to attend some special cooking course. When's that start?"

"It's ongoing," she says. "But I might have to postpone it now that I'm going to have houseguests."

"Don't change your plans, Bernie. John Jr. knows how to take care of our—I mean your—house. If it would make you feel better, they can stay at mine. What's this course about?"

"The catering business." This is the first thing that pops into her head. It also doesn't make any sense. But John wouldn't know this.

"That's great. So you're coming back to where you belong," he says. "As the song goes."

"Maybe I am," Bernadine says. "I think I need to get home. It feels like I'm going downhill fast."

"Will you be all right?"

"I just need to lie down before whatever this is kicks into gear." They hug each other for the second time in fifteen years. This one is quick. On the drive home Bernadine has to pull over twice. As soon as she walks inside the house she runs upstairs, slides open the nightstand drawer, takes two Xanax and chases them with a half cup of cold tea. Without taking off her clothes or sandals, Bernadine slides under the covers. She tells herself that Taylor was on to something and that as soon as her head stops spinning, she should probably make that call.

140/90

"So, how long do we have?" Joseph wants to know after Gloria had finally spoken with the leasing agent.

"Sixty days. But they're willing to extend it at the same rate on a month-to-month basis for a maximum of four months."

"How generous of them."

"So that gives us until January," Gloria says, and takes a long sip from her twenty-four-ounce Pepsi.

"Did you say *us*?"

"I believe I did. Everybody has to go, not just Oasis," she says. "Next year this time this whole block will be condos."

"Ask me if I care?"

"Do you care, Joseph?" Gloria asks, just to mess with him.

"More than you will ever know. We need to start looking for a space if you want to do this, Glo. And sooner rather than later."

"I know. I just don't want you to worry, Joseph."

"Me? I'm not worried. I don't want you to worry. That's my main concern."

"It seems like such a defeat to just give up all I've worked for, but I still need to figure out what I'm doing

257

and how." Gloria cleans the smudges off her reading glasses with the cuff of her white blouse. The frames are metallic candy-apple red. They look good on her. In fact, she bought the same pair in cobalt blue. Now she can see everything clearly. She has to move the shop to a different location. But where?

She's sitting on the grape sofa meant for clients. It's low to the floor and, she now realizes, uncomfortable. Gloria tries to cross her legs, hoping this will cause her back to tip backward, but her thighs are too thick and feel like the sticky stuff on Post-Its. This is just one more thing she doesn't feel like thinking about.

"Well, this is where I come in," Joseph says. "A rent increase that's ridiculously out of reach is really an opportunity to make a change. Maybe you should thank the bastards."

"Thank you, bastards!" Gloria yells. "I'm going home." But when she goes to push herself up to a standing position, she can't do it. Joseph extends his hand. Gloria takes it. She shakes her head in embarrassment as he pulls her to a standing position.

"And this, too, shall pass," he says, and gives her a kiss on her forehead.

——

After Joseph left, Gloria still didn't want to go home, because there was no reason to. She'd been lollygagging around the salon, telling herself it was to miss rush-hour traffic.

She enters the freeway and heads in the opposite direction from home. She's doing about seventy but is now aware of the glassy whir of headlights passing her by.

In a split second she hears and then sees a motorcycle in her rearview mirror fly past her with only inches between it and the car in the next lane, and a Hummer on her left cuts her off. She is tempted to honk but in a sudden panic her heart makes one long hard beat and she decides against it. She grips the steering wheel, then puts on her blinkers and gets off at the next exit and pulls over. Her heart is beating fast and her head drops against the steering wheel. She starts crying uncontrollably. Finally, she stops. Reaches in the glove compartment and gets a napkin. Wipes her eyes. But then here come more tears. "When is this going to stop?" she says out loud. Gloria had no idea how much it hurts to lose someone you love. How hard it is to keep going. How it takes all the strength you have to just go through the motions to get from one day to the next. And sometimes, one minute to the next. Sometimes the grief strikes like an earthquake and there is nothing she can do except hold on to something solid and wait for it to pass.

"What in God's name am I doing way out here?" she asks herself. She pulls onto the road, looking for a place to turn around. This stretch of road offers nothing but blackness. Finally, after five or six more minutes, she sees signs for an Indian casino. When Gloria spots a gas station, to her own surprise she keeps driving. "Oh, why not?" she asks herself. "Maybe I'll have some fun. Maybe I'll hit a jackpot! Maybe I'll run into Sister Monroe!" Knowing she may have spoken too soon, she says, "I take that back, Lord. Please, don't let me run into that woman. Please."

Gloria is surprised when she starts laughing and for the next fifteen minutes travels farther down this two-lane road until the casino appears out of nowhere. She follows the curved driveway lined with giant ferns and palm trees whose fronds are lit with colored lights. If she didn't know better, Gloria might think she was in the Caribbean, that she could expect to hear slow waves hitting a sandy shore-line. This is definitely Arizona and it's also ninety degrees and humid, and this casino is on a real Indian reservation in the middle of the desert; make no mistake about it.

She pulls right up to valet parking.

"Good evening, madam. And will you be checking in or just here for gaming?"

"Both," she hears herself say. Gloria thinks maybe she's losing her mind, doing something this impulsive without even considering what she's going to do in a hotel room all by herself and all of forty minutes from where she lives. She barely knows how to gamble. Slots don't count and she has never had the heart to play anything higher than the quarter machines. Craps scare her because she has never understood how the game works and there are far too many numbers that mean far too many things.

Blackjack is another story. As a kid, she played it with her dad but he just called it "twenty-one" and the word *blackjack* came up only when you were dealt a hand that added up to twenty-one. Go figure. By the time she was in middle and then high school, Gloria played for nickels and dimes and usually cleaned up. She became unpopular when it came to all card games even though blackjack was the only one she was good at. Well, there was also spades.

Before she reaches the building, Gloria is taken aback by the lines of seniors being escorted onto buses. Many of them are using canes or in wheelchairs. Once she gets closer to the entrance, the doors open and close even when no one's walking through them. Gloria tries not to stare at an elderly black woman with oxygen tubes stuffed in both nostrils struggling to smoke a cigarette as she drags her ventilator along as if it's one of those carts you get at a Laundromat to hang your clothes on.

Once she is inside, the smoke-filled air looks like smog and yet it doesn't seem to be bothering anybody. It looks more like a geriatric convention than a casino. It's definitely not Vegas. This place is about the size of a big barn and is packed to capacity. There are probably close to a thousand people in here, huddled around craps tables, crouched in front of slot machines, arms crossed tightly in front of the roulette table, staring at the cards falling onto the blackjack table as if they are hoping for a miracle. Most of them look like they're in a trance, and almost everybody looks scared or desperate. It doesn't look like they're having much fun, even those with stacks of chips.

Gloria heads over to the hotel registration counter. Her cell phone rings. It's Tarik but she decides to let it go to voice mail. She'll call him back after she's all settled in.

When she looks up, even the young bleached blonde whose name tag reads "Cindy W." looks damaged, like she's been through too much already. "Checking in?" she asks Gloria. Cindy can't be more than twenty-five but she looks thirty-five. Her hair looks like uncooked spaghetti, her roots the color of weak coffee. Her skin is sallow and dried zit marks dot her cheeks, which only draws more attention to the pale peach lipstick that's working against her on every level. Gloria tries to ignore what nails she has left. Cindy's eyes are glazed and her pupils dilated. She must not get tested very often, Gloria thinks. Cindy flits back and forth behind the counter for at least a minute before returning to the spot where she can actually give Gloria her full attention. Something's making her act this revved up. "I'll be with you in a few minutes," Cindy says. "I have to put out a small fire." And off she goes. She should not be welcoming anybody.

While she waits, Gloria looks around. She has no idea what she's doing here. Row after row of slot machines are lined up like soldiers at Buckingham Palace. But this is no palace. There are no gates and there is nothing to protect. The craps tables are surrounded by people who appear to be looking for UFOs more than the right dots on the dice. There are no earsplitting jackpot squeals. No one seems to be laughing or smiling. There is no delight in this place. And to top it off, no bells are ringing. No one seems to be getting what they came here for, which was to win. Gloria knows there's nothing in here for her to win.

"Is your husband parking your car?" Cindy asks.

Gloria is startled. "No, he isn't."

"Then shall I go ahead and book a room for you?"

"I don't think so," Gloria says. "But thanks for your help anyway."

She heads back outside, where the woman with emphysema is now sitting. She is not smoking, thank God. She looks like a brown skeleton, especially her arms and fingers. Gloria stands here and smiles even though she wants to scream at her because she cannot for the life of her understand why this woman is out here all alone and why she is still smoking cigarettes knowing she is so close to death. Maybe that's precisely why, Gloria thinks as she waits for the valet to bring her car around.

"Your luck couldn'ta ran out this fast," the old woman says. She is trying very hard to smile.

"It didn't," Gloria says. "I just didn't feel like betting on anything when the odds aren't in my favor."

———

On her way home, Gloria decides to stop by the grocery store. She's almost out of everything she needs: toilet paper, paper towels, orange juice, candy corn, chips and salsa, chocolate milk (that she knows she shouldn't be drinking), those frozen apple and raisin turnovers (that she knows she shouldn't be eating), frozen waffles, sausage links, macaroni and cheese and a twelve-pack of Diet Pepsi. It's been hard trying to do everything right, which is why Gloria often rewards herself with food for what she does manage.

She knows the danger. It's called a heart attack. If she listened to her doctor and started eating like she knows she should, lost at least twenty but preferably thirty pounds, did at least a half hour of any kind of exercise five but preferably seven days a week, she could eliminate almost all of the medication she takes. The good news: her mammogram was negative. Everything else was a little too high. Her glucose was 180. Her cholesterol 205. Blood pressure 140/90. This was the one that scared her the most.

Gloria was not about to panic, because that was part of the problem. But trying not to worry was the same as worrying. You can't trick your body, because it's smarter than you are. Gloria's been doing her very best pretending that in the very near future she's going to miraculously wake up one morning and eat a piece of fruit with some yogurt, then she'll take ten thousand steps before she starts her workday. She'll eat steamed vegetables and a salad with baked fish or chicken and she'll have pasta and she'll be able to live without the twenty different desserts she once couldn't live without. She will lose weight sensibly. She will look better. She'll feel better. She'll be one of the smart ones, who learned how to live like she really wanted to.

"Is that you, Gloria?" someone calls out. It's a voice she doesn't recognize. Even after she turns, she just sees an elderly black woman in one of those wheelchair carts.

"Yes, my name is Gloria. Do I know you from somewhere? I'm terrible with names, I'm sorry to say."

"Girl, I'm Dottie. Dottie Knox."

Gloria is trying to go through her memory bank, but it's locked. She also doesn't feel like trying to remember Dottie.

"From Black Women on the Move! Ringing any bells yet?"

Now Gloria looks more closely at this frail woman in a wig meant more for transvestites, what appeared to be bifocals, and slacks that should've been dry-cleaned but had clearly been ironed too many times, because they are shiny, and that's when it hits Gloria that the other Dottie used to be an almost good-looking, well-dressed pain in the ass. In fact, she was quite a few years younger than Gloria. Dottie also thought she was fine as wine back then, but she was destined to be a spinster because she had no tolerance for other people's shortcomings. Dottie was the one who complained about everything at the meetings (which is why they went on for hours) and always objected to just about every fund-raising idea anybody made, and nobody could really stand her. She was also the treasurer and always had to be in control. But after years of declining membership and due to a lack of focus, Gloria, Bernadine, Robin and Savannah stopped going to the meetings because that's all they were: meetings.

"Dottie! Of course I remember you, girl. How are you?"

Dottie throws her arms up in the air. "How does it look like I'm doing?"

Gloria is ashamed of herself for even thinking it, but once a bitch always a bitch, and this is a word she stopped using a long time ago. "Did you have an accident?"

"That would be called a stroke and that would be nine years ago, and that also makes me grateful that our Lord Jesus Christ who is our savior spared me, so now I do His work and do everything in His name. Are you saved?"

Damn, Gloria thinks. I just came in here to get a few groceries. "I was saved a long time ago, Dottie. Are you doing okay, though, for real? It looks like you're able to get around pretty good."

"Some things aren't what they appear to be. I never did get up the courage to marry. I was very sorry to hear about the tragic death of your husband. Wasn't his name Marlin?"

"Marvin."

"Yes, I read about it in the paper quite a few months back. How are you doing? You're looking healthy. Grief sneaks up on you and you have to get through it the best you can. Look at me, would you?"

"You look pretty good, Dottie, considering what you've been through."

"Why are you still wearing your wedding ring?"

Gloria looks down. She's never thought about it until now. "I just haven't gotten around to not wearing it."

"Anyway, how's your son?"

"He's fine. Lives over in Gilbert. Happily married with three beautiful kids. He's a lieutenant on the police force."

"That's so nice to hear. And you? What are you doing for yourself these days besides eating?" She actually chuckles like this was meant to be a joke, but Gloria didn't think it was the least bit funny.

"Well, I still have Oasis although I'm about to move into a much bigger space and add a day spa—a wellness, holistic-type spa—so you might want to watch the papers for our grand opening."

"When might that be?"

"I'd say in the next four or five months, depending on how much renovating we have to do."

Dottie is almost impressed but doesn't want to act like it. "Well, you know, I can walk. Sometimes I just get better treatment riding around in this thing. Will you be having those massages with the hot rocks?"

"Yes."

"Un-hun. Do you have a Web site?"

"It's under construction."

"Un-hun. I bet it is."

"Excuse me?"

"I said I bet it's going to be lovely. I'll be on the lookout."

"By the way, Dottie, is BWOTM still active at all?"

"I doubt it. There was some talk about getting it going again, but they can count me out."

"I bet they can," Gloria mumbles, as she swipes her debit card. "Who does your hair?"

Dottie grabs her head. "I do it myself. Why?"

"You should stop by Oasis if you can when you have time and let us give you a deep conditioner and shampoo and any style you want. On me. For old times' sake."

"You would do that for me, Gloria?"

"Yes, I would."

"But I always thought you didn't like me."

"I didn't," Gloria says and puts Dottie's saltines, two cans of Campbell's chicken noodle soup and Quaker Instant Oatmeal onto the moving belt. "But you seem much nicer now."

"I am," Dottie says. "Praise the Lord."

———

Gloria feels different on the drive home. Stronger. More connected. It wasn't just Dottie. Or being in that casino. She's grateful for what she can still do. For how much she has left. It was also daunting, seeing what time can do to some folks and not others. Maybe it's neglect. Maybe it's apathy. Whatever it is, Gloria doesn't want any. In fact, she's thinking about giving a call to those real estate agents Marvin had been dealing with when he was trying to help her find a space to accommodate the kind of spa he knew she wanted. How many square feet would they need, she's wondering. *They?* That's exactly what she's thinking. They. As she dials Tarik's number, Gloria smiles because this means her mind has made the decision for her.

"Ma, where are you?" Tarik asks.

Gloria doesn't want to tell him she's been to a casino and didn't win anything because she didn't spend a penny. "I stopped off at Safeway to pick up a few things, and I'm on my way home. Is everything all right with you?"

"No."

As soon as she hears him say this, Gloria pulls into someone's driveway and puts the car in park. She leaves the parking lights on. "What do you mean, 'no'? It doesn't have anything to do with the kids, I hope?"

"The kids are fine, Ma. It's Nickida."

Gloria has never heard Tarik call her Nickida. "What about her?"

"I think we might be getting a divorce."

"What on earth are you talking about, Tarik?"

"She's been cheating on me."

"How do you know that?"

"I don't want to go into any details, Ma. But it's all good."

"Slow down, would you, Tarik. You don't end a marriage over one infidelity, do you?"

"You do when it's her ex-husband," he says.

"No, she didn't!"

"Oh yes, she did."

"That sneaky little bitch!" Gloria says. Too late to take it back.

I Need a Fucking Vacation

GoGo isn't coming because he's in jail. Sheila isn't coming because she's too upset GoGo's in jail. Mama told me if it was a train ticket, she'd come in their place. Since 9/11, she refuses to get on an airplane. "It's what Sheila gets for thinking so far ahead. You can't plan mistakes." I was relieved I wasn't home last night when they left these messages.

I went to see *Hustle & Flow* with Robin, which was a big mistake. She talked off and on during the entire fucking movie about that stupid Black Angel dude standing her up and Russell finally getting off the chain gang. "I'm about to give up on this online dating thing and maybe think about speed dating because at least you meet the person up front and can tell right off the bat if there's any chemistry." I pray for her. It was a good movie and I was on the verge of falling in love with that Terrence Howard but Robin just kept jacking off at the mouth no matter how many times I asked her to zip it. So I'm going to have to see it again by myself or pray Gloria gets it on bootleg soon.

Right now, I'm getting dressed for work. I did not sleep well. I must have gone to the bathroom two or three times last night. I don't know what this is about but maybe it's because I've been drinking so much water. It's what you do in Arizona in the summertime. Hydrate. After I make coffee and put a bran muffin in the microwave and slather it with I Can't Believe It's Not Butter, I go outside and sit on the deck my ex-husband built. I'm also sitting next to the cabinet he built. It houses the flat-screen television that pops up for spectators or bootleg DVD viewers. Now that I'm out here, I can't help but look at the bed he built. It's perched on a platform. Green-and-white-striped canvas drapes hang from metal bars on three sides. He built that bar at the end of the pool. That redwood fence. Isaac certainly added a lot of beauty to this place.

I take one long gulp from my coffee before I dial my sister's number, which I'm dreading doing. She said it was urgent that I call her as soon as I got the message. Everything is urgent these days, though, isn't it? "Hey, Sheila."

"I was just about to call you. Didn't you get my message last night?"

"I did but I got in too late."

"If somebody says it's urgent, what does that mean to you, Savannah?"

"If it was super-urgent then you should've called back. So GoGo's in jail? For what?"

"That's not important right now but we need your help getting him out."

"How much help, Sheila?"

"His bail is set at a hundred thousand and we need ten to get GoGo out of there as soon as humanly possible, but we don't have that kind of money and we need to know if you could lend it to us. Please tell me you can do it, Savannah, and you know I wouldn't ask if we had other options."

"You know, some things just don't change. Everybody must think that money grows on palm trees in Phoenix or something. Do I need to remind you who's been paying for Mama's housing for the last twenty years? And who supplements her social security? I'm not rich, Sheila. Damn."

"I know that, sis, and I wouldn't ask, but we don't have nothing left to borrow against this house."

"Then tell me, what did he do?"

"He got caught supposedly selling something to somebody he shouldn't have been selling it to."

"You mean as in drugs?"

"It was just marijuana. And he didn't have that much on him. But it was a few too many joints. Can you help us out or not, Savannah? We're going crazy back here trying to figure out what to do. And GoGo is a wreck."

What I'm thinking is: *just* marijuana? And poor GoGo is a *wreck*? I swear to God. On top of this, after taking out a second mortgage and paying off Isaac, I ended up with about eighteen thousand bucks, which I decided to use to pay off a few credit cards and the balance on my Land Rover and to surprise Mama by sending her a few extra dollars to play with. I've also been thinking about taking a long-overdue vacation—anywhere—to celebrate my new life. However, I do have an open line of credit at my credit union. So what the hell. Family is family. "How soon do you need it?"

"How soon can you get it to us? And thank you so much, Savannah. GoGo will thank you personally."

"That won't be necessary. Anyway, I'll Federal Express a check today."

"Can you make sure it's certified?"

"Of course."

"You know, it still might be a good thing for him to come out there, even if it's just for a week. GoGo is very interested in entertainment."

"That's an understatement," I say. "Maybe next year, Sheila. Love you."

———

I sit here for a few more minutes thinking this is why prisons are so overpopulated with black men. This is how it starts. It breaks my heart, how easy breaking the law is for some of us. And how hard it is to deal with when they get caught. On one hand, I now wish GoGo had made it out here. Of course, I have no clue what to talk to a seventeen-year-old black boy about, but I think I would've come up with something that wouldn't have landed him in jail.

I feel like sliding back under the covers. I think I might be somewhat depressed. I've got all the symptoms. Some mornings it's been hard rolling out of bed, and regardless of what time I go to sleep I still feel sluggish when I wake up. There is no pep in my step and I don't get all that worked up over too much of anything these days.

"The going rate for postdivorce depression is two years," Thora had said right after mine was official. "But there are things you can do to speed up the process, especially since you don't have kids. Count those seven months you were separated and add the year or two you were biding your time before you took that leap. All of this knocks off a lot from the time you need to get used to being single."

I nod.

"The stages of grief are the same as when someone close to you dies but after you accept that you aren't a failure at love, and that you wanted to end your marriage because you were unhappy, you can actually begin thinking of being happy again. It's a chance to build a new life, and hopefully with someone else one day."

"How do you build a new life?" I remember asking, not like she was a divorce guru or anything.

"You're already doing it," she said.

I wasn't completely sure what she was talking about because I didn't know what I was doing. I do know I've had a lot of things on my mind, although not enough to warrant this kind of lethargy. I pray I don't have cancer. Or a brain tumor. Or—what is it called?—narcolepsy. During lunch, I have found myself putting my head down and actually dozing off. I mean, I'm always doing research for two or three potential stories—which is pretty normal. I'm also trying to figure out when I might be able to get back to Pittsburgh to see everybody. And I want to take a class.

Since Isaac has been gone I've had to get used to a lot. Besides not having him to complain about, I've had to get used to doing almost everything alone: eating, sleeping, watching television, cooking, getting my truck washed, getting the oil changed. I realized how much stuff Isaac used to do around here and how little I actually know how to do. I am not good with tools. I don't like the shapes of most of them, except the hammer. That's an easy one to use. I've been amazed at how many things require tools. Even simple stuff. I'm tired of paying the handyman and I wonder if they have classes to teach you how to fix stuff around the house, especially if you don't have a husband to do it. I can't help but be reminded how Mama always used to sing, "It's so nice to have a man around the house . . ." even though she never had one.

After finishing my coffee, I still feel like curling up for another twenty minutes. But I don't. I have to stop by my dry cleaners because they sent me a notice telling me I've had some things that have been there since right after the New Year. I stop by my credit union first, and then pick up the dry cleaning. There are a lot more clothes than I'd thought. I hang them in the back and then feel a sudden sense of dread coming on. I just remembered Thora's bringing her four-year-old twin boys in this afternoon. They're the most spoiled-rotten little kids I've ever been close to in my life. For the life of me, I cannot remember their names. I decide to call Sally, one of the other producers. She'll know. "Hey there, Sal," I say when she answers. "I've got a question for you, but please don't let anyone know I asked, okay?"

"Okay. Is this juicy? If so, I'm loving it!"

"Not even close. What are Thora's boys' names?"

"Oh, fuck. Those little monsters? I'm thinking. I know it starts with a 'J' but she should've named them Jason I and Jason II. Hold on a sec, Savannah, and let me ask Richard."

In the rearview mirror, mixed in with my dry cleaning, I spot Isaac's yellow shirt, black linen slacks and the mint green linen sports jacket I always loved him in. I'm surprised he hasn't asked about them after all this time. I suppose I could call him and just tell him I'll leave them with the receptionist or something.

"The little devils are Jake and Joshua. See you soon. Oh! Could you stop at Starbucks and pick me up a cappuccino? I'll reimburse."

"No problem, Sally."

"Breve."

"What does that mean?"

"I'm ashamed to admit it, but it means they use half and half instead of milk."

"You're skinny. You can afford it."

"Thanks."

She didn't bother to comment about me being thin, of course. As soon as I get over boredomitis—and now divorcitis—I intend to start taking much better care of myself.

I sneak into the studio and hand Sally her coffee and head back to my office. I actually broke down and bought one of those delicious apple fritter things because it was beckoning me. I also decided to try that breve drink. It was like an orgasm in a cup. (It's been eight months.) I'm not getting into the habit of eating or drinking this stuff. Not even.

Oh-oh! Here they come. "Hi, Thora," I say with feigned enthusiasm. She's got them by their hands. They dash into my office, and just stand there and stare at me like they've never seen me or a black person before. Thora acts like she's afraid of them. These kids think the world revolves around them, that they should get whatever they ask for when they ask for it. They don't know or care what the word *no* means. Imagine what sort of men they're going to turn into. The kind we end up marrying and divorcing.

"Say hello to Savannah, boys."

"Hello, Savannah," they say simultaneously. She should stop with the plaid shirts and those coverall shorts. And wash their sneakers or buy new ones, for crying out loud. Their pacifiers are hanging around their necks. I wish I could take the scissors I'm looking at and cut them off.

"Savannah, would you mind terribly if the boys stayed in here for a few minutes while I run to the ladies' room?"

"No, I don't mind."

"Oh, before I forget, Jasper wants to know when we could set something up for you two to meet. Did you ever Google him?"

"I hate to admit it, but I haven't gotten around to it. I did see the picture you sent. He's a handsome man."

"I'll tell him we might be able to work something out soon. How's that sound to you?"

"Foreign." I haven't figured out a polite way to tell her I'm not interested in meeting anybody yet. On the other hand, I also don't know when you're supposed to know.

"I think it's exciting. Okay, boys, promise Mommy you'll be on your best behavior until I get back?"

"We promise," they say simultaneously. I find this to be spooky. They push those pacifiers into their mouths and start pressing the keys on my laptop.

"Please don't touch those keys," I say.

One lets his pacifier fall on his bib. "Why not? Mommy lets us!"

"Because you could break it."

"Then you get it fixed," one says and shoves that pacifier back into his mouth.

"Why do such big boys like you still suck on pacifiers?"

"Because we like them." They say this in sync.

"But I thought they were for babies."

"We are babies," they say together.

"I thought you were four years old."

"We are. Four-year-old babies." One speaks for both this time.

I didn't dare ask about those pull-ups they still sleep in at night. When I started chuckling under my breath, they didn't. I was thinking that if they'd had my mama for a mother, she'd have snatched those pacifiers out of their mouths as soon as they could say a whole word, thrown those things in the trash and dared them to cry.

Dilbert sets a stack of mail on my desk and salutes the twins. They lick their tongues out at him. He winks at me while shaking his head. He has a crush on me and about six other women who work here. Dilbert is old enough to be my grandfather. I wink back. The boys start flipping through my envelopes like they must do at home, and when I recognize the logo from my credit union, I pull it out, open it and read:

Dear Member:
Our records indicate one or more payments remain due for the loan shown above. Perhaps this matter

was simply overlooked. As coborrower, you are equally responsible for payments on this account. Please be advised that thirty day or more delinquencies become a part of your permanent credit file. As required by law, you are hereby notified that a negative report reflecting on your credit record may be submitted to a credit reporting agency if you fail to fulfill the terms of your credit obligation. This is an attempt to collect a debt. We thank you for giving this account the prompt attention it deserves. Please do not hesitate to call us at the number below.

Sincerely,

Asset & Recovery Department

"Oh no the hell you didn't, Isaac!"

"That's a bad word!" one of them says.

"Hell yeah, it is!" the other one says, and they both start laughing.

Thora appears in the doorway. "I'm going to make the rounds with the boys, and they said they want to go to the park so it looks like I have to take them. Let's talk next week about the domestic violence piece. We'll stop by and say goodbye on our way out. Right, fellas?"

They just look at me over their shoulders as they leave. I want to stick my tongue out at them, but of course I don't. I dial the number at the bottom of this letter. Of course I get a computerized voice that asks me to punch in my account number. When I hear how delinquent *my* loan is—three fucking months—I feel myself going ice cold. I don't believe this son of a bitch! Not once did it ever occur to me that Isaac would default on this loan. He knew that if he ever missed a payment, I, as the cosigner, would be the one stuck paying it. I feel like I could detonate.

I call him on his cell and am shocked to hear, "I'm sorry but that number is no longer in service. Please check the number you are calling and—"

I try not to slam the phone down and place it as gently as possible in the cradle but then snatch it back up and dial his mama. She answers on the first ring. "Hello, Teretha. This is Savannah. How are you?"

"I'm doing just fine. And yourself?"

"I'm doing pretty good. Look, it seems like your son has gotten some urgent mail I think he might want to know about. But his number's been changed. Do you have his new one?"

"I sure do. He'll probably be glad to hear from you. He's not doing so well."

"Is he sick?"

"Not that I know of."

"Well, I'm glad to hear it's not his health. Can you give me the number now, Teretha, because I have to be somewhere in ten minutes."

She rattles it off and I tell her another lie about taking her to lunch or something. I dial the new number. It rings twice. "How you doing, Savannah?"

"Not so good. You probably know why I'm calling, don't you?"

"I have a pretty good idea."

"Why haven't you been making the fucking payments on the loan?"

"Do you have to swear?"

"Yes, I do. Answer the fucking question, Isaac."

"Because I've been having some financial difficulties."

"I just lent your sorry ass three thousand dollars. What did you do with it that fast?"

"I had a few other pressing issues."

"More pressing than your bills?"

"I got hurt."

"Well, so did I, but I still pay my bills."

"My back went out."

"Sorry to hear that. Isn't it always the back, Isaac?"

"I might end up being on disability for a while."

"Did your fingers get hurt, too? Out of common fucking courtesy, why couldn't you have picked up the phone and just told me you couldn't make the payments? Huh?"

"Because I was trying to make them."

"My credit union doesn't count 'trying' as a payment, Isaac. Should I just add this to the long list of parting gifts? I thought we were going to be civil about this."

"I'm trying to be civil, Savannah. There's a chance I might end up being forced to retire."

"Well, yahoo. Did you have to go to the hospital?"

"No."

"Have you had an MRI?"

"No."

"So what makes you think you might need to retire? Are you seeing a spiritual guide or something?"

"I could recover, but right now I just don't know."

"Hypothetically, do you really think at forty-nine you could actually retire, Isaac?"

"I don't know. There may be other options. I'll have to wait and see. I'm just trying to figure a lot of things out."

"Well, join the club. What about your bills? How do they fit into your plans for the near future, huh?"

"I might have to file Chapter Seven."

"File WHAT?"

"Look, you don't have to yell, Savannah."

"Let me ask you something, Isaac."

"I'm listening."

"Are you still a Republican?"

There is a long silence. And then, "To be honest with you, Savannah, I don't know what I am anymore."

"Good luck figuring it out. I hate to say it, but I'm glad I divorced your sorry ass. It's men like you who give the good ones a bad name. Have a good life." I hang up, open my laptop and log on to FICO to see if my credit rating has changed. The first thing it says on top is: "Score Watch: Your score has dropped 36 points."

My mouth drops another ten.

I jump up from my desk and walk out into the studio until I spot Thora. I don't see the twins but I spot them in Sally's office, taking turns drinking out of her Starbucks cup. "Thora, I need to ask you something."

"Shoot."

"Remember when you told me about your flat in Paris?"

"I do, indeed."

"And you said if I ever wanted to go you'd be happy to rent it to me."

"I didn't say *rent*. You're welcome to stay there any-time. We have caretakers and would just need to give them a few weeks' notice to get everything in tip-top shape. How soon would you like to go?"

"I wish I could go today but all I know is I need a fucking vacation so bad I can almost taste it."

"Don't let him get to you. They're like ghosts who haunt you, but pretty soon he'll have no effect on you whatsoever."

"I'm waiting for that moment. Right now I feel like I need to do something or I'm going to explode."

"Don't we all? I'll be honest. I love these boys to death but some days I wish to hell I could drop them off at day care for about a month."

"How long could I stay?"

"How long do you need?"

"A couple of weeks would help."

"That's all? Are you sure?"

"Well, how long do you think I could get off?"

"Are you kidding me? You can work from Paris. They've got the Internet over there, too. Duh."

"Maybe I need to give this a little more thought."

"Don't think. That's part of our problem. When we get to be our age we're too fucking practical. Just go, and think about it once you're on the plane."

"You could be right, Thora."

"Of course I am. Start brushing up on your French and get back in that office and book your flight and make sure it's a nonrefundable one so you won't be inclined to change your mind. Wait. Is there any way you could squeeze in a coffee with Jasper before you leave?"

I want to say no but since she's being so nice, I say, "Sure."

She gives me a hug and then the boys appear out of nowhere and start tugging at her skirt.

"Thanks a million, Thora. Goodbye, boys. Hope to see you again soon." I smile and wave and I can't believe it when those little fuckers give me the finger! Where do they learn this stuff?

I book a fully refundable flight for a month from now. Not because I think I might change my mind. Not even. But as is becoming more and more obvious to me: shit happens. Right now, my heart is pounding like crazy because I can't believe I'm actually doing this. I lean back in my chair and slowly rock until the confirmation lands in my in-box. It's at this moment I decide not to tell my girlfriends, at least not until I'm almost packed. They'd probably freak out to know I'm going alone. But I need to go by myself. I need to hear myself think. Or not think. Mostly I just want to see if I remember who I am. And what I'm going to do about it.

Returns

"Yes, I'd like to return this dress," I say to the cashier after taking it out of their nice shiny shopping bag.

She looks at my receipt. "You can't return items after ten days. Sorry," she says and hands it back to me.

"What are you talking about?"

"It's store policy."

"But I've shopped here for years and I've never had any problems returning anything."

"Well, I've worked here for ten years and it's always been store policy."

What a little bitch. First of all, it looks like everything on her body has been purchased and she still looks bad. Be nice, Robin, be nice. "As you can see, I haven't worn the dress."

"I can see that, ma'am. However, in order for me to accept it I have to be able to restock it, and I can't do that after ten days."

"Why not?"

"As I previously stated: it's store policy."

"Look, I paid two hundred eight dollars for this dress. Now it's on sale for one forty-eight. All I want to do is exchange it so I can get it at the cheaper price."

She looks bored. I would really like to slap her ass

into next week, but I take my raspberry knit dress I absolutely love and walk down the aisle to a different register. This clerk is young and carefree. Her hair is black and green. Her minidress is orange and yellow. She looks like a toucan. And she's cute. She's also chewing gum, which is a very good sign.

"Hello," I say in my friendliest "return" voice.

"Hello to you back. How may I help you today?"

"I have a return." I hand her the dress and the receipt. She starts punching numbers on the cash register, tosses the dress on top of a pile of other returns, and hands me the receipt. "You'll see a credit on your next statement. Anything else I can do for you today?"

"Nope. You've been quite helpful."

And off she goes. She sits in an empty chair, crosses her legs and prepares to people-watch. I pick my dress up and take it to another register out of her line of vision.

"Yes, I'd like to get this dress," I say to the new clerk, whose hair is feathered like Farrah Fawcett wore back in the seventies. I didn't know that look was back! "I love your hair."

"Thanks. It's supposed to look like Farrah Fawcett. You know, from the seventies or eighties."

"Well, it works in 2005, too."

"Thanks again. Shall I put this in a dressing room for you?"

"No, that's okay."

"You sure you wouldn't like to try it on first?"

"No, I'm pretty sure it'll fit."

"Okay. This is a final sale, which means the dress

can't be returned, sweetheart. Are you sure you don't want to try it on?"

"I'm sure. I think it'll fit. What is the sale price?"

"Well, you're in luck today. This gorgeous dress has been marked down from two hundred eight to one forty-eight!"

"Wow, that's super! But tell me something . . ." I say, looking at her name tag ". . . Claudia. May I use this twenty-five-dollar coupon in addition to the sale price?"

"You most certainly may! Wow. You're quite the smart shopper, because you are now getting this lovely dress for the super-deluxe low price of one hundred twenty-three dollars. Would you like another shopping bag?"

"No, this one's fine." I open my bag wide enough for her to drop the now tissue-papered dress right on in.

"Enjoy!" she says. "I hope you're going somewhere nice to wear it!"

If only.

———

I've been trying not to remind myself I got stood up by somebody I never even met. Sparrow didn't bother to ask how it went, because she saw the look on my face when I stormed past her and went into my room and slammed the door. I also didn't bother to mention I'd run into her trifling father. The first thing I did was wipe off my makeup. Then I took an extra-long shower and put my favorite yellow jammies on. I sat on the bed with the television off and called Dark Angel. He actually had the nerve to answer.

"What happened to you?" I asked.

"Tiger Lady?"

"Expecting someone else? How many of us have you stood up, Dark Angel?"

"Whoa. Wait a minute. I thought our date was tomorrow."

"That is so not true. That is so lame. What do you take me for?"

"Seriously. Maybe I'm tripping, but I've got you in my BlackBerry for tomorrow."

"Is that a baby I hear crying in the background?" I get up and take the portable down to my office. Sparrow had set the mail on my chair. I put it on the desk and sit down.

"That's my sister's baby."

All of this was just a little too shaky. "Look, Dark Angel, I'm curious about something."

"I'm listening, baby."

"Please don't call me baby."

"Okay, I'm listening, Tiger Lady."

"My name is not Tiger Lady. It's Robin." This was when I saw that manila envelope I sent him a couple of weeks ago. "No Such Address" was stamped on the front. I opened it, took out the copy of *Selected Poems of Langston Hughes* and ripped up the three-hundred-dollar check I thought might help him self-publish his book.

"Okay, Robin, Tiger Lady, whatever works for you."

"Did you ever get the book I sent?"

"Of course I did."

"Have you had a chance to read any of the poems?"

"Yes, I have."

"Tell me one of your favorites."

"I've got lots of them, Robin. Tell me one of yours."

" 'One Hundred Years of Solitude.' "

"I loved that one, too. It was beautiful."

"So, Dark Angel . . . who is that I hear talking in the background?"

"That's my sister."

"Are you at her house?"

"Yes, I am."

"In Phoenix?"

"Glendale."

"She sounds upset about something."

"She's always upset."

"And where is it you live again?"

"Well, I have more than one residence."

"Oh, really? Funny, you never mentioned that in any of your e-mail."

"I didn't think it was important. So look, I'm kinda in the middle of something and I'm wondering if we can get a rain check. I'm feeling a little under the weather."

"So, you can't say thank you for the check?"

"What check?"

"I put a three-hundred-dollar check inside the book of poems to help you get yours published. Didn't it fall out when you were reading?"

"I didn't notice it. Let me give you a different address. Maybe you could stop payment on that one and resend it."

"Oh, my bad. I think I'm looking at it right here. Looks like I sent it to the wrong address. So you know what, Dark fucking Angel, tell your wife and baby I said 'Hey.'"

He chuckled. "Well, this has been fun, Tiger Lady. No harm done. I'm glad you dug that poem. Good luck on your search. And by the way, do yourself a solid and stop lying about your age. You look fifty, not forty-two."

"Then you should do yourself a favor and stop writing such infantile, sophomoric, sentimental, corny and just plain bad poetry. In case you weren't aware, this is not a game, Dark Angel. There are millions of women out here hoping to meet a decent man online, and if your behavior represents what's out there, I'm bowing out now. I'd also change my screen name if I were you because I'm going to post it as one to avoid. Enjoy your life." And I hung up.

Since then, I've been wondering just how common it is for these guys to manufacture a personality and a life to see who takes the bait. I don't want to find out. I thought online dating was meant to save you time and help you get around the riffraff and avoid playing the usual games so you'd stand a better chance of meeting that special someone. Maybe I'm turning into a skeptic. I don't think so. I'm too old for this shit. That much I do know. I'm bored on top of being tired of wading through hundreds of e-mail week after week only to realize how much time I'd wasted. It's felt like I've been preparing for a test I'm never going to take, which is ridiculous. Dark Angel is my last icebreaker. I didn't bother to erase his number. I used the remaining twenty-nine minutes, then hit the phone with a hammer a few times and tossed it in the trash. If I ever meet someone who truly is worthy, I'll be more than happy to give him my home number.

—

"Sparrow! Have you eaten anything?" I've just come in from the gym. The dogs, of course, rush to greet me. I forgot about their vet appointment this morning. Things have been crazy at work. Looks like there could be a merger, but no one's saying anything. Even Norman is mum these days. Lucille is still beating everyone in. Her loyalty is sickening sometimes.

"No, I haven't, Mom! I'm on the phone! I'll be down in a few!"

I feed the dogs, and out of sheer habit, I'm about to head upstairs to log in. I stop myself. I'm not that hungry. I had a late lunch.

"You want me to order something in?"

She doesn't answer. I curl up on the sofa. I don't want to watch another stupid anything on television tonight. I look at the coffee table, which offers a few magazine options. I decide on *Bark*. It's the only one free of violence and bad news.

"Hey there, Mom. How was your day?" Sparrow bends down and lays one on my forehead. I'm surprised she's in her pajamas already. Or, I should say, the plaid pajama bottoms she probably wore to school, over which is a T-shirt meant for football players.

"I had a hectic day at work and then had to return a dress, which turned out to be a very smart move. It was marked down and they were nice and gave me the sale price. Anyway, what do you feel like for dinner?"

"I ate after practice."

"Good."

"You'll never guess in a million years who I was just talking to, Mom."

"I can't begin to guess, Sparrow, so spare me."

"My dad."

I sit up.

"Your who?"

"You heard right."

"He called you?"

"No, I called him."

"How'd you know he was out? And how'd you get his number?"

"You told me the approximate time, remember? I Googled him and found him in the white pages."

"But what made you call him?"

"I just wanted to reach out."

"But why, Sparrow?"

"Why not? Because he's my dad."

"I thought you didn't want anything to do with him."

"That was when I was young and stupid."

"It was a few months ago."

"You know what occurred to me? That my very own father lives in the same city as I do, and I'm his daughter and I wouldn't know him if I passed him on the street."

"I understand. But this is just not at all what I was expecting from you. This is quite a shock, to be honest."

"He's actually a nice person who made some stupid choices and he's paid for them. I want to get to know him."

"I think this is a really nice gesture, Sparrow."

"Gesture? His blood flows through my veins, Mom. Just like yours. And don't worry, he's not going to be coming over or anything."

"You mean you've made plans to see each other?"

"Duh. Not like tomorrow or anything. He says he wants to get himself grounded and get used to the idea that I don't hate him and that I really do want to see him."

"That's touching," I say. "It really is." I'm trying to sound sincere.

"You have to open your heart and learn how to forgive others when they disappoint you, Mom. Haven't you always told me that?"

"I have. And I subscribe to it."

"Cool."

"Just keep him away from me."

"No problem. So you're really not upset about this, are you, Mom?"

"No. Like I said, I'm just a little surprised."

"Good. Because this isn't an act of betrayal. It's just that I have two parents and I might finally get to know the other one."

She darts off.

I sit here and read about more dogs. I'm trying not to think about Russell eking his way back into any crevices of my life. But my daughter is right. She should be able to find out who her father is and what parts of him she might be able to love.

———

I doze off for a solid hour. I'm now starving. While I microwave a Healthy Choice chicken-something I run up and get the mail. There's a flyer for the upcoming winter schedule for the black ski club I belong to. I'm excited. I missed out last season and promised myself I wouldn't miss the next one. I scroll down until I find Vail, my most favorite ski area of all. After fifteen years you'd think I'd be doing black diamond runs. Not even. I ski blue. I'm what's called a PI: permanent intermediate. I know my comfort zone. I'm not trying to win a slalom. I just like to inhale the thin air, spread my arms and shake out all the tension and stress before I dig my poles into the snow and sail down that mountain.

Sparrow, of course, thinks belonging to anything based on race is racist. That skiing is a bourgeois sport because you need to have money to burn. I earn a decent salary and I don't feel guilty spending a little on recreation. This is such a done deal. I eat my bland dinner and chase it with a Heineken. I go upstairs to my office but this time when I go online, it's to renew an annual membership for something I know exactly what it is I'm going to get in return.

Play Areas

Tarik and Gloria are sitting in two lawn chairs at the boat dock. Her son asked if she would meet him out here, and she agreed without thinking of how she might feel seeing that boat again. At first sight, she felt a pang in her stomach, then her chest. She fanned her face and shook out her hands and decided not to let it hold her hostage because her son's heart is breaking. She came out here to listen, to find out if he has any ideas about how he's going to mend it. Nickida has apparently admitted she made a mistake, that she does not want to break up her family.

Gloria does not want to pass judgment on her—again—but she is not feeling any love for her daughter-in-law. None whatsoever. She also doesn't want to give her grown son any advice unless he asks for it. In all honesty, Gloria doesn't really know what she'll tell him to do if he does ask, because she's not sure what she'd do if she were in his shoes.

"You want one of these Snapples?" she asks him.

"Thanks, Ma." He pulls the bill of his red Diamondbacks cap down to shield his eyes from the sun.

She hands him a bottle and she takes a sip of hers. They look out at the lake, which is pretty calm for such a balmy afternoon. It's almost five, and it's monsoon season, so this means nothing. In fact, those thunderheads are growing taller above the mountains, which are less than fifteen miles from here. Again, Gloria and Tarik know this means nothing, that it could all change in a matter of minutes. Gloria could care less right now. She's just waiting for Tarik to say something.

"Ma, would you mind picking Blaze and Diamond up from preschool tomorrow?"

"Of course I don't mind. What about Stone and Brass?"

"Didn't I tell you? Brass is spending a few weeks with his grandparents and Stone's at overnight camp for two weeks."

"No, you didn't."

"He's at space camp down in Tucson."

"Good Lord. He's finally old enough, huh?"

"Yep. He wanted to go for the entire two weeks, too."

"I remember when you first went to sleepaway camp. That's what we called it back then. You didn't want to come home when I went to get you. Do you remember that?"

He just nods his head yes, and Gloria sees a smile emerge on his face.

Gloria tugs on the hem of her denim capris, hoping to loosen them a little. She's been trying to give her son as much time as he needs to say what he wants to say, but she also knows they won't last too much longer out here before the weather breaks. "So, talk to me, Tarik. Tell me what's going on? I don't understand what has happened here."

He takes a sip of the iced tea and twists the top back

on. "What has happened in my house and in my bed is my wife saw fit to *entertain* her ex-husband when he came to pick up his son that I've been caring for and feeding for fifteen days out of each and every month for the past seven and a half years, and our four-year-old daughter happened to walk into her mommy and daddy's bedroom. Then she told her daddy what she saw."

"Oh my goodness," Gloria says and covers her mouth. "Little Blazie saw *that* mess?"

"She didn't know exactly what they were doing but she knew Luther wasn't supposed to be under the covers in her daddy and mommy's bed. Anyway, she's fine."

Gloria just sits there, wanting to ask a million questions but she will wait and listen. And while she does she begins to tap her feet against the asphalt.

"Ma, you don't do this kind of stuff to someone you're supposed to love. Do you?"

"Well, not ordinarily. But a lot of us are known for exercising poor judgment."

"Poor judgment? Is that what you think this is?"

"You know, Tarik, it doesn't matter what I think. It's how you and Nickida want to handle it. I just want you to be happy. And my grandchildren."

"You never liked her, did you?"

Shit. Now she's going to have to lie. And Gloria is not good at it. She takes another sip of her Snapple. It's getting warm. She doesn't like it warm. "First of all, I do like a lot of things about Nickida. I have to admit she's given me pause on some occasions, but I'm sure the feeling is mutual. I just think she's strong-willed and some-what of a worrier—"

"She's a hypochondriac. I know that."

"But that's not a reason to not like somebody."

"She's also a bitch."

Gloria is shocked to hear her son say this about his wife. She's finally glad to know Tarik has some clue that Nickida is not an easy person to appreciate. "That's not true," Gloria says.

"It is true, Ma. And she's a sneaky bitch."

"You know, I don't like hearing you call her that even if she's not your favorite person right now, okay?"

"I'm sorry. You're right. I'm just angry as hell."

"I know. What does Nickida have to say for herself?"

"She's just been bawling her eyes out, trying to get me to believe she has no idea how Luther was able to coerce her into doing something like this. That she isn't even attracted to him, and hasn't been for years."

"So how did he end up in your bed with her? Did she try to fight him off and it failed?"

In slow motion, he begins to shake his head. "She said the kids were playing video games and she went outside and smoked a joint with him and one thing led to another."

"You mean as in a marijuana joint?"

He nods his head.

"Did that shock you?"

He shakes his head no.

"So you mean you knew she smoked it?"

He nods again.

"So does this mean she smokes this stuff on a regular basis?"

He nods his head up and down.

"Do you smoke it, too, Tarik?"

"Of course not, Ma. I'm an officer of the law."

"But apparently that doesn't matter to her, then, huh?"

"She told me she had quit."

"Quit?" Gloria takes the last swallow of her drink, twists the cap back on tighter than necessary and sets it next to her right foot. Her sandals are under the chair. The first few sprinkles hit her red toenails. Ripples are forming in the water and most of the boaters are docking.

"Ma, you know it's gonna be pouring in a few minutes. You see those thunderheads up there? See how dark they are? We should get going."

Something told her coming out here wasn't a good idea. She gets up and starts folding up her chair.

"Is Nickida at home with the kids?"

"Afraid not. She's at her sister's house, where she'll be until we can be civil."

"Then who's watching the girls?"

"The neighbor's oldest daughter. You know Regina, who lives two doors down?"

Gloria nods. Nice people.

Without any warning, thunder begins to roar. And as if someone snapped their fingers to make it happen, raindrops start falling like they're being shot out of a BB gun. Gloria grabs her sandals, runs as fast as she can (which isn't very fast), heads toward the parking lot and jumps inside Tarik's SUV. He tosses both chairs in the back, over the kids' car seats, and then hops in. Everybody's running to their RVs and parked vehicles because those who live here know the combination of wind and lightning and rain can sometimes be a life-threatening cocktail.

"Can you call and see if it's raining over by your house?" Gloria asks. Even though it's pouring down here, it could be sunny on the other side of town.

Tarik calls the babysitter. "Hey, Regina, how's everybody doing? That's good. Is it storming over there? Oh, it just left? Well, we got it out here. I'm at Lake Pleasant. That's good to hear. Tell the girls I'll be home in about an hour. Thanks a lot. I appreciate it." He hangs up.

"So everybody's good?"

"Yep. They're eating pizza and watching cartoons."

"Have you said anything to the kids or have they asked where their mom is?"

"I just told them their mom was visiting their auntie for a few days."

"Have you thought about what impact all of this might have on them, Tarik?" Gloria asks.

"I haven't gotten that far yet."

"Okay," she says with a sigh. Gloria crosses her hands and lets them rest in her lap. What a mess. Treated his wife like she was Princess Di, and this is how she shows her gratitude and love? Gloria would really like to kick her ass. Or slap the shit out of her.

The sky is getting darker, and three flashes of lavender lightning just pierced through it. It is a spectacular light show but one Gloria would appreciate more seeing from inside the comfort of her home. They sit tight waiting for it to stop. It could be a while.

"So, I've been hoping she would stop smoking that stuff but it doesn't look like that's going to happen anytime soon. She's been jeopardizing our kids, not to mention putting me in a precarious position. I don't know when she smokes it. But I think I know where she gets it, and apparently she's been giving Luther something in kind. Something I thought was mine. This whole ordeal makes me sick, Ma."

"I know, baby."

"What would you do?"

"I don't know what I'd do, to be honest. But sometimes it's best not to make rash decisions, especially if you might end up regretting them later."

"I don't think I can trust her, Ma. In fact, I'm sure I can't. I mean, she brought this motha—sorry, she brought another man into our bed. With the kids downstairs? Who does she think she is?"

Gloria keeps quiet.

"I want out."

Gloria could ask a ton of questions, but she doesn't want to press him. Tarik needs some breathing room. Right now, as the rain hits the roof of the truck like bullets, she will sit here for what will amount to another forty-five minutes, waiting for her son to let his heart admit how much this hurts, which he will not do. When the rain stops, it will be abrupt, and she will give him a big hug and get in her car and hope neither of them gets caught in the gushing silt rushing through one of the gullies.

———

The next afternoon, Gloria arrives at the Shelton Academy for Primary Education, registers at the front desk and gets a pass to enter the school. The hallway walls are plastered with drawings and paintings. When she sees a teacher holding a tiny girl's hand—apparently taking her to the bathroom—Gloria asks her where the preschool classroom is and the teacher, who looks like she can't be more than twenty-one, points two doors down.

As soon as she finds the room, it looks like Santa's workshop of little black elves. There must be at least twenty of them. The walls are a potpourri of giant letters and numbers, animals in their natural habitat, the sun and the moon side by side and mountains observing them all. The children appear to be divided into groups, and everybody is busy and preoccupied. A small circle of children are peering up at a teacher as she tells them a story. Others are sitting at round tables, drawing or coloring. A few are curled up in fat-cushioned chairs, sound asleep. Diamond is one of them.

When Gloria spots Blaze, she's standing in front of a pink-and-lavender sink full of plastic dishes in what appears to be a miniature kitchen. She is surrounded by four other little girls who are apparently preparing a meal on a pink stove with the tiniest plastic pots and pans Gloria has ever seen. One has a little spoon and is just stirring away. Another girl standing next to Blaze is talking to someone on the headset of an old white princess phone. Gloria forgot how big those things used to be. It's almost as big as Blaze is.

"Gawa!" Blaze yells when she spots Gloria. "This is my gawa everybody!"

"Hi, Gawa!" they all seem to say at the same time.

"Hello there, everybody!" Gloria says. "What are you guys doing?"

"We're not guys," the little one on the phone says. "We're girls." She has two thick braids that fall like ropes past her shoulders and those big black eyes show she doesn't miss too much of anything. The others are nodding in agreement. Ms. Operator smiles, displaying eye teeth that look like tiny vampire fangs. Gloria laughs. The little girl laughs, too. They're all as cute as they can be.

"I'm sorry, *girls*. What are you doing, Blazie?"

Blaze looks up at Gloria, as do the other girls, as if to ask, "What does it look like I'm doing?" but instead she says, "I'm washing dishes."

The other girls nod, as if saying that's right, that's what she's doing. "Well, I came to pick you and Diamond up, Blazie, but it looks like she's still sleeping."

"This is nap time for the little kids," Ms. Operator says.

"Oh," Gloria says. "And who are you talking to?"

"Her not talking to anybody," a little chocolate-chip girl says. She looks like she's already seen some things. Her clothes are old and her hair looks like it hasn't been combed in days.

"I am, too!"

"Well, I was wondering, I would really like to get my hair done today."

"We're too little, Gawa," Blazie says, still rubbing her dry dishes and putting them into the dish rack. She positions them as if they're actually going to drain into her waterless sink.

"Well, I was hoping to get my makeup done, too, while I'm waiting."

"I can do your makeup," Ms. Chocolate Chip says, raising her hand to make sure she gets Gloria's attention.

"I have to call upstairs to the big kids and see if they

have any abailability to do your hair. Want me to?" Ms. Operator asks.

"I would like that."

"Hol' on a minute," she says while punching at least twenty numbers on that giant phone, so hard that the white cord hanging at the end of it swings back and forth. "Yes, I'm calling to see if you have any abailability for Blazie's gawa to get her hair done today? Hol' on a minute."

"They wanna know what you want done," she says to Gloria.

"I could sure use a new weave."

"They don't do weaves. You wanna get it braided?"

"How much does it cost?"

"Five hundred dollars," she says.

"Will they take a check?"

"No! They don't take no checks only credit cards," Ms. Chocolate Chip butts in as if she has had run-ins like this before.

"Then maybe I'll get it done a different day."

Gloria spots Diamond walking toward her with a sleepy smile on her face.

"You know, girls, it's been such a pleasure to have met you but I'm going to have to take my granddaughters home now."

"Can you come back and play with us again?" Ms. Chocolate Chip asks, as if she's pleading.

"Yes, I will," Gloria says.

"When?"

"Soon," Gloria says.

"Can you give me a hug?" she asks.

Gloria is surprised and moved by this request, but happy to oblige.

"I want one, too," Ms. Operator says.

"Me, too," another one says.

The next thing Gloria knows, the other girls descend upon her as well. All she feels are warm little arms and hands squeezing her thighs and waist. She's thinking that all these miniature people are real people. That one day they'll grow up and become real adults and they'll fall in love, and some of them will have their hearts broken and cry and wonder if they'll ever recover. Some of them will probably get married and have babies and their husbands might die when they least expect it. Or one day they'll be grandparents and their adult children will need them again, which is why Gloria is going to take two of these children to her house until their father, her only son, tells her just how long he needs all of them to stay.

Blockbuster Night

"Open this door before I break it down!" Robin yells.

"It's open!" Savannah yells back as she heads on out to the backyard. "And I hope you didn't bring those whiny little dogs with you, because we can never hear the dog-gone movie. Get it?"

"Oh, shut up, Savannah," Robin says, coming through the double doors that lead to the deck. "I dropped them off at Macy's. They're looking for new outfits. What can I do to help?"

"Don't ask a question you don't really want the answer to," Bernadine says after Robin passes her in the kitchen.

Savannah and Gloria are putting mint green sheets on the bed that Isaac built. It looks like something out of a movie. None of them has ever seen a bed in anybody's backyard. At least not one you'd want to sleep in. What Savannah's friends don't know is she hasn't so much as sat on it since she's been living alone.

"Who'd you get all dressed up for?" Gloria asks as Savannah tugs to get the sheet snug under her corner.

"I got this dress at Target. Thirty-nine bucks. I'm tired of looking like a slob just because I'm not at work." The dress is orange cotton, sleeveless, with a box-pleated skirt.

"Did I just hear you say you got that dress at Tarj'et? For under forty bucks?" Robin asks.

Savannah nods. They all know Robin can't pass up a good deal.

"Does it come in any other colors? I can't do orange."

"White and bright yellow."

"Why don't you make those mojitos and settle down," Gloria says. Robin obeys, heading over to the deck bar where Savannah has all the fixings ready and waiting. Perched high on top of a cabinet, the flat-screen TV awaits. Gloria has already slid *Crash* into the DVD player. It was the movie everybody wanted to see, since they missed it at the theater. Savannah has the remote, so Gloria started the movie manually. The previews are playing.

"What's the longest you've ever gone without shopping?" Gloria asks Robin.

"I don't know. Two, three days, tops. Why?"

"Were you sick and shut in?" Savannah asks.

"So I like to shop. Big deal."

"That's an understatement," Bernadine yells from the kitchen, where she is, of course, spreading out the food she has prepared, as she has done for every Blockbuster Night. She always surprises and outdoes herself.

"Do you ever ask yourself why you buy so much stuff you don't need?" Gloria is looking her dead in the face.

Robin turns the blender on high a little longer than it takes. Does a taste test. She's pleased. "It's not about need. I buy things because I like them."

"I like monkeys, too, but I'm not going to run out and buy one," Bernadine says, still from the kitchen.

"Don't make enough for me. I'm drinking water or iced tea this evening."

Everyone tries hard not to look suspicious.

"Just tell us when we can eat, please." Robin pours the mix into three martini glasses and takes a sip of hers.

"Anytime is the right time," Bernadine says.

"I'll bet you a hundred dollars you can't go a week without shopping," Savannah says.

"I don't need to prove anything to you."

"You're right," Savannah says. "So, let's fix our plates and come back and watch this movie. I heard it's probably gonna get nominated for an Oscar."

During the next ten minutes or so they fill their plates with everything they see: chicken and sweet potato salad, tomato and olive pasta with giant prawns piled on top, and everybody's favorite (which Bernadine borrowed from Tanya Holland's *New Soul Cooking*), that mouthwatering confetti cornbread. For dessert: summer pudding, an English recipe. Bernadine usually makes huge bowls of it for everybody down at Oasis. She can almost make it with her eyes closed: fresh raspberries and sugar boiled to a thick liquid then poured over layers of stiff white bread. She staggers them with the same concoction of blueberries and blackberries, puts it in the refrigerator overnight and uses sprigs of mint as a garnish and ultrarich clotted cream to top it off.

"Anybody want to hear a good joke while the previews are on? It's hecka funny," Robin says.

"No," Gloria says.

"Save it," Bernadine says.

"E-mail it to me," Savannah says.

They head back outside and sit in their usual places, Gloria and Robin on the deck in chaises, Bernadine and Savannah on the bed, leaning against the headboard. Savannah looks over at Bernadine. She's never seen anyone except Isaac in that spot.

"We couldn't have picked a nicer night to be outside, huh, girls?" Robin says. "No rain tonight."

Because Robin answered her own question, nobody bothers to respond. Gloria reaches over and presses PLAY on the DVD player.

Savannah hits the PAUSE button on the remote control. "So how's everybody doing and what's everybody been up to lately?"

Gloria rolls her eyes and lets out a long sigh. This is going to take all night. She can already feel it.

"Before I forget!" Robin yells out. "Lucille is selling—"

"I'm not buying another ticket to another one of those tired dances," Savannah says.

"I think I'll pass, too." Gloria sets her now empty plate on the deck.

"When is it?" Bernadine asks.

"Are we gonna ever watch this movie tonight or not? I'll be asleep in a few minutes if we don't." Gloria crosses her arms and legs and peers at everyone, hoping someone agrees with her.

Savannah sticks her tongue out at Gloria and presses the PLAY button. More previews.

"Early September. Did I tell you guys I'm going skiing with the black ski club this winter?"

"No," Bernadine says. "Why?"

"Because I'm tired of not having any fun."

"But aren't they all, like, twenty-one?" Savannah asks.

"No. Most twenty-one-year-olds can't afford to ski. Anyway, I'm buying four tickets to the dance, and if you don't come you will hurt Lucille's feelings. It's for a good cause."

"I believe in supporting a good cause but it doesn't mean I have to go to the boring dance. Which one is it for?" Savannah asks.

"It'll provide scholarships for black high school kids who have good grades but still need money for college. We need to stop being so selfish."

"I agree," Savannah says. "Okay. I'll go if everybody else goes. Damn."

"I'll buy a ticket," Gloria says.

"Since you put it that way, Robin. It's sad but true. None of us does anything for other folks the way we used to when we were in Black Women on the Move," Bernadine says. "Does anybody know whatever happened to them?"

"I ran into Dottie a little while ago. Remember her?"

"You mean Miss Meany? *That* Dottie?" Robin asks.

Gloria nods. "She didn't look so good."

"Neither do we," Bernadine says.

Gloria nods again. "Anyway, she had a stroke and she was in a wheelchair."

"I'm sorry to hear that," Savannah says. "She got on everybody's nerves but I hope she's going to be okay."

"You just never know when tragedy might strike," Bernadine says.

"Dottie told me there was some talk about starting it back up, but I think she was just saying it to be saying it. I'm thinking of giving Etta-Mae a call. She was the brain behind BWOTM."

"I heard she died a few years ago," Bernadine said.

"Let's talk about this again. After we see if we can locate any of the old members," Savannah says.

"I'll look into it," Gloria says.

"How much are the tickets this time, Robin?" Bernadine asks.

"Seventy-five, *but* it includes dinner and of course live entertainment and a raffle!"

"Remember a long time ago when Robin screwed one of the band members?" Bernadine asks. "And his wife was gonna kick her ass?"

Robin ignores this. Everybody is trying hard not to laugh. The credits finally start rolling. Now everybody seems to be daydreaming.

"I have to see if I can find something I can fit into," Gloria says. "Maybe this'll give me enough time to lose a few pounds. Everybody always overdresses. Like they're going to a ball or something."

"And do they love wearing sequins and rhinestones or what?" Savannah says while flipping the remote back and forth from one hand to the other. "I'll tell you right now, when the DJ plays the middle-age theme song, I'm not doing the Electric Slide. I mean it."

"I love doing the Electric Slide," Robin says.

"I don't," Gloria says.

"I can take it or leave it," Bernadine says.

"I'll tell you what you can do for me, Robin," Gloria

says, trying hard not to laugh. "Ask Lucille if she can ask somebody on the food committee if they can try not to be so stingy with it."

"Tell me about it. Something besides that choke-me-to-death chicken breast, that tablespoon of rice and those two tiny-ass carrots, on top of that tasteless sponge cake with that white frosting," Savannah says.

"Okay! I get it. Eat before you leave home. Damn," Robin says. "It's for a good cause so stop complaining."

The screen is still frozen on the credits and no one is paying attention to them now.

"You're entirely too cynical, Savannah—you know that?" Robin says. "And stop swearing so damn much."

Savannah's mouth is in the shape of an O. She doesn't say a word because she knows Robin is probably right. "I'll work on being sweeter."

Gloria goes inside the house and comes back out with two blankets. She tosses one to Robin.

"No one has yet to answer my question. How's everybody doing? For real," says Savannah.

Everybody's thinking how best to answer.

"I'm lonely and bored," Robin says.

"I'm frustrated with myself," Bernadine says.

"I miss my husband and I'm worried about my son and my grandkids," Gloria says, pulling the blanket up to her shoulders. "What about you, Savannah?"

"I'm getting better. But I won't lie. This is some hard shit to go through. I wish I was telepathic and could see how long it's going to be before we're all in high spirits again."

"You and me both," Bernadine says.

Gloria just nods.

Robin lets out a sigh, then finishes what's left of her mojito.

"Doesn't it seem like we're always making adjustments to things we weren't responsible for or had no control over?"

They look at her: dumb-ass question, Savannah.

"And I've been thinking."

"Oh, hell," Gloria says.

"Please don't take half the night telling us," Robin says.

"Hold up," Bernadine interrupts. "First of all, the whole point of us getting together like this was meant to catch up, maybe give each other booster shots, and *then* watch the frigging movie. Otherwise, we could just watch it in the comfort of our own living rooms or curled up under our fluffy comforters. Right?"

Everybody nods their heads. True.

"I think we owe it to ourselves to start doing as much as we possibly can to make ourselves as happy as we possibly can for as long as we possibly can and to hell with all the bullshit that doesn't."

"Well, that's quite a tall order, Oprah, so why don't you tell us how in the hell we might do this?" Robin asks.

"Yeah, I'm way behind in my aha! moments," Bernadine says.

"I don't know. If I had the formula, don't you think I'd be bottling the shit and selling it?"

"Good point," Robin says. "I'm making more drinks. Who wants another mojito?" She gets up without looking to see.

"Oh, never mind. Where's the remote?" Savannah asks.

"It's in your hand," Gloria says. "I was listening, Savannah."

She presses PLAY anyway.

"I was too," Bernadine says. "I didn't know Sandra Bullock was in this movie. I like her."

"That fine-ass Terrence Howard is the one I'm waiting to see," Robin says. "I hope there's a nude scene in this one. I didn't like him when he played that pimp. Remember, Savannah?"

She shakes her head because she doesn't want to remember. "There's bottled water in the cooler," Savannah says. She's clearly annoyed by their apathy, and wants to be taken seriously. She needs their help with this.

"Finish what you were saying, girl. You know I'm interested," Bernadine says as she turns to give Savannah her full attention.

She hits the PAUSE button. "Look. We love each other like sisters, don't we?"

The three women nod. Of course they do.

"And we know we've got one another's backs at all times, right?"

They nod again.

"Then why don't we do something to try to help each other out?" Savannah says.

With their eyes, the three women are asking: Like what?

"I was reading somewhere that—"

"Hold it a minute," Bernadine says. "If this is some

kind of New Age stuff, forget it. It took us years to get Robin to stop faxing us our daily horoscopes."

"Shut up. I read online somewhere—and never mind where—that sometimes we have to reinvent ourselves."

"Okay," Gloria says.

Robin makes a face at Bernadine and presses the START button on the blender. Savannah is getting on her nerves. She's wondering what Sparrow is doing. And if she took out the trash.

"We've probably lived two thirds of our entire lives, which means if our life was a play, you could say this is our third act."

"What about intermission?"

"Would you please be quiet, Robin!" Gloria says.

"Anyway," Savannah continues, "sometimes we need somebody to just tell us what to do even though we already know it. What I'm saying is, we shouldn't be afraid to ask for help. Since we're closer than family, why don't we try to give one another one good piece of advice that might help us get stronger or whatever?"

"Savannah, you already do that," Robin says.

"I don't mean it like that, heffa. I mean, we all know some of the things we've been struggling with. Granted, some stuff we have to figure out how to deal with on our own. But there are a lot of other things we can offer each other, you know. Sound advice. Good suggestions. We weigh the pros and forget the cons. Then try whatever it is for thirty days or something. If we see some improvement we just keep doing it."

"For example?" Bernadine asks.

Gloria's thinking. She accidentally takes a sip of Robin's drink. Turns up her nose. Then takes another one.

"Let's start with me. What's the one thing you know I've been wanting to do but haven't been able to?"

"Lose weight," Bernadine says.

Savannah gives her the finger.

"Get over Isaac," Robin says.

"Getting over your ex-husband isn't a goal, because the goal was accomplished when he became the ex. What do I whine about all the time?"

"Everything," Robin says, and they all laugh, including Savannah.

"That you never do anything adventurous or interesting," Robin says.

"Well, that's about to change."

"What's that supposed to mean?" Gloria asks.

"Nothing. Strike that from the record."

"Good. Curious minds don't want to know tonight—whatever it is," Robin says. "Here's my advice to you, Savannah. Take a yoga class. Go visit your family in Pittsburgh. Get a puppy."

"I'm not getting a puppy."

"Do the story on gangs," Gloria says.

Savannah points her index finger at Gloria. "That's a good one."

"Drop your guard," Bernadine says. "Don't end up like me." She gives Savannah a little nudge with her shoulder.

"Do you guys realize how long we've been here and have yet to see five minutes of the movie? I've gotta be at work a little early tomorrow. There's been a lot of talk about a big merger so we're probably being prepped for it."

"I can tell you what you complain about all the time, Robin," Gloria says to her.

"My job, I know. And as soon as I figure out a way to quit, I'll be on it."

"Can I just tell her what I think she should do right now? Is that how we can play this game?" Gloria asks.

"This doesn't feel like a game," Bernadine says.

Gloria turns and looks directly at Robin. "I wish you would think about what else you get a charge out of doing so you can leave that job once and for all. You've been bored too long. I'd be willing to give you sixty days. How's that for starters?"

"Wait! I've got one for you, too," Savannah says. "I wish you would stop this scavenger hunt you've been on, trying to find a husband on the Internet, because you have yet to go on a decent date. At least give it a break. Try it for a month and see if you can handle the withdrawal."

"You can take that one off my to-do list. I canceled my memberships. So there."

"I'm on the same page as everybody else as far as you go, Ms. Birdie. Now, Gloria," Bernadine says. "We all know you've put a few back on since Marvin went to Heaven but we don't want to see you have another damn heart attack, okay?"

"I already know this," Gloria says. "And you're right. So I suppose this means I'm going to have to stop relying on Doritos for a kiss, gelato for a hug, sorbet for a really big hug and Jelly Bellies for sex, huh?"

Laughter. Hoots.

"As for you, Miss Bernadine," Savannah says, turning to look at her. It's obvious Bernadine is terrified she's about to say something about the pills, but they've already talked about that. "We want a new restaurant, don't we, ladies?" Savannah winks at Bernadine.

Gloria and Robin nod and nod and nod.

Bernadine looks relieved when she sees the smiles on her friends' faces. "This is the real deal. I've got four years left on the lease for Sweet Tooth. My money is starting to get a little funny since I closed, so I'm working on what my next move should be."

"Can't you turn it into a different kind of restaurant?" Gloria asks.

"It's a pretty good size," Savannah says.

"And a good location," Robin says.

"Let me tell you guys this and just get it over with. I don't know if I have it in me to run another restaurant."

"Who said you have to run it? Isn't that why folks have employees?" Savannah says.

"It's the reason why I stopped doing hair," Gloria says. "I'm the overseer."

"All you need to do is come up with some of those fancy-schmancy menus you were telling us all about and hire some of those kids fresh out of culinary school and just teach them how to prepare it," Robin adds.

"Well put, Robin. It could be fun, Bernie. You could design it the hip way we talked about, remember?" Savannah says.

"Yeah, and think about having some live music, 'cause Lord knows we need somewhere to go," Robin says.

"If you're getting low on funds, Bernie, you know all you have to do is pick up the phone," Gloria says.

"Ain't that the truth," Robin says.

"I've got access to a little loot if you need it," Savannah says. "Take some time to think about this. But not too long."

Bernadine is humbled. She can't say a word.

"I wish I had some talent," Robin says.

"Sometimes I would just like to smack you, Robin—you know that?" Savannah says.

"You and me both," Gloria says. "What *you* need to do is be a personal shopper or clean out your closets and start one of those consignment stores."

"I like the second one," Bernadine says. "I've got years' worth of stuff you can have to start your inventory."

Savannah raises her hand to ditto that.

"Actually, I think that's kind of a cool idea," Robin says.

"Just for the record: your daughter is a testament to what a good mother you are," Gloria says.

"She's a spoiled brat, but it's okay. She's smarter than I ever was and she's going to be a fantastic violinist one day. Did I tell you guys she called Russell?"

Everybody shakes their heads no.

"Yep, she reached out to him. Wants to get to know his stupid ass after all these years."

"What's wrong with that?" Bernie asks.

"Nothing, I suppose. I just don't want her to be badly influenced."

"I doubt that," Savannah says. "Russell thought he

was Mac Daddy way back when but he's not a bad guy when you get right down to it."

"You're going to have to learn how to share her," Gloria says.

"Whatever."

"Did you have a start date in mind for us, Lady Guru?" Gloria looks at Savannah.

"Shut up, Gloria. We've been friends a long time. I always thought friends tried to do things to make one another's lives better. I know I run my mouth a lot and I'm an idealist, so you guys can tell me to go straight to hell if you want to. I'm just tired of us feeling like there's no tomorrow."

"Well, let's not worry about any start dates tonight since it's not a game," Bernadine says. "Let's start by taking baby steps and see if we notice one another's progress. How's that sound to everybody?"

Nods all around.

Savannah presses PLAY again.

From the television they hear Don Cheadle: ". . . in L.A. nobody touches you. . . always behind this metal and glass. I think we miss that touch so much that we crash into each other just so we can feel something."

This time, Bernadine grabs the remote and presses PAUSE. "Has anybody noticed what I haven't mentioned this evening?"

"I thought my prayers had been answered," Savannah says.

"We thought you were finally on the road to recovery," Robin says.

"There's nothing you can say that we haven't already heard," Gloria says. "We're your friends, so say it."

"Not even close. Well, maybe a little. You know what I'd love to see happen? I would love it if every woman in America who's ever been played, betrayed, deceived or hurt by their significant other staged a one-day moratorium—no, make it a whole week—no sex, no cooking, no laundry, no housecleaning, no *nothing*, just so they can see how valuable we are."

"They still wouldn't get it," Robin says. "There are too many women out here willing to do just about anything to keep them. I should know, since I used to be one of them."

"Can I say one more thing since we're on the subject?" Savannah asks.

Gloria crosses her arms. "Do we have a choice?"

"Should I ever get an opportunity to stumble on another member of the opposite sex who rocks me even at this late stage in my life, I'm not jumping on the first train that pulls into my station. I don't want another husband. I just want somebody to have dinner with a couple of times a month. Sex twice a month—three times would be better. Somebody to travel with. Go to a concert with. The movies. And maybe spend the night every once in a while. And then send his ass home. I'll date until I'm dead."

"Well, you won't be dead before you go on your little blind date, I hope. Did you tell them about Jasper?" Bernadine asks.

"Who's Jasper?" Gloria asks.

"He's some guy my boss wants me to have coffee with in the very near future. I'm actually dreading it."

"Is he white?" Gloria asks. "With a name like Jasper."

"No, he's black. He's a surgeon. The kind that travels all over the world to help people who need it."

"I'm thinking about crossing over," Robin says.

"Crossing over what?" Gloria asks.

"The color line."

"Really?"

"You guys have never considered it?"

They all pretty much shake their heads no.

"We're stupid. Men will fuck anything, and here we are still holding on to blackness," Robin says. "We can still be black and love whoever we want to. It's about time we gave ourselves more options."

"You've got a point," Savannah says.

"They're all the same," Bernadine says.

"I've always loved black men," Gloria says.

"Because you had a good one," Robin says. "Anyway, I'm thinking about going Asian. Maybe Japanese. You know that fine Watanabe guy who was in *The Last Samurai* with Tom Cruise?"

"He's Japanese?" Savannah asks.

"Yes, Lord. And fine as he wants to be. He's also tall."

"I thought he was black. Just mixed with something."

"Nope. He's one hundred percent Japanese. I'd give him some in a heartbeat."

"Not too many black men want old pussy, Robin. What makes you think a Japanese guy would want it?" Bernadine asks.

"'Cause I still know how to make it snap."

Bernadine presses PLAY.

"Pause it, Bernie! You guys are gonna hear my joke, since the movie's not going to start anytime this year."

"Tell the doggone joke, Robin," Gloria says. "And it better be funny."

"Okay. You guys are gonna love this: Su Wong marries Lee Wong. The next year, the Wongs have a new baby. The nurse brings over a lovely, healthy, bouncy, but definitely Caucasian, white baby boy.

"'Congratulations,' says the nurse to the new parents.

"'Well, Mr. Wong, what will you and Mrs. Wong name the baby?'

"The puzzled father looks at his new baby boy and says, 'Well, two Wongs don't make a white, so I think we will name him . . . Sum Ting Wong.'"

All three are laughing.

Robin is pleased. "See, I told you it was funny."

"Thanks for sharing, you silly bitch," Bernadine says.

"I think we should stop calling each other bitches. It just doesn't sound right anymore," Savannah says.

"I agree, bitch," Robin says to her.

"Okay, maybe if we say it like that, because that was touching, Robin."

"It was," Gloria says, "but I don't like that word or the N word or the F word either. I took them out of my vocabulary a long time ago. We can live without all of them."

"Then let's just agree not to refer to any woman—black or white or otherwise—this way. If we say it to each other with affection, we'll take it as such?" Bernadine asks.

"That'll work for me, bitch." Robin giggles.

"You guys will always be my bitches," Savannah says, keeling over. "What about *ho*?" Savannah asks.

"That one stays," Robin says.

"I don't know any," Bernadine says.

"I know one and her name is Nickida," Gloria says.

They've all gotten the lowdown and were equally shocked.

"I hope Tarik puts her out to pasture and leaves her there. Some things you just don't do," Bernadine says.

"I have never cheated on a boyfriend, let alone my husband," Savannah says. "Have any of you?"

They shake their heads no.

"Are they going to get divorced?" Robin asks. "That's probably a dumb question."

"He filed a few days ago."

"What about the kids?" Bernadine asks.

"The court'll decide if she's fit to share custody. I'm praying she only gets supervised visits."

"I wouldn't trust her with my dogs," Robin says.

"I'm sure it wasn't the first time she'd done the nasty with her ex, and Lord only knows who else," Bernadine says.

"Something like this could cost Tarik his job," Savannah says.

"Well, I might be going to rehab," Bernadine says.

"Thank you, thank you, thank you!" Savannah reaches over and hugs her. Robin and Gloria charge down the steps and do the same.

"Is this the only way you know how to tell us important stuff, Bernie? Just dropping it out of nowhere like this?" Gloria asks.

"Sometimes I'm too scared."

"I hear you, girl. And I'm sorry for saying it like that. You don't have to explain a thing," Gloria says.

"You certainly don't," Robin says. "We've just been waiting for you to do something about this."

"Then why didn't anybody say anything?"

"We've tried," Robin says.

"You didn't hear us," Savannah says. "We figured when you got tired you'd hold up that white flag. We weren't about to let anything happen to you—that much we can say, right?"

Robin and Gloria nod their heads.

"So, how long and when and where do you think you might be going?" Savannah asks.

"I've been looking at some places online. There's a good one in Tucson but it's really expensive and they don't accept insurance. There are a lot of reputable ones in California that do."

"Have you talked to anybody yet?" Robin asks.

"I've called and hung up. I'm not sure what to say."

"Try telling them the truth, Bernie," Gloria says.

"I don't know what that is."

"Do you really think you're addicted?" Robin asks.

Bernadine nods. "I don't take a lot of them but I've been taking them too long."

"Have you ever tried just stopping?" Robin asks.

Before Bernadine can answer, Gloria says, "She could get really messed trying to quit cold turkey. It's better to do it under the care of a doctor or people who can help her get through the detoxing stage. That's the hardest part."

"How do you know so much about this?" Savannah asks her.

"Girl, I have heard and seen some of everything down at Oasis. Joline even told me how she kicked a sixty-pill-a-day Vicodin habit."

"Sixty?" Robin says. "How could you swallow that many pills in one day?"

"You'd be surprised," Gloria says. "They've done specials on every kind of drug you can think of. Haven't you guys ever seen them? Especially you, Savannah."

"I've seen some on alcohol, crystal meth and that OxyContin stuff, but not tranquilizers."

"And an occasional sleeping pill," Bernadine throws in.

"Do whatever you have to do, Bernie. And whatever you need us to do, we'll do it. We're very proud of you, girl," Savannah says and sits straight up. "Since we're confessing. I'm going somewhere too. Paris."

"Where?" Bernadine asks. She turns to look at Savannah as if she doesn't know who she is.

"Did you just say Paris?" Robin asks.

"Yes, I said Paris."

"When? How? And when did you decide to do this? I know you're not going by yourself," Robin says.

"I most certainly am."

"Can I go with you?"

"Robin, shut up," Bernadine says. "You could certainly use a vacation, Savannah."

"We all could. And Robin? No, you cannot go with me. Maybe next time."

"Why not? Don't you need somebody to keep you company?"

Savannah shakes her head. "I'm going for two weeks. For the same reason Bernie's going to rehab. To find my center. I need a break from everything. So I can accept the reality that I'm a fifty-one-year-old single woman. Which means I need to launch a whole new program to help me live like this is a new beginning instead of an ending."

"Well, when did you decide all this? Without telling anybody?" Robin is pissed.

Gloria shakes her head at Robin, then looks at Savannah and says, "You go on, girl, and go."

"I wasn't trying to keep it a secret, Robin. I just wanted to put it in motion before I talked myself out of it."

"Smart move," Bernadine says. "Very smart."

"Anyway, my boss has a gorgeous apartment over there and she's letting me stay in it for free."

"I think it's wonderful and exciting, and one day I'd like to do something like this," Gloria says.

"I know you'd let me come with you, huh, Glo?"

Gloria rolls her eyes at Robin, then smiles. "I pray you find a husband soon, so you can drive him crazy everywhere you go."

"Hey," Savannah says. "We can go anywhere we feel like going. All we have to do is whip out a credit card and buy the damn ticket and go."

"Won't you be scared, going by yourself?" Robin asks.

"Scared of what?"

"Strangers."

"You deal with strangers every single day online. Are you scared?"

"I closed all six of my accounts. I'm finished with all of that."

"Hallelujah!" Gloria says.

"You were on six different sites? You should've had four or five husbands by now," Savannah says.

"What happened to Hark Angel?" Bernadine asks.

"*Dark* Angel. Don't even mention him. He's history. If I do anything else, it'll be speed dating."

No one wants to respond to this.

"Anyway," Savannah says. "A change of scenery is good for the soul. As the saying goes, sometimes you have to step outside of yourself in order to see yourself. So I'm going to Paris to rejuvenate." She lets out a huge sigh. "And to shop."

Bernadine presses PLAY, then tosses the remote onto a patch of grass. They all curl up. And watch the movie. Finally.

I'd Rather Work at Walmart

When I walk into the office, something isn't right. My department head isn't in his glass cage like he's been for the past two hundred years. It's lit up, so that means nothing has happened to him. Thank God. His name is Horace Mann. For years I got his name confused with Thomas Mann, the guy who wrote *Death in Venice*. I paid attention in high school, of course, but I'm now an official member of the CRS—Can't Remember Shit—club, along with every other woman pushing fifty. I wonder where he could be. He's like a voyeur. Watches everybody come and go. He also lives on his computer.

I don't see Lucille either, which is weird. She's usually the first one here and the last to leave. Lucille is a VP—same as me and Norman. She's rather bitchy, with a headmistress demeanor. For the past twelve years she's worn a number of stingy black wigs with tight curls, and black-rimmed glasses that push the hair out and away from her ears. It adds ten years to her fifty-three. Lucille also dresses like she's going to a funeral, which makes her unattractive. She's divorced, and it's no wonder. She's all work and no play. Word around the office is Lucille hasn't had sex in a decade. It certainly shows. She rarely smiles. But I still like her.

Her office, which is right before you get to mine, is always spotless. This morning it looks even more like an ad in the Office Depot catalog. I don't see Norman. This is about the time he goes downstairs to get the paper and his Earl Grey tea. Fernando is sitting in his little cubicle, pretending to be engrossed in his work. He is such a bullshitter. He's a smart one. If only he could step up to the plate more often, he'd have a bright future with this company.

"Robin," I hear Horace say before I reach my office.

"Good morning, Horace." I turn to face him. He's six-five and shaped like an egg. "Is there a meeting or something going on that I wasn't told about?"

"Well, yes and no. However, would you mind meeting me in the conference room?"

"Sure, just let me put my things in my office. Do I have time to run downstairs to get a latte?"

"No. This won't take long. In fact, it'd be best if you could join us now."

"Okay." I follow him. I'm wondering if this is about that merger. It probably is. I'm feeling suspicious, especially since Lucille isn't around to tell me what the hell is going on. "Has anybody heard from Lucille? It's not like her to be late. I hope she's not sick."

"I'm not sure," he says.

When we get to the conference room, there's a red-headed fellow with a tan who I know works in Human Resources. He's sitting at the conference table closest to the window. This morning, the mountains, which I normally don't pay much attention to, seem bigger, closer, much more imposing than their normal postcard backdrop.

"Good morning, Ms. Stokes. I'm Daniel Merrick, from Human Resources. Would you mind having a seat?"

"If this won't take long, I'd prefer to stand, if you don't mind."

I'm wondering what's in that manila envelope, although I think I already know. I still want to hear it. Mr. Mann is standing at the far end of the table. He looks pasty. His jawbone is jumping. The sweat on his freshly shaved skin is glistening. "What's this about?" I ask the HR guy before either of them has a chance to speak. I'm not stupid. I've heard about how these things go down. Nevertheless, I want freckle-face here to tell me in his very own hit-the-road language.

"As you know, Ms. Stokes, the company has been undergoing some tough times over the past few years. Profits are down and losses are up. This is one of the reasons for our impending merger."

I feel my hips rock. My weight shifts to one leg. I know this is tacky and ghetto, but sometimes my body has its own brain. I feel like I'm rolling my eyes at him but I will them to stop. I also want to cross my arms. I don't do this either. Instead, I stand there like a slave about to be sold—all for their live entertainment. I'm just waiting for those magic words to roll off his tongue.

He clears his throat. "As a result of this shift, we're being forced to make some adjustments in personnel—namely a reduction." He opens that large manila envelope, pulls out the company's white one and hands it to me. What a fucked-up job he has. "We have truly valued your contribution to the company over the past eighteen years, and you'll see evidence of this outlined in the severance package we're offering you."

I reach down and pick up the envelope. "Am I supposed to open this right now?"

"Yes."

"I'd rather take it to my office and read it."

"We'd appreciate it if you would take a look at the terms and conditions now. Someone will then escort you out of the building."

"Escort me out of the building?"

"Yes, Ms. Stokes. Your office has already been packed up and all of your personal belongings are in those boxes over there."

I look down and see all the stuff I've accumulated over the years. This office was my second home. I can't believe these bastards had the nerve to go through my cabinets and drawers and apparently even the closet. This feels exactly the same as when my apartment got robbed right after college. It is such a violation. Such an invasion of my fucking privacy. In those boxes are everything from my feminine hygiene products and makeup to workout clothes along with soiled socks stuck inside a pair of running shoes. Panty hose. I even see my snacks and perishable food they took out of the little fridge behind my desk. These bastards. Two of my favorite umbrellas and my black patent-leather raincoat. It's balled up. These bastards. Worst of all, on top of one box in a double frame are two pictures of my mom and dad: when they were married in 1942, and on their fiftieth wedding anniversary. These bastards. Beside them is a picture of Romeo and Juliet dressed in red and white, sitting on Santa's lap with Sparrow, who looks bored. Then there are my yellow tulips in two glass vases sitting in water. Everybody thinks they're real. I am not, however, like them: dead in the water. Not even close.

I rip open the envelope. There is a check inside I don't bother to look at because no matter what the amount, it couldn't possibly be enough to compensate me for all the fucking years I've given this fucking company. I don't feel like reading the letter. I fold the papers and shove them back inside the envelope. "What about what's on my computer?"

"It's company property."

"But I've got personal as well as private information on that computer!"

"It's company property, Ms. Stokes. We're also going to need your parking pass and your BlackBerry, as well as the security card that lets you into the building."

"Anything else?" I ask while whipping all of this stuff out of my purse and tossing it on the table. Some of it slides right in front of Mr. HR.

"We would like you to know you are eligible for rehire should things change. We've paid you for all sick and vacation days, and you have the option of continuing your health insurance through COBRA. To show our appreciation for your contribution to the company, we've given you two weeks' severance pay for each year of service. We hope you'll find this agreeable."

"I can't thank you enough." I turn to leave.

"Oh, one last thing, Ms. Stokes. The terms of your termination must be kept confidential insofar as other employees are concerned."

"So you're saying I'm not allowed to tell anybody who works here why or how you fired me?"

"We're not firing you."

"Well, thanks for the advance notice. But you want to know something?"

Mr. Mann looks fearful and Mr. HR looks like he's prepared to call security, which I will learn when I walk out of here is standing right outside the door. I guess this is why people go *postal*, but they have no idea what a favor they've done for me, which is why I look at them and say, "I'd like to thank you both for giving me the opportunity to work here for the past eighteen years, but now I think I'd rather work at Walmart."

I'm so pissed off, I'm shaking. I pick up one of my boxes and push the other one with my foot. The security guard offers to help and I tell him no thank you. I can manage. When I glance around the corner to see if Lucille is here—and of course she's not—I hope she realizes now how coming in early all these years didn't pay off. As I press the elevator button and get on, I see Norman. He doesn't see me yet. His instincts were right this time. Norman's a quiet yet friendly guy, widowed forever and with no children. He's shown us photos of property he bought in Costa Rica because he was planning to build on it when he retired in four years. Mr. Mann is leading him toward the conference room, too. Poor Norman. I push the boxes over to the side and pretend to be searching for something in my purse. I want to look as frazzled as I usually do when I'm on my way to a meeting. I don't bother to look up until after the doors squish shut. *We are all just a fucking number* is what I'm thinking when the doors pop open to the parking garage.

The boxes barely fit in my car. I put one on the backseat and the other on the passenger seat. I get behind the wheel and sit for what feels like hours. Eventually I put the key in the ignition. I'm wondering if what just happened really happened. If I really and truly no longer have a job. I suddenly feel scared as hell and yet relieved at the same time. It is not a good feeling, because I don't know which one I should trust. I turn the key hard. I gun the engine. It sounds loud down here. Not loud enough. I gun it again and again and again, until I see the exhaust coming from the tailpipe.

When I come to my senses, I look around to see if anyone has noticed, and there, standing a few feet away, is Norman. He has no boxes, just an outdated attaché case and a plaque he got ten years ago for doing something none of us who went into his office ever paid any attention to. Right now, those spider veins on his face look like a map. That brown plaid jacket he has worn on a weekly basis no matter what the temperature is drooping off his shoulders. Norman looks like he's lost weight. Our eyes meet. Mine say, "What are you going to do now, Norman?" His say, "I don't know."

He waves. I try to smile as I wave back, and then I back out of my parking space. I have no idea what a person is supposed to do when they don't have a job anymore. What on earth do you do when you have nothing but free time?

I decide to go to one of my favorite outlets. I float in and out of one store after another, trying on expensive clothes

I wouldn't ordinarily look at twice. Almost all of them are orange. I'm waiting for that thrill I usually get. I don't feel it. It doesn't stop me from trying. After three hours, the only thing I remember buying is a pair of snakeskin cowboy boots (I don't even like cowboy boots); sexy lingerie from Victoria's Secret that I'll probably never wear; a neon blue Nano for Sparrow and a silver one for me. I get new outfits for Romeo and Juliet, one of which they already have.

I buy so much stuff I have to make four trips to the parking lot because I can't carry it all. I shove so many bags into my Porsche, I have no idea how they all fit. The sound of each bag rubbing against another is so pronounced, I feel like throwing them all out the window.

—

I'm hoping Sparrow is still at practice. However, the first thing I see when I hit the garage door opener is her hybrid. I can't tell where that hole was she made in the wall. The damage to my Porsche wasn't as bad as she thought. I leave everything I bought in the car. I'll get it when I get it. The kids jump and bounce and bark when they see me. It doesn't seem cute today.

Sparrow appears at the top of the stairwell. "Are you all right, Mom?"

"Why wouldn't I be?"

"Because I know what happened."

"And just how would you know what happened to me today?"

"Because I called you at work and they said you didn't work there anymore. And I know you didn't quit. You got riffed. We study this in civics class, and a hecka lot of my friends' parents have had the exact same thing happen to them. I'm really sorry, Mom." She comes down and puts her arms around me like I'm her little girl. "We'll be fine. I'll start looking for a part-time job tomorrow. You can have as much of my check as you need. All of it."

"Thank you, baby. We don't have to worry about any of that right now. This is probably for the best. It just knocks the wind out of you. I'll be fine. We'll be fine. How are you?"

She turns to run back upstairs and then stops. "I think my heart was broken today, too. Gustav broke up with me."

"Why?"

"He says he thinks he's gay. I asked him how do you *think* it? Anyway, I told him never mind trying to explain it. We're still going to hang out and do stuff because we like each other's heads. So, I guess I've got a new friend. Anyway, I've got studying to do. I'm going to say good night. Good night, Mom. I love you." She trounces up the stairs and closes her door, and within minutes I hear her playing the violin.

I want to tell somebody what happened today but don't think I have any energy left to repeat it. When the phone rings I answer it without bothering to check caller ID.

"What're you up to?" Savannah asks.

"Oh, not much. I went on a shopping spree today."

"So, what else is new?"

"Oh, nothing, really. Oh yeah, I almost forgot. I did get canned today."

"You got *what*?"

"You heard right."

"You're not saying you were fired?"

"They call it downsizing since we . . . I mean, they're going through a merger. Same thing. They do it like they're the Gestapo and you're a spy or something. They actually put all of my shit in boxes and wouldn't even let me go into my office."

"Damn. I'm really, really sorry to hear this, Robin."

"I know. I'm still trying to digest it. But at least they gave me a decent-enough severance package. Enough to keep me going for a while."

"I know this is a stupid question, and you may not have had time to think about it yet: but what are you going to do?"

"I have no idea, Savannah. None whatsoever."

"Wanna go to Paris?"

Before I can register that Savannah is really inviting me to go with her, and before I can even think long enough about whether I could afford it, and before I can take another three seconds to weigh the pros and cons, but mostly before she has a chance to come to her senses and change her mind, I say, "Hell yeah!"

Stick a Fork in Me: I'm Done

"I'm a little nervous," Bernadine says.

"It's okay. I understand," the woman on the other end of the phone says. "So you think you have a problem with tranquilizers and sleeping pills. Is that right?"

"Yes."

"What kinds of tranquilizers are you taking?"

"Xanax."

"Five milligram?"

"No. Two point five."

"How many a day?"

"One. Sometimes two."

"And this is the maximum you've ever taken?"

"Yes."

"Any opiates?"

"What's that?"

"Vicodin, Percocet, things of that nature."

"No."

"That's good. Anything else?"

"Ambien."

"Five milligrams?"

"Yes."

"Every night?"

"No. But often."

"About how often?"

"It depends. Last week I took two. Some weeks none. Rarely more than two nights in a row."

"Are you taking any other types of medication?"

"Zoloft."

"Have they helped?"

"I don't know."

"And how long have you been taking these?"

"Which ones?"

"All three."

"Off and on about six years."

"What did you do during the off years?"

"Nothing."

"Any alcohol?"

"A glass of wine or a beer every now and then. But never after I've taken a Xanax."

"Do you consume any caffeine?"

"Coffee. No soda."

"How much?"

"One to two cups a day."

"When was the last time you had a Xanax?"

"Yesterday."

"What's the longest you've gone without taking one?"

"Three days."

"And how did you feel?"

"On the third day: weird."

"Did you experience any tremors?"

"No."

"Nausea?"

"Yes."

"Vomiting?"

"Yes."

"Sweats?"

"Yes."

"Any mental health diagnosis?"

"No."

"Have you ever been to any facility before?"

"No."

"Are the medications you're taking prescribed to you by your physician?"

"Of course."

"Why were they prescribed?"

"Because I was going through a bad divorce situation."

"Then you *do* have mental health issues."

"I didn't have a nervous breakdown or anything."

"That's not what we mean by it."

"Well, I don't know what you mean."

"It's okay. When was your divorce?"

"Actually, my marriage was annulled. Six years ago."

"What happened that made it tough for you?"

"I found out he was also married to another woman."

"Shut up!"

"In another state. So I've been angry and sort of numbing myself off and on all these years."

"Well, no wonder. We would call this a traumatic experience here at A New Day."

"It was very traumatic, to say the least."

"We can help you deal with the substance-abuse issue and help you begin to address some of the emotional ones, since they're obviously linked. So, you're interested in our twenty-eight-day inpatient program?"

"That's correct."

"I see you've already given us your insurance information. Is everything still current?"

"Yes, it is. I just sent it this morning."

"Okay. Let me ask you a few more questions and then I'll be able to process your application."

"May I ask you one, if you don't mind?"

"Sure," she says.

"Based on what I've told you, how long do you think it'll take me to detox?"

"Our intake specialist could better answer that. However, between us, based on your usage, and with supervision, it might take four or five days."

"Is it painful? I mean, will I freak out or anything?"

She actually chuckles. "No, you won't freak out. They'll give you medication that will keep you comfortable during detoxification."

"Thank God."

"But detoxing alone doesn't solve the problem."

"What problem is that?"

"Addiction. It's a disease."

"I've read that."

"It's a chronic illness. Just like cancer. There's no cure. But you can learn how to manage the disease."

Damn. Bernadine didn't think she had a chronic illness. She certainly didn't think taking these pills should be compared to having cancer. But she wasn't in a position to argue about that with this woman. "Thanks for clearing this up for me."

"You're quite welcome. I just have a few more questions for you. Are you having or have you had any thoughts of suicide?"

Bernadine felt like saying "Are you fucking crazy? Kill myself?" Instead, she says, "Absolutely not."

"Glad to hear that. Okay. So how soon would you like to come for treatment?"

"I don't know. Soon."

"What kind of support system do you have?"

"Really good friends."

"And do you work outside of the home?"

"No."

"And how would you feel about going to a meeting tonight?"

"What kind of meeting?"

"Narcotics Anonymous."

Bernadine wanted to ask, "Aren't those meetings full of die-hard drug addicts and junkies?" Instead she says: "I don't think I can make it tonight. I'm exhausted just doing this."

"Not to worry. But for now, you're okay, then?"

"Yes."

"Then I'll try to push your application through. After we get confirmation from your insurance company, someone will be in touch with you. How's that sound?"

"Good," she says. "And thank you."

"Thank you for calling A New Day."

Bernadine hangs up and just sits there without moving for about an hour. For some reason, she decides to check her e-mail—something she hasn't done in weeks. There are three jokes from Robin. She opens the first one: "Two little old ladies were sitting on a park bench outside the local town hall where a flower show was in progress . . ."

When the phone rings, it's Savannah. "I think I made a big mistake inviting Robin to go to Paris with me."

"I couldn't agree more."

"You do?"

"Of course. It was a nice gesture, Savannah, all things considered. But let's face it. Robin's a latte with two shots and no foam. Although she's our friend, you need to do this the way you planned it. Hold on, I've got another call coming in."

"No. Go ahead and take it. We can talk later. Thanks, girl."

Bernadine doesn't bother checking to see who it is before clicking over. "Hello."

"Yes, is Bernadine Harris available?"

"May I ask who's calling?" Bernadine doesn't recognize the voice.

"Yes, my name is Rowena and I'm calling from A New Day Recovery Center."

"Yes," Bernadine says suspiciously, as she pushes herself forward in the chair so her bare feet are flat on the floor.

"I've got good news for you. Your insurance company is willing to cover all but twenty percent of the cost of treatment."

"Really?"

"That's pretty good. So does this mean you'd be able to pay the difference?"

"Yes, I can."

"Fantastic. How soon would you be able to come?"

"I don't know. How soon could I come?"

"How does day after tomorrow sound?"

"You mean this Sunday?"

"Will that not work for you?"

Bernadine almost can't breathe. The thought of actually going through with this has been in her head for so long—now that the reality of it is here, she's panicking. It's difficult for her to take in air. She tries not to pant, but it's impossible.

"Are you all right?"

She reaches inside her purse, takes out a Xanax and swallows it. Her forehead is wet. She wipes it dry. "I'm fine," Bernadine says. "Sunday works for me."

———

She calls John.

"I need to tell you something," she says. Bernadine has no idea what made her call him first.

"I think I may already know. Whatever you need, Bernie: just say the word."

"I need your help." She also can't believe she just came out and said this to her ex-husband. She has never asked him or anybody for help—until an hour and a half ago. "I have a problem," she says.

"I know, Bernie. This is me you're talking to."

She's trying her damnedest not to cry but it's hard.

"It's okay. Taylor told me you might be going some-where. I found out it wasn't a class. I told you, you can't trust her with a secret, didn't I?"

Bernadine starts laughing.

"She said she lost one mother, she didn't want to lose another one."

"Thank Ms. Big Mouth for me, would you, John? It's Xanax and an occasional sleeping pill. I just want to get my life back."

"Don't we all? May I please say something?"

"Go ahead," she says, somewhat apprehensively.

"I think I may have something to do with this."

"What are you talking about, John?"

"I broke your heart."

"You didn't break my heart. You betrayed me but that was so long ago I barely remember it."

"I'm the one who started this. Not James. I'm the one who disappointed you on a grand level."

"Can we not go there?"

"No. I think it's important that you know I accept some responsibility for the invisible bruises you've been walking around with all these years. James's bullshit only exacerbated it. You haven't deserved any of this, Bernie."

"Okay. I thank you for caring."

"Don't try to brush this off. I've thought about this for years. Don't think Kathleen's exit wasn't my comeuppance. I'm very much aware of that."

"She made you happy, though, for years, John. Come on."

"The same holds true for us, doesn't it? We fell in love in college, Bernie. We were married for eleven wonderful years and I just took all of it for granted. Look where I am now."

"You'll be fine. Maybe Kathleen will come back."

"She won't be coming back anytime soon. We're divorced. I'm glad, if you can believe that. She also wants Taylor to come visit her in London, but Taylor doesn't want to."

"Why can't she come here?"

"Apparently she hates Phoenix."

"Well, isn't that just too fucking bad."

"Taylor feels the same way. Anyway, we'll be fine. I just want to make sure you're going to be."

"Thanks for what you just said, John."

"May I ask you something, Bernie?"

"I'm listening."

"When did you stop hating me?"

"I never really hated you."

"You most certainly did."

"Okay. I can't remember."

"Do you remember forgiving me?"

Bernadine gives that one some thought. Draws a blank.

"Something happened that allowed you to let me off the hook. You don't remember what that was?"

Her chest sinks. She does remember. "It wasn't one thing, John. After a while, I realized it was wearing me out inside. Not you. That resenting you, holding you hostage and blaming you for my pain wasn't making it go away. You were living your life. I wasn't. That's when I decided to let it go."

"Why can't you do the same thing with James?"

"Because I haven't tried," she hears herself say. "Because I've felt that the longer I hate him, eventually he'll feel it."

"If that were possible, hypothetically speaking, then what?"

"Then we'd be even."

"Is that what you really think?"

"No."

"I hope not, Bernie. You need to let yourself off the

hook. Because this isn't about James anymore. Don't you get that?"

"I'm moving in that direction. What I do know is all this negative energy has contaminated too many areas of my life. And I'm starting to see that my happiness is more important than my unhappiness. That's the pill I need to swallow."

"Okay. So tell me what I can do. You need me to pay for this? Just say the word."

"No."

"I know these places are off the chart. I don't care how much, Bernie."

"My insurance covers most of it."

"That's good. But what about your bills? The mortgage payment."

"What about my bills, and what makes you think I have a mortgage payment?"

"I know how hard it's been for you, Bernie. I know what that asshole did to you financially. You've just been too damn stubborn and proud to say anything to anybody."

"What else do you think you know?"

"I know I've paid off the second mortgage and the lease on your old café for the next four years, and I cannot wait to see what kind of hip new restaurant you plan to put in it after you get back home and get your bearings."

"Who said anything about a new restaurant?"

"Taylor. Who else? Well, she told me all about your menus and she said she saw some design ideas from photos you've ripped out of magazines."

"That girl."

"Do something exciting, Bernie. Something outrageous and different. Make it joyful. I'll pay for the architect. Renovations. Whatever it takes. Don't fight this. Please."

Bernadine is literally speechless. Her lips are trembling. She does not know what to say. Finally, she says, "Thank you, John."

"No worries. By the way, check your in-box. I sent you the floor plans for some of the properties I'd like you to take a look at. None of them would work for a restaurant. You could certainly lease them out. Nothing like income property."

"You're the best ex-husband, John."

"I'm your friend, Bernie. Now. You still haven't asked me to do anything yet. I'm listening."

"Would you be able to drive me to Palm Springs?"

"Of course."

"In two days?"

"The sooner the better is what I always say."

"Oh shit! Wait! I forgot! John Jr.'s coming next week! There's no way I can—"

"You can and you will. He'll be fine. Our son is a grown man who's going to be a father soon, so he'll just have to be patient."

"What can you tell him, John?"

"The truth, Bernie. It's fine. And I'll tell Onika when she gets home in two weeks. They know what time it is—as they say—so this shouldn't be anything they can't handle."

Bernadine feels a sense of calmness inside. Xanax has never made her feel this way.

"Anything else you can think of?" he asks.

"No. Except. Thank you, again."

"You're quite welcome. It's the least I can do."

Is That Your Final Answer?

I've been having a fantastic pity party. I'm on day three. Tomorrow it ends. I'm suffering in bed because I feel worthless. I even think my soul hurts. I'm not sure yet if this sauvignon blanc is helping, but I'm giving this bottle the opportunity to lift my spirits. I can't remember how to tell if you're drunk or not. Savannah is coming over sometime this evening so I'm trying very hard to pace myself. I'm also watching Halle Berry in *Catwoman*. I would kill for her body and those cheekbones. Bitch. Whoops! Not supposed to say that anymore. Huzzie!

I've been trying to read *What Should I Do with My Life?* by that fine-ass Po Bronson. Now that's a white boy I would go out with. Maybe he could help me find another job. He did say something I thought was deep and totally agree with. Po said: "We want to know where we're headed—not to spoil our own ending by ruining the surprise, but we want to ensure that when the ending comes, it won't be shallow. We will have done something. We will not have squandered our time here."

I don't mind doing a little squandering today. Sometimes you need a break from the pressures of the real world. This is why I bought two bottles of this blanco. On top of trying to find a new direction for my life, I figured I could also be entertained. I'm surrounded by a sea of novels I've been meaning to read since forever: *What You Owe Me, Soul Kiss, Discretion, You Know Better, A Love of My Own* and *Understand This.* But where to start? I don't know. You can get a lot of inspiration from books. First, you actually have to read them. What is Halle doing out on that ledge? Trying to save a cat? Is she crazy? I can't remember how long it takes her to turn into Cat-woman. I do not have all night. That's not true. I do. I'm bored. For the hundredth time today. I wish I could con-centrate on something for more than a few minutes. I fast-forward Halle a few scenes, then decide to watch TV until it gets to the good part. I saw bits and pieces of this movie with Sparrow and of course she had to narrate.

I'm still in my pajamas and I'm glad Sparrow's out with her friends and not practicing the violin, which would probably send me right over the edge this evening. It's so melancholy. I'm also glad she understands that her mom's been feeling a little purple since she got axed. And I just need to play this all the way out before I get it back together. She's never seen me like this although she seems to enjoy taking care of me. I can't eat her so-called cooking. I also haven't had much of an appetite. I've had oatmeal and raisins for breakfast and lunch. I have self-pity for dinner.

I wish Savannah would hurry up and get here so I can tell her I'm not going to Paris with her. I don't want to be a burden. I know she was just feeling sorry for me. Well, maybe not *sorry*. She was caught up in the moment and, because she cares about me, opened her big mouth and invited me. I bet it was probably a matter of hours before she called Bernie up and said: "Girl, I think I made a major mistake." And then Bernie would have asked her: "How?" And Savannah probably said, "I opened my big fucking mouth and invited Robin to go to Paris with me because she sounded so pathetic right after she got fired." Savannah made it crystal clear on Blockbuster Night she didn't want anybody going over there with her.

I don't need to spend money for a vacation when I don't have any coming in. Thanks to my dad, I'm somewhat set up, but I need to know what it feels like to be frugal. I spend way too much money on bullshit. Plus, Savannah didn't say a thing about my staying in that apartment with her. I wasn't about to ask. Everybody knows how expensive hotels are all over Europe.

I stare at the television and here comes yet another commercial about a cure for suffering from something. I take a tiny sip of my wine instead of a long, slow one. Yes, I wanted to change jobs. One day. Yes, I did my job by rote. No, I wasn't challenged. Yes, I'm worried about how I want to spend the rest of my life. No, I haven't thought that far ahead. Of course I'm probably supposed to look at this as some kind of blessing. I'm not feeling it. Of course things happen for a reason and this is probably a chance for me to reevaluate what I might really enjoy doing. As of this moment, I have yet to think of anything that would lift my skirt.

If I see one more commercial for Viagra, I swear to God, I might just go out and find me a guy who's been stricken with all the side effects, because at this point, I'd take a sixty-year-old blind deaf-mute on Viagra with a four-hour erection, three or four times a month, and call it a fucking day. How lucky could a woman get?

This wine is good.

What is *going on*? This is like the third or fourth or fifth commercial for an antidepressant I've seen tonight. As a matter of fact I've been noticing just how many prime-time ads all seem to be pushing pills for whatever might ail you. Apparently it's a lot. Are we baby boomers the new geriatrics or what? One week I wondered if I had restless leg syndrome. Then I worried about fibromyalgia—whatever it is. Whatever happened to Crest? And Oil of Olay and "Where's the beef?"

There are so many commercials for antidepressants that if you aren't depressed you feel like maybe you're the one missing out. I'm starting to wonder if I should get a few months' supply of Cymbalta to help me wade through this rough patch, although I don't think I make a good candidate for depression. Feeling sorry for myself takes too much time and energy. I'm also finding out how hard it is to do nothing. Three days is long enough to be blue. Tomorrow I hit the gym. I'm going to sweat out every drop of despair. And booze.

I switch back to *Catwoman* and there is Halle in her tight black jumpsuit, looking like the sexiest cat I have ever seen on two legs. You go, Halle. After a few more minutes I realize I'm not in the mood for watching her prey on folks.

Uh-oh. Savannah's here. Romeo and Juliet look nervous. I hear her knocking hard. She never rings the doorbell. "I'm coming! Hold your horses!" I dash down the stairs, feeling a little light-headed, so I cool my jets.

Before I open the door I press my cheek against it: "Don't say a word about how bad I look, because I haven't been in any mood for dressing up, okay?"

"Okay! Open the door, please, Robin! I have to go to the bathroom, badly!"

She dashes past me in very tight denim capris. "Savannah, have you lost a few pounds?"

"You must be delusional," she says from behind the door.

"I think you have. Your ass looks smaller."

"It's not. Believe me. It's called Lycra."

"So, how was your date?"

"It's a week from Sunday."

"Are you psyched?"

She comes out, stands in the hallway and crosses her arms. "Not really. I'm not looking for a new love just yet, Robin. How long have you been in those pajamas?"

I look down. "Three days."

"Does that mean you haven't bathed?"

"I guess not."

"We're going to change that."

"I don't feel like being clean."

"You'll feel better. Come on." She takes me by the arm and pulls me upstairs to my bathroom. She begins to run me a bath, pours in my favorite bubble bath. I sit on the toilet. "Stand up, Robin."

I do. She puts the seat cover down. "I see you've had a few, huh?"

"A girl's just gotta have fun, sometimes."

"Can you get out of those pajamas?"

I look down. Why are there so many buttons on this top?

"Don't worry about it. Where do you keep your hairbrush?"

I point to a drawer.

She gets it out, along with a scrunchie, and pulls my hair up into a ponytail. "Stand up, Robin." She unbuttons my top and pulls my bottoms down. I hold on to her shoulder for balance. She tests the water. "Go ahead, sweetie. Get in."

I do exactly that.

"This all makes sense, Robin. And mark my words, it'll be better soon."

"What makes you so sure?"

"Because this is just a transition."

She hands me my sponge ball.

"It's bullshit. That's what this is, Savannah."

"I know. But you have a chance to start fresh."

"Fresh?"

"When we're in Paris. You can think about which direction you might want to explore."

"I'm not going to Paris with you, Savannah."

"Yes, you are." She flops down on the toilet seat a little too hard. I kind of chuckle.

"It was a nice gesture. And you know I appreciate it, but I really need to stay here and get my life together."

"Your life hasn't fallen apart, Robin. You just don't have a job. Where's Sparrow?"

"At midnight bowling."

"But it's not midnight."

"They start early."

"It sounds like fun."

"It is. It's more like a club. Neon lights. A DJ who plays nothing but hip-hop music. They dance and every-thing."

"Is it only for teenagers?"

"No."

"We should go."

"Not on the nights they go."

"We could start a night for us boomers."

"Do you know how to bowl?"

"Roll the ball down the middle of the lane and knock over the fucking pins. Duh."

This is funny. Savannah is a hoot sometimes. I'm glad she's here, glad she's my friend.

"I still like to dance. Don't you?" she asks.

"Speaking of dances."

"Don't go there. Please! Give it a rest or I'll get up from this toilet seat and drown your ass!"

"Okay, okay. How long were you planning on staying this evening?" I ask her.

"Until we work this out."

"Work what out?"

"Your future. Paris."

"I already said I'm not going, Savannah."

"But I invited you."

"I'm uninviting me."

"You should come anyway."

"Are you deaf? You *should* go by yourself. Just the way you planned. I need to stay here and figure out what I'm going to do next."

"Are you sure you won't come?"

"Not now. Another time."

"And that's your final answer?"

"That's it. And thank you for inviting me, Savannah."

"You're quite welcome."

She stands up. "All right, get your ass out of there. You should be sparkling clean. I didn't see you wash those ears! Where's a clean towel?"

"Open that cabinet. They're in there. You want some wine?"

"No, thank you. And you're not having any more either."

She hands me the towel. I wrap it around myself.

"You're in good shape, Robin. I swear you make me want to exercise."

"You will when it's important enough to you."

"That would be, like, last year. Anyway, put on a pair of fresh pajamas and meet me downstairs."

"Yes, ma'am."

I do as I'm told. When I get downstairs, Savannah is helping herself to one of my Lean Cuisines. I sit at the table in the nook and cup my chin inside my hand. "It looks like I'm still unemployed."

"You know, Robin, let's get this over with, okay?"

"Okay."

"We all know you were tired of that boring-ass job and you'd reached that stupid glass ceiling, right?"

I nod.

"Think of this as a blessing."

"Please don't start with that blessing stuff. It's so lame."

"I'll put it this way. You have no idea what opportunities might be out there waiting for you to seize them."

"That's another one! Have you started going back to church again?"

"Shut up, Robin. No. Although it's not a bad idea."

"I don't know how to handle this, okay? I've never been unemployed before."

"You have a degree in business. You also have something most people who lose their jobs don't have. Backup funds."

"I don't think about that money because it's for when I'm older."

"And when does that start?"

"I need some new skills. The kind that are marketable."

"Then go back to school and get some."

"I'm too old to go back to college, Savannah."

"That is the biggest crock of shit I've heard in a long time. Too old to learn?"

"What would I look like sitting in a classroom with kids fresh out of high school?"

"Times have changed, Robin. Interspersed in most of those classes are students of all ages and backgrounds. There's a lot of people who've decided to change lanes, even after years of being successful. You tell me where it's written that you have to be eighteen to get into college?"

"You've got a point. I don't think I'd feel right."

"Then you should think about what Gloria suggested."

"You mean opening my own consignment shop?"

"I looked it up. Check your in-box for a change. There's more than fifteen thousand of them all over the United States. That should tell you something. You'd be your own boss. Blah blah blah. I'm not trying to do a hard sell, but it sounds like it's right up your alley."

"I do love to shop. I wonder if I'd get the same charge watching other people do it?"

"Have you been back to that yoga class?"

"No. I was waiting for you."

"Don't hold your breath."

"Okay, so can you, like, go home now? I'm tired."

"You're buzzed. There's a big difference."

"Show yourself out. And thanks again." I give her a hug then head back up to my room. I fall across the bed. I think I hear the door close. Then again, it could be Halle, kicking her neighbors' door in when they refuse to turn that music down.

———

I keep my word. In the morning, I go to the gym. I do not want to believe I have a hangover. I think I do. I've been on this treadmill for forty-three minutes. I'm dripping with perspiration and it probably reeks of sauvignon whatever. I'm taking a long sip of Cytomax when I hear a voice I haven't heard in years: "Robin Stokes. As I live and breathe."

I turn to match the voice with the face. Standing next to me is Michael, obviously reincarnated. He is not fat by a long shot. He's also handsome. What happened to those puffy cheeks? He must be gay now because he's buff. I'll bet it's from steroids. I press the STOP button. "Is that really you, Michael?"

"It is I. I was pretty sure that was you," he says. "You have just made my day. I don't believe this. I was just thinking about you this morning. Wondering what you might be up to. I kid you not."

"What are you doing here? I thought you were living in Miami?"

"I moved back to Phoenix about a year ago. I have a CPA firm. My kids have graduated from college. And I just bought a house not far from here, which is why I joined this gym. You look fantastic, Robin."

"So do you, Michael. I almost didn't recognize you."

"I've lost a few pounds since the last time we saw each other. So how are you? What are you up to? Are you still in underwriting? Ever get married? You don't look like you've had any kids."

"As a matter of fact, I just got riffed from our old firm if you can believe it, and no, I never got married but I do have a sixteen-year-old daughter."

"You won't have any problem finding another job—that is, assuming you're looking for something in the same field."

"I don't know what I'm looking for, to be honest with you. I'll figure it out. It just happened. So, how about you, Michael? Did you ever remarry?"

"No," he says and winks at me. "Maybe I've been waiting for you."

Thank You

Gloria had no idea why the policeman was pulling her over.

She wasn't speeding. She came to complete stops when she was supposed to. She definitely wasn't tailgating. Or weaving. And Blaze and Diamond were securely strapped in their car seats. This Tahoe was much bigger than her Volvo but Gloria knew how to handle it. She hadn't broken any laws.

"Here comes the policeman, Gawa," Blaze said with a tinge of excitement in her voice. Even Diamond, who was sucking her thumb, looked rather eager.

Gloria put her flashers on and rolled the window down. "Yes, Officer. Did I do something wrong?"

"First, may I see your license and registration and proof of insurance, please? Hi there, kids."

They merely gazed at him.

After Gloria handed him the items, she turned to the kids. "It'll be okay. Don't worry."

"Well, ma'am, you were doing thirty-one in a twenty-five-mile-per-hour zone. And," he said, looking into the backseat, "I'm not sure this is such a safe way to drive with these little ones in here."

"I understand, Officer, but my speedometer is digi-

tal and it said I was only doing twenty-six. I've been driving in this neighborhood for over twenty years. It's the
route I take to work. I obey all speed limits."

"That's good to hear. For now, however, I'm going
to have to issue you a citation. I'll be right back. It'll only
take a few minutes."

"Gawa," Blaze said, and leaned forward in her car
seat so the straps made her look like a prisoner. "Fight it!
Don't pay it! Just go to court!"

Gloria turned to face her five-year-old granddaughter. "What do you know about fighting and going to
court, young lady?"

"Every time the policemens stopped my mommy, as
soon as he leaved she would say: 'I'm going to fight this
damn ticket! I'm not paying this! I'll just go to court! I
was not speeding!'"

"Oh, really," Gloria said.

Diamond was nodding her head in agreement. That
thumb was probably wrinkled by now.

When the officer returned, he handed Gloria her
papers. "You know what, ma'am? Two things. First, I saw
that you have not had any prior infractions, and two,
you're related to my buddy Tarik. Aren't you his mom?"

"I am indeed."

"He's our daddy!" Blaze yelled. Diamond nodded.

"You kids have a great dad, you know. And tell your
mom Officer Bell said hello. Would you do that for me?"

"We can't," Blaze said.

"And why not, sweetheart?"

"Because she's away on vacation," Gloria inter-
rupted.

"No, she's not on vacation, Gawa! She's in jail. We can't go see her there. We can't call either. But she'll be out soon."

First of all, this was news to Gloria—shocking news. "You know how silly kids can be," she said.

"I do. What imaginations they have. Too much TV. Anyway, ma'am, what I'm going to do today is issue you a warning. You don't have to do anything. Remember, it's always better to stay a little under the posted limit, okay?"

"I'll do that, Officer. And thank you."

After Gloria pulled off, he waved. The kids didn't wave back.

"Where are we going now, Gawa?"

"First, we're going to stop by a jewelry store. Then we're going to Gawa's hair salon for a little while. Your dad said he'd bring Stone over to Gawa's after his Cub Scout meeting. And he'll pick you guys up later."

"Goodie. Can we get our nails polished?"

Diamond took that thumb out of her mouth and pointed to her toes.

"Yes, you may."

"And can we have McDonald's? Please, Gawa?"

"We'll see. Blazie, how do you know your mommy's in jail?"

"Because Brass told me and Stone."

"When did you talk to Brass?"

"Yesterday or last week. I can't remember."

"Does your dad know your mommy's in jail?"

"I don't know."

"Do you miss your mommy being at home?"

"Sometimes. But not all the time."

"Why not?"

"Because she's mean."

"Is that because she tells you no sometimes?"

Diamond started shaking her head no; that's not it at all.

"Because she hits hard. And lots of times."

"Really. Does she hit you with her hand?"

"She hit Stone with Harry Potter one time and she hit me with some shoes. Those Nikes."

Gloria gripped the steering wheel.

"What about Diamond?"

"She just always shaked her back and forth but one time Diamond hit her head on the bathroom sink when she shaked her too much."

Gloria tried not to scream or swear and had to stop herself from speed-dialing her son. She didn't want the kids to hear what she would've said to him even though she didn't know what that would've been. "Why was your mommy shaking her?"

"Because she was trying to make her talk."

"Does your daddy know your mommy did this to Diamond?"

"I don't know."

"Did you ever tell him?"

"No."

"Why not?"

"I don't know. Can we get a Happy Meal, Gawa, please?"

"Yes, you can have a Happy Meal," Gloria said, trying her best not to let her granddaughters know tears were burning her cheeks.

———

She'd been thinking about doing this for a while, but hadn't had the nerve. Or the courage. However, Gloria promised herself she would do it today. Whenever she needed a plumber or electrician or handyman—even the new gardeners—her wedding ring told them she did not live alone. It protected her. This was the reason she'd been relying on it for almost eight months. She was afraid to take it off. It would make more things final. She was no longer married. And she didn't have a husband anymore. To Gloria, they meant two very different things.

Dottie had noticed it. Her friends were probably wondering when she was going to stop wearing it, too. They wouldn't ask her, though. Not yet. Even that young girl at the casino assumed her husband was parking the car.

Gloria unbuckled the kids and, with both in tow, walked up to the door. She let them both press the buzzer. This was a reputable jeweler. Joseph had told her about it. After they were buzzed in, Gloria reminded the girls how to behave. A nice older Jewish man with a thick white mustache stood behind a glass case full of diamonds on top of diamonds. "Hello, my little darlings." Blaze and Diamond appeared to be afraid of him. "It's the mustache," he said to Gloria. He then pulled both sides through his fingers, causing the tips to curl up.

The girls laughed at this.

"You look like Santa Claus but you're not fat," Blaze said.

"I hear that a lot. Would you girls like a peppermint

or a chocolate kiss?" He held out a bowl of wrapped candies.

They looked up at Gloria for an okay. She nodded.

"Thank you," Blaze said.

"Thank you," Diamond said.

Gloria thought she must not have heard what she thought she'd heard. She looked hard at Diamond. "Can you say that again, sweetheart?"

"Thank you," she repeated. Gloria's mouth formed a circle, and even though she felt the air enter, she could not exhale. A moment later she bent down and gave her granddaughter a hug so strong it lifted Diamond high off the floor.

"She can say more than that," Blaze said. "She just talks when she feels like it."

"Well, I'm glad she's talking, ma'am. Now, how may I help you today?" he asked a still-in-shock Gloria.

"I believe I'm interested in having my wedding rings turned into a pendant. Or something else nice. I was told you were the best jeweler in town for this."

"Thank whoever said that for me. We certainly don't like to disappoint. Let's see what you've got there."

She held out her left hand.

"Would you mind taking them off, ma'am?"

Would you mind taking them off? It sounded like an echo. However, Gloria watched as two fingers on her right hand slid the diamond ring and wedding band off her left finger. She looked at that finger. The skin was two or three shades lighter than the rest. She hadn't seen that finger bare in almost fifteen years. She handed the rings to the jeweler as if she didn't trust him.

"Is your husband deceased?"

Gloria nodded and then said, "Yes, he is."

"I'm very sorry for your loss." The jeweler put a metal contraption around his head, turned on a pin light, pushed it behind a round magnifying glass and began inspecting the diamond. "I know this is difficult for you to do," he said, "but it's a very good way of keeping your loved one close while accepting that they're also gone. Tell me if you see any settings in the cases that you might like."

Gloria was looking. They were all pretty. She almost didn't care which one. After a few minutes, she pointed. "I like that one."

"Me, too," Blaze said.

Diamond nodded.

"This is a very nice stone—almost a carat and a half, as I'm sure you're aware. It looks like there's a small chip on a corner there. I could have it repaired for you quite easily."

"That would be fine."

"I can repolish it and it'll look like new. I could have it all done in about two weeks if that suits you."

"I'm in no rush."

"I'd be happy to fax you an estimate once I talk to my gem guy, and I can let you know later if this would be in your price range."

"I'm sure it's in my price range."

"My prices are fair. Here's your wedding band. Can't do much with that."

Gloria turned her palm up. He placed it in the center. It was already cold. She'd forgotten they weren't attached.

Hadn't thought about that. And now she wasn't sure what she was going to do with it. Maybe put it with other keepsakes. Maybe. She didn't know. She slid it inside the zippered part of her purse. Outside the shop she snapped the kids into their car seats and got behind the wheel. As she drove, Gloria kept staring at her ringless finger. Her entire left hand felt naked. Cold. Despite how hard the sun was trying to warm it up.

———

As soon as they arrived at Oasis, the girls waved hello and dashed straight to the area where two empty pedicure chairs awaited them. They opened their bags and started eating those McNuggets and fries like they were about to disappear. One of the new hires—Ming Su—would paint flowers on their fingers and toes. Probably pink and blue ones.

Today was Old School Saturday, which was why Jackie Wilson's "Baby Workout!" had just finished playing. After the first few bars, Gloria recognized Barbara Mason's "Hello Stranger." It was one of her favorite songs. "Hi, everybody." Instead of the usual enthusiastic "Hey, Ms. Glo," everybody just nodded and said hello with their eyes. Something was going on in here. Gloria felt two different kinds of vibes at work. There was a stillness in here she wasn't used to. And despite the music, it was too quiet. No one was talking.

Sister Monroe was tapping her feet and rolling her eyes at Twyla, who looked like she might have a good forty-five minutes to go before she'd be finished doing a weave. This wasn't it. Joline was talking on her cell phone with an earpiece, chewing gum and putting individual blond braids on a woman who was darker than an espresso. Nothing unusual about this.

There were quite a few regulars, some asleep, some under hot hooded dryers. Others were reading *Jet* and *Essence, Black Enterprise* and *People*. There was, however, one woman Gloria didn't recognize. She reminded her of somebody. She was sitting on the sofa, clutching a tissue in each hand. It was obvious she'd been crying. Her wig was balled up in her lap. Inside out. A knitted skullcap sat tightly on her matted gray hair.

Joseph stopped cutting his male customer's hair and gave him an "I'll be right back" tap on the shoulder. He motioned Gloria with his finger and headed toward her office. He abruptly stopped, pivoted and pointed to a stack of photographs: "Don't let anybody touch those until I come back, okay?"

"You let everybody else look at them. Why not me?" Sister Monroe asked.

"I didn't mean to be rude. I didn't think you'd be interested." He walked back and handed her the photos.

"Who are these cute little boys?"

"Those are my and my husband's sons. We just adopted them."

Gloria gave Joseph a great big hug, then took some of the pictures from Sister Monroe. "You guys finally did it! I'm so happy for you, baby! We all know this was a long process. But now you're proud parents! Congratulations, Joseph."

"Wait a minute, now," Sister Monroe said. "You mean to tell me they let faggots adopt little boys?"

Everybody in the salon stopped doing what they

were doing and gave her the evil eye. It was Gloria who decided to handle this before Joseph could. She walked right over and stood so close, Sister Monroe could probably smell Gloria's breath. "You know what, Sister Monroe? I've been tolerating you for years. But you've pushed the envelope this time. This is it. I would appreciate it if you would take your business elsewhere. We cannot nor do we want to do your hair anymore since you don't seem to know what respect means or when you're making a complete fool out of yourself, not to mention being rude as hell."

"All I said was . . ."

Gloria turned to the patrons and her stylists. "Does anybody see any faggots in here?"

Every single person in there—including the woman who'd been crying—either shook their head no or came out and said, "Hell no!"

"For somebody who's supposed to be so full of the holy spirit, you are one of the biggest hypocrites I've ever met. Now please, go. I mean it. And read the sign on your way out," Gloria said, putting her hands on her hips.

Sister Monroe didn't say a word. She did exactly what she was told. Everybody, but no one more than Twyla, was tickled pink. She didn't have to have that woman in her chair, telling her how to do her job.

Joseph gave Gloria a high five on the way to her office. "Thank you, baby," he said. "And good riddance, Johnnie Lee. This was a long time coming."

"Johnnie Lee, my foot."

"Anyway, you see the woman sitting on the sofa?"

"Yes."

"She's here without an appointment but somebody close to her has apparently passed on and she needed to get her hair done to go to the funeral. She said your friend Dottie recommended that she come see you."

"Did she really?" Gloria said, looking out into the salon. The woman looked lost, like she needed more than her hair done.

"I'll go talk to her. I just need a minute to make a quick call. Would you mind telling her I'll be with her in a few minutes?"

"Of course I don't mind. Oh. You just missed Savannah. She was in here at the crack of dawn and none other than Miss Blond Sleep-In herself was on time! Joline gave her some kind of new twists and added a little hair for body, and girlfriend is ready for what is apparently a hot blind date tomorrow, not to mention the fact that she's on her way to Paris. She is too tough! I've got one more surprise for you."

Gloria wanted to say she'd already had two that made her day. Her granddaughter had said two words. She didn't know how or why and she wasn't about to question it. And now Joseph and Javier were finally daddies. She didn't feel like waiting for the third surprise. "Tell me what it is now, Joseph? Come on, baby. It's been a long day."

"I'm ninety-nine percent sure I found us the perfect space! I e-mailed you about twenty pictures, plus the floor plan, which you will not believe. Check them out as soon as you get a chance. If you like what you see we can go take a look. Like, tomorrow!" He held up his sons' pictures and Gloria winked at him.

She dialed Tarik's cell phone.

"Hey, Ma. How's it going?"

"Tarik, when did Nickida go to jail? And for what?"

"Let me put it this way, Ma. She's been busy in more ways than I ever imagined. Which explains a lot."

"Could you get to the damn point, Tarik? I have a customer who's not in the best shape and I can't talk. The girls are getting their nails and toes polished. Wait a minute! I heard Diamond talk! Have you ever heard her speak?"

"Yes, I have."

"Well, why couldn't somebody tell me she could talk?"

"Because she doesn't do it very often. What did she say?"

"Thank you. She said thank you. I almost had a heart attack when I heard her. Anyway, what did Nickida do and what does this all mean for you and the kids? That's all I want to know."

"Well, she's been helping Luther do a little distributing of his goods and she's been fired by the IRS and is being investigated for purportedly creating her own little repayment plans on the side."

"You mean she's been doing that under-the-table kind of stuff?"

"Yes, indeed, which explains her so-called raises. This is a federal offense, Ma. I couldn't help her out of this even if I wanted to."

"I'm so sorry, Tarik. I really, truly am sorry. About all of it. Are you okay?"

"I'm fine. Me and my kids will be fine. Most likely Brass is going to be staying with us, too. I can't leave him over there with that lowlife he thinks is his father when he's not his biological."

"You mean to tell me you've known all this time?"

"Of course I did. But since Luther claimed him, I went along with it. Until he got ugly. Brass is *my* son."

"I hope this all works out for the best. Tarik. Baby. I have to go for now. Someone's waiting for me. I'll see you in a couple of hours. Don't rush." After she hung up, Gloria shook her head. "Lord have mercy on us all."

She walked out to the woman sitting on the sofa. "Hello, I'm Gloria. And what's your name?"

"I'm Marlene. Dottie's baby sister."

"Nice to meet you," Gloria said. "I knew you reminded me of somebody. I just couldn't put my finger on it. Can I offer you something cool to drink?"

"That would be nice."

"I'll get it," Twyla said. "Is bottled water okay?" Marlene nodded.

Blaze came running out and stood next to Gloria. "Excuse me, Gawa. Diamond is getting her toes done first. I'm next. Hello," she said to Marlene.

"Hello, baby."

"Why are you crying?"

"Oh, sometimes things make you sad."

"I know. I get sad, too. What made you sad?"

"Well, my sister just died."

"You mean Dottie is dead?" Gloria asked to be sure.

"Who shot her?" Blaze asked.

"Nobody, baby. She died in her sleep. She's in Heaven now."

"So is Grandpa Marvin. Maybe she could tell him hello for me and Diamond and Stone and Brass."

"I'm sure she will."

"I am so sorry to hear this, Marlene. I just saw Dottie not that long ago."

"I know. She was so happy to see you. She talked about how good you looked and how you wanted to start a whole new chapter of Black Women on the Move with those other friends of yours she always thought so highly of."

"Really?" Gloria felt terrible. She had called Dottie that awful *B* word. Never again would it slip and pass her lips.

"She'd been telling me to get rid of this wig and come over here to Oasis and you would fix me right up. I know I should've called to make an appointment but I'm not thinking straight. Me and my sister have lived together for the last thirty-one years. Now she's gone."

Gloria rubbed her arm to let her know it was okay. "Why don't you let me get you a smock and you come on back here to the sink. I'll give you a long shampoo and massage your scalp and give you a deep conditioner and a hot oil treatment. Then maybe a good cut and a nice new style. Would you like that?"

"I'll take whatever you want to give me, sugar," Marlene said as she leaned her head back and closed her eyes. Gloria turned the water on and tested it to make sure it wasn't too hot. "Thank you," Marlene said. And squeezed Gloria's hand.

Blind Date

Brunch is what we agreed to. At one of my favorite resort hotels. It's on a cliff and overlooks the entire valley of Phoenix. Today is so clear I can actually see it. I'm driving up the side of this mountain like a tourist. I feel great. In fact, I would go so far as to say I'm stoked. None of which has anything to do with Jasper. I leave for Paris in three days. I've already packed about ten books. They're too heavy. Some probably won't make this trip. I can't even sleep in my bed because it's covered with clothes. I don't care. I can't decide what to take. I want to make sure everything I wear projects what I'm feeling and makes a statement about who I am when I walk down those Parisian streets.

I valet park. I'm tempted to check my makeup and hair in the ladies' room, but convince myself I haven't changed since I left home twenty minutes ago. I'm wearing something forgettable. A peach top. Cantaloupe pants. Gauze. Layered to camouflage my stomach and my behind. I don't want Jasper to get any ideas I'm trying to lure him. I'm also starving, as I forgot to eat breakfast. I was too busy trying on shoes. Most for comfort, a few with heels. I have every intention of doing in Paris what I hardly ever do in Phoenix. Dance. Hear live music. Walk. Read a whole book. Eat out alone. And be still.

I'm also relieved. Bernie's on her way to Palm Springs. She sent the three of us an e-mail at six o'clock this morning, said we probably wouldn't hear from her for the next twenty-eight days and not to worry. John was driving her. How about that? I used to hate him almost as much as I did James. Unlike James, John has redeemed himself. We're all praying Bernie's able to break free from those pills and that the time she spends at that place is what she needs to jump-start her way back.

And then there's Miss Robin. Word on the street is she ran into a blast from the past and has been tweeting ever since. "We have a connection," she wrote in the subject line of an e-mail I was all set to delete because I thought it was another of her stupid jokes. However, my instincts told me to open it. "Michael is the same kind, sweet, thoughtful man he always was. There have been quite a few major improvements in other areas, if you get my drift. I like him. A lot. I particularly like what he stands for. He's been making me laugh, which is pretty hard to do, considering my employment status. He also suggested I not rush to look for another job. That I give myself more credit. You guys have pretty much been telling me the same thing. I'm getting there. Sparrow likes him, too. So do Romeo and Juliet, which is always a good sign. They can smell a scumbag. Michael remembers you guys and hopes we can all have dinner one day soon. And guess what? He still dances! I think I might want to keep him. He makes me feel good inside. At our age, it doesn't take a long courtship to know if your key fits. And, Savannah, please don't snicker or lecture me this time. Be happy for me." I responded with three smiley faces and one of those pumping red hearts.

I suppose I should be nervous, but I'm not. If I were secretly praying Jasper might be husband number two, maybe I would be. I don't care if I ever get married again. That much I do know. I just want to get this over with so I can get home and pack a little more. I haven't even considered jewelry. I already have an exit strategy. If he turns out to be a creepy crawler or acts like a nerdy white guy because he's a surgeon, I'll be respectful and figure out a nice way to wade through the forty-five minutes to an hour I've set aside before thanking him for a lovely meal and yes, maybe we could get together again sometime. In case he turns out to be a nice guy, maybe I'll make a new friend. I don't have many of those of the male variety. I hope his teeth are straight. And white. If not, they could turn into my focal point, which would make it difficult not to stare. Doctors and dentists are notorious for having jacked-up teeth. Why is that? I always wondered.

I don't see him anywhere inside. I do, however, see the back of a black man in a pink polo shirt taking a sip from a glass of something. He's outside on the terrace. "Hello, Jasper," I say and hold out my hand. He stands up, shakes my hand like he hasn't seen me in years.

"Nice to finally meet you, Savannah. For a minute there, I thought I might be getting stood up."

"That would be rude, Jasper. I was raised better."

"Well, hats off to your parents for good home training. Do you mind sitting out here? Can't beat this view, can we?"

"I was thinking about that on the drive up here. This is fine."

I'm surprised Jasper is more handsome in person

than he is in his picture. Which is clearly dated. His hair is still black and kinky but there's a whole new family of gray making a home along his temples. I find it grossly unfair that God rigged this whole thing so men seem to get better-looking as they get older and women simply age out. Why is it that their wrinkles make them sexy and more distinguished while ours make us look old and unattractive?

"Have you ever eaten here?" he asks.

"Yes, but it's been a while." I didn't want to say what I was thinking: that it was with the son-of-a-bitch I was married to even though he was lovable back then. I remind myself to smile. I don't want to come across as if I'm just going through the motions. At the same time, I'm not interested in trying to get below the surface with this man. I don't care how good he looks.

"What are you in the mood for?" he asks.

"They used to make the absolute best Caesar salad."

"That sounds good," he says. "I'll have the same. How about a glass of wine?"

"It's a little early for me. A glass of sparkling water with lime would be nice."

He flags a waiter. "So, Savannah. Have you ever been on a blind date?"

"No, I haven't. What about you?"

"Once."

"Was it weird?"

"Well, that's a matter of opinion. I married her."

"So it worked out pretty well."

"For about fourteen years it was fine."

He orders our salads and a large bottle of Pellegrino

with lime on the side. So far, he seems pleasant enough. I still wonder if he's as normal as he appears to be. He probably has a dark side. You never see it at first. They always put their best foot forward out of the starting gate. Anything to get an A when the date is over. I've fallen for this tactic once too often. He's probably sizing me up, too, looking for my obvious flaws, or, like me, waiting for me to say the one stupid thing that will turn him off so he'll have to figure out how to tell Thora and Bert why he's not going to make that follow-up phone call.

"Thora told me you have two sons."

"Yep. Both in college. Maxwell's a freshman at NYU and Kenan's a sophomore at Boston U."

"That's where I went for undergrad!"

"You know, I do remember Thora mentioning that. Who knows, this could be a link we'll share forever. Wait. Don't take that the wrong way. I'm trying to loosen up. And failing."

"Why are you nervous?"

"Because I'm a little rusty."

"I haven't been on a date in twelve years. How's that for rusty?"

"May I make a suggestion, then?" he asks.

"Sure."

"How about we not think of this as a real date? This way we can get rid of all those superficial expectations and just relax."

"That gets me out of the hot seat."

"That makes two of us. We could think of this as the beginning of a budding friendship."

"First I need to decide if I want to be your friend, Jasper, or if I want you to be mine."

"I hear you. Then let's see what we can learn about each other today and take it from there. How does that grab you?"

"As long as you don't get too personal."

He rakes his bottom lip with his teeth and then tilts his head to the side as if I wasn't listening to what he just said. I think he's flirting with me! He may not realize he's doing it, but he is. I forgot how this works. I'm too old to blush and yet my face is heating up. Maybe I'm reading more into this than I should. "So what made you want to practice medicine, Jasper?"

"Honestly?"

"Honestly."

"It might sound strange, but I always found science and biology fascinating. It helped me discover how our bodies work, how everything is connected and how—because of science and technology—some things can be fixed. I wanted to be a human mechanic, so to speak."

"And here I'm trying to learn how to change my oil."

He cracks up. His teeth are as straight as dentures. And wedding-dress white. I bet he uses those strips. He must have had braces when he was a teenager. His voice is raspy. It suits him. I'm not giving him points for being attractive, because he can't help it. Isaac had the same kind of magnetism.

"Technically, I'm a retired orthopedic surgeon although I travel all over the world, mostly to third-world countries with a group of volunteer doctors. We treat people who're victims of disasters, various deformities, all of whom have no access to medical treatment. I work on children, mostly. But I teach at the Mayo Clinic here in Phoenix."

"That's really wonderful, Jasper."

"Okay," he says, leaning forward, and he looks me dead in the eye. "Ask me anything you want."

"First, I have to be honest."

"Okay."

"When I told my girlfriends I was going on a blind date, one of them told me about a Web site that had about two hundred date questions. I wasn't sure what I wanted to know about you, if anything, so I picked about twenty or thirty of them, in case you turned out to be boring and we had nothing to talk about."

"Am I boring?"

"So far you're not."

"Neither are you. So, go ahead. Ask me anything."

The waitress brings our salads and pours us a glass of water. We squeeze our limes at the same time. "I only remember a few of them and it feels a little silly to me now."

"Come on. This might be fun."

"Okay, but don't answer them if you don't want to."

He looks excited.

"What's the last book you read?"

"*Harry Potter and the Order of the Phoenix.*"

"No shit? Whoops, sorry. I didn't mean to swear."

"No shit, and I did. What about you?"

"*Brief Interviews with Hideous Men.*"

"I hope it's fiction."

"It is," I say. "What's the most beautiful place you've ever seen?"

It looks like he's mentally traveling through a scrapbook. "Too many to pick just one," he says. "But. Fiji and Kenya. That's two, so fire me."

At least he has a sense of humor and he's not a nerd or a fuddy-duddy. I still sneak an occasional peek at my watch. I know how charm works. It's right up there with sex appeal. I'm wearing an invisible repellent to keep them away from me. For now.

"How do you measure success, Jasper?"

"Doing what you love even if the pay isn't good. And you?"

"We're on the same page on that one," I say. "How do you measure happiness?"

He thinks about this one. And as if he's talking to himself, he says: "It's a feeling of calm that comes from inside. When you figure out what's important. When you have nothing to prove. Giving everything you do everything you've got and being satisfied, regardless of the outcome. What about you?"

I take a long sip of water. I hadn't considered answering these questions when I was going through them. "When you're willing to surrender to goodness and joy. Give yourself permission to feel it. Not holding yourself hostage for making mistakes. Doing what you love. Doing for others. Learning to cherish the beauty of right now. When you can make yourself smile and laugh without depending on anybody else."

"I like yours. Maybe we can combine them."

I look at him like, what?

"Come on, Savannah. You're intelligent enough to know what I meant. So don't even go there."

"Your three worst qualities?"

"My three worst qualities? Hard to narrow it down to just three. Okay. One: I'm impatient. Two: I'm opinionated. And three: I'm a perfectionist. And I'm listening," he says, putting his chin in his hands.

"I'm impatient, opinionated and I, too, am a perfectionist. If you wouldn't mind, I'd like to add two more."

"Be my guest. I could've kept going, too, you know. But I wouldn't want to frighten you off."

"I'm shaking like a leaf. I'm prone to gossip and sometimes I'm not as empathetic as I could be."

"Who is?"

"What about your best qualities?" I ask.

"I'm not the one to answer that. Yours?"

"I'm brutally honest. I'm prone to gossip and I'm definitely opinionated. It's how I know where I stand. Last one?"

"Are you in a hurry?"

"No. I just have a million things I have to do today. I also have to be somewhere in less than an hour."

"Did you have a time limit set for me? Tell the truth."

"Of course not," I say as I finish the last of my salad.

Jasper hasn't touched his. I feel his eyes on me. I'm almost afraid to look up. "This was delicious," I say. "Why aren't you eating yours?"

"I seem to have lost my appetite, which is strange

because I haven't eaten since this morning. I loved those questions. I hope we can do this again one day."

I look at my salad. One day? "Maybe we can, Jasper."

"Once more with feeling," he says. "Look, I'll be frank. I know a lot about you, Savannah, which is why I wanted to meet you."

"What is it you think you know about me?"

"You're independent and smart and interesting. You know who you are. I respect the topics you explore on your shows. I know you collect black art—and so do I, by the way. You're an avid reader. And from what I can tell, pretty open-minded. Did I mention that you're also beautiful?"

"Thank you, Jasper. Especially for the nice things you said about my work."

"How much time do we have?" He's got a smirk on his face.

"About twenty minutes or so."

"Tell me. What kinds of things do you like to do in your spare time? Was this question on that list?"

"No. You mean, as in hobbies?"

He nods. Nibbles on a long leaf.

"I don't really have any specific hobbies."

"I don't believe that."

"I'm ashamed to admit it, but I don't."

"Have you ever golfed?"

"No. I've been thinking about taking lessons. I take it you do?"

"Every chance I get. Maybe we could go out on the driving range one day. I could teach you a few things."

"Wait! I do have a hobby. I love to travel."

"I don't know if traveling is what I'd call a hobby. I could be wrong. I'd like to hear about some of the places you've been. Maybe another time. For now, how about this: Where's your next trip?"

"Paris. I leave in three days. For two weeks."

His eyes widen and brighten. "Right on! Paris is probably my most favorite city in the world. In fact, I almost moved there. Have you been before?"

"Twice."

"Do you speak French?"

"No, I don't."

"Neither do I. If you don't mind my asking, are you going with someone?"

"No, I'm not."

"Good for you, Savannah! My kind of woman! Forgive me. I just haven't met very many sisters who travel the world solo. That's all I meant. I hope I didn't offend you."

"No offense taken."

"God, I sure wish I could go. We could hang out in one of those fabulous lounges and have a drink and sit on a sofa and listen to live music and talk some and boogie some and then chase it with a few shots of espresso and maybe walk along the Seine . . ."

"Earth to Jasper. That sounds very intriguing but right now we're here in Phoenix and it's been very nice having brunch with you."

He folds his hands, leans forward and looks directly into my eyes. "Before you go, can I ask you one last question just to satisfy my curiosity?"

"It depends on the question."

"Of course Thora told me you're a recent divorcee."

"That I am."

"I also understand we're not supposed to talk about our divorces. Was this a no-no on the list?"

"It sure was."

"If you don't want to answer this, you can tell me to go to hell and that'll be the end of it."

"Okay."

"So what made you want to divorce him? Unless it's way too personal."

"He bored me to death."

"That's the same reason my wife wanted to split! But she was right. I was boring as hell back then. I was working seventy, eighty hours a week. It's one of the reasons I retired. I made a horrible husband. I don't want to make the same mistake twice."

"And he was a porn addict."

"There's that."

"Are you on good terms with your ex-wife?"

"I would say so. After years of pure hell. Time does help you heal. What about you? We're breaking the first-date rules, Savannah."

"It's okay. It's not a date, remember?"

He hunches his shoulders. It is what it is.

"Anyway. We parted ways on pretty good terms. It's his postdivorce actions that have gotten me a little pissed. Sorry."

"Don't apologize. I hated my wife's guts for years because it turned out she'd been having an affair with one of my best friends. End of divorce stories. Okay?"

I nod.

"Trust me. Pretty soon he'll just be someone you used to love."

"If only."

"Well, whether you realize it or not, you're already starting a new life, for lack of a better cliché."

"You don't know that, Jasper."

"You're on your way to Paris. Alone. And you're here," he says, tapping the table." On a blind date with me. No one twisted your arm—at least I don't think Thora did, though she can be quite persuasive. Seriously, your willingness to meet me for a salad is a big deal. You have every right to be gun shy. However, should we end up becoming friends, I hope we can still meet in Paris for a drink one day. No strings attached. On the other hand, if you think I'm a complete jerk and you never want to see me again, I want you to know I give you a lot of credit for realizing what you can live with and what you can live without."

Well, damn, since he put it like that.

Recovery Road

"So, what are you on?" Bernadine's new roommate asked her.

"Nothing," she said, and sat up in her twin-size bed.

"Well, I can see you're not wearing your purple wrist-band. And you're in your own clothes, so you've already been through the hardest part. I'm Belinda," she said, reaching out her shaking hand. "So, put another way. What *were* you on?"

"Xanax and Ambien."

"Well, I've got you beat by a long shot, honey. What were your numbers?"

"What do you mean?"

"How many a day?"

"One or two Xanax. And—"

"Stop right there. Did you just say 'one or two'?"

Bernadine nodded. "Sometimes two or three Ambien a week."

"Then what the fuck are you doing in here? I'm sorry for swearing. You're not one of those religious ones, are you?"

Bernadine shook her head. Belinda looked like she'd been on something for a long time. Her brown hair was greasy. Her skin was so pasty it looked like she never went outside. Her blue eyes looked like glass. The sockets under them were so swollen, Bernadine saw a freeway of veins. "What are you on?"

"Looks like that morphine drip got me again."

"I'm confused."

"Aren't we all?" Belinda said. "I'm a nurse. Or I should say, I was a nurse. Thanks to my loving husband, who turned me in this time. Anyway, I cared for terminally ill patients and unfortunately, after some of them died, there was still a little of my drug of choice left, so I figured, what a waste to toss it."

"Well, you couldn't have had people dying every day."

She pulled her hospital gown to cover her shoulders, then pointed her index finger at Bernadine. "You are correct. Which is why I started helping myself. Anyway, you may find this hard to believe, but I took Xanax and Vicodin to detox off morphine. To the tune of about ten or twenty a day. Don't even ask how many milligrams. It's a moot point."

Bernadine swallowed hard. "Didn't you ever worry about overdosing?"

Belinda just looked at her. "Haven't you met any of the other honorary members at A New Day yet?"

"Yesterday was my first full day participating."

"Wasn't it fun? Especially the meet and greet. 'Hi, I'm Belinda and I'm a drug addict from San Bernardino.' So you got the addiction-is-a-*disease* lecture and you have to find your Higher Power or you're doomed. Right?"

"Somewhat. I learned a lot."

"Oh, they're just warming up, honey bunny. Take a

look at the schedule of lectures and movies. You'll be able to run your own facility by the time you're ready to go home."

There were about thirty people there. Some were there because it was either rehab or jail. Some were there due to intervention. Addiction certainly didn't discriminate. There was a judge, a schoolteacher, a college professor, at least three doctors, a couple of lawyers, housewives, musicians, an accountant, a model Bernadine had never seen anywhere, a vineyard manager, a few local politicians and even a police chief. Bernadine was the only black person. Not that it bothered her. She just couldn't help noticing.

"Who's your counselor? You better pray you get Mignon. She's the only one around here who has a soft heart. Her approach isn't from some rehab bible. She looks at your situation as yours. Don't judge her by those Hush Puppies. Check your paperwork over there."

Bernadine walked over to their shared dresser. "Yep. It is Mignon."

"Have you been to group yet?"

"You mean group therapy?"

"Yes."

"Tomorrow."

"You'll be able to get up close and personal with a few of your fellow alcoholics and druggies. It's quite intimate. You're going to hear some horror stories that'll make your mouth drop. Lots of tears. So be prepared. And believe everything you hear so you don't ever come back to one of these fucking places."

"So, you've obviously been here before."

She holds up three fingers. "They say five is the magic

number. This is my second stint at A New Day. I like this place better than the others. Anyway, you're gonna have to pour your heart out in group, you know. Right before you split, they make you write this dreadful letter to explain how and why you think you got here and how you plan to stay sober. Plead the fifth when they start badgering you afterward."

"Will you be there?"

"Honey, I'm just getting started. In a matter of hours I'll be in a coma. I'm just kidding. Seriously, I probably won't leave this room for at least a week. They have to give me the hard stuff to keep me from jumping out the window. But may I ask you a big favor?"

"It depends."

"First, I should warn you. Watch out for Nurse Ratched. Her real name is Mary. She's the one who dispenses all the meds at night. She's just like the nurse from *Cuckoo's Nest*. I kid you not. She's on a power trip. Everybody hates her. If you tell her you're in pain or hyper or can't sleep, she won't give you any more meds. She likes watching us suffer. Are you taking any of yours?"

"No. They told me I could refuse them. Since everything is out of my system now, popping another pill doesn't make any sense to me. The only thing I'm taking is a multivitamin, iron and a new antidepressant they put me on until I see my doctor when I get home."

"May I have yours, then? All you have to do is tell Nurse Ratched you've changed your mind."

"But won't she be suspicious?"

"They have your stats behind that desk. They know you're a kindergartener, that you might be a little scared being in here for the first time. Anyway, if you don't feel comfortable doing it, I understand."

"I'll see."

"Well, I've said more than I thought I could. Good luck to you. Bernadine, wasn't it?"

"You sound like you're going somewhere."

"It's gonna be lights out in the reptile house for me in a matter of minutes. That's why I'm chattering away now."

"Did they give you something to help you?"

"Of course. Otherwise I could go through hell at home. Oh, a few more pieces of advice from an alumna. Do all the physical stuff. The walks. The yoga. Pick up those weights. Good luck trying to meditate. Some people swear it helps them relax. One last thing: don't fall for the guilt trips they try to lay on you doing those Steps. I'm not kidding. I think the people who run AA and NA are all part of one big cult. They want you to drink the Kool-Aid. Just go along with them until you get back to your real life. After you see some of the folks in here, myself included, you should never want to pop anything heavier than an Advil, sister. End of rehab lecture. I'm headed for a comfort zone."

"Thanks for the insight. Get some rest."

Belinda pulled the covers over her head. "You seem like you're going to be a cool roommate," she said. "I need a friend."

———

"Hi, I'm Bernadine, and I'm an addict from Phoenix," she said when it was her turn to introduce herself. Hearing herself say this was like scratching her fingernails on a chalkboard. Bernadine didn't feel like a drug addict. She'd developed a dependency on pills. She didn't take them to get high, and she certainly didn't enjoy taking them. Didn't that make a difference? Over the next few weeks, she would get tired of saying this and even more tired of hearing it. What she wanted to say was "Hi, I'm Bernadine. I'm a great cook. I live in Scottsdale. I'm here because I've been doing a number on myself for years, but guess what? Game over."

By the time she got back from her walk, went to breakfast, sat in on two lectures about the nature of addiction and getting clean, went to a yoga class, ate lunch, watched a film about the history of Alcoholics Anonymous and how following the Twelve Steps could help you on the road to recovery, Bernadine was exhausted.

She returned to their room. Belinda wasn't in her bed. Bernadine wondered where she could be. She went to the kitchen, the reading room, both ladies' rooms. The gym and yoga studio, the meditation room, the steam room and sauna. Belinda wasn't there. Finally, Bernadine went to the front desk. "Has anyone seen Belinda?"

"She's gone," Polly said. She was not Nurse Ratched, although Bernadine would discover that Polly ran a close second. She had greeted Bernadine when she arrived. After John had left, Polly looked at Bernadine's two large suitcases and said, "Where do you think you're going? To a resort?"

"What do you mean, she's gone?" Bernadine said. "She just got here."

"Her insurance company refused to cover her treatment."

"I thought you guys verified this before we get here?"

"This happens more than we care to acknowledge.

It's more paperwork for us. Is there anything else I can do for you?"

Bernadine shook her head. It wasn't until she walked back into the room that she noticed Belinda's quilted overnight bag was gone.

———

The sound of moaning woke Bernadine up. It was the middle of the night. She hadn't had a roommate since Belinda had been sent packing over a week ago. Bernadine looked over at the other bed. Whoever it was, she was bone thin. Another hour went by. The girl fell out of the bed. Bernadine helped her get back in, then walked down to the front desk.

"The girl in the bed next to me is not doing so well. She seems to be in a lot of pain," Bernadine told Mary, a/k/a Nurse Ratched.

"She's just having a tough time. Do you need a sleep aid?"

"No, I don't want a sleep aid."

"I've got earplugs."

"I just want to know how long she's going to go through this."

"It depends. She could be better tomorrow. Maybe worse. This is what happens in rehab, honey."

"If she isn't any better, would it be possible to change rooms?"

Nurse Ratched chuckled. "If this were a hotel, we could upgrade you to a suite. We're short on rooms, sweetheart. See how she does tomorrow."

The next night was just as bad. Her legs seemed to kick uncontrollably. She complained she was freezing. A new nurse wrapped her in blankets and gave her something that eventually calmed her down. This made her snore like a trucker. As it turned out, this girl was only nineteen, was detoxing off that Oxycontin, another new pill Bernadine never knew existed. When she saw daylight peeking through the blinds, Bernadine got up. She drank a small glass of orange juice in the kitchen, grabbed a bottle of water, then joined the small group who walked four miles every morning. She was up to two.

———

"I don't like it here," Bernadine told Mignon at the end of her second week.

"What don't you like about it?"

"Being forced to go to those AA or NA meetings. Saying that serenity prayer over and over. Hearing all those depressing stories and testimonials. And the lectures. I've learned enough about addiction to last the rest of my life. Don't get me wrong—it's good to know. But I would love to talk about something else."

"Like what?"

"Like what to do once you leave here."

"That's next week. It's under recovery."

"I mean, I'm not ungrateful. I'm getting a lot out of being here. I haven't had a pill for thirteen days and I feel great."

"So what do you like about being here?"

"Honestly?"

Mignon nods. Pushes her glasses up. Crosses her legs. Those gray Hush Puppies are dreadful.

"Going to yoga class and meditation. The morning walks."

"What about group?"

"I mean, the impact letters are pretty powerful, but I'm not sure what they prove."

"Why don't you see how you feel after you share yours next week? Then tell me if it mattered. How's that sound?"

"It sounds good."

"I'd like to share something with you, Bernadine."

"Sure."

"Please keep this between us—it's not meant to be shared with the other counselors, during discussion after the lectures or with any other people in the program."

"Okay."

"One of the things you said in your written statement was how the horrible way your marriage ended made you feel like a victim."

"That's true."

"That you still feel a great deal of anger and resentment toward your ex-husband."

"That's putting it mildly."

"What if I told you these emotions and thoughts were totally justified?"

"It's what I've been trying to get my friends and everybody to understand for years!"

"What if I also told you it doesn't make a bit of difference if they're justified or not?"

"I thought you just said you *got* it?"

"I do. But so what? Tell me what holding on to all of this anger and resentment has helped you to do."

"Pop pills."

"What else?"

"Be unhappy."

"So, would it be safe to say that you've been letting the pain from your past turn the present into the enemy?"

"That's one way to look at it."

"Tell me in your own words what you hoped to accomplish by coming to A New Day."

"I wanted to stop taking pills and learn how to live a healthy life again."

"That means you're pretty damn tired of living like a victim, right?"

"Absolutely."

"Then I'm going to ask you to try something."

"Look, Mignon. I don't want you to think I think I'm better than any of the people in this program. Or that I don't have a problem. Watching what drugs and alcohol have done to some of these people is exhausting, not to mention depressing as hell. I'm just trying to figure out how to get to happy."

"This is precisely why the steps are so important for so many people."

Bernadine shook her head. She was thinking about what Belinda had said. She was also wondering where she was and how she might be doing. "I have a problem with the idea that if God could remove all of our defects and shortcomings, then we'd all be perfect."

"I totally agree. This is one reason why I'm going to ask you to take what you need from the program during the next two weeks."

"I'm glad you understand."

"There's something I'd like you to try after you leave my office."

Bernadine looked a bit apprehensive. "Like what?"

"If you can, try to pretend that your life is a one-thousand-page book. You're how old?"

"Fifty-one."

"At fifty-one you've already lived, say, six hundred of those pages."

"Okay."

"You've got four hundred more to go. Today, you're starting on page six hundred and one. You can live these next four hundred pages without clinging to what appeared on pages one to six hundred. Keep in mind that no one's asking you to forget what's on those other six hundred. For now, leave them just where they are. At least until you're ready to accept whatever it was that was painful. The idea is to live the next four hundred pages the way you wish to. How's that sound?"

"This is the kind of stuff they need to suggest in those lectures. Instead of scaring the hell out of you."

"I know, Bernadine. But a lot of what some people hear doesn't scare them enough."

"Thank you," Bernadine said.

"You're welcome. See you in group?"

Bonjour

The day after my surprisingly pleasant date, my doctor left me a message saying she wanted to see me right away but there was no need to be alarmed. I could drop by at my convenience. This freaked me out. I'm probably dying. They never want to give you bad news over the phone. I bet it's some kind of cancer. Or my liver or kidneys. Something that can't be fixed. I'll have to cancel my trip because I'll probably be getting prepped for chemo. Fuck.

I should never have done drugs in college and after graduate school. I should never have smoked those stupid cigarettes! I should've stopped with the French fries and double cheeseburgers and large Cokes once I hit twenty-three. Just said no to those second and third helpings of peach cobbler and sweet potato pie and fried chicken and macaroni and cheese and that extra dollop of sour cream on my baked potato, knowing I'm lactose intolerant. But no. I have always said yes to Savannah, and now look at the price I'm going to have to pay for being so self-indulgent.

Is this what happens after fifty? Your body starts turning against you? Years ago, it seemed as if every time I called Mama she was either on her way to, or just coming back from, the doctor. Or going to pick up a prescription.

Now my friends and I are doing the exact same thing. There's always some mandatory test we have to take. Some new ailment or complaint. We're always getting repaired.

———

I was sitting on the exam table, waiting for the doctor to walk in and give me the bad news. My heart was beating like crazy. I looked at all the disease pamphlets on the wall to see which one I might be lucky enough to get. As soon as Dr. Mizrahi walked in, she gave me a reassuring pat on the knee. "So. You're producing too much glucose, which is the same as sugar, which means you've got diabetes two."

My chest sank. "I know what diabetes is. But what does this mean for me?"

"That your glucose levels are much higher than they should be. Your mother was diabetic, right?" she asked, flipping the pages of my chart.

"*Is.* She's still alive."

"What about your father?"

"Never met him."

She gave me a prescription. At least it wasn't cancer.

———

I got lucky. I had enough miles to upgrade to business class. I sat upstairs. It was very cool up there. The seats reclined to a horizontal position. I pulled out six books from my carry-on. I knew I wouldn't be able to read all of them in two weeks, but I liked having options: *Krik? Krak!, All Over but the Shoutin', Breaking Her Fall, Giovanni's Room, One Hundred Years of Solitude* (my third time), *Avalanche,* and *White Teeth.* I don't count the book of French phrases, which was in my purse. I also broke down and bought one of those little translator gizmos.

"Warm nuts, mademoiselle?" the flight attendant asked.

I wanted to say, "Yes, but not that kind." Instead I just smiled, shook my head and said, "No, thank you." I'm afraid of nuts. I don't know which ones are good for me. I'm already thinking about what I put in my mouth before I put it in my mouth. Nothing like a little diabetes diagnosis to act as a wake-up call.

It was pouring when we landed in Paris. The taxi driver drove past a cemetery that looked like the kind you saw in old horror movies. Three short blocks from there, he stopped in front of a drab building from the early twentieth century. I thought Thora said it was hip. Which to me meant modern. I pulled my big suitcase into the dark hallway and a dim light came on. This was already too creepy. I was looking for the elevator. No such luck. I had to drag my heavy suitcase up two flights of thinly carpeted stairs. It smelled like mildew. When I heard trash bags falling down an air shaft, I almost lost it.

As soon as I walked inside the apartment, I thought I could have been standing in the foyer. I was trying to get my bearings. I took a few steps past the stairs, saw the kitchen on my right, and realized I was in the living room. Nothing looked the way it did on those fucking pictures Thora had posted on the bulletin board. She must have used a special lens to make everything look bigger. Now that I was at the other end of the living room, I needed to sit down. There was no sofa because there was no room for one. Just two ugly over-stuffed chairs: one was olive green and the other some kind of tweed. The kitchen appliances were probably from the '80s. They were baby doodoo yellow. The glass coffeepot was brown from not being fully cleaned after sitting too long on the burner. There was only half a refrigerator. The wooden cabinets looked sticky. I didn't dare touch anything.

I flipped on a few more lights so I could find my way upstairs. The circuit breaker tripped. I had to duck going up the steps. It was hot as hell up there. I didn't want to concern myself with the thought of air-conditioning. The bed was on the floor. The duvet—or whatever it used to be—was thin and grayish blue. Who would choose such an ugly color? I couldn't help from turning it back. The sheets looked as if they'd been slept on. I got a lump in my throat. This was also when I hit my head on the damn ceiling. Which sloped. This meant I had to stay close to the wall because it was the only place I could stand upright. Thora had the nerve to call this place a duplex?

Someone obviously loved watching *Friends* in French, because there were stacks of DVDs sitting on an outdated television set. The bathroom was the only modern thing in here. It was all white. Except only one person could stand in it at a time. The tub was deep and had a handheld shower. The sink was so small that when I bent over to rinse my face, water splashed all over the floor. I didn't trust the towels so I used my sleeve. The "second bedroom" was adjacent to this one. There was no door. A twin-size bed was pushed against the wall. An empty desk on the other side. French novels from yesteryear sat on a shelf. A dwarf wouldn't be comfortable in there.

I ran downstairs and collapsed in one of those chairs. There was no fucking way I was spending a single night in there. The thought of sleeping in that bed was enough to make me itch. Where was I going to find a nice hotel at this time of night? I looked inside a cabinet and found a phonebook, which of course I couldn't fucking read. Thank God hotel was spelled the same. I was trying to remember the name of the one I stayed at before. Couldn't. That's when I remembered I had one of those guides in my purse. I went by the pictures of the rooms. Found one. Didn't care how many Euros. Yes, I did. I could afford it. They answered in French. *"Bonjour,"* I said. *"Un hotel reservation?"*

"Votre nom, s'il vous plaît?"

"American," I said, trying to find my translation book or that little contraption.

"You are American. Do you wish to reserve a room?"

"Yes, ma'am. If you have anything available tonight, I would really appreciate it."

"We do indeed, madam."

I pushed my luggage down the stairs using my feet, pulled it out to the street and trudged my way to the corner. I was happy when a taxi stopped in less than a minute. I sat in that backseat and pressed my forehead against the glass. I looked up as we passed lighted apartments. Beautiful apartments. When it started raining again, I didn't care. The hotel was modern, hip and gorgeous. Right across the street from Radio France, close to the Statue of Liberty. A few blocks from the Eiffel Tower. And a half block from the Seine. All they had available was a junior suite, which was somewhat expensive, but I was worth it. When the bellman opened the door to my room, I felt like hugging him. It was not only twice the size of Thora's flat, it looked like a page from *Elle Décor.* The furniture was Italian, dark and smooth. Everything else was the color of straw: the duvet, the carpet, the shades. There was a flat-screen TV that I would not turn on once.

The sun streaming into the room woke me up. I looked around to make sure I was really in Paris. The honking horns outside the window and the smell of coffee and fresh-baked pastry downstairs confirmed it. I was on the second floor. I ordered breakfast: poached eggs, whole wheat toast, a few slices of melon and two shots of espresso. I checked my glucose before I ate *anything*. Took my medication after I swallowed the last bite.

I dreaded calling Thora, but figured I should get it over with. I rehearsed my upbeat tone in the shower. Thank God she wasn't there. "Bonjour, Mademoiselle Thora. Everything is fine here except I was allergic to something in your lovely flat so I've had to check into a hotel. It's all good. I'll speak to you as soon as I get back. Thanks much."

With my map in tow, I crossed over the main avenue and started walking along the Seine. I had to stop just to take this in. I am in Paris, I thought. I wanted to give myself a few minutes to appreciate how I got here. I sat on the grass. Watched the tugboats. The floating restaurants. The charters. I inhaled the scent of river water and fresh air. The cars behind me went silent. I was awestruck looking up at the Eiffel Tower. To my right: the Statue of Liberty. Directly across this river was the Left Bank. It felt surreal, looking at so much history.

I had a history, too. I was raised in a Pittsburgh ghetto. Thanks to my mama, I never felt deprived or disadvantaged. In fact, she had me believing that when I grew up, my life was going to be remarkable. Exciting. Possibly even thrilling. She was right. I graduated from a well-respected college, have a great job and love what I do. I married a good man, but one who made me feel as if I were disintegrating inside. I opted out because I was too smart to settle for mediocrity. I don't care what Sheila thinks. My life didn't end just because my marriage did. I've got plenty of reasons to live, and much to look forward to.

Otherwise, I wouldn't be here. I didn't come to Paris to run from myself. I came here to run back to myself. As soon as I stepped off that plane, I already felt like Cinder-fucking-ella except I didn't have to wait for a prince to find my other slipper. I brought quite a few pairs with me. In my twenties, I used to think people in their fifties were old. Too old to have any fun. I felt sorry for them because their best years were behind them. It was all downhill from there. I beg to differ. I like my life. I'm free. I can do anything I want to. Go anywhere I want and don't have to depend on anybody to orchestrate it. I'm my own conductor.

I got up, stretched and kept walking. I felt lighter. I must have been smiling because people smiled back. *"Bonjour,"* they said. *"Bonjour, à vous aussi,"* I said. Originally, I'd thought about trekking back up to the top of the Eiffel Tower. Why repeat myself? I passed over the tunnel where Princess Diana was killed. There were wreaths of plastic flowers everywhere. I couldn't help thinking how quickly tragedy can strike. This one impacted the world. By the time I made it to the Place de la Concorde, I moved in slow motion in order to appreciate the cascade of those fountains. I headed on down the Champs-Elysees, past all the shops to the avenue of trees. For someone just diagnosed with a life-changing disease, I had energy to spare. As if diabetes was a wake-up call to finally get healthy.

I still took a cab back to the hotel.

———

I'd been there three days when I decided to call Mama so she would know where I was. "Did you get my e-mail text message?" she asked.

"No. I haven't checked either one in a couple of days."

"Why not?"

"Because I haven't felt like it."

"Why not?"

"Because I'm in Paris."

"What in the world are you doing in Paris?"

"Having fun," I said, knowing this was the wrong answer.

"Did you go with somebody?"

"Nope. Came all by myself."

"You ain't been divorced but fifteen minutes and you had to run all the way to Paris, France, by yourself to prove what?"

"I'm not trying to prove anything, Mama. I just needed to get away."

"Then why didn't you come to Pittsburgh?"

"It just wouldn't have worked right now."

"What's wrong with Pittsburgh?"

"Nothing, Mama. I needed to go someplace far away. Someplace beautiful and foreign."

"Hell, Pittsburgh is foreign to you. It ain't exactly no postcard but you ain't been here in years."

"I would like to come home for Christmas if that's all right with you."

"I have to see this to believe it. Do you get the news about what's going on over here in the United States?"

"I'm taking a much-needed break from the news, which is why I'm not watching any TV or reading any newspapers while I'm here. I'm not even going on the Internet, and I didn't bring my laptop. I'm not checking voice messages—nada—until I get back home. Why?"

"What's wrong with you, Savannah?"

"Nothing, Mama. The world won't come to an end while I'm on vacation. Was there a particular reason why you asked?"

"Nope. You go on and do your thang, baby."

I was thinking about telling Mama about my diagnosis, but something told me to just wait until I got there. "I'm going to have to hang up now, Mama. It's expensive."

"A few more minutes won't break you. Guess what? They dropped them charges against GoGo."

"Well, that's good news."

"That's one way to look at it. The police violated his Molinda rights or some such mess. Anyway, you have a good time over there and be careful. Don't talk to strangers." She let out a little chuckle. "Wait. Do you speak French, Savannah?"

"No, I don't."

"Then how you suppose to understand them folks?"

"I have my ways."

"What in the world would you do if you met a nice French man and you can't understand a damn thang he's saying?"

"Bye, Mama. I love you."

"Of course you do. Call me when you get home. And bring me back some French perfume. But not that stinky kind that make you smell like you old."

Right after I hung up, I ordered a pot of tea. I decided to call Sheila to get it over with. She would be jealous as hell if I didn't. She answered on the first ring.

"What in the world are you doing in Paris?"

"How do you know I'm in Paris?"

"Because Mama just texted me and said you were."

"You have got to be kidding."

"GoGo's been giving her tutorials. Anyway, what in the hell are you doing in Paris by yourself and why in the hell didn't you invite me to come along to keep you company when you know I've got this unused ticket just laying around and it could've been applied toward a ticket to Paris? And how much does it cost to get over there? Oh hell, never mind because I don't have no interest in going to nobody's Paris, but Rio de Janeiro would be a whole different story. What are you doing over there?"

"Don't you need to swallow?"

"You go straight to hell. Aren't you scared, being all the way in Europe by yourself? This is when you need a man."

"If it wasn't for shame, I swear to God, I'd hang up this phone right now, but I won't. Mama just told me the good news about GoGo."

"Yeah, but unfortunately those bond people don't

give you your money back even if the charges get dropped. They're nothing but gangsters. Anyway, Paul just found out about some kind of new home loan we might qualify for. Interest only or something. I'll let you know as soon as we hear."

"Not to worry."

"Can you speak French?"

"Yes, I can."

"Say something in French."

"Je vous aime à mort mais vous montez vraiment dans mon dernier nerf baisant."

"What did you just say?"

"I said, 'I'm coming home for Christmas.'"

"I don't believe that's what you said. And I'll believe it when you get here."

"Bye, Sheila. I'll talk to you when I get back."

"Would you please bring me back a bottle of French perfume but not the kind with that real Frenchy smell?"

Family.

———

During the rest of my trip, I did everything I said I was going to do. I walked every day, except the two I spent reading in bed. I finished three of the six books sitting at outside cafés and brasseries. Men flirted with me. I flirted with them, too. I felt my power. I saw more black people on the streets of Paris in two weeks than I saw in a whole year in Phoenix. French isn't a color. I was fascinated watching how these folks used their hands and eyes to tell each other how they felt. They like to touch. I saw so many people of all ages kissing in public places, it made me hopeful. Romance isn't out of the question. And I haven't given up on men. I'm just not going to act like a hitchhiker on a two-lane highway waiting to get picked up. I've decided to take a more proactive approach. I'm going to start asking men out. All they can do is say no. One monkey doesn't stop the whole show.

Because I always wanted to see some of the French countryside, I took a two-hour train ride outside of Paris. I saw herds of fat sheep. Farm after farm. Rolling dark green hills. I got off in a small village. I saw a castle. A real castle. I took pictures of it for the girls. I'm going to lie and tell them I went inside, ran up and down the stairs and stuck my head out the window like Rapunzel. On the ride back, I was thinking that there's a lot worth seeing in this world. In fact, I was trying to decide where I might go next. Venice. Bora Bora. Or Kenya. I've always wanted to go on a safari.

I shopped. Ate what I could. And ate late at night. I skipped the Louvre and Moulin Rouge and most of the museums. I wanted to do things I hadn't done before. So I went to two swanky spas. Had many treatments. There is no better feeling than being pampered. I was glowing inside and out. I always wanted to see the Hotel de Ville. Almost broke my neck looking up at the ceiling. Those breathtaking blues. I sat for hours in the Jardin des Tuileries and didn't read anything except people. I took a taxi to the Palace of Versailles. Even did the tour. Then I sat on a bench and watched tourists walk through that giant garden.

On my last night, I put on a pair of high heels and what could pass for a sexy dress and went downstairs to the Zebra Lounge. The place was packed. People were sitting on sofas, deep in conversation. Some were whispering into each other's ears. Laughing. Others were dancing to the mellow music the band was playing. I thought about Jasper after I walked out onto the dance floor, found my rhythm for three or four songs in a row, had a glass of wine, then chased it with a double espresso.

Velvet Handcuffs

"I know you'll never wear this again, Mom," Sparrow says, holding up a skirt I don't remember.

"I don't care if I do or not. Put it in the bag."

We're in my closet. It's a walk-in. We've been in here so long, we've filled up six black trash bags with my clothes and now have two laundry baskets of empty hangers. I've got a fan on in the doorway, even though it's not helping all that much. It's too bad. Ever since those levees broke in New Orleans, it's been hard trying to grasp what's happening. It doesn't seem real, but it is. We've been glued to the television, gasping as we watched the devastation continue to multiply. We've stamped our feet on the floor, hoping and praying help would come a lot faster. So far, it hasn't. What's taking so damn long?

We couldn't imagine waking up to this. Sparrow and I had to do something. I started with towels and sheets and blankets we could live without. We emptied out our dresser drawers and put every piece of clothing, pajamas and even socks we don't need in boxes. I did the same with shoes and purses; some I've never even worn or carried. Too much is sometimes just too much. It has made me sick standing in this closet, looking at how much I have, knowing so many people don't have anything. I've been a slave to the good life. Which is precisely why I'm taking off these velvet handcuffs.

———

"Wasn't that the doorbell?" I ask Sparrow. She's blasting one of my favorite country songs of the moment, "Redneck Woman." Romeo and Juliet dash downstairs. I look around my closet one more time. I don't think I have anything left to give. I take a sip of water. It's now lukewarm. I wonder who it could be. I go out and peek over the banister.

Sparrow's looking through the peephole. "It's the mailperson." She opens the door, signs something, runs up two steps at a time and hands me a manila envelope.

There's no name on it, just a return address. I open it and out fall four tickets to the dance. There's a note card from Lucille paper-clipped to them:

Hello, Robin! It's me, Lucille! I hope you're faring well. I've decided to retire although I now do floral arrangements. I enjoy it. I should also let you know I'm dating! Yes, me! My high school sweetheart! Because of the damage Katrina has caused, all of the proceeds from this event will go to the victims. It's being announced on the black radio station. Since you've always been so nice to me over the years, and so supportive of our causes, I thought I'd treat you to these four tickets with the hope that you'll bring your funny girlfriends—or anyone else you might like. Let me know if you need additional tickets. They've increased the price to one hundred dollars. Hope to see you in a few weeks. Very best, Lucille.

I almost can't believe it. This was so nice of her. And to think I used to dog her. I'm sorry, Lucille. I can't wait to tell the girls. I wonder if Michael might want to go?

When the phone rings, I almost knock Sparrow over to get it. "Hello," I say calmly.

"And how are you this afternoon?"

"I'm fine, Michael. And you?"

"Are you still in the closet?"

"Nope. We finally finished."

"I've got quite a few boxes I was going to drop off. I can pick yours up, too, if you want."

"That would be great. This whole thing is just so draining and nothing has even happened to us."

"Well, I've got a few friends who've got relatives down there. They need our prayers and all the support they can get."

"This feels a lot like nine-eleven. Doesn't it?"

"It does. Which brings me to the other reason I called. If you don't want to go, I'll understand. But I could sure use a short break."

"Go where, Michael?"

"I don't want to bore you, but about a year ago, I did a favor for a college buddy. He inherited a share of a vineyard in Napa. I helped him with the corporate tax restructuring. The long and short of it, things worked out, and to show his gratitude he's given me a nice long weekend at a resort over there. I was wondering if you'd like to come with me."

"Napa, huh? I've never been to that part of California. I need to check my schedule. Hold on a second. Sparrow, am I free this weekend?"

"I believe you are!" she yells from upstairs. "But I'm not."

"I think I could squeeze you in."

"I hoped you would."

"Tell me what to do."

"Start packing," he says. "My travel agent's just waiting for me to give her the go-ahead. What about Sparrow? Do you need to make some kind of arrangements for her?"

"She's sixteen. She'll be fine. Plus, I've got friends who'll keep an eye on her."

"Good. Tell her I said hello. And I hope to hear her play that violin one of these days—if I'm still around."

"No comment, Michael. I'm hanging up now. E-mail me the particulars, dude."

I run up the stairs three at a time. "Sparrow! Michael's invited me to go to the wine country in California this weekend. What're your plans?"

She almost runs into me. "Forget about my plans. Just go, Mom, please."

"I need to make sure you're covered."

"At first, a few of the group members wanted to come over to practice a really cool song, but we're all so bummed out by Katrina, we volunteered to make calls to help raise money instead. Is it okay if they come over, Mom? You know we're all responsible."

I think about this for a few minutes.

"I'll call you if there's an emergency. Please?"

"Just don't forget the rules."

———

Michael rents a convertible. We drive from Oakland to Napa in a little over an hour. The Bay Area is so pretty. In my opinion, much prettier than L.A. It's lush. And green. No rush hour traffic when it's not rush hour. Michael and I talked about me. Him. Me and him. How good we feel. How good this is. How lucky we are to have this second chance. We decide to milk it, play it all the way out. Neither of us was specific, although I have a pretty good idea what he meant. "I'm not playing," he said as we passed over some bridge that wasn't the Bay Bridge or the Golden Gate.

"I'm not either," I said. "I like you, Michael."

"Not half as much as I like you," he said.

And we left it at that.

"How much farther?"

"About ten or fifteen minutes. You need me to stop? Do you have to go to the restroom?"

"Nope. I'm good."

A few minutes later, we pass a designer outlet and I almost have a stroke. "Oh my God! There's a Barney's! Coach! BCBG and Cole Haan! Are they serious?"

"I can turn around if you want to check it out."

"No!" I say, pressing both hands against the dashboard.

"I don't mind, Robin."

"There's nothing in those shops I need. So keep driving, dude."

The hotel is unassuming. After we check in, they put our bags on a golf cart and drive us to our room. When the bellman opens the door, I almost have a heart attack. It feels like we're in the Mediterranean. There are two huge rooms. A fireplace. A sofa. A table with settings for two. The bed is up high and stuffed with pillows. Everything is white and gold. "Is this their honeymoon suite, or what?" I ask Michael.

"I have no idea. But it's ours for two nights."

He takes me by the hand and walks me out to a terrace that overlooks what appears to be the entire Napa Valley. I have never seen anything quite like this except in movies. We lean over the wooden railing and look down at a grove of olive trees. "This is unbelievable." It's about all I can say.

"Okay," Michael says, "this is the plan. We can change any part of it if you want. Tonight: we have dinner upstairs in the hotel's restaurant. They have a tasting menu that's supposed to be out of this world, and then tomorrow morning we have reservations for a four-handed massage."

"How many hands?"

"Four. Two people massage you at the same time. We'll be in separate rooms. After that, we go on a wine-tasting tour. Later, dinner on the wine train. It travels through the vineyards. And Sunday, we sleep in until they kick us out, then head back to the real world."

"This is real, isn't it, Michael?"

"Very much so," he says. "Very much so."

We miss dinner.

———

"Will I get a chance to meet your friend?" I ask. We're lying by the pool. It's one of those infinity kind. We just had our four-handed massage. Out of this world. Then we took a steam bath. I don't know how we got out here.

"He's in New York. You'll meet him one day. Not to worry. He's a golfer."

"Okay," I say and close my eyes. This sure feels like a honeymoon. I look over at Michael. "Would you like to marry me?"

He opens his eyes like he's just had those drops they put in at the optometrist. "I thought you'd never ask."

We lie there for a few minutes and look at each other. He gets up from his chaise and comes over to mine. Drops his towel on the purple concrete and gets on his knees. He kisses me on one cheek. Then the other. He looks into my eyes and smiles. "Are you sure you want me to be your husband?"

"Absolutely positively sure."

"Why?"

"Because I love you."

"Are you sure about that, Robin?"

"Absolutely positively sure."

"But why?" he asks as I make room for him.

"Because I really *like* you, Michael. I like who you are. What you stand for. I like that you have integrity. I like what you value, and I like your values. Always have. You respect me. You make me feel smart, even though I am smart. You make me feel good inside. Like warm pudding. And you make me feel luscious and beautiful and important. I know you love me, don't you?"

"From the beginning."

"It's also nice not to have to apologize for what I'm not."

"What are you talking about? You've got it all. You've got charm and energy and sass and moxy and you drive a fast car and you're smart and sexy. You're a good parent. And I repeat: What on earth are you talking about?"

"I don't have a job."

"And?"

"I don't know what I'm going to do for the rest of my life, Michael."

"Who does? We think we do. I wish you would stop acting like a clock is ticking or some such nonsense."

"But it is."

"You've still got a few minutes left, I think. Come on, baby. You don't have to have it all figured out today or next week. You've got me for life."

"Oh. That's a given. I can tell you right now that divorce is out of the question. I don't care how pissed off we get, we will work it out. Deal?"

He repositions himself and shakes my hand. "Deal."

"Even if you put those forty pounds back on, join a circus, get a job flipping burgers at Micky D's—you ain't going nowhere, boyfriend."

"Is that a promise?"

"It is."

"So you know. I'm willing to do everything I can to help you figure out what you think you might want to do."

"I think I'm going to have to figure it out on my own, Michael."

"I know. I just don't want you to have to worry about money, because I've got some."

"So do I. So you don't have to worry about taking care of me."

"What do you think your girlfriends are going to think about this? Us?"

"You think I'm worried about that?"

"I didn't say that. But what if they ask you what made you want to do this so soon when you haven't seen me in years?"

"I'll just say because I wanted to. And that'll be the end of it."

I push him off my lounge chair.

"So, is that a yes or a no?"

"Make that a yes, Robin. I'd love to be your husband."

———

"I must be seeing things," I say to Michael when he pulls up in front of my house. "That looks like Russell's raggedy car parked in the driveway."

"Were you expecting him?"

"No, I wasn't. And I want to know what he's doing here." Before I get out of the car, Sparrow comes running out of the house toward me and Russell is walking behind her. I slam the door after I get out.

"Mom, I'm so sorry," she says, hugging me hard. She's also crying.

I push her away. "What's going on? What's wrong? Did something happen? And what are you doing here?" I say to Russell. The look on his face tells me *something* has happened.

"Well, Mom. You know that the group came over and we were supposed to make calls on behalf of Katrina victims, right?"

"And?"

"Well, Samuel told someone at school he was coming over and it got out and then, like, I didn't even have a chance to open the door when they rang the doorbell and then the next thing I knew there were, like, sixty kids in the house and they were, like, playing music and drinking stuff out of the bar and I was yelling at them, telling them to leave but they wouldn't and so I got scared and didn't want to call you on your vacation and so I called my dad."

"I just stopped them from destroying your crib," Russell says.

"And how did you do that, Russell?"

"I just locked the door and told them that if they didn't clean this mess up, I was going to call the police and every single one of them would be arrested for trespassing and breaking and entering."

"That's true, Mom."

I hear Michael get out of the car. "Hi, Sparrow. You okay?"

"I'm fine."

"How's it going, man?" he says to Russell.

"It's all good," he says. "Just tried to protect my daughter."

"Thank you," I say. "Thank you for protecting our daughter, Russell. Really."

"You're quite welcome."

"Oh, one more thing, Mom. I think Romeo got out."

"Got out how? Where is he?"

"I don't know."

"We've been looking everywhere for him," Russell

says. "And you know little dogs like that don't stand much of a chance out here in the desert. I'm really sorry, Robin."

"Where's Juliet?"

"Hiding," Sparrow says.

"Then wherever she is, Romeo won't be far."

I charge inside the house and pass through one beer-smelling room after another. I yell both of their names and sling open my bedroom door, hoping that these kids didn't have the nerve to come in here. I stand there, looking around, making sure everything is intact. It doesn't look like anything has been touched. This is when I hear whimpering coming from under my bed. I bend down and there those two little munchkins are, just shivering away. "It's okay, kids, come on out. It's okay," I say as they creep out on all fours, but not before looking around to make sure the coast is clear.

Payments

As soon as I got to the airport, I stood frozen in one spot for so long—watching in horror what was on every TV monitor—I almost missed my flight. I could not believe what I was seeing. That there had been a hurricane. The bitch's name was Katrina and she had caused the levees to break and much of New Orleans was underwater. Hundreds of thousands of people were now homeless, lost, dead or injured? That twenty thousand people had been living in the Superdome with no toilets, no food, no air-conditioning and no drinking water? And no help from the United States government? They were Johnnie on the spot when that tsunami hit Thailand last year, though, weren't they? This was like watching a science fiction movie. I hadn't seen this look of panic and helplessness on people's faces since 9/11. I listened as men and women described their futile search for loved ones. Children separated from their parents. There was no power. No buses. No trains. No nothing. By the time I boarded and sank into my comfortable business-class seat, I was crying so hard I couldn't stop. I was wrong. For some, the world can come to an end while you're on vacation.

"Are you all right, mademoiselle? Are you ill?" the flight attendant asked as she put her hand on my shoulder.

I shook my head. "I'll be okay," I said. "Thank you."

I closed my eyes and leaned back in my seat. I kept seeing people running and screaming and crying and walking through waist-high water. I wanted to know how they were going to survive that. I wanted to know how it feels to lose everything. How do you plan for tomorrow when all you have is today? *As soon as this plane lands, I'm calling Thora,* I thought.

After getting my luggage and waiting in line for a taxi, I sent Thora a text message explaining the reasons why I wanted and needed to go to New Orleans. On the ride home, I decided to check my messages. I only had seven, since I give my cell number only to friends, Mama and Sheila and a few close associates. The first one was from Isaac, last week:

Hey, Savannah. Hope you're doing well. Just wanted you to know that I got the settlement. Thank you very much. I slid an envelope under your doormat with a certified check in it to cover the three thousand I owe you plus a couple of the back payments on the loan. That's the best I can do for now. I'm really sorry about all this, Savannah, and will keep you posted as my situation improves. By the way, I went fishing a few days ago. Caught some beautiful striped bass. Couldn't make them taste the way you always did to save my life. Well, anyway, you take good care.

His message made me smile. I really needed a reason. I wished I could take back what I'd said to him. That I regretted ever marrying him. Because it wasn't true. Isaac filled years of my life with love and magic and comfort. No one can ever take that from me. Not even him.

By the time the taxi neared my exit, I waited to hear the second message. It was from Jasper:

Bonjour, Mademoiselle Savannah. This is Jasper calling to say I hope you had a wonderful time in Paris and I'm sorry you had to come home to such tragic news. I'm in New Orleans, trying to help with the medical problems many people are facing, and not sure how long I'm going to be here, so it looks like we're going to have to postpone going to the driving range for a minute, but I'll try to be in touch. Take good care. I look forward to seeing you soon.

Right on, Jasper. I think I might like to get to know him better. I think I might like him. A little bit. He's definitely interesting. He might even be fun.

Next was Thora.

So sorry you had an allergic reaction to something in the flat but I'm sure you found a wonderful hotel, since there are so many to choose from. Anyway, I wanted to know if you've been thinking more about that new format for your shows you mentioned before you left. We can talk more about specifics after you get over your jet lag. Oh, let me know if you have time to come to the boys' fifth birthday party. It's going to be at Chuck E Cheese. But no clowns. They scare the bejeezers out of them.

There is no way in hell I'm going to a birthday party for those five-year-old little Chuckys. I think I'm going to be honest and tell Thora as nicely as possible that I don't think I'd enjoy the party as much as she will.

Robin:
Okay, so don't freak out. Michael and I are getting married. We haven't set a date but you guys have to help me find a dress! I hope you had a hella good time in Paris and you brought me back some expensive perfume. And just so you know, I've got our tickets to the you-know-what next weekend and all the proceeds are going to the Katrina Relief Fund, so you and Gloria and Bernie are going whether you want to or not. Call me if you need a ride from the airport. I'll send Sparrow to pick your behind up! Not! I'm happy, girl.

Well, well, well. You finally found him, Robin. It looks like this is one time it pays not to forget the past. I always liked Michael. We all did. He was a good guy. I never thought he was fat—maybe a little on the pudgy side, but that didn't make him unattractive. Well, maybe a little bit. Oh who cares! Our girl has found her Mr. Wonderful. It's amazing how on any given day or in any given moment, one person's life can begin again while another one's falls apart. We've waited a hundred years to witness this. She deserves to be loved. I wouldn't get in a car with Sparrow behind the wheel to save my life. So I guess I have to go find a new dress to wear to this shindig due to the fact that I seem to have lost four whole pounds. Maybe three. Depending on the scale.

Gloria:

Savannah, are you back? I can't keep up with everybody's schedule since I'm running around with little
people all the time. You know we found a new spot
and it's almost perfect, because these idiots got
deported for embezzling but they sure had good
taste, so we hardly have to do anything to the space.
Anyway, I hope you had a good time in Paris and you
brought me back a really expensive bottle of perfume.
If you need a ride from the airport, let me know. Oh,
as an FYI: I joined Weight Watchers and want to know
if you guys want to start walking together—at least
once a week. I've already started, and even though it
reminds me of Marvin, it doesn't make me sad. I
heard about your diabetes diagnosis. Join the club.
We can manage this. My pressure is almost where it
should be. Welcome back, girl.

Bernadine:

I know you're probably on your way back from Paris
and I hope you had a good time. I'm still in rehab
and we're not supposed to have cell phones in here
but somebody snuck one in and let me use it for a
few minutes. I'll be home in another week or so. This
is the most life-affirming experience I've had in years,
Savannah. I feel good. My body is clean and I can't
wait to see your ass. I've been walking twice a day
since I detoxed. You won't believe this, but I'm doing
yoga. As soon as I get home, I'm signing you guys
up for an introductory class. Yes, I said yoga! I want
to show you guys how to meditate. Don't laugh. I've

learned how to breathe. You don't have to chant or anything like that. You better not have forgotten to bring me a bottle of perfume. I don't even care if it's cheap. Love you, girl. Gotta run.

Thank God for girlfriends.

———

The next morning, it took forever to unroll ten bottles of reasonably priced French perfume from inside ten wash-cloths I'd borrowed from the hotel. I think I need a dis-tributor. I went to the bank and deposited Isaac's loot. When I got back in the car, I found myself making an illegal U-turn when I saw an ASPCA. Before I knew it, I was walking out with a brand-new brown-and-white kitten. I named her Mocha. She is seven weeks old. When I got home, I got her all settled in and set up. Like an idiot I went and dug out an old picture of my first cat, Yasmine, and showed it to her. Mocha wasn't moved.

I took my laptop out on the deck and ate my deli-cious lunch: a cup of lentil soup with a half turkey-breast sandwich made on high-fiber whole-wheat bread, with one teaspoon—not tablespoon—of mayonnaise and mus-tard, a few slices of honeydew and a half cup of steamed broccoli.

I put the dirty dishes in the sink, rinsed them off and, as soon as I finished, turned the faucet off. It continued to drip. I leaned on the counter, placed my chin in the palm of my hand and watched that drip until it felt like I was being hypnotized. I knew all it needed was a new washer. I don't know how to do that, and I was not call-ing a plumber for a hundred and fifty dollars an hour to change it. Instead, I went back outside and sat in front of my laptop. I logged on to the junior college closest to my house and found a continuing education class called Household Survival. I was happy there was still room. It starts in two weeks. That drip can wait.

I spent the next hour wading through all the Web sites that had been set up for sending money for Katrina victims. I was looking for the most legitimate ones that would guarantee the money you sent online would actually get to its intended destination. And since I really hadn't been counting on Isaac paying me back, I added a couple of thousand to it and sent a third toward hospitalization and medical help, another third for books and school supplies and the rest for food and clothing. It looked like temporary housing was *finally* starting to happen since George Bush had *finally* come home from his fucking vacation and *finally* declared this to be a state of emergency.

I'll be so glad when we get a new president.

Today I Got a Letter

Bernadine talked John's ear off the first two hours of the drive home. He hadn't seen her this animated and energetic in years. "I feel like I've been in hiding," she said.

"Well, I'm glad our daughter doesn't have to hide anymore either."

This threw Bernadine completely off. "So, she finally told you."

"She did."

"What was your reaction?"

"It was tougher than I thought. Hearing her say it. But then I thought about how hard this has been for her. So. I told myself this wasn't about me. I needed to put my feelings aside."

"What exactly does that mean?"

"Look, Bernie. You and I've known this about Onika for years."

"Why didn't you ever say anything to me?"

"What would've been the point?"

"Maybe we could've made it easier for her."

"I think she was waiting to feel comfortable."

"So, you're okay with it?"

"What difference does it make? I'm not about to

make my daughter feel bad because she's a lesbian. My biggest regret is her not giving us a grandchild or two."

"She's not sterile, John. Gay and lesbian couples have babies like everybody else. They can also adopt. Joseph and Javier just adopted two little boys."

"No shit? Well, Onika won't be doing much of anything with that Shy girl."

"You mean it's over?"

He nods. "It was another camp counselor."

"Is Onika okay?"

"Seems like it. She's just happy to see her brother and her soon-to-be sister-in-law. That Bronwyn is a real nice girl. She's smart as a whip and I love that Texas accent. Our son is happy."

Bernadine smiled.

"They're not sure if you want them to stay with you since you're just getting your bearings back."

"Of course I do."

"That's what I figured and that's what I told them."

The melody of George Benson's "Breezin'" started coming from John's cell phone. As soon as he pressed TALK, Bernadine heard him say, "We don't need to talk about Katrina right now, okay?" Without waiting for an answer, he handed the phone to Bernadine. "It's my other daughter."

"*Our,*" Bernadine said. "Who's Katrina? Hello, Ms. Taylor. And what is it you could possibly have to say to me?"

"She's a female disaster who's been stirring up a lot of trouble trying to get President Bush's attention, but he blew her off. Enough about her. I missed you, Mom-Mom. And guess what?"

"I can't even begin to."

"We're making dinner for you. It's a surprise. So act surprised, okay?"

"Okay."

"Did everything go okay?"

"Everything went fine, Taylor."

"I'm glad to hear it, MomMom. So. The other thing is this. I've been doing some serious thinking and I have come to the conclusion that it would be better if I stayed with my dad because he's lonely and he's got that big prostate issue and I think he needs me. Plus, he's been coming home earlier and we've been talking about all kinds of things. I never knew he was so interesting."

"I always thought he was."

"I'm starting to like him more as the weeks go by. Anyway, I just want you to know I'll be more than happy to spend weekends with you should you wish to have the pleasure of my company. That is, if your social life isn't too hectic."

"What social life?"

"Exactly. I understand this is one of the things you'll be working on."

"Who told you that?"

"Auntie Robin. You may or may not know her love life has certainly picked up since you've been away."

"How do you know this?"

"Sparrow. She said her mom has finally gotten laid and how much nicer she is. That she's fallen for this super-nice guy Michael, a real blast from her past, and things have gotten hot and heavy and are picking up more steam than a locomotive around their crib, and this weekend they're in Napa Valley—you know, that big wine area in California—but they're not picking any grapes. They're bonding."

Bernadine's mouth dropped open. This girl reminded her so much of Rona Barrett from way, way back, it wasn't funny. She was just glad it was good news. So Michael's back? Welcome back, Kotter. Wow. Go away for a month and look what happens.

"MomMom, you still there?"

"I'm still here. Any more news to report?"

"Actually, yes. Can I help it if people trust me enough to confide in me?"

"I suppose you can't."

"Anyway, Auntie Gloria and Uncle Joseph found a fresh new spot for Oasis, and Bonnie is still in deep shit. Sorry. You know I meant to say *trouble*. But she's drowning in it."

"Who's Bonnie?"

"Nickida. As in Bonnie and Clyde? Me and Sparrow would like to kick her sneaky ass. She is such a ho. So you're not upset about my not moving in?"

Bernadine didn't feel like reacting to Taylor's swearing. She was actually getting a kick out of it. "No, I'm not upset."

"Good. You might want to know that Auntie Savannah has diabetes. Not the kind you have to shoot up. She just has to take a pill. Anyway, she's not freaking out about it. She takes her meds and I hear she's actually lost a pound or two since she's now eating with a conscience. Anyway, she had an amazing time in Paris. She bought us all some perfume. Mine smells like formaldehyde. If you like it, you can have it. I left it on your desk."

"Diabetes? How do you know all this, Taylor?"

"Because she called to make sure you were doing okay in rehab. She was talking to Dad on speaker."

"Is there anything else you haven't mentioned?"

"I think that pretty much covers it. Anyway, Mom-Mom, we're all looking forward to seeing you in a couple of hours. I love you! Tell my dad I have nothing else to say to him right now. Byeeeeee!"

Bernadine handed the phone back to him.

"She's a talker, isn't she?" John said.

"That's putting it mildly."

———

As soon as they walked in the door, Bernadine was greeted with hugs and kisses and high fives and we-missed-yous and you-sure-look-great-Mom and this-is-Bronwyn and so-nice-to-finally-meet-you-and-thank-you-for-letting-us-stay-here-we-promise-not-to-get-on-your-nerves-or-overstay-our-welcome-and-yes-we-do-windows and here-feel-it's-in-there and we-don't-know-if-what-we've-cooked-will-compare-with-what-you-do-in-the-kitchen-but-you-will-eat-it-and-love-it.

"Please let me take a shower first," Bernadine begged. They ushered her through them like she was in the *Soul Train* line. She headed upstairs.

Ten minutes or so later, Onika tapped on Bernadine's door and eased her way in. "Mom, are you almost out of the shower?"

"Drying off," she said. Bernadine wrapped the towel

around herself and walked out into the bedroom. "I'm almost ready. Five minutes is all I need."

"No one's rushing you, Mom." Onika acted as if she wanted to sit but decided against it.

"Come in here while I put on a little makeup and comb my hair."

Onika leaned against the doorway. "So how are you feeling, Mom? You sure sound good."

"I feel good, O. I do. I'm giving myself another chance to get this right."

"You haven't been doing it wrong, Mom. You've just been on a detour. And we're all glad to have you back."

"How about you? How are you feeling after telling your dad?"

"Okay, I guess. He's trying so hard to put up a good front. I give him credit for that."

"He'll come around. I heard about Shy. How're you holding up on that end?"

"Shy and I are cool. We're young. She broke my heart but there are more mermaids in the sea." She smiled when she said this. So did Bernadine.

"Can I ask you something, sweetie, if you promise not to get upset or offended by it?"

Onika sat down on the floor in a lotus position. She looked up at her mother, all ears.

"What's it like being a lesbian? No, strike that. That's not what I want to know. Have you ever been with a boy or guy?"

"Yes, Mom."

"What was it like for you?"

"I didn't like it."

"Why not?"

"You have to work too hard."

"For what?"

"Everything."

"Not with all of them," Bernadine said.

"I can't sleep with all of them. Plus, I had to explain myself too much."

"What's that supposed to mean?"

"It means that women understand women. We can skip the bullshit—forgive me."

Bernadine chuckled. "I wonder if I should try it."

Onika chuckled, too. "To answer your original question, Mom, it's not about *being* with a woman. You have to be drawn. And it's not all sexual. Too much emphasis is placed on the physical. It's a feeling of comfort I get. And safety. Something I've never felt with a guy."

"Well, I feel like this toward my girlfriends, but I can't say I've ever had a desire to *be* with a woman."

"Then take this off your list of things to do, Mom."

"Consider it done." Bernadine headed for her closet.

Onika followed. She took a deep breath. "I have something for you," she said as she pulled an envelope from her back pocket and handed it to Bernadine.

"What's this?"

"It's from James. I've held on to it for five years. You seem strong enough now. I hope you're not mad at me."

Bernadine looked at Onika. And smiled. "There's no reason to be mad. You were just looking out for me."

"Cool. I'll meet you downstairs," Onika said, and she closed the door behind her.

Bernadine sat on the edge of the bed and slowly opened the envelope:

Dear Bernadine:

Even though you may not even read this, it will make me feel better knowing I reached out to you. There are not enough words in the dictionary to describe how ashamed I am for the harm I caused you. I'm sorry for violating your trust, for deceiving you, and I hope I didn't ruin it for any man that may have come after me. If so, please don't punish him or short-change your heart because of what I did. You deserve to be happy. You're a wonderful human being and a beautiful, intelligent woman. I just wanted to be smarter than you. I've hurt a lot of people because of my selfishness. My punishment doesn't cover the impact of the emotional crimes I've committed. My life is a wreck. I've been in prison almost two years and have three more to go. No one has visited me since I've been here, and I don't blame them. My daughters don't know who I am anymore. I'm not feeling sorry for myself. I just wanted you to know that when people do bad things to others, it always catches up to them. I'm a good example. Anyway, I hope your children are thriving. I'm sure they are. You don't have to tell them I said hello, because I know they probably hate my guts. Who could blame them? Bernadine, please know that from the bottom of my heart I am truly, truly sorry. Jesse.

How long had she waited to hear those words: I'm sorry?

And now here they were. It didn't change a thing. She folded the letter and put it back in the envelope, then dropped it in the trash basket. As she got dressed, Bernadine wondered what he went to prison for. If his children were back in his life. If he'd ever had a visitor. If he was doing okay.

She hoped so.

Choosing a Future

"So are we good to go?" Joseph asked Gloria.

"We're good to go, sweetheart."

"You're absolutely sure?"

"I said I loved all the swatches, Joseph. I wouldn't say it if I didn't mean it."

"Okey-dokey, then. My, are we awful testy today."

"Would you mind bringing me a strawberry-kiwi smoothie when you come back?" Joline asked Gloria.

"I would if I were coming back, Joline."

"Where are you going?"

"To take care of some personal business, if that's all right with you." Gloria winked at her. Joseph winked at Gloria. *Tell her, honey.*

Just then two of the three DVD boys strutted in. *Oh, hell,* Gloria thought. She didn't have time to go through all those stupid movies right then. What were they doing here so early anyway?

"Hello, Miss Gloria. Everybody."

"Hey," the others said.

"Hi," Gloria said. "Before you ask, I have to give you guys some bad news. We're moving in the next couple of months and I don't think we're going to be able to keep supporting your venture, but please don't be offended, because we have truly appreciated your services. Where's Marvin?"

"Well, that's one of the reasons we stopped by. He decided he was finished with hustling so he's, like, in retirement and everythang. He just started his first semester at Arizona State."

"That's nice to hear," Gloria said.

"Yeah, he twenty-one and everythang but better late than never, if ya know what I mean."

Gloria nodded. She didn't know either of their names and wasn't about to ask. "So what are you two going to do?"

"Not this. It's illegal and they cracking down and we in no way, shape or form are interested in seeing the inside of nobody's jail over this bullmess. You know we twins? Fraternal. Anyway, we gotta get real jobs or our mom said we gots to move outta her crib. College may not be in our cards, but we might be looking into trade schools."

"I hope so. For both of your sakes. Please tell Marvin we wish him all the best."

"Will do. Hold up. As our way of saying sayonara, we got a few freebies you can choose from. Is that all right, Miss Gloria?"

"That's fine, baby. And thank you for being so nice. I've gotta run or I'm going to be late."

"Well, for the little ones we got *The Aristocats, The Bad News Bears*—"

"Hold on a minute, son." Gloria raised her hand. "I'll take those two. What else do you have in that bag?" she asked as she put all her weight on one leg and her hand on her hip.

"Well, Miss Gloria—and clientele and employees— we've got *Charlie and the Chocolate Factory, Wedding Crashers, The Fantastic Four, Hustle and Flow, Happy Endings* and, just in this morning, *The 40-Year-Old Virgin.* Yours for the asking."

"I'll take one of each. Here." Gloria whipped out two one-hundred-dollar bills and handed them to one of the twins. "Split it three ways and if I find out you didn't, I will personally go over to ASU and sit on that campus until Marvin walks by me and I'll ask him myself!" She started laughing, and then they started laughing and then Joseph along with Joline and Twyla and everybody else started cracking up, too. Nobody was doing hair or nails or pedicures. They were too busy rummaging through those satchels as if they were on a scavenger hunt.

"Thank you, Miss Gloria," the young men said and politely put those bills in their pockets. "Good luck to you at your new spot. We'll tell everybody we know with some money to come see you guys when they need to get their hair did and when their feet and nails is toe-up. You know they come in large numbers. Peace out," one of them said as they walked out the front door with two fingers above each head.

Gloria hadn't told anybody where she was going, not even her new partner. She still liked the sound of that—*partner*—but no one more than Joseph. He told just about everybody who walked in the front door. "Do be on the lookout for me and my partner's new salon." And: "Never been to Oasis before? Let me introduce you to my partner, Gloria Matthews-King." Gloria had almost forgotten her maiden name was Matthews. She wondered if she would ever have a reason to stop using King. She couldn't imagine it.

As she gathered up her DVDs, Gloria was a little nervous for a number of reasons. She had a check in her purse for $300,000. It had been in a drawer at home ever since the insurance company sent it to her months ago. She never bothered to deposit it. There was no reason to. Now that Tarik was going to be a single parent, he needed all the help he could get. Although he had balked at the idea, Gloria was going to give half of it to him for obvious reasons. He was planning to finish up those last nine units to get his master's in criminology, but until then, one income wasn't enough to feed, clothe and educate three kids. Make that four, since Tarik had filed for temporary custody of Brass. Adoption papers were next.

Gloria also intended to pay off that boat even though Tarik insisted they sell it. She put up a fuss until he insisted she name it, which she did: *What's Going On?* What else could she call it? She had also agreed it was time she set foot on it, and today was the day. She wouldn't fall apart; at least, she didn't think she would. She needed to do this. Just like she needed to take off her wedding ring. She had picked up the pendant a few days ago and was wearing it right now.

They were taking the kids fishing in a few hours and Gloria was going to surprise them. Last night she bought Diamond a pink-and-lavender *Little Mermaid* pole. Blaze, a black-and-white *Dalmatians* one. Stone, who was all of eight now, got *Spider-Man*. She bought a real one for Brass, even though she would soon find out that he had a special type since he and Tarik were serious about this whole fishing thing.

She was also going to send five thousand of her money for the Katrina victims. Savannah had sent her a link to the same Web site she, Robin, Michael and Bernadine—who sent what she could—had all used.

Gloria was setting aside a nice sum to guarantee Oasis was going to be one of the hippest, sexiest, up-to-the-minute state-of-the-art salon-and-spas in Phoenix. Her partner was matching this amount. The workstations were being custom-made by some guy who ripped off Italian designers. The Web site was going to be "off the hook," thanks to her nephew John Jr. Years ago when she had a bar, most of the clients thought "open bar" meant "never closed." She closed it. Some folks were often sipping and no one knew who they were. But times had changed. Gloria and Joseph decided that most of those young alcoholics were now middle-aged and their credit cards didn't get declined, not to mention that they acquired something that can come with age when you do in fact mature, and it is called discretion.

Everybody was excited about the new all-natural hair and skin product lines, not to mention unique jewelry (some of which would be made by Ms. Sparrow), and if all went according to plan, Gloria and Joseph were considering interviewing four new stylists.

"I'll see you guys tomorrow afternoon," she said and waved to everybody.

———

Her first stop was Weight Watchers. To weigh in. Nothing lost yet, but that's okay. Soon.

Next, she drove to Good Vibrations and parked right in front.

"Welcome back," the same young woman who was there before said.

"I can't believe you remember me," Gloria said.

"Sista, I never forget a face."

———

When Gloria pulled up to the dock with the little fishing poles in tow, the kids ran toward her, then stopped and stared at their poles as if they were something foreign. "What's that, Gawa?" Blaze asked. *Lord is she getting tall,* Gloria thought.

"I think they're called fishing poles," Gloria said.

Diamond smiled and walked over to Gloria and stood on her toes. "Thank you," she whispered as they both ran back toward Tarik and the boys. They were standing on the pier with their lines already in the water. "Hey, Ma," Tarik said. "We might have to stop by Fish and Chips tonight because you know not much is running this time of year."

"Gawa, is that a *Spider-Man* fishing pole?" Stone asked.

"Sure looks like it," she said.

And Brass, who, at fourteen, was now almost as tall as Tarik—six feet and a few inches—walked over and gave Gloria a hug. "Hi, Grandma," he said. She held out a grown-up pole for him. "Oh wow!" he said, and instantly became eight years old again. "Dad, check this out! You must have spent a mint on this, Grandma! This is sweeeeet!"

"Ma, where's mine?" Tarik asked and winked at her.

Gloria smiled but couldn't take her eyes off the boat, which was over to their left. After they helped the kids get their little poles assembled—which didn't take much—

Gloria decided to walk over to take a look at the boat while they fished. "I'll be right back," she said to them.

"Are you sure you don't want me to come with you, Ma?"

"I'll come with you, Gawa," Blaze said and dropped her pole on the rocks.

"No, it's okay. Gawa would like to go on the boat alone, if you don't mind. Please pick up that fishing pole, Blaze. Money does not grow on trees."

"No, it does not!" Diamond yelled and then giggled.

Blaze did exactly as she was told but stuck her tongue out at Diamond. The boys were staring into the water as if they could will the fish to jump on the end of their lines.

As Gloria got near the boat, she looked at the name *What's Going On?* and smiled. She ran her hands across the smooth wood and walked up the ramp until she was standing on the boat. Her heartbeat was steady. In fact, as she walked around the deck and headed below, Gloria was calm. She sat on the little sofa and rubbed the cushion, feeling the thick threads that formed the tapestry. "Marvin, you would've liked this boat, baby," she said. "But guess what? I like it, too. I wish you were here to enjoy it. You're probably on a golf course up there. Just do me a favor, baby. Every time you see Tarik taking this boat out, know you're welcome to come aboard."

And she got up.

"Gawa, where are you?" Blaze asked, ducking her head until she saw Gloria.

"Ma, you all right down there?" Tarik asked, coming

down the steps behind Blaze, with Diamond on his back. Stone and Brass stood behind them.

"I'm fine," she said. "Really, I am."

"Good," he said.

"So, how many did you guys catch so far?"

"That would be a negative," Brass said. "But ask us if we care?"

Breathe

"I knew I wasn't going to like yoga," Savannah says to her girlfriends. They're heading toward the parking lot. They've just finished taking a yoga class.

"It was hard doing that stuff," Gloria says. "I was embarrassed as hell when I fell over trying to do that doggie pose."

"It was kind of funny, Glo," Robin says. "But I didn't laugh. Just so you know."

"Savannah," Bernadine says. "You and Robin have been saying you wanted to try yoga for months. So stop whining."

"I liked it," Robin said.

"Because you're already flexible, that's why," Savannah says. "Why was everybody so serious? You'd think they'd at least crack a smile doing those poses, since yoga's supposed to make you feel so good."

"You smile from inside," Bernadine says.

"You need to stop talking like this," Savannah says.

"You are going a little far," Robin says.

"First of all, Bernie, we know you got off doing this New Age stuff when you were in rehab, and we know yoga is all the rage and it's good for the soul and everything, but don't expect us to just fall in place on our very first time. Damn," Savannah says.

"You're right."

"Plus, you told us the class was for beginners," Gloria says.

"You were supposed to do as much as you could. Didn't you hear the teacher? She showed you how to modify the poses."

"Why was her voice so soft?" Robin asks.

"She was talking to us in her 'inside' voice. That's what I tell my grandkids to use. It did seem a little weird hearing a grown-up talking like that."

"I could barely hear her," Savannah says.

"Because you weren't listening," Bernadine says.

"She was whispering."

"What I really liked was when she sprayed that little mist of lavender water on us as we were leaving," Gloria says.

"I liked that, too," Savannah says.

"I don't think yoga is my cup of tea, though," Gloria says.

"I'm definitely coming back," Robin says.

"I'm not saying I wouldn't try it again. I suppose I need to be more open-minded," Savannah says.

"Anyway, I'll meet you guys at my house," Bernadine says.

"How long will it take us to learn how to meditate?" Gloria asks.

"Yeah, Swami Bernie," Savannah says. "You promised us lunch after our morning of spiritual enlightenment."

"Ten minutes," Bernadine says.

———

"Okay, so the first thing you do is close your eyes, inhale and then exhale."

"You know, I think this is the major reason we're all alive, Bernie," Savannah says.

Robin giggles. They're sitting on Bernadine's kitchen chairs, which have been pulled away from the table.

"She's got a point," Gloria says. "What's the trick to doing this?"

"There is no trick. If you guys would shut the hell up long enough so I can finish showing you, maybe we could all see what it feels like to be relaxed."

"I am relaxed," Gloria says.

"I am, too," Savannah says.

"I'm a little hyper myself," Robin says. "You guys, stop messing with Bernie. This is kind of a big deal to her. Besides, people in India have been doing this and yoga for centuries, so there must be something to it. Keep going, Bernie."

"Okay, so the whole idea is to inhale through your nose and exhale through your mouth. Do it slowly."

"How many times?" Robin asks.

"You don't count, Robin. Anyway, if you guys would just let me finish explaining, we can try it and you can see for yourself how it makes you feel."

"Can't see if your eyes are closed," Savannah says. "Sorry. Couldn't resist. Okay," she says. "I'm being quiet and paying attention."

"So when you inhale, try to do it on the count of four. And when you exhale, on the count of seven."

"Why'd you change the guidelines already?" Gloria asks.

"I'm not answering that. Anyway, the idea is to focus

on each breath. All you want to do is keep your mind on your breathing."

"How are we supposed to do that?" Savannah asks.

"By trying it, Savannah. This is the deal. Your mind is going to jump all over the place. The idea is each time it happens, bring your focus back to your breathing. And that's it."

"That's it?" Robin asks.

"I can do that," Gloria says.

"Let's try it," Savannah says. "Wait. Why do we want to do this again?"

"I told you to Google it so I wouldn't have to explain it."

"I forgot," Savannah says.

"Me, too," Robin says.

"I made a mistake and looked up *mediate* instead of *meditate,* and then Diamond fell and busted her lip, so I never got back around to it."

"Is this the same way you did it in rehab?" Robin asks.

"At first."

"I just want to know what they showed you that's made you such a believer," Savannah says.

"All the yoga teacher kept telling us to do was focus on our breathing, too. So there's something to this whole breathing thing. What is it? Break it down so we know what we're supposed to be looking for," Robin says.

"That's just it. You're not supposed to be *looking* for anything. At first we did the breathing exercise I just described. But then they told us to become aware of our thoughts and especially the disturbing ones."

"Like what?" Robin asked.

"Like when you feel anger and hurt and resentment and worry and fear, to name a few. Anyway, they told us to imagine that when we inhale, we're breathing in hope and vitality, and when we exhale, we're breathing out hurt and anger. You can breathe in faith and confidence and breathe out doubt and despair. And so on."

"No shit," Savannah says. "And you think it works?"

"I don't hate James."

"You mean you forgave him?" Robin asks.

"I didn't make a conscious decision. I just didn't fee' any of it the more I did this. I can't explain it."

"You don't have to," Savannah says.

"So this is why you've been so upbeat since you've been home," Gloria says.

"It's not magic. All I know is when you do this breathing exercise, especially on a daily basis, you feel more focused and relaxed and even jazzed. There's lots of different ways people meditate. All I know is it helps me concentrate better and think clearer, and I have a helluva lot more energy. Anyway, that's pretty much it."

"How long are you supposed to do it?" Gloria asks.

"There's no specific time. Some people do it for five minutes at a time, two and three times a day. We started out doing it a couple of minutes. By the time I left, I was up to fifteen."

"You mean, just sitting there breathing?" Robin asks.

Bernadine nods.

"Let's try it again," Robin says.

"This seems a lot easier than yoga," Savannah says.

"Okay, so you want to sit up straight and maybe put your hands in your lap, palms up."

"Why?" Robin asks.

Bernadine lets out a long sigh. "Just do it."

"How about some meditation music?" Savannah says.

"Yeah, that would definitely stop my mind from drifting," Gloria says.

"I don't have any," Bernadine says. "We don't need music."

"Whatever," Savannah says.

"Okay. Let's try it for three minutes," Bernadine says. "Close your eyes and breathe."

Everybody does.

Robin peeks at Savannah and Gloria to see if their eyes are closed. They are, so she closes hers. She sees herself standing in front of a classroom. She's laughing at something one of the kids said. Michael's swimming in the ocean. He's got on too much sunblock. Someone hands her a mojito. It's the best she's ever had. Did I pay my cell phone bill? Sparrow's throwing another party. Russell's at the door. Admission is a dollar.

Gloria is smiling. Her new salon is the bomb. People are flocking in. Marvin Gaye is singing "I Heard It Through the Grapevine." Gloria is popping her fingers. Is that her on the TV? She's now a spokesperson for Jenny Craig. She goes to visit Nickida. Opens her eyes. No frigging way. Closes them. "Has it been three minutes yet? My mind is jumping around like crazy."

Savannah is snoring.

"Wake her ass up," Bernadine says. "It's been five minutes."

"Wow," Savannah says. She opens her eyes as if she's waking up from a good dream. "I'm calm as can be. I'll do this again. At home. Without an audience."

"What about that kitten?" Robin asks.

"She doesn't judge," Savannah says.

"Okay, so we've done yoga and we've meditated. Can we please eat now?" Gloria asks.

"I thought you'd never ask," Bernadine says.

White Dress

"This better be the one!" Bernadine says.

"Hurry up! We don't have all day!" Savannah says.

"Both of you, be quiet," Gloria whispers as she shoves Savannah, who in turn bumps into Bernadine.

They're at a bridal salon, sitting on a round velvet sofa, surrounded by fifteen or twenty mannequins in wedding gowns.

"They don't look very excited, do they?" Savannah says to Bernadine and Gloria.

"They're virgins. They're scared. Tonight's the big night," Bernadine says. "That one over by the window couldn't wait. She's pregnant. Look how she's sucking in her stomach. Ho."

All three burst into laughter.

"They need some plus-size brides in here," Gloria says.

"And some maternity gowns," Savannah says. "I don't see any Latinas representing."

"Asians get married in Phoenix, too," Bernadine says.

"At least there's one black one in here. She looks more like Britney Spears, though, doesn't she?" Gloria asks.

Okay. So that killed a few more minutes.

Over the past couple of weeks, Robin had been to every bridal salon listed in the yellow pages. She liked this one best. Had narrowed it down to four dresses. They'd seen three. Though all of them were gorgeous, so far, none looked like they were made for Robin.

"I can't do this by myself," she'd said to them. "I'm too nervous. I need you guys to help me decide."

"Hold your horses, ladies!" Robin yells from behind a white door.

A middle-aged woman, in a black tailored suit and support hose, comes out and stands in front of them. She smiles, then crosses her arms. "She'll be out shortly, ladies. Some of the gowns take a little extra doing to get into and out of. May I get any of you a glass of water, coffee, anything?"

They shake their heads no but thanks.

"I think you'll love this one." She pivots like an usher and disappears behind that door.

"She should rethink those shoes," Savannah says.

"She's on her feet all day," Gloria says. "I'd be in flats, too."

"Nobody has come through that door and we've been here over an hour. Two-inch heels wouldn't kill her," Savannah says.

"Did anybody hear what Sparrow suggested Robin wear?" Bernadine asked.

"I'm afraid to hear this," Gloria says.

"A long white slip."

"It could work," Savannah says.

"What do you guys think of this one?" Robin asks as she tiptoes over and stops directly in front of them. They stand up. Robin takes a few steps back so they can get a better look. Her friends don't say a word. After Robin twirls around, all they can do is cover their mouths with both hands.

Everybody Dance Now

"Here we go again," Savannah says with a sigh. She and Bernadine have been driving around the parking lot of the Scottsdale Princess Hotel and Resort for almost ten minutes without any luck.

"There's one!" Bernadine says as she checks her lipstick in the visor mirror. "And do us all a favor tonight, Savannah—please don't complain about how people are dressed or how tired the band is or how the DJ is stuck in the eighties, and especially when he plays "It's Electric"—which you already know is going to happen, okay?"

"Just so you know, I wasn't planning on complaining about anything. I'm trying to get into the habit of not being so critical."

"I have to see this to believe it."

"Did I mention how snazzy you look this evening?"

Bernadine pops her upside the head. She's wearing a dark gold dress with black spaghetti straps. It wants to shine but stops short. Savannah has on a two-tiered teal-and-cream floor-length dress. It's cotton knit and shows some of her curves.

"You don't look like such a slouch yourself. Now hurry up," Bernadine says. "My feet are already killing me."

"Yours? I just bought these suckers today. I

should've worn them around the house a few hours to break them in."

"Don't tell me you plan on dancing, Savannah?"

"If the spirit moves me. You never know."

"Did you know this is where I met James?"

"I thought it was the Biltmore."

"Nope, right in that bar over there."

"You never said a word about this, Bernie."

"Well, I'm telling you now."

"And you're all right?"

"Do you think I'd be here if I wasn't?"

A parade of black folks are heading inside. It looks like they're on a moving walkway. The women are sparkling and glittering. The men are tuxedoed.

Bernadine flips her cell phone open when she feels it vibrate. "Where are you guys? Already seated? Are you the first ones there or what? Anyway, we're walking in the door right now. Table twenty-six. You see anybody you know yet? Get out! That's so nice. Bye," she says. "Can you believe our girl is really getting hitched, Savannah?"

"I can. Michael's a good guy. I think it's going to last."

"What makes you say that?"

"When you get married at fifty, what reasons could you possibly have to get a divorce? Besides, Robin is live entertainment."

"Anyway, she and Gloria are already at our table and apparently there are some elderly people sitting with us, too."

"Good, then we'll be with our peers."

As they walk into the gigantic ballroom they look

around until they spot their friends. The band isn't on stage yet but their instruments are waiting for them. Herbie Hancock's music is playing in the background. The parquet dance floor is empty. There must be well over a thousand people here. Most of the big round tables are already full. Candles flicker. The centerpieces are desert bouquets.

"Hello," Bernadine and Savannah say to the two elderly couples. All four have silver hair. Their skin is the color of molasses.

"Hello to you, ladies. Where are your husbands tonight? Left them at home, did you?"

"We did," Robin says before anyone has a chance to respond. "You know what happens when football season starts, sir."

"That I do," he says.

"Are you all planning to cut a rug this evening?" Savannah asks.

"We're just excited we could be here for this important occasion. We feel blessed to be alive and have so much to be thankful for. We can't stay long, but we're ready to hit the dance floor as soon as they play something we can dance to."

Robin is nodding and smiling from ear to ear. Instead of the simple black, slinky dress she told everybody she was wearing, she's draped in a sequined explosion of every color you could find on a Las Vegas showgirl.

"Is that dress new?" Bernadine asks her.

"Girl, Michael bought this for me. He helped me pick it out. I'm on a shopping diet."

"What's that supposed to mean?" Gloria asks.

"It means I'm not buying anything I don't need. Until I get a job."

"How many hours has it been so far?" Savannah asks.

"Sixteen *days,* and it's killing me. I won't lie. They're having a twice-yearly sale at Nordstrom starting tomorrow but guess who's not going?" She points to her chest.

"I didn't mean to say that," Savannah says.

"Yes, you did. It's just you being you, Savannah. Can I get anybody a drink?" Robin stands tall. Gets her bag. She isn't the least bit upset.

All three women shake their heads no.

"Well, times have sure changed," she says. "I would love a glass of chardonnay. I'll be right back."

Before she makes it to the bar, Robin can't believe it when she sees Lucille all gussied up and sporting a new hairstyle. There's Norman, sitting next to an elderly woman in a wheelchair. And Fernando! "Well, hello there to all my ex-coworkers! How's everybody doing? Lucille, you look wonderful! Retirement is certainly agreeing with you! And thanks again for the tickets."

"You're quite welcome. I wanted you to meet Hank, but his sciatic nerve flared up so he's at home icing away. Your dress is just gorgeous, Robin."

"It *is* working for you, lady," Fernando says. "Hey, what's that on your left hand?"

"An engagement ring."

"You mean you're getting married?" he asks.

"That's what it usually means, Fernando!"

"Well, congratulations!" Lucille says.

"So where are you hiding him?" Fernando asks.

"At home. It's a girls' night."

"That's just super," Norman says. "Robin, I'd like you to meet my mother, Mary. She can't hear, so there's no need to say anything."

Robin smiles and waves.

"And this is Lupe," Fernando says. "Remember the ex-con and amateur golfer?"

"The infamous Lupe?"

"Yes, ma'am. I didn't take your advice, though. Instead of a job, I opted for barber school. Fernando, too."

"Well, this is just great. It's so nice to see you guys. And everybody doing so well. It really is. Are you holding up okay, Norm?"

"I'm great. I'm not going to Costa Rica. Sold my land. I'm doing lots of gardening and taking care of my mother. If all goes well, I hope to see you back here next year. The music is super and the people are very kind."

Robin gives them a thumbs-up. Changes her mind about the wine. She heads back to the table. "I'll have what you guys are having." She looks at her friends and smiles.

They people-watch and enjoy the mellow jazz. It'll be a while before the DJ starts playing dance music. The band members are coming to the stage. They look to be in their late fifties. The drummer taps his snare. As soon as they begin to play "I've Got You Under My Skin," both of the elderly gentlemen stand up, pull their wives' chairs out and take them by the hand. "We're going to dance a little," one of them says. The women are smiling as if this is their prom night. "And then we're going to head on home. It was very nice to have met you all."

"Don't you want to stay for dinner?" Gloria asks.

"We always eat before we come to this type of affair. We also have a long drive ahead of us."

"Where are you headed?" Savannah asks.

"Tucson. We live in a senior facility down there."

"What's the name of it?" Robin asks.

"Fiesta Village," one says.

"Do you know Pearl Stokes?"

"Of course we do!" one of the women says, holding her husband's hand tight. "We were at her birthday party earlier this summer. We had the time of our lives. Are you Robin?"

"I am!"

"She talks about you and a different bird . . . oh . . ."

"Sparrow," the other woman says. "All the time. We'll be sure to give her your love and tell her how nice you looked."

"Thank you," Robin says.

The four of them wave goodbye and head for the dance floor.

"We should be so lucky," Savannah says.

"Excuse me," Bernadine says to Gloria. She's staring at her left hand. "Where's your wedding ring?"

Gloria points to the diamond pendant around her neck. "Right here."

"That's nice," Bernadine says.

The other women nod in agreement. They know what a big deal this is. What they don't know is that for the first time in almost nine months, Gloria has started sleeping in her own bed. That she has taken down all the pictures of Marvin except the one of him fishing and another of the two of them sitting by the pool, reading the newspaper. Tarik took it. Gloria stored the others with her keepsakes.

"Speaking of jewelry, where did you get those earrings, Robin?" Savannah asks.

"I made them."

"Don't make any more," Bernadine says.

"I have to agree," Gloria says. "Let your daughter make the jewelry."

"They don't look like they move even though they dangle," Bernadine says.

"Is that blood on your neck?" Savannah asks.

"Damn it! Sparrow told me to use those little round silver things but I couldn't get them on." She takes them off and slips them into her purse.

"I hope this isn't your new hobby," Gloria says.

"You know what I just remembered, you guys? I used to have a real hobby."

"Used to doesn't count," Bernadine says. "We're trying to live in the present and leave the past where it belongs. But what was it?"

"I used to make pottery."

"Good pottery or that fucked-up-looking pottery?" Savannah asks.

"It was the fucked-up kind. My mom and dad used to display it in parts of the house where company never went. I still enjoyed doing it. It wasn't like I was trying to get it in Target or anything."

The music stops. A balding black man stands at the podium and taps on the microphone, looks out at the audience. He is pleased all the tables are full. He begins what will be a long list of awards and speeches. How much money they raised for the Katrina victims and that they should be proud. The women will listen and applaud as dinner is being served.

Savannah is excited when she recognizes the chicken breast she was expecting. Gloria says yes to the roast beef, but passes on the gravy. They smile at three limp carrots with a lonely asparagus tip asleep on top. On the other side of the plate is a small island of white rice. Neither Savannah nor Gloria will touch it. Their goal is to avoid eating anything white. When dessert arrives, they push the coconut cake to the side. The only person who eats it is Robin. She can afford to.

"I'm going back to school. To get my teaching credentials," Robin says matter-of-factly.

Everybody looks stunned, then happy.

"This is the best news I've heard since you told us you were getting married," Savannah says.

"When did you decide to do this?" Gloria asks.

"In Napa. On a train. During a massage. When I was eating eggs Benedict. When I was meditating! After going online and looking at all the great teaching opportunities. I can picture myself in a classroom. I really can."

"I'm proud of you, Robin," Bernadine says. "Make that two of us going back to school. I just enrolled in a one-year program at the Culinary Institute."

"Oh, shit, I forgot! Michael stole the tasting menu from our hotel restaurant. His buddy's going to get one from that French Laundry for you, too."

"Thanks for thinking of me, honey. And thank Michael for stealing for his soon-to-be sister-in-law."

464 | Terry McMillan

"So finish what you were saying," Robin says.

"Before I open another restaurant, this time I intend to do it up right. I hope it'll be the talk of Phoenix. I'm going to learn how to prepare all the dishes I love so they not only taste good but are good for you."

"I'll do a show about you and your restaurant whenever you open it."

"Seriously?"

"I'm getting a new format. It could be called a talk show."

"Hallelujah," Robin says. "It's about time."

"The station's sending me to New Orleans in a few weeks. I'm going to interview some folks to find out how they're managing."

"Isn't Casper down there?" Bernadine asks.

"*Jasper*. Yes, he is."

"Didn't you kind of like him a little bit?" Robin asks.

"I think he's nice."

"Are you going to go out with him again?" Gloria asks.

"I think so."

"Don't think too hard or you'll talk yourself out of feeling it. Remember, every relationship starts with a date," Robin says.

"That's not always true," Savannah says.

"Just give him some the next time you see him so you can get that out of the way. Then decide if you want to take it to the next level."

"I kind of agree with Robin," Bernadine says. "You better get it while the getting's good. What do you have to lose at this point?"

"I agree with you both," Gloria says.

"This is how I ended up marrying Isaac. I'm not making the same mistake twice. I just want to have some fun."

"You don't think having sex is fun?"

"Shut up, Robin."

"I hope to do it again one day," Bernadine says.

"You couldn't possibly be talking about sex," Savannah says.

"That, too. Maybe meeting someone. Possibly dating again."

The women look like they've seen a ghost.

"What did they put in the water when you were at rehab?" Robin asks. "Whatever it was, I hope you brought some home."

"I'm not dead. I've been frozen for a while. As you guys can tell, I'm thawing out."

"This is fan-fucking-tabulous," Savannah says. "You keep on doing those poses and meditating your behind off. Hey! Remember when you talked about having one of those progressive dinners or something?"

"I do."

"Why don't you start planning one?"

"You can have the first course at my house," Gloria says.

"We all know somebody that nobody knows, so let's invite some new somebodies and expand our circle of friends. Not just men."

"Bernie, does he have to know how to meditate and do yoga?"

"Go to hell, Robin."

"I thought you and John were getting kind of close again," Gloria says.

"He's like an old friend I happened to be married to a long time ago. He's definitely been there for me. Question, ladies: When and where's the next Blockbuster Night?"

They all look at one another.

Gloria raises her hand. "Two weeks."

"What movie?" Robin asks.

"Well, since our bootleg days are over and we've seen all the latest . . ." Savannah says. "Did anybody ever see *Monsoon Wedding*? It's hilarious."

"You've already seen it?" Gloria asks.

"I could watch it again. Easy."

"And keep your mouth shut during the movie?" Bernadine says.

"I promise."

"I'll control the remote," Gloria says. "Let's give ourselves a half hour, forty-five minutes to an hour tops, to catch up and weigh in, so to speak."

"Rent it," Robin says. "Speaking of weddings. I know you guys have been dying to know: Michael and I have decided to get married in Vail."

"Vail?" Bernadine says. "Colorado?"

"That's where I think it is," Robin says. She makes a face.

"I thought you wanted to get married in Tucson so your mom could come," Savannah says like it's a protest.

"Without my dad being here, she didn't think she could handle it. She asked if I could just send her pictures. I know she's happy for me. She's getting older, you guys."

"Looks like I have to buy a ski outfit," Bernadine says. "I'm not getting on anybody's skis. That much I can tell you."

"I will," Savannah says.

"I'd try it," Gloria says.

"I didn't say we were getting married on a ski run, you guys. Damn."

———

After coffee, the band finally starts playing R&B from the '70s and '80s and a few from the '90s but doesn't quite make it to the new millennium. No one seems to care. The dance floor becomes a menagerie of jerky as well as smooth swirling hips. Men who could once cut up are now glad they still have rhythm. Women are flirting with their dance partners. Bernadine, Robin, Gloria and Savannah watch while moving their shoulders to the beat.

"Even though I wanted to, I'm glad I didn't go to Paris," Robin says as if she's talking to herself. "I think we should all go on a cruise."

"I don't like cruises," Savannah says.

"I've never been on one," Gloria says. "Why don't you like cruises, Savannah?"

"Don't even get me started. First of all, they make you claustrophobic just knowing you can't get off even if you want to. The hallways are too narrow, and when that ship rocks, you rock, too. I threw up twice when I went with Mama and Sheila. The rooms are like closets, and if you can afford a window, what can you see besides water? I don't like all those ice sculptures and those corny stage shows and those slot machines that never pay off, not to mention those expensive-ass watered-down drinks and all

that heart attack food and kids running around screaming
and splashing you with water and—"

"Okay! We get it!" Bernadine says.

"Count me out," Gloria says.

"Me, too," Robin says. "It doesn't sound like much
fun at all. And cruises aren't cheap."

"What would you do about your husband?" Bernadine asks.

"My *husband* already knows I'm not going to stop
doing things with my friends just because I have a *husband*.
The same holds true for him. We've already talked about
this. We're not twenty-two. We're grown-ups. We know
who we are, what we've got and what we're doing."

"Cool," Savannah says, and then she starts looking
up at a chandelier as if she's daydreaming. "How about
we go somewhere exotic next year—early next year—on
a plane. Someplace none of us has ever been."

"And the purpose of this trip, since you always have
some kind of agenda for us, Savannah, is . . . ?" Robin
asks.

"To have fun."

"That's it?"

"Everything doesn't have to have a purpose, does it?"

"Where would you suggest we go?" Robin asks her.

"Where would you suggest we go, Robin?"

"I don't know."

"There has to be somewhere you've always wanted
to go," Savannah says with a sigh.

"I've always wanted to go to Tahiti," Gloria says.

"Rio," Robin says.

"I'm dying to go to Venice and Rio and I could do

Tahiti," Savannah says. "I've always wanted to go to Kenya. On a safari."

"I'm not going near any wild animals," Robin says. "Jeep or no jeep."

"Me neither," Gloria says. "Rio, maybe. But I'll be damned if I get naked prancing around anybody's beach."

"What about Barcelo—oh-oh," Bernadine says and stands up. "I think I hear our anthem!"

The DJ is indeed spinning the first few bars of "It's Electric," and as if this is about to be one huge baptism, hundreds of people flock to the dance floor and immediately start bending over and rocking their shoulders.

"I'm not going out there," Savannah says. "I'll watch." She crosses her arms tightly.

"Oh, yes, the hell you are," Bernadine says, as she and Robin and Gloria surround her and tug on her arms until they fall apart.

"Wait! My shoes are under the table!" she says.

"I thought you said they hurt," Robin says.

"They do!"

"Mine are killing me, too," Bernadine says, and kicks hers off.

"Wait a minute," Robin says. "Did you get those at Nordstrom?"

"Shut up!" Gloria, of all people, yells. "Everybody leave their damn shoes right where they are!"

And they do. The four of them dash out to the dance floor like they're on *So You Think You Can Dance* and wiggle their hips to carve out enough room, but only two can fit in the same row, so Robin and Gloria slip in behind Savannah and Bernadine. The crowd is already moving, and it takes a few seconds for them to get into the groove. Savannah looks over her shoulder and rolls her eyes at Gloria and Robin and then at Bernadine. They just roll theirs right back.

Seconds later, all four of them are popping their fingers, and when they take three steps back and tap their feet, then take three steps forward and tap again, by the time they cross one leg over the other and slide left to right and back, they start getting fancy and add an extra skip here and an extra dip there, but the next few times they sashay backward and forward their hips seem to have a mind of their own, because even when the song ends and the DJ overlaps it with a jam that takes them way back—"Everybody Dance Now"—they don't lose the beat and not a soul leaves the dance floor. When someone yells out, "Party over here!" these four women—these four friends—cannot stop swaying and shimmying to this brand-new beat, and the next thing they know they are jump-jump-jumping up and down and waving their hands in the air like they just don't care. But they do. They definitely do.

ACKNOWLEDGMENTS

The last few years have been rough. It's hard to write when you're angry, or numb. It's hard to do anything when you're angry or numb. There are, however, quite a few folks I would like to thank for their ongoing support, understanding, and patience; who helped me to relocate my center and get back to doing what I love to do: Molly Friedrich, my agent, tops this list, for letting me drive her crazy with rough drafts before they were meant to be read; Carole DeSanti, my amazing editor, for respecting me as a writer and for "getting" these women's plights; Lucy Carson, for knowing how to read, and for being so smart and tactful; Beena Kamlani, for her keen eye and ears and first-rate work on the book; Blanche Richardson, my long-time friend, for everything, but mostly for listening to me read passages and chapters over the phone and for lying to me that the dreadful drafts were good; my wonderful and efficient assistant, Roberta Ponder; my smart and organized cousin, Jacqueline Dixon; Jeffery Banks, for all his help on lakes and fish in Arizona; my friends who kept me afloat: Lynda and Leon Drummer, Gilda Kihneman, Valari Adams, Susan Taylor and Khephra Burns; and Bonnie Ross. I am thankful for my sisters: Vicki, Crystal and Rosalyn, who held on tight and made me feel loved. I am also grateful to the Corporation of Yaddo for giving me uninterrupted time to write; to the W Hotel where I edited and ordered room service and didn't do dishes or clean for weeks; and to NYC for helping me feel electric again! More than anyone, I want to thank my son, Solomon, for his faith in me, for his concern for my well-being, for being the man in my life who made sure I was going to flourish, and for asking me, "Mom, do you have anything I can listen to today?" as he sat down in a chair in my office time after time, giving me high fives along with the warmest hugs ever. He is the best thing that has ever happened to me.

Read on for a selection from

WAITING TO EXHALE

Terry McMillan's beloved prequel to
Getting to Happy.

Available now.

Right now I'm supposed to be all geeked up because I'm getting ready for a New Year's Eve party that some guy named Lionel invited me to. Sheila, my baby sister, insisted on giving me his phone number because he lives here in Denver and her simple-ass husband played basketball with him eleven years ago at the University of Washington, and since I'm still single (which is downright pitiful to her, considering I'm the oldest of four kids and the only one who has yet to say "I do"), she's worried about me. She and Mama both think I'm out here dying of loneliness, which is not true. I mean, I have my days and I have my nights, but I haven't gotten to the point where I'll take whatever I can get. There's a big difference between being thirsty and being dehydrated.

But Sheila and Mama have always thought that something was better than nothing, and look where it's gotten them. Mama, who thinks she's an expert on everything, hasn't had a whole man in her life for seventeen years, and if I knew where my daddy was, I'd probably kill him for making her such a bitter woman. He broke her heart, and she's never recovered. And Sheila? She files for divorce on an annual basis and calls me collect from some cheap motel where she and the kids are hiding out until she can serve the papers on Paul. I listen to her whine for hours about how sick she is of him and that there's nothing he can do or say that would make her go back this time. But then, like a fool, she turns right around and calls him up, repeats her long list of needs that aren't being met, and he promises to give her anything she wants. She refuses to believe him, so he begs on a daily basis for two weeks, and by then he's convinced her that he means it, so she gives in and goes on back home. I rarely hear from her while they're "honeymooning," except maybe a three-minute synopsis of how hunky-dory everything is now, and because he's given her permission to go ahead and rip out the old carpet or buy some new dining room furniture, she's watching her money, which is why she can't talk long. One of my brothers is in prison for doing some stupid shit, passing counterfeit money, but he's not a criminal; and the other one's a lifer in the Marine Corps. So as far as taking advice from *any* of them goes, I'm skeptical.

The deal is, the men are dead in Denver. Which is only one reason why I'm leaving. I'm tired of this altitude, all this damn snow, and this obsession with the Denver Broncos. For the last three years, my life has felt inconsequential, like nobody really gives a shit what I'm doing or how well I do it. From the outside, everything looks good: I've got a decent job, money in the bank, live in a nice condo, and drive a respectable car. I've got everything I need except a man. And I'm not one of these women who think that a man is the answer to everything, but I'm tired of being by myself. Being single isn't half as much fun as it used to be. Ever since I broke up with Kenneth, I haven't even come close to being in love, and that was almost four years ago, when I lived in Boston. I miss that feeling, and I want it back. But I'm also not the type to sit around and wait for too much of anything. If I want something to happen, I know I have to make it happen. And as hard as I've tried, nothing unforgettable has happened to me since I've been in Denver, which is why I'm getting the hell out of here.

My baby sister has also never appreciated or understood taking real risks, so she wasn't all that thrilled when I called her two weeks ago to tell her I was moving to Phoenix. "Why would anybody in their right mind want to live in Arizona?" she asked me. "Are there any black folks out there? And isn't that where that governor rescinded the King holiday after it had already been passed?" I had to remind her that my best friend, Bernadine—the girl who was my roommate in college, the girl whose wedding I drove sixty miles in a snowstorm to get to because I was her bridesmaid—lives in Scottsdale. She's been black all her life, and she seems to like it there. And as far as the King holiday goes, all I could say was that I'd be one of the first people at the polls when the time came.

Bernadine had talked me into coming out there to spend my birthday, which I had to remind Sheila was October 14 and not the twenty-second, which was the day I got her card. She damn near has a stroke if hers is late. Anyway, I couldn't believe how pretty and warm and cheap it was to live there. We went to this Urban League affair, and I got to talking to one of Bernadine's husband's friends, and he told me about this opening in the publicity department at one of the local TV stations, so I applied, and after flying back and forth for three different interviews, I had just found out that I got the job, and hell, it's a welcome change from the gas company, and plenty of opportunities to advance. What I didn't tell her was that I was taking a twelve-thousand-dollar-a-year pay cut, which probably would've sent her soaring through the roof, because I'm the one who's basically been supporting Mama for the past three years while everybody else just watched. Mama gets a whopping $407 a month from Social Security and $104 worth of food stamps, but who the hell can live off of that? She lives in a Section Eight apartment. I pay her portion of the rent and send her a few extra dollars a month so she can at least go to a movie, but all she does is spend it in thrift shops or put furniture on layaway that'll take years to get out. If my condo doesn't sell, I'll be up shit's creek. I'll be cutting it close as it is, but I'm hoping it won't take me that long to get into producing, which is what I really want to do.

Sheila's got three kids, doesn't work, and has never lived anywhere except Pittsburgh. "This'll make the fourth city you've lived in in fifteen years. I can't keep track, Savannah. When are you gonna be still long enough to settle down?" All I could say was, "When I find what I'm looking for." I didn't feel like telling her for the umpteenth time what it was, because she doesn't understand it: peace of mind; a place I can call home; feeling important to somebody; and just trying to live a meaningful, significant, and positive life. Of course she didn't bother asking this time. But Sheila did manage to remind me for the zillionth time that I'm running out of *time*, because here I am all of thirty-six years old without so much as a prospect in sight; and on top of that, she said that my swinging-singles lifestyle doesn't amount to shit, that I run the gamut when it comes to stereotypes of buppiedom because I put too much energy into my career, that without a husband and children my life really has no meaning, that I'm traversing down that road less traveled, and that by now I should've been divorced at least once and be the mother of at least 2.5 children. Sheila said I'm too choosy, that my standards are too high, and because they seem to be nonnegotiable, she swears up and down that if I don't loosen up, the only person who'll ever meet my qualifications is God. I love her to death, but I swear, she gets on my last nerve.

Also from

Terry McMillan

The *New York Times* bestselling
prequel to *Getting to Happy*

WAITING TO EXHALE

From the critically acclaimed author of *A Day Late
and a Dollar Short* and *The Interruption of Everything*,
a wise, earthy story of a friendship between four
African American women who lean on each other
while "waiting to exhale": waiting for that man who
will take their breath away.

**"Terry McMillan is perhaps the world's finest
chronicler of modern life among
African-American men and women."
*—San Francisco Chronicle***

Available wherever books are sold or at
penguin.com